Asking For Trouble

Elizabeth Young started writing after a variety of jobs that included being part of an airline cabin crew, modelling for TV commercials in Cyprus and working for the Sultan's Armed Forces in Oman. She lives in Surrey with a fat cat, a barmy spaniel and a saintly other half.

D0595738

ASKING FOR TROUBLE

Elizabeth Young

arrow books

Published by Arrow Books in 2000

5 7 9 10 8 6 4

First published in the United Kingdom in 2000 by William Heinemann

Arrow Books Limited
The Random House Group Ltd
20 Vauxhall Bridge Road, London SW1V 2SA

Random House Australia (Pty) Limited
20 Alfred Street, Milsons Point, Sydney,
New South Wales 2061, Australia

Random House New Zealand Limited
18 Poland Road, Glenfield
Auckland 10, New Zealand

Random House (Pty) Limited
Endulini, 5a Jubilee Road, Parktown 2193, South Africa

The Random House Group Ltd Reg. No. 954009

www.randomhouse.co.uk

ISBN 0 09 941506 2

Typeset by SX Composing DTP, Rayleigh, Essex
Printed and bound in Great Britain by
Bookmarque Ltd, Croydon, Surrey

For my father, who loved a good, rolling, alliterative curse, and made everybody laugh.

Acknowledgements

Special thanks to:

Sarah Molloy, my agent, for her enthusiasm and all those phone calls I thought I'd never hear.

Lynne Drew and Kate Elton at Arrow, for making all my efforts worth it fifty times over.

Mothers of daughters everywhere, especially Mrs Bennett, who was so greatly vexed when Mr Bingley danced with Charlotte.

And of course to my lovely Andrew, Phil and Alex, for their love, laughs, and support when I needed it most.

Prologue

The invitation came on a Saturday morning, just in time to wreck my weekend. On stiff, crinkly edged card it read:

Mrs and Mrs Edward Metcalfe
request the pleasure of the company of
Sophy and Dominic
at the wedding of their daughter
Belinda Anne
To Mr Paul Fairfax
At
The Inn by the Beck
On Saturday, 11th May, at 1.00 p.m.
RSVP

It wasn't that it came as a shock. When your sister's wedding date's been set, you don't have to wait for the invitation to arrive to find out. If you have a mother like mine, BT lines are buzzing instantly. She'd probably announced it in the *Telegraph*, the *Manchester Evening News*, and very possibly the *South China Morning Post*, too. For all I knew she might even have announced it on the Internet. Not to be outdone by an arch-rival neighbour, Mum had recently acquired a Toshiba laptop.

There had been an engagement bash back in January, but three months had whizzed by since then, and if ever a party had been thrown from mixed motives, it was Belinda's. You only had to listen to my mother.

To Maggie Freeman, the arch-rival neighbour, there was a barely concealed hint of up-yours: 'Oh, yes, he whisked her off to Florence just last week – proposed right on the Ponte Vecchio – I suppose you've seen her ring?'

To neighbours she actually liked it was: 'Well, of course, Ted and I are delighted – he's doing terribly well and obviously besotted . . .'

To me, while we were whipping satay sticks from the oven, it was a whispered, '. . . and I feel he'll be *good* for Belinda – nothing *wishy-washy* about him, if you know what I mean. Don't ever tell her I told you, but I always thought she'd end up with one of those wishy-washy boys she could never say no to. Daddy was afraid it might be that Tim – a nice enough boy, of course, but not much use in a crisis, if you ask me. I won't tell you what Daddy called him – it was terribly rude.'

There must have been forty-odd guests at Belinda's party, which wasn't bad at short notice. Two-thirds were specifically her friends; the rest assorted family and friends, all milling pleasantly in my folks' party-sized sitting room and spilling into hall and kitchen, as they do. As always at any bash thrown by my folks, foody-drinky warmth hit you the instant you walked in the door, which was just as well, given the sub-zero frost outside.

In case you're a normally nosy person (like me) let me share some more eavesdroppings. From assorted friends of Belinda's I heard this:

'He bought her that dress, you know. In Florence. She won't say, but it looks like Versace to me. Mind you, Belinda could almost make British Home Stores look like Versace.'

'Makes you sick, doesn't it? The most Ian's ever bought me is a satin teddy from Knickerbox.'

'Mind you, I'm not sure I'd actually *want* a bloke like Paul. I'd never relax for a second – there'd always be half a dozen bitches trying to pinch him.'

Belinda, as you may have gathered, was floating on a euphoric pink cloud. The dress was little, black, and possessed that simple yet out-of-the-ordinary something that screams megabucks. And if Paul's arm scarcely left her waist all evening, you could hardly blame him.

Nobody ever believes we're sisters. She modelled for a bit, among other things (cookery course, secretarial stuff) but wasn't tall enough to make the grade. I have the inches, at five foot eight, but Belinda has the rest. A perfect size ten, the kind of creamy-honey skin that never goes pink and pasty even in the depths of winter, a luxuriant mane of dark-honey hair, and hazel eyes with lashes you would swear came from Boots Over-The-Top range. And a face, well . . . A friend of hers once confided to me, 'I hate to say it, but when someone looks like that you almost wish she was an utter cow so you could hate her with a clear conscience.'

I'm not an Ugly Sister, exactly, but with competition

3

like that you can't help feeling like one. I'm a perfect size thirteen and three-quarters: 36C top, 37D bottom, skin of cream without the honey, and a luxuriant-ish mane of common-or-garden dark brown hair like Mum's. I have Mum's eyes, too: big, navy-blue jobs which I may modestly say are my best feature.

I'd only met Paul a couple of times before, and since he'd fit right into a mail-order catalogue of Grade A men, it had been a relief to find I didn't actually fancy him. About six foot one, he had the lithe build of a tennis pro, with that medium olive skin that looks brilliant against white. He had dark brown eyes to match and hair the colour of very old, polished mahogany. At thirty-one, four years older than Belinda, he was a meteorically rising star in some management consultancy.

'Great to see you again – how's London treating you?' he asked, when I finally made it to the happy couple. 'Hope the traffic wasn't a complete bitch.'

'Fairly bitchy, but never mind.' I'd driven up and been a bit late. 'Well, what can I say? Congratulations, and all that . . . I think you should have warned us all to wear sunglasses before looking at that ring.'

It was a mega-watt diamond cluster, not so huge as to be knuckle-dusterish – her fingers wouldn't take it – but the stones flashed a blue fire that made you blink.

Belinda gave a guiltily pleased little laugh. 'I'm sure it was horribly extravagant . . .'

His hand was still on her waist in that *she's mine* fashion. 'Sweetheart, you should know me by now. If a thing's worth doing . . .'

'You did the whole thing properly,' I said. 'Right out of the romantic rule book. Men like you are an extinct species in London.'

'Sophy, how can you say that?' Belinda tutted. 'Didn't Dominic whisk you off from some boring party to some flash restaurant right after you met?'

'Yes, he has potential,' I said lightly. 'As long as he doesn't start asking me to sew buttons on his shirts I might tolerate him till Valentine's day.'

Belinda gave another little laugh. 'Sure sign she's mad about him,' she stage-whispered to Paul. 'Any madder and she'd be saying she was going right off him already, just so as not to tempt Fate.'

'Sweetheart, Fate is for losers,' Paul said crisply. 'If you want something, you go out and *make* it happen.'

When I caught her alone for a minute, later on, free-flowing alcohol had only heightened her glow. 'I just couldn't believe it,' she gushed happily. 'I mean, we'd only just arrived and he took me straight to the bridge, and there we were at sunset, and suddenly he took this little box out of his pocket – it was like a dream. And later, back at the hotel . . .' She drew me aside and whispered, 'All I wore for practically the next twenty-four hours was the ring.'

'And a big fat grin, I bet.'

'You bet.' She went on in a giggly whisper, 'I've never met anyone who turns me on like he does. I never have to say "left hand down a bit" – he just seems to *know*, if you get what I mean.'

'Trollop,' I said severely, thinking: Lucky old you. 'No wonder you're walking like Clint Eastwood.'

During the next hour I did plenty more eaves-dropping – I couldn't avoid it, not that I actually tried. From a couple of Mum's friends from the golf club I heard, '. . . mind you, I always think it's a shame when the younger sister gets married first. Sophy must be coming up to thirty and it's so hard for girls these days. Half the chaps are raging poofs.'

'Trudi, you're not supposed to say that word nowa-days. Anyway, Sophy *is* seeing someone, Sue told me: a merchant banker, apparently. She was hoping she'd bring him tonight but it's probably a bit soon for family dos.'

From another knot of Belinda's friends I heard: 'Does that Paul ever let go of her? He's had a proprietary arm around her all bloody night.'

'She probably likes it. By all accounts they hardly got out of bed their first four weekends – I'm only surprised she hasn't moved in with him already. Mind you, all that rampant non-stop bonking gave her cystitis. It bruises your tissues.'

'Christ. Still, if you'd like a dose of that from rampant non-stop bonking, I'm willing and able.'

'Oh, grow up. And stop gawping at her legs, will you? If you start sticking a rifle in my back at three o'clock in the morning I'll know who you've been dreaming about.'

Around half-nine I opened the door to a latecomer. 'Tamara! We'd just about given you up.'

'Hi, ratbag,' she grinned. 'Long time no see. Quick, let me in, it's freezing – I walked all the way from The Bear. I got waylaid by Dave Doodah earlier and he dragged me off for a quick one, only it turned into three and a game of pool. I'm a bit pissed already, actually.'

'So am I,' I replied happily. The Bear was half a mile up the road. Tamara Dixon, an old schoolfriend of mine, lived four doors away. She'd been abroad for three years on and off, so I hadn't seen much of her lately, and at Christmas she'd been skiing, so I hadn't even seen her then. Under a halo of red-gold curls and the kind of innocent-angel face you see in sentimental Victorian paintings, Tamara possessed a blithely wicked streak. She could be on the dippy side, too, but she was a good laugh.

'Glad to be back?' I asked, once she'd warmed up.

'Not sure yet, but Mum's so chuffed to have me home, she's even doing my ironing. So how's this Dominic?' she added, with a grin. 'Belinda's told me all about him.'

'I'm surprised she had to. Mum's already told half of north-west England.'

She laughed. 'Did you meet him through Posh Whatsit?'

'Are you kidding? We don't quite deal in big-league stuff.'

By 'Posh Whatsit' she meant Aristos Recruitment, who had twenty branches in London and the south-east, of which I was supposed to manage one. 'Aristos' wasn't meant to have 'posh' connotations, exactly. Pronounced 'Aristoss', it apparently means 'best' in ancient Greek, which is a laugh if you could see some of the people taking our literacy and numeracy tests.

'I gather Paul's big-league,' she said, nodding towards the star guests. 'Or well on his way. No wonder your mum's looking like the cat that got the goldfish.'

Later, as people were drifting off, I heard someone say, 'So when's the wedding?'

You should have seen Mum's face. Radiant glory, wreathed in beaming smiles. 'They haven't *quite* fixed a date yet, but I'm sure it won't be long . . .'

Which brings me neatly back to that invitation hitting the mat. With it came a note:

It's all going to be a terrible rush – barely six weeks to organise everything – I really must lose a few pounds before I even *think* about looking for something to wear – but they were very lucky to get a cancellation. I do hope Dominic'll be able to come. We're so looking forward to meeting him. Much love in haste,
    M x
    And a x from D, of course.

I stuck the invitation on the mantelpiece, where it glared balefully at me. 'Well?' it seemed to say. 'Are you going to sort this out, or what?'

Mum phoned that same evening. 'You will bring him, won't you, dear? I've told absolutely everybody about him and you do want to keep your end up – Zoe Freeman's still seeing that Oliver – I had to invite him, of course – he looks a bit chinless to me but that's all the more reason for you to indulge in a little bit of flaunting—'

'Mum—'

'Yes, I know it sounds bitchy, dear, but Maggie's on and on about Oliver this and Oliver that – I really will murder that woman one day – you'd think a corporate lawyer was a cross between God and Mel Hudson to hear her carry on—'

'*Gibson*, Mum. Mel Gibson.'

'You know what I mean. Please do tell Dominic we'd love to see him – he surely can't be booked up six weeks in advance – if he thinks enough of you I'm sure he'll be only too pleased . . .'

After another minute of this I said weakly that yes, I was sure he'd love to come, yes, I was fine, everything was fine, give my love to Dad and Belinda, see you soon, and hung up.

'She wants me to keep *my* end up,' I said. 'Permit me a hollow little laugh.'

Alix, my friend, flatmate and unpaid counsellor was giving me her *God, You're hopeless* look. 'God, you're hopeless,' she said. 'Why can't you just dump him and be done with it?'

'I can't just *do* it! I've got to psych myself up first – think of an utterly unarguable reason why we're no longer compatible.'

'I can think of a brilliant one,' she said. 'Death is generally considered the perfect grounds for ending an inconvenient relationship. Have him mugged to death for his gold cards.'

I don't mind telling you, such callousness appalled me. 'Wouldn't it seem just a bit ungrateful, after I've used him so shamelessly?'

'Stuff that. Have it done next week – quick, clean, and no chance of a reconciliation. You can't take a corpse to a wedding.'

'A messy murder would cast a bit of a cloud over the wedding,' I pointed out. 'I don't want to be a killjoy, with everyone feeling sorry for me. And how on earth would I look heartbroken when I was actually thinking: Thank God for that – pass me another large vodka and the best man, please?'

'You think of something, then!' She gave an up-to-here sigh. 'I hate to say I told you so, but I *did*. If you will invent some perfect, pain-in-the-arse bloke just to get your mum off your back—'

'He wasn't *entirely* invented,' I pointed out.

'Don't split hairs.' She sloshed me out a third glass of Jackdaw Ridge. 'You made him up, you get shot of him.'

ONE

I blame it entirely on pressure of work, but for the next couple of weeks Dominic and I were still officially an item at the bottom of my in-tray. Every time it rose to the surface, saying, 'Well?' I told it to bugger off, I was far too busy and important to deal with it just now.

After a lull we were suddenly inundated. IT, marketing, accounts: you name it, they wanted it, and that was without the temps. We were trawling old candidate files and advertising everywhere but the backs of cornflake packets. There was barely even time to discuss really crucial stuff, like the previous night's *Friends*, or that irritating woman in the sandwich shop.

I didn't tackle Dominic properly until Sunday morning, nineteen days before the wedding. Having *him* dump *me* would have been the simplest way out, but that wouldn't keep anybody's end up, least of all mine. I suppose I'd been hoping my imagination would suddenly whack me on the head with the perfect way out. It had been very creative once. I'd had brilliant fantasies about being in the Famous Five (instead of that wet Anne with her dolls) or plotting against the Sheriff with Robin Hood (instead of that wet Maid Marian).

Mind you, I hadn't exercised it much lately, except with the kind of fantasies you don't tell your mother

11

about, so since all it had come up with was 'Abduction by Aliens', I was still dithering over alternatives.

Nobody was helping me, either. Alix was still asleep, and although a vaguely human body was sprawled on the sofa, it was absorbed in the football pages. Its beloved Tossers United had screwed up yet again so it was serious stuff. I was up against a bad case of TMD, a.k.a. Temporary Male Deafness.

The body belonged to Alix's 'little' brother Ace, all five foot eleven of him. He was twenty-six, quite nice-looking under the scruff, and his light-brown ponytail was in vibrant condition, thanks to my Pantene 2 in 1, which he pinched constantly. With it he wore one gold earring and, except when Tossers had screwed up, a chilled-out air I defy anyone to beat.

'You might make *some* suggestion, even if it's completely brainless,' I muttered. 'You could at least show *willing*.'

Not so much as a primeval grunt.

Currently occupying the cupboard that passed as a third bedroom in this flat, Ace had moved in for a week a couple of months back, and had stayed because he preferred paying cupboard-sized rent to the room-sized variety. Despite nicking Pantene and everything else, Ace had his uses. If you had a sudden craving for Jaffa Cakes just before *EastEnders*, he'd nip to the Pop-In News 'n' Grocery if you asked him very nicely.

After a thirty-second time lapse, something got through the footie fog. 'I'd make him a perve, if I were you,' he announced. 'Tell your mum you went round

12

one night and found him poncing around in high heels and one of your bras, all upset because he couldn't find enough socks to stuff it with.'

'Dominic's not like you,' I said testily. 'He doesn't have to hunt under the bed every morning for any putrid socks that haven't actually walked to the washing machine by themselves. He's got whole drawers full, all neatly rolled up and colour-coded.'

'S&M, then.' The little toad was grinning his face off. 'What if he suddenly asked you to do the Miss Bumwhack bit?' He put on a lecherous, gasp-and-pant voice. 'I've been a really, *really* bad boy – I was playing with my winkle all night—'

'For God's sake, he'd never call it a *winkle*. Anyway, I refuse to have a relationship with a perve.'

'Suit yourself. Sling me a couple of those chocolate fingers, will you?'

I slung. There were four left in the packet on the coffee table. *Four*, and I'd bought them only an hour previously, while picking up the papers at the Pop-In.

Ace bit half off both of them and continued with his mouth full, 'Your mum was bound to resort to emotional blackmail in the end. It's a mum's favourite weapon and if you haven't sussed that out by now, then quite frankly, I despair of you.'

I could almost have written a dissertation on Emotional Blackmail, Maternal Variety Of. Before phoning home an hour and a half previously I'd been psyching myself up for a hefty dose of precisely that. I'd decided to be strong, harden my heart, not give in

13

to it. I'd worked out exactly what I was going to say.

I'd started all brisk and no-nonsense, as you do. I was very sorry but I didn't think Dominic was going to be able to make it, after all. He was terribly busy.

Cue for, 'Oh, Sophy, *really*! I knew you'd let me down again, just when everybody's dying to meet him. I told wretched Maggie he was almost definitely coming and you know what that woman's like . . .' She went on a bit.

Eventually Mum'd gone all plaintive on me: 'Sometimes I wonder whether you're ashamed of me and Daddy. Every single time you've promised to bring him home . . .' Etc.

To distract myself from the memory of Mum's soulful voice and Ace's demolition of the biscuits, I leafed through the *Mag on Sunday*; the lovelorn small ads are always good for a laugh. As usual they were crawling with slim, attractive, bubbly women who WLTM unmarried, un-sad, un-ugly blokes for caring and sharing. You had to admire their optimism.

'Maybe I should put an ad in,' I said now. '"Daft cow, 30, needs passable blokes for one day only. No polyester shirts, no creeps, positively no sex, fifty quid."'

'I'll do it for fifty quid,' the little toad grinned. 'Only you'll have to buy me a flash suit first.'

'Brilliant. You look *exactly* like Mum's idea of a thirty-five-year-old merchant banker.'

I mooched to the window. This corner of south-west London could occasionally look quite passable; for once there wasn't so much as a crisp packet dancing in the breeze. The sun was pointing shining fingers at our grubby Edwardian sashes, making sanctimonious observations about lazy cows and Mr Muscle.

I ignored it. 'I'll just have to say I've dumped him. Maybe he's turning horrendously jealous and possessive.'

'That'll never wash with your old lady. She'll only think it shows how keen he is.'

True.

'Course, you could always do what I usually do when up to my nuts in hassle,' he went on, turning the pages noisily. 'Leg it. Or wing it. I'll take a quick look in the cheap flights bit . . .'

Constructive suggestions from Ace had always come under the heading of 'Forlorn Hope'. Working on autopilot, my hand conveyed another chocolate finger to my mouth. The previous fifteen or so were making me vaguely sick, but what the hell?

'The basic problem is that old hag Maggie Freeman,' I explained. 'Mum's bragged to her about him, so if I don't produce this hot favourite in the perfect-potential-son-in-law stakes, she stands to lose about three million points.'

Maggie Freeman had been my mother's 'friend' and neighbour for nearly twenty-five years. Neither could stand the other really, but they pretended for the sake of form. It all stemmed from them each having two daughters of similar ages. Arch-rivalry, in other words, from the time we were old enough to do anything to brag about.

Take our first ballet exam, when Sarah Freeman

15

and I were six. At the end of a doorstep conversation Maggie had dropped a casual, 'Oh, by the way, Sue, did I tell you Sarah got a Highly Commended?' This had been uttered in the smug knowledge that I'd only got a Fairy-Elephant Pass, and the neighbourly rot had started there, so to speak. But Mum had got her own back later, when I got my Junior Dolphin swimming badge a whole term before Sarah. Fifty points to the Freemans, fifty to the Metcalfes. And so it had gone on: me *versus* Sarah, Belinda *versus* Zoe.

The scores had been relatively even until three years ago, when Maggie had notched up fifty trillion points in one go. Sarah Freeman had Got Engaged. And not to just anybody: to some minor landowner with a country house and a second cousin who was a *Sir*.

Maggie's smugness had known no bounds. For months she'd popped round every other day with pictures of pageboys' outfits, saying, 'What do you think, Sue? We're still dithering over transport – can't decide between the white vintage Rolls and the horse-drawn carriage. Such a pity you can't rely on the weather.'

At first Mum had smiled nicely and made her a cup of tea. Later she'd smiled through clenched teeth and made her a cup of tea. Later still she'd smiled through clenched teeth, made her a cup of tea, and wished to God she had some arsenic to put in it.

So Belinda's wedding, to my mother, was the rough equivalent of a rollover lottery jackpot. There were no ancestral acres or Sir-type cousins to brag about, but in one respect at least, she could outdo Maggie. While

Sarah, Zoe and I are what you might call passably attractive – at least nobody's ever asked us to stick a bag over our heads – Belinda, as I said before, is Something Else. Mum's hour of glorious getting-her-own-back was about to come. All she needed to ice her perfect wedding cake was one thing: to cap Zoe Freeman's chinless Oliver with my tall, suave, handsome, witty, I-think-he-must-be-getting-serious Dominic Walsh, merchant banker.

Ace had gone quiet. I thought he was back with the Tossers until he jabbed his finger at the paper. 'Blimey, I'm a genius. Take a look at that.'

Half expecting a one-way cheapie to Outer Mongolia, I humoured him and cast it a glance. And another.

'Ace, this is an escort agency!'

He gave me that noble patience look blokes do so well. 'I'd hardly be showing you an ad for a male impotence clinic.'

'There's no way I'm going to an escort agency! They'd think I was desperate. The *bloke*'d think I was desperate.'

'You *are* desperate.'

'You know what I mean. What kind of man does that, anyway?'

He considered. 'OK, a bloke who fancies himself and wants money for old rope. Still, worth a try.'

I scanned the blurb. It was worded to persuade cynics like me that hiring an escort was no iffier than hiring a carpet shampooer, and a lot more fun.

Nice try, I thought, but Ace was giving me a *Well?* look.

'I'd feel a prat, explaining the situation,' I protested. 'They'd crack up.'

'Course they wouldn't.'

'I bet they would.' The woman in the advertisement looked as if 'desperate' had never entered her vocabulary. Cool. Classy. In control. The type who hasn't done anything stupid or embarrassing since she was three and half and knows she never will again. 'I'd have to check the small print, but I have a feeling that paying a man for his company is against my principles.'

'Look at it this way, Sophe. If you hadn't got a car for the day, you'd hire one. You haven't got a bloke for the day, so hire one.'

'Ace, hiring a Dominic is not precisely the same as hiring a Ford Escort with airbag. The men are bound to think you're dying to inspect their credentials.'

'You could always say you're a lezzie but you haven't got the nerve to tell your folks.'

'Any more helpful suggestions?' Still eyeing the smug, skinny blonde in the ad, I consoled myself with the thought that she probably had no boobs to speak of, unless they were silicone implants. 'I bet they charge an arm and a leg.'

'Probably. You wouldn't want some cheap bloke, would you?'

Well, no.

At this point Alix staggered in, yawning as if she'd been up half the night. Which she had, if the crawling-in noises I'd heard at roughly four fifteen were anything to go by. Actually, I was surprised she'd crawled in at all. As her current bloke was turning out better than expected, I didn't see much of her lately. I missed her, especially when there was someone particularly annoying on the television and I had no one to have a friendly bitch with. Alix and I always found precisely the same people annoying, which was one of the reasons we got on. She was five foot six, a grey-eyed natural blonde, 34A top and bottom, but since she envied my cleavage bitterly I had to love her.

Wrapped in a long, fleecy dressing gown patterned with teddies, she flopped into an armchair and yawned. 'Ace, if you make me a cup of tea I'll give you two quid.'

'Bugger off,' he said.

'Three quid,' she pleaded. 'Before I quietly die of dehydration.'

'You'll have to die, then. I'm trying to talk Sophe into giving this a go.'

'Giving what a go?'

He passed her the paper. 'See? Perfect answer to her little problem, or what?' He really looked unbelievably pleased with himself.

Alix's sleep-fogged eye slowly de-misted. 'Ace, this is an escort agency!'

He raised his eyes to the ceiling. 'I know, thicko! She needs a bloke for the wedding! Only she's got this idea that the bloke'd think she's panting for it.'

'He probably would,' she yawned. 'Most blokes think all women are panting for it anyway.'

'No, we just hope. It's what you call eternal optimism.'

'It's what you call eternal obsession with your dangly bits,' she retorted.

'Can we please get back to the *subject*?' With a pained expression, he pointed at the ad again. 'I mean, I'm a bloke and I don't think most other blokes'd think old Sophe's that desperate for a Melvyn.'

Dear little boy. I felt my self-esteem positively soaring.

Poor Alix wasn't quite with it. 'It's a Dominic she's desperate for, not a bloody Melvyn.'

I reached for the last chocolate finger. 'A Melvyn *Bragg*, dopey.'

Alix made the *might-have-known* face that often followed Ace's utterances. 'He really is a bit much first thing in the morning. I've told Mum often enough he should have been drowned at birth but she just says, "I know, dear, but at least I cut his tail off."'

Inured to this sort of thing, Ace was gaping at the empty packet. 'She's eaten the whole lot!' He waved it at Alix. 'Look at that! She'll be moaning next week that her knickers have shrunk!'

'She's stressed!' she snapped. 'Go and do something useful, will you? Like sticking a tea-bag in a cup.'

'Why can't your regular slave do it?' he demanded.

'He's still asleep and you're not. If you do me some toast and Marmite as well, I'll make it five quid.'

'OK.' He departed for the kitchen.

While Alix re-bent her head over the paper, I thought about toast and Marmite. Even better, one of Ace's Marlboro Lights. After months of worthy abstinence I could suddenly have killed for one really good nicotine hit. As a bonus it would probably taste vile and make me throw up all those chocolate fingers.

Alix was reading the ad. 'You're not actually going to do this, are you? I thought you were going to phone your mum this morning and say he couldn't make it.'

'I tried. She gave me a load of emotional blackmail about being ashamed of them, then, to ensure she had the last word, made an excuse about being busy, and hung up. So yes, I might just clutch the odd straw.'

'Sophy, you can't *pay* for a man! It goes right against the grain.'

I'd almost known her first, instinctive reaction would be the same as mine. Alix and I went back a long way, to our third day at university, where we'd had rooms in the same hall. We'd both been desperately homesick, while pretending to be the height of cool as we downed gallons of beer at Freshers' Nights. After getting drunk enough to throw up in adjacent loos, we'd confessed to each other how we wished we were dead and were terrified of lectures starting, in case everybody else was cleverer than us and made us look thick. From then on, things had improved no end.

Maybe it was desperation, maybe it was the thought of that conversation with Mum, but although we were invariably right about absolutely everything else, I was beginning to think Alix and I were both overreacting on this one. 'It's a service, like any other,' I said tentatively. 'After all, what if you fancied a civilised evening of *La Bohème* and wanted someone else to fight their way to the bar in the interval?'

'Oh, come on! What kind of "service" are they going

to think you're after? I saw a chat show about escorts not so long ago. You should have seen them – all bragging about how much they made on the optional extras and how the poor desperate women were so grateful. And believe me, none of them looked remotely like a Dominic.'

'Perhaps this place isn't like that. Surely there's no harm trying. If they haven't got anyone suitable, I'll forget it.'

'You should have forgotten it weeks ago. You should have dumped him before your mother started hoping it was Getting Serious.'

Exactly. So why hadn't I? Because it was easier not to, that's why. I'd have been back to square one.

Square one had started like this. About eight months back I'd split up with Kit. Kit and I had been an item for ages, until he'd told me he was terribly sorry, he was still very fond of me, but to be honest, he thought we'd turned into a *comfortable habit*.

Unlike me, Kit would barely have scraped a GCSE in fibbing. He'd delivered his dump-line in the awkward, stumbling tones of a hopeless liar and I'd known at once what was behind it.

Or rather, *who*. I'd met her at a do thrown by a colleague of his a couple of weeks previously. She'd given me that poisoned-honey smile such women always give you when they fancy your man like mad and are hoping you'll conveniently get run over on the way home. I'd poison-honeyed back (as you do) and hoped she'd come out in nipple warts for her pains.

On the way home afterwards Kit had said reproach-fully, 'I thought you were just a bit off with Jocasta.'

Jocasta. I ask you. 'Of course I was!' I'd retorted. 'She fancies the pants off you! She was giving you the eye half the night, only you're too thick to see it!'

'She was doing nothing of the sort,' he'd said irritably. 'God, women can be so unbelievably *bitchy*. She's a really nice girl.'

Bloke-speak for, *I wouldn't kick her out of bed, either*.

So when we'd come to that hideous, 'Sophy, we need to talk,' bit, I don't know how he could have imagined I was too thick to put two and two together. Too devastated to be dignified, I'd screamed it through a throatful of tears. The word 'cow' had figured prominently, I'm not ashamed to say, and faced with that, he'd admitted it. He was terribly sorry but you didn't choose these things, they just happened.

If Belinda hadn't been occupying our cupboard at the time, my loving mother would never have known the extent of my misery. But as it was, Belinda was doing a sort of foreign correspondent of the love-war zone, reporting back with messages like, 'Emergency supplies of vodka and tissues are being rushed in but the situation is frankly desperate.'

Which naturally resulted in worried maternal phone calls every other day, to check that any over-doses were only of the Nutella variety: 'Are you *sure* you're all right, dear?' etc. Eventually these had pro-gressed to anxious variations on, 'You really must get out more, dear, and find somebody else,' so one night, just to keep her happy (all right, to shut her up) I'd lied. Dominic had just slipped out, perfectly formed, but as I said before, he wasn't *entirely* plucked out of thin air.

Four nights before the fateful phone call, I'd gone to a party. I hadn't been in the mood, but the hostess was Jess, my number two at Aristos, who was thirty-six and even more blokeless than me (not so much as a damp squib in eighteen months). Jess was what my mother called 'a worrier', she'd been worrying about this do for days: what if hardly anyone turned up and she was left among her M&S nibbles like a female version of Mrs Merton's Malcolm?

So I'd taken along a duty-free bottle of Stolichnaya and prepared to be a party animal. I'd even put on a little black dress with a tiny bit of fluff just above my left nipple, as I'd read somewhere that it's a foolproof way of pulling; blokes are irresistibly drawn to said fluff and itch to brush it off. Nobody had told Jess this, however, as two minutes after I'd got there she said, 'Oh, look, there's a bit of fluff on your dress,' and flicked it off herself. Well, that's the last time I donate my duty-free booze to her.

At first it had looked as if her nightmare was coming true. Guests were thin, conversation strained, and people were starting to give their watches furtive glances. Knowing I could hardly desert a sinking do, I just carried on hitting the vodka, grinning fatuously and trying to break awkward silences with stupid jokes.

But lo, suddenly there arrived a raucous horde, courtesy of Luke and Neil from the estate agent's next door to Aristos. (I quite fancied Luke but he was a serial three-night-stand man.) They had a dozen friends in tow, most of whom Jess knew not at all, but who cared?

And there he was, across a crowded room, dressed from some previous do in a dinner jacket and dress shirt, open at the neck, his bow-tie wrenched undone. In short, the type to make your worst female enemy hate you even more if you had him on your arm. So I charged off to Jess's loo to look for another bit of fluff, but since she's one of those irritating houseworky types I couldn't find any. Not that it would have made any difference if I had.

For the next three hours, Dominic Walsh (for it was he) had assorted size-ten women hanging on to him. After an initial, perfunctory introduction I only managed to catch his eye twice and my alluring smile (perfected in bathroom mirror at age sixteen) had sod-all effect. So I carried on hitting the vodka and let some bloke called Clive chat me up. I phone a taxi about one fifteen, and would you believe, just as I was about to leave, Dominic came up, eyed my cleavage and said, 'Not off already?'

Story of my life.

If I'd been sensible and switched to Evian an hour previously, I might have said, 'Well, maybe not,' while metaphorically punching the air and yelling, 'Yes! Yes! Yes!' However, since I was Sophy Metcalfe, with incipient hiccups and a horrible feeling I might actually throw up within the next twenty minutes, I gave an enigmatic (drunken) smile, said, 'Afraid so,' and thought: Shit.

But then (I've only ever done this when really far gone) I grabbed a pen from Jess's side table and took his arm in what I imagined was a seductively inviting manner. In a huskily inviting tone (thank God no hiccups came out) I said, 'But feel free to give me a call,' and wrote my number on his wrist. I smiled again, floated out without falling over, and threw up the minute I got home.

Needless to say the bastard never phoned, but he served my devious purpose. I embroidered him nicely and he went down like a dream. I never told Belinda he was merely a Mum-pacifying concoction. She'd gone home by then and had seemed so pleased for me, I hadn't liked to disillusion her.

Back to our unhoovered living room, however, and still tea-less Alix.

'My mother was going on just as much as yours, and I didn't invent anybody. And I was in just as bad a state as you were. Worse, if anything. I mean, Simon just told me straight out that there was somebody else.'

Shortly after Kit had given me the elbow, Alix had suffered exactly the same. 'You always knew he was basically a reptile,' I pointed out. 'You always used to fall for reptiles.'

'So did you. Kit was too "nice", if you ask me. You'd only have got bored with him in the end.'

'I was nowhere near bored with him! He was the first decent bloke I'd had in ages!' However, I have to confess that she'd uttered a crumb of truth. Just occasionally his 'niceness' had made me guiltily irritated;

for example, he'd always refused to bitch about anybody, no matter how bitchy or bastardy they were. I'd almost wished he'd show a normal, human, bloke-ish crack.

And of course, I'd got my wish.

'Couldn't you ask that Luke bloke to do the honours?' she asked. 'I mean, I know he's an estate agent but he looks the part, at least.'

'Are you kidding? The real Dominic's a friend of his, or at least an acquaintance. I'd never tell him I'd invented a bloke, anyway. He'd crack up.' I hadn't even told Jess about Dominic, in case she let it out. More than once I'd nearly told Harriet, who was new and much more on my wavelength than Jess, but there'd always been an interruption.

'What about that Adam bloke at the gym?' she said. 'You used to quite fancy him.'

'I went off him. He's besotted with someone else.'

'Who?'

'Himself.' I hadn't been to the gym for weeks anyway – my sub had run out.

'Belinda's never met Calum,' she mused. 'I suppose you could ask him.'

Calum was the slumbering 'slave'. Alix had met him one freezing afternoon a couple of months back, after 'accidentally' spraying him with foam at the car wash. 'He looked marginally less primeval-slime-ish than the average,' she'd explained, 'so I thought, sod it, live dangerously.' Lately Alix, for her, was going right over the complimentary top, e.g. 'He looks quite sweet when he's asleep.'

27

Much as I appreciated the offer, I wouldn't have dreamt of inflicting my entire family on Calum for the day. I wasn't sure his relationship with Alix was on a firm enough footing to stand it. Besides which, Calum wasn't exactly how I pictured Dominic. He reminded me of a big, shaggy dog – very loveable, but not quite groomed enough. And very slightly portly about the tummy, if you want the truth.

'I couldn't possibly ask, if only because he's far too nice to say no,' I extemporised.

She didn't persist, 'I still think this agency business is mad. They'll all be slimeballs, you mark my words.'

'There's no harm in giving them a ring. I would like to keep Mum's end up, if only for a day.'

'You mean she'll be "off" with you for six months if you don't,' Alix corrected me sharply. She glanced over her shoulder towards the kitchen, whence came merry banging and crashing. 'God, he can't even make a cup of tea without creating a racket. If he wakes Calum up, I'll kill him. He looks really sweet when he's asleep.'

You see?

Ace's return, with sustenance, restored her humour. 'Thanks, *mon ange*. There should be a fiver in my bag, if you can find it.'

'Nah,' he said. 'You can iron me a couple of T-shirts.'

This was intended as a wind-up. Alix was supposed to echo, '*Iron*? What the hell do you think I am?' whereupon Ace would grin, 'A woman.'

Ignoring this bait, she made a face at her toast.

'You've put far too much Marmite on. How many times do I have tell you to scrape it?'

'God, I can't do anything right.' Ace shot me a hurt look that was rather spoilt by the wicked little wink he added. 'Bitch, bitch, bitch – moan, moan, moan – she's getting just like dear old Mum.'

'I'll tell her you said that!' Alix threw a cushion at him, Ace threw it back and a fight ensued. I didn't care whether it ended with Alix's tea going all over the carpet, but I retrieved the paper before it got torn or tea-soaked, or both.

We know the feeling, the blurb said. *We are Sally and Julia and we started Just For Tonight because we know exactly what it's like to be missing that one vital accessory for important occasions. If you've got the perfect dress, the perfect jewellery, the perfect shoes, why not choose the perfect man to complement them?*

Just too easy for words.

TWO

It wasn't, of course. The whole process reminded me of going out for dinner when you're feeling vaguely sick and the only dish you could really fancy picking at is 'off'. Still, my second choice was not only passable, but also available.

'He's prepared to do it,' I told Alix on the Tuesday evening. 'Julia Thingy rang this morning and said "no problem".'

'No problem?' she echoed. 'No problem for her, maybe – all she's got to do is take the money. You haven't thought this through, Sophy. It's a disaster just waiting to happen.'

The last thing I needed was anybody fanning my butterflies, so to speak. 'Will you stop being so bloody *negative*? It'll be fine. I'm meeting him on Friday for a quick drink.'

'*Fine*?' At it again like a human echo-chamber, she picked at morsels of red pepper from our stir-fry mix. 'How can a quick drink possibly guarantee it'll be "fine"? What if he bumps into somebody he knows at the reception and they give him away in front of everybody?'

'Then I'll commit instant hara-kiri with that lovely big knife they always provide for cake-cutting.'

'For God's sake! I wasn't joking!'

Neither was I. 'The odds are millions to one,' I pointed out.

'Don't kid yourself. People bump into old acquaintances all the time.'

'OK, thousands to one. And even if it was only ten to one, I can't cancel him now. I told Mum he's almost certainly coming and she practically had an orgasm on the phone.'

'And I'm damned if I'd drive a man I didn't known from Fred Flintstone to darkest Lancashire,' she went on, regardless. 'I'm sure even total psychos can seem perfectly charming over a pint in a pub. Don't come running to me when they find you dead in a ditch by Newport Pagnell Services.'

'He's been vetted! They *all* have!'

'What "vetting"? A couple of references? Look at all those paedophiles who were "vetted" before they got jobs in children's homes.'

Nutter tendencies were the least of my worries. If he murdered me on the way up, at least I wouldn't have to go through with it.

'What's his name, anyway?' she asked.

'Colin Davies.'

'And what does he do when he's not escorting?'

I didn't quite like the tiny emphasis she put on 'escorting'. She managed to make it sound exactly like 'male prostituting'.

'He used to be with one of the high-street banks, but he's taking a career break.'

'He's been made redundant, in other words.'

'So what if he has? It probably wasn't his fault! He

looked nice on the video – looked like he'd got a twinkle in his eye and if ever I needed a man with a GSOH, it's now.'

'If he's short of cash I suppose it's almost legit,' she conceded. 'I mean, what sort of man would do that if he didn't need the money?'

'There's nothing wrong with it!'

'Oh, come on. You've changed your tune. Would you want to be involved with a man who did that from *choice*?'

I refused to answer this on the grounds that I preferred not to think about it. 'I'll have hours to brief him on the journey up,' I said instead. 'About where we met, precisely how pissed I was at the time, my addiction to hot Ribena, and so on.'

'I just hope you can remember everything you told your mother. You'd better write it all down beforehand, so you can synchronise your lies. And I bet you anything he'll be a prat. I just can't bear the thought of some aren't-I-gorgeous prat thinking you can't get yourself a man. Make sure he knows desperation is not in your vocabulary – you're just incredibly choosy.'

I wasn't particularly desperate, in spite of having no carnal knowledge since Kit. I once read that unlike men, who get progressively more obsessed with sex the longer they go without, women do the exact opposite. The longer they go without, the more they think they'd prefer *Pride and Prejudice* and a Nutella sandwich. I wouldn't say it *exactly* applied to me. In the absence of anything both fanciable and available I'd indulged in the odd fantasy about the unavailable, e.g. George Clooney and Mr Darcy (not both at once, though now I come to think of it such a fantasy might steam-clean the windows nicely). I was beginning to prefer fantasy men to real ones, to be honest. Everything else in my life was perfectly satisfactory – why muck it up with heartache and covers yanked off you in the night? As for those heady first stages of a relationship, forget it. The buzz was great, but it was such hard work, looking perfect all the time and pretending to be too ladylike to fart.

I had wedding nightmares that night, complete with Colin. First he got drunk and told Mum they'd given him a bonus for taking me on, and then the Old Bill turned up and nicked him for fraud, deception, and impersonating a Dominic. I woke in a cold sweat at four o'clock, couldn't get back to sleep, and was consequently ratty at work.

Jess didn't help either. A memo from head office had just informed us that as we now wore the *Investors in People* logo, and the training budget was robust and healthy, Jess and I had been selected for some robust, healthy training in Wales. This would provide us with tough new challenges and improve our teamwork and problem-solving skills no end. Could we please contact them a.s.a.p., with any unacceptable dates between now and October?

Jess practically wet herself forthwith. 'I've heard about these courses! They make you go potholing! And abseiling! I'll *hate* it! I get vertigo! And what about my cat?'

She kept this up half the morning. At lunchtime I escaped, collided with Luke on his way to the pub and accepted his kind offer of a jar. 'Anyone'd think they were sending her to Colditz,' I muttered, over a large V&T. 'I don't want to go bloody potholing, either.'

'You'll love it,' he grinned. 'Ritual humiliation, from what I've heard. The instructors are all ex-SAS sadists. They make you crap yourself with terror and charge two thousand quid a head for the privilege. Fancy another?'

I had two more, two packets of smoky bacon, and a headache to follow. I was beginning to wish I were Alix, who'd recently gone freelance in graphic design. Nobody wanted to send her potholing and if she sloped off to the pub at lunchtime at least she could have a siesta afterwards.

I still had the headache when Mum phoned that evening. 'I don't know how this wedding's ever going to get organised,' she said, back in plaintive mode. 'Belinda still hasn't found any shoes and can you believe they haven't even booked the honeymoon yet?'

'You book it then. Tell them you've fixed up a week in Mablethorpe – that'll sort them out.'

'There's no need to be rude about Mablethorpe, dear. They were about to book a safari but Belinda suddenly went off the idea – the thought of all those horrible big wigglies was putting her off. They were going to be camping in the bush and you know what Belinda's like with wigglies. Still, she came round in the end – I really thought she was being very silly – but by then the hotels were booked up – I think they had a little tiff about it. Lord knows where they're going now – Paul's still trying for cancellations.'

After wittering on for ages about everything else that a) had already gone wrong, or b) hadn't yet, but undoubtedly would, she went on, 'I expect you'd like a word with Belinda – I'll just call her . . .'

I wasn't in the mood for this. If my main worry had consisted of where to stick a pin in Faraway brochures, I'd have been happiness made flesh. I'd even have gone around dispensing beatific smiles to traffic wardens and those irritating old people who hold you up in post offices.

I didn't even try not to sound exasperated. 'For God's sake, haven't you grown out of this wiggly thing yet?'

'It wasn't the wigglies! OK, I hate the thought of them crawling over the bed, but it's just so unbelievably expensive – nearly three *weeks* – Malindi and a tip to Zanzibar too – and he only wants to stay in really swanky hotels. It seems obscene when the people are so poor.'

She might have had a point but I wasn't in the mood to admit it. 'It's your honeymoon, for God's sake. If he wants to lash out, do you have to make an ideological thing of it? Give everybody massive tips if it'll make you feel better!'

'*Please* don't start having a go at me! I'm just about up to here – Mum's driving me mad – on and on non-stop about dresses and presents and speeches till I want to scream. I'm just so worn out with the whole business, and, well . . .'

35

I suddenly realised that under the tension, she sounded almost tearful. 'Well what?'

'Oh, nothing. I suppose I'm just hormonal, but everything's getting on top of me and Paul was getting impatient over the honeymoon, and now the wretched hotels are booked up . . .'

I began to see light. 'Mum said you'd had a little tiff – you have made up, haven't you?'

'Yes!' She gave a little laugh, but her voice was still wobbly. 'It's just me being daft, as usual. I knew I should never have watched *Weddings From Hell* . . .'

More megawatts of light. A 'real-life' reconstruction thing, *Weddings From Hell* had been screened a week or so ago; we'd caught the last half after the news. After two minutes Alix had summed it up thus: 'Typical commercial pandering to brain-dead voyeurism – dontcha just love it?'

Five minutes later, as some Neanderthal groom had chickened out at the last minute, she said, 'God, I hope Belinda's not watching this,' and I'd said, 'God, so do I.' But we'd been laughing. Half laughing, anyway.

I wasn't laughing now, I was back in maximum exasperation mode. 'For God's sake, don't tell me you've worked yourself into a thing about Paul not turning up?'

A moment's defensive silence was answer enough.

'You had a *tiff*,' I went on. 'People do, Belinda, so, for God's sake, get a grip. I bet you've been watching that wretched film again, haven't you? On top of *Weddings From Hell*?'

'No! Well, not lately . . .'

Not that it would have made any difference; she'd watched *Four Weddings* so often, it must have worn a smooth groove in her brain. 'Belinda, you are not poor old Duck-face. Paul is not going to do a Hugh Grant and chicken out at the altar. Though quite frankly, if you turn your nose up at five-star honeymoons I wouldn't blame him if he did slope off to the pub instead!'

'Will you *please* stop having a go at me? I can do without it! And I wasn't thinking any such thing, so just shut up, will you?'

Her tone, angry and tearful together, gave me a jolt, but also told me I was spot-on and she felt too daft to admit it.

So I said, 'Sorry – I didn't mean to have a go at you. I'm just jealous. I'd give anything to be off to exotic sunsets and sex siestas. Not to mention long exotic drinks, with exotic wigglies plopping into them from the shady umbongo tree.'

She gave a wan little laugh. 'Sorry – I know I shouldn't be moaning but Mum's so paranoid about something going wrong, she's making me a nervous wreck, too. I've been having visions of tripping over my dress and Dad making embarrassing speeches. After a few drinks he's bound to tell that bath story that makes me cringe.'

I wouldn't quite put it past him. 'Tell him you'll kill him. Tell him *I'll* kill him, if you like. And try to be patient with Mum. It's only because she's so desperate for everything to be absolutely perfect.'

'Do you think *I* don't know that? The food, the

37

weather, even you and Dominic. You'll never believe what Maggie said, a couple of days ago.'

I nearly had a heart attack here. What if, by some foul and devious jungle telegraph, Maggie had got wind of my deception? 'What?'

'She asked whether he was coming and Mum said, "Yes, I think so," and Maggie gave her one of those smug, knowing looks that get right up Mum's nose, and said, "Well, we'll see," and Mum prickled like an irate mother hedgehog – you know how she does – and said, "Just what do you mean by that?" and Maggie said, "Well, Sue, the number of times he *hasn't* turned up, it makes you wonder whether Sophy's invented him." She pretended it was a joke, of course, but Mum said she'll never know how she didn't brain her with a frozen leg of lamb – they were in the supermarket at the time.'

My coronary receded. If Maggie really had heard anything she'd have told a couple of cronies at the golf club and it would have got back to Mum by now. 'That bloody woman!' I said – with pretty convincing indignation, I thought.

'Yes, Mum was livid. She went on and on: "How *dare* she imply that my own daughter'd lie to me?" – and all that. She only shut up about it when *Emmerdale* came on. She's feeling bad for not inviting Alix, by the way – so do I, come to that, only the numbers were going through the roof—'

'For heaven's sake, she never *expected* to be invited!' She hadn't. Hardly a way-back friend of Belinda's, she didn't quite fall into the 'family friend' category either.

'I suppose not. Give her my love anyway, will you? Oh, bum, *now* what?' Her voice took on a weary note. 'She's calling me. I'd better go . . .'

Over a takeaway *souvlaki* I recounted the conversation to Alix. 'Honestly, I could strangle that girl sometimes. Africa! Gorgeous sunsets and elephants and the snows of Kilimanjaro! If some chap was planning to make *me* suffer three weeks in obscenely expensive hotels, I think I'd manage to grit my teeth and think of England. And whatever she says, she *had* worked herself into a tizz about Paul, I swear. That girl's her own worst enemy – always expects the worst, bloke-wise.'

'Especially if they've just had a tiff.'

'And especially after bloody Marc.'

Bloody Marc was the reason Belinda had been occupying our cupboard last year. They'd been an item for months, until she'd seen him out one night (when Marc was supposed to have been working, naturally) with a certain Melanie, who was supposed to be a friend of Belinda's.

Don't hold your breath – she didn't go and pour a pint of Guinness over them. She didn't even confront them. She went home, cried, and agonised over whether to leave a go-and-screw-yourself message on his answerphone.

And chickened out.

Belinda, alas, had never been made of very stern emotional stuff. Only last Christmas, when dragged by Mum to the old dears' day centre bazaar, she'd bought a sad-looking knitted teddy (reduced to a pound) because everything else had been sold and she'd thought they might chuck him in the rubbish. (All right, so I might have bought him too – such soppiness does tend to run in families – but you get the picture.)

For another week she pretended ignorance while Marc made more excuses about working late. But instead of chucking him and finding someone else sharpish, she spun him some supposedly casual line about wanting to get away from home and work in London for a bit.

The object of this whopper, naturally, was to shock Marc into Realising Just How Much He Cared. And naturally, it backfired. He'd made vague, *Well, if that's what you want* . . . noises, and Belinda could hardly lose face by staying put. That was when I'd had a tearful phone call, asking whether our cupboard was available. She'd turned up on the doorstep, all wounded and beautiful, deposited by a cabbie who'd evidently fallen in love with her en route from Euston and only charged three quid.

After a couple of weeks' languishing on our sofa, wearing out the video with *Four Weddings and a Funeral* and waiting for Marc to call, she'd eventually got a grip: registered with an emergency-nanny agency and taken comfort from the sweet little babies. (Belinda had come late to nursery nursing and loved it. Well, it takes all sorts.)

Still, Marc had gradually worn off. She'd just started talking about returning home when Kit had done the dirty and she'd stayed, in order to offer sisterly support, tissues, etc. and only ten days later, poor Alix had been raiding the tissues, too. As Belinda had despairingly observed, our flat had turned into a sort of serial dumping ground; she'd jinxed the pair of us and had better clear off before anything worse happened.

She had met Paul only three weeks later.

I was meeting Colin on the Friday evening. By Friday lunchtime I felt so sick with apprehension, it showed. Jess said, 'You're looking a bit funny. You haven't got this horrible tummy bug, have you?'

'I hope not.' On top of dozens of aggressive butter-flies, that was all I needed. While Jess went for her sandwich I nearly confided in Harriet, but she started telling me about a friend who'd fallen wildly in love on some exotic beach. All very nice, until she found out the bloke was married and lived in Singapore, and her coil had forgotten to read its job description.

'And you thought you had problems,' I told myself, but it didn't help. By the time I left, I was tizzing for England.

He was there, bang on time. 'Sophy? How do you do? What can I get you?'

Phew. He looked right, in an un-special way. No white socks or halitosis. His smile didn't even look put on. 'Just a mineral water, please – no, make that a vodka and tonic.'

For the entire forty minutes we were there he was perfectly pleasant, perfectly non-prat-ish. He even managed to make me feel that inventing blokes was a perfectly normal female activity. I couldn't really have fancied him, but I felt comfortable with him. I was so relieved I got a bit pissed, but I don't think he noticed.

I phoned Mum when I got home and told her Dominic was definitely coming. 'So she had another orgasm,' I told Alix later, over the phone. (She was at Calum's, just for a change.) 'And then *I* nearly had a fit when she said she'd book us a double room at the hotel.'

'You can't share a *bed*!' Alix screeched.

'Don't panic. We're not even sharing a room. God knows why I didn't think of it before. Half the family are staying over so she was bound to assume we would too. After a frantic panic I think I said we couldn't possibly stay over, he was zooming off to Kuala Lumpur the next day.'

'Kuala Lumpur?' she echoed.

'It was the first thing that came into my head! I thought it was rather good,' I added, in hurt tones. 'He's got a top-level meeting with local bankers or something. Maybe ministers, too. Excellencies, and all that. I said it was a terrible shame but he'd have to leave at a reasonable time on the Saturday. He might still have work to do first thing on Sunday morning. So by the time I'd laid all *that* on with a shovel, she was overwhelmed with gratitude that he was sparing the time to come at all.'

'So how many lies does that make?' Alix demanded. 'Or have you lost count? All this is asking for trouble; you're just begging to trip yourself up.'

'Will you stop nit-picking? It'll be fine!' (If I kept

saying it, I might even convince myself.)

'Will *you* stay over?' she demanded.

'I thought about it, but I've already told the agency I'll drive him back. Seems an awful shame to have to leave early but I suspect I'll be dying to get away after all the strain anyway. I told Mum I'd have to drive him so he wouldn't be too knackered on the Sunday. It's an exhausting flight to KL, you know, even when you go First Class.'

'I'm surprised you haven't invented a company Learjet,' she snorted.

I had thought of it. 'So it's all sorted,' I went on brightly.

'*Sorted*?' she echoed. 'If that's "sorted" I'd like to see what total imminent disaster looks like. Sorry, but I've got to go. I'm in the middle of making a rhubarb crumble.'

'You *hate* rhubarb!'

'I know, but Calum loves it.'

The writing was on the wall.

Disaster struck early. Two days before the wedding, the agency called.

'Sophy Metcalfe? It's Julia Wright from Just For Tonight. I'm terribly sorry, but there's been a little hitch. Colin's been rushed to hospital with suspected peritonitis.'

Little? 'Can I call you back?' (I was in the office and preferred to throw up in private.)

'Look, don't worry,' she said, when I got back to her. 'I think I can suggest a replacement.'

'Nobody else'll do!' I wondered whether to strangle myself now, and save my mother the trouble. 'None of the others looked quite right—'

'Maybe not, but this one's new. He wasn't on the books when you called. Josh Carmichael – really very personable. I've already explained your little predicament and he's quite prepared to do it.'

If not for the thought of Maggie's smug triumph . . . 'Is "personable" a euphemism for good-looking? Because I really do need somebody pretty "personable". My mother's emotional health depends on it.'

She paused delicately. 'I wouldn't say he's pin-up stuff, exactly, but he's very *nice*-looking, if you know what I mean. I'd be quite happy to take him home to meet my mother. You know when a man's going to appeal to your mother, don't you? You can just tell.'

Knowing Julia's mother would have helped here. Some mothers go a bundle on those sad, wet types – 'Such a *nice* boy, dear, and personally I think an upholstery class a splendid way for him to make friends' – but I needed something more impressive. 'I don't want to appear over-picky, but I hope he's not the earnest spaniel type.'

'Oh, no,' she said. 'Definitely not *wet*, if that's what you mean. He's an ex-Royal Marine.'

These might not come in 'wet', but they very possibly came in 'macho brute'; even in 'sublimated psycho'.

'Presumably he's been vetted?' I asked, feeling both desperate and reluctant.

'I assure you, I'd never offer anybody who hadn't

been most thoroughly vetted.'

'And you're sure he's prepared to do it?'

'Quite prepared.'

'How tall?'

'Six two and a half.'

'Hair?'

'Mid brown.'

'Age?'

'Thirty-four.'

Near enough. 'Any designer stubble? My father's got a thing about designer stubble.'

'No, he's clean-shaven. I'm quite sure you won't be disappointed.'

Oh God, decisions. 'I'll pop in later and check the video.'

'Oh, dear . . .' There was a slight flurry on the other end. 'I'm afraid we haven't got the video yet – just the little passport photo he sent in with his application, but it doesn't really do him justice. They never do, do they?'

'Could I meet him tonight? Just for ten minutes?'

'I'll have to check. I'll ring you back.'

She got back to me ten minutes later. 'I'm so sorry, but he's tied up till Saturday morning.'

Oh, bum. Bum and buggeration. And, as my dear father is wont to roar when he can't find something in the cupboard under the stairs, 'Crap and Corruption! Shit and seduction!' Dad likes a good, rolling, alliterative curse, especially when Mum's calling helpfully from the kitchen, 'It *is* in there, dear, if you'll just look *properly* . . .'

'I'm sure he'd fit the bill very nicely,' Julia went on.

Oh, to hell. What choice did I have? 'All right then, book him. Please tell him to be here by eight o'clock. I daren't take any risks with the traffic. He can bring his suit on a hanger. We'll change when we get there. And – oh Lord – I forgot to say this before, but not a brown suit, please. My mother can't stand brown suits. And I do hope Colin'll be better soon.'

Alix was as close to dumbstruck as I've ever seen her. 'You *booked* him? Without even seeing his photo?'

'I didn't have much choice!'

'Sophy, you're off your trolley.'

'Leave her alone, can't you?' said dear little Ace. 'She's in enough of a state already. Have a fag, Sophe. Calm you down.'

'Don't you dare!' Alix snatched back his Marlboro Lights. 'You're supposed to be having *sex* with this bloke, for God's sake – what if he makes you shudder?'

She said nothing I hadn't already thought at least a million times. In my mind's eye I'd pictured a) a smarmy, pompous, crawly handed creep who'd instantly assume I was lusting after his body, and b) a macho, sexist, iron-pumped brute who'd instantly assume I was lusting after his body. 'If I don't like the look of him I'll just tell him thank you very much, but I've changed my mind.'

'Oh, really? And what will you tell your mother?'

Naturally, I'd prepared another little fib for insurance purposes. 'I'll tell her we had a seafood dinner the night before, he ate an iffy oyster, and is consequently suffering from non-stop runs.'

'See?' said Ace. 'She's got it all under control.'

If only.

At ten to eight on the morning of the wedding, I phoned home. A certain amount of psyching-up was necessary first; I needed to sound like someone cheerfully looking forward to a lovely day, not like a *Titanic* passenger who's just had a ghastly premonition and is about to embark anyway.

'Morning, Mum. Everything under control?'

'Yes, dear, fine. I'm just about to take Belinda breakfast in bed.'

I began working up to my devious point. 'Dominic's due any minute – I hope he hasn't overslept – he had some urgent work to do last night.' Here I cunningly inserted my porkie. 'We had a lovely seafood dinner before he had to dash. Gorgeous *fruits de mer* for two – langoustines, oysters, you name it.'

'Well, you know what they say about oysters, dear.'

I swear I almost saw her wink over the phone, 'Yes, Mother – full of essential vitamins and minerals.' And salmonella, if required. 'Anyway, must go.' I made a kissy noise into the phone. 'Give my love to Dad and Belinda, see you later . . .'

With jittery hands, I checked my things. Suit on hanger, shoes, directions, spare tights, spare knickers in case I actually did wet myself, hot brush, emergency suicide pills . . .

Quick, the loo.

Twenty minutes later 'Dominic' still hadn't shown

up and all butterflies had long since flown from my stomach, leaving several dozen earthworms in their place. Huge, squirmy worms, all under instructions to make me puke from nerves.

'Where the hell *is* he?' I fumed, torn between wanting to a) throw up and b) kill myself, in roughly equal proportions.

Clad in only a pair of Simpsons boxers, Ace poured himself a bowl of Rice Krispies. Alix was still asleep and therefore not hovering around in her dressing gown saying, 'Calm down – it'll be fine', while thinking: I *knew* it'd be a disaster.

Ace said, 'Don't panic. He'll show up.'

That was what I was beginning to be afraid of. Compared to a gut full of worms that I wouldn't even be able to drown in vodka, dodgy-oysters runs suddenly seemed a sweetly restful option. 'If he's not here in two minutes, I'm going.'

Suddenly beset by craving, I glanced around. 'Where are your fags? I could murder one.'

'Sorry, Sophe – I've run out.'

'For God's *sake*! I can't rely on *any*body!' I went for another emergency pee, asking myself for the millionth time why I'd ever got into this.

When I emerged, Ace was standing by the living-room window. 'A cab just pulled in,' he called, with his mouth full. 'Looks like Rent-a-Stud's here.'

I could hardly bear to look.

Ever since waking at five thirty, I'd had a male nightmare in my head. To give its full Latin name: *Young-fogeyus cravaticus, becoming rarer, but may still be seen in country pubs, where it emits distinctive, braying calls.*

'Wotcher think?' Ace asked.

On the pavement was a back-view blur of beigey chinos and olivey polo shirt, paying the cabbie. It straightened up, turned around, and looked directly up at the window where Ace and I stood.

No cravat, thank God. 'He'll do,' I muttered. 'And he bloody well ought to – he's costing enough.'

With jittery hands, I grabbed my things. 'If I get through the day without having to commit hara-kiri, I'll see you later.'

'Ta-ta, Sophe, have fun.'

Ha bloody ha. I'd wrenched the door open almost before he'd rung the bell. 'Where the hell have you been? I said *eight*!'

'I'm sorry. I overslept. It's only sixteen minutes past,' he added, glancing at his watch.

Close up, I saw a further reason for wobbly-throwing. 'You haven't even shaved!'

'I'm sorry. I was going to give myself a quick electric job in the cab, but I hardly ever use the thing and the batteries were more or less dead. If you can stop for two minutes at a petrol station, I'll buy some.' He added a decidedly wary smile and a hand. 'Josh Carmichael.'

He might well be wary: I was almost too cross to take it. 'Not now, you're not. You're Dominic Walsh, bachelor of this parish. So, for God's sake, let's go.'

My newish black Clio was freshly washed for once, the inside hoovered, all Mars bar wrappers removed from door compartments.

49

As I turned my head for reversing purposes, I caught his eye. 'Oh God, your eyes are wrong. I swear I told my mother they were blue.'

'Not much I can do about that, I'm afraid.'

Eye colour notwithstanding, a trickle of relief began to drown my worms. Once he'd had a shave he'd definitely do; mother-pleasing potential was certainly present. And Maggie-pissing-off potential, which was even more important. As Julia had said, he wasn't pin-up stuff, exactly; there was something vaguely crooked about his nose and mouth, but not enough to make you think: My God, haven't you ever thought about plastic surgery?

The eyes were sort of browny-green and went with his hair, which was indeed mid-brown and still damp from the wash. 'She probably won't remember,' I said, inching out of my space. 'If she does, I'll just say I was ratso the first time we met.'

He made no comment, which instantly made me wonder whether he was thinking a) that I got ratso on a regular and dangerous basis, and b) that he might therefore end the day in a body bag. Or, perhaps more likely, whether he was recalling agency warnings, e.g. '. . . and she did seem a trifle neurotic. Well, I dare say she must be if she's invented an other half, poor thing, so I do hope it won't be too much of a trial. I think I should warn you that some of them can turn into raging nymphos after three vodkas – they need very tactful handling. The trick is to appear sincerely flattered but terribly regretful that it's strictly against agency rules.'

Just in case, I went on, very crisply, 'Not that I'll be

getting remotely ratso today. Quite apart from the driving, I'm going to need all my wits about me.' After oozing out into the traffic, I headed round the corner to the Pop-In. 'They should have your batteries. Would you get me a packet of, erm, wine gums?'

'Will do.'

Damn it. What I'd actually meant to say was, 'a packet of Silk Cut', but had chickened out.

While waiting, I tried to ignore my desiccated mouth and fed myself soothing platitudes instead: so far so good, could be worse, etc. In one respect he was exactly what I'd have chosen. I'd had to specify 'tall'. If you're five ten and a half in your heels you need an absolute minimum of six foot. What I hadn't specified was, 'hefty enough to make me feel delicately slim by comparison.' I mean, I really can't do with men whose thighs are thinner than my own.

In his absence I gave myself a quick facial check. Not too gruesome. Considering the amount of sleep I'd had, even my eyes didn't look too bad. My hair was a mess, but since I was going to shove it up later, I didn't care.

However, what amazed me for about the zillionth time was the fact that I looked like any reasonably together, grown-up type of person. People *did* think I was reasonably grown-up and together. I'd often wondered how long I could keep the act up and what'd happen when I finally got found out.

I put the mirror away and watched 'Dominic' return. 'Happy little bunny' was not how I'd describe his expression. It bore all the marks of a man wishing to God he were anywhere else, doing anything else, but nobly determined to grit his teeth and suffer.

That acid snapping had been a mistake; I needed him on my side. I sort of smiled as he handed me the wine gums. 'It's very good of you to do this at such short notice. I hope you didn't have to come far.'

'Only about fifteen minutes in the cab.'

Nice voice, too: nothing nasal or irritating.

As I headed for the North Circular he finished his shave. 'Not perfect,' he observed, running a hand over the result. 'If we have time to stop at the services, I'll buy a wet razor and do it properly.'

'*If* we have time. The M6 can be a nightmare.' I felt I should say something about our situation here. 'I expect you're wondering what on earth makes a relatively sane woman invent a relationship.'

'They told me you had to fob off a relentlessly questioning mother.'

Now Mum might get on my nerves now and then, but I didn't want him thinking she was a complete pain. 'She was just concerned. I'm only doing this to keep her end up with the neighbours.'

I told him about Maggie. I couldn't exactly see his face; I was just aware of it out of the corner of my eye. A certain little smile seemed to be busying itself around the side of his mouth.

Laughing, the bastard.

Still, I couldn't altogether blame him. To somebody detached, the situation had all the makings of a first-class theatrical farce.

'If she's really that bad, why is your mother inviting

her today?' he asked.

'Because they're supposed to be friends. Haven't you got any friends you can't stand?'

'They wouldn't be friends if I couldn't stand them. They'd be acquaintances.'

Trust a man to apply irritating logic. 'You know what I mean. She had to be invited, anyway. We were all invited to her daughter's wedding.' Which was absolutely perfect, of course. Mum had valiantly smiled through it all, praying for a chance to do it even better, preferably in St Paul's Cathedral with a heavenly choir thrown in.

The pretty little village church where Sarah had got hitched had been booked solid for ages but the Inn by the Beck, the venue for Belinda's wedding, was the next best thing, so everyone said. Quaintly pretty, it had a restaurant that got reasonable write-ups in the papers.

At a roundabout I nipped out in the right-hand lane past one of those dithery little old men whose head just reaches a position where he can peer over the wheel. He always wears a hat that makes his ears stick out and he always takes his little old wife to the shops on a Saturday morning, even though he's got the rest of the week to do it.

'Where did we meet?' Josh asked.

'At a party.'

'How very conventional.'

'I'm terribly sorry.' I couldn't keep back a trace of acid here. 'I'd prefer to have crash-landed my clapped-out old Cessna in your back garden and had

53

you pull me from the wreckage, but unfortunately you were an impulse invention.'

Since I hadn't intended this to be funny – I was far too wound up to be thinking of jokes – I was a tad taken aback when he laughed.

'Whose party was it?' he asked.

'Jess from work, but it wasn't the most scintillating do in the world.' Sorry, Jess. 'We escaped as soon as decently possible and went for dinner.'

'It was instant sparks, then?'

'No, we were just starving. She'd only allowed four M&S nibbles per head.'

He was quietly laughing again but I didn't mind; some miserable bugger with zero sense of humour was the last thing I needed. 'By the way, you were working last night,' I told him. 'Just in case my mother says she hopes you weren't too terribly late to bed. We had a seafood dinner first and you pigged out on oysters. It had to be something potentially dodgy in case you turned out to be a total creep and I had to send you home.'

'I'm relieved to know I "passed". I wouldn't have liked to spend the entire weekend suffering from dodgy-oyster gut.'

'You very nearly did. I was just about to go when you showed up.'

'What sort of guy am I?' he asked. 'Laid-back? Possessive? Any dark skeletons in the closet?'

'You're a Mr Poppins among men,' I told him. 'Practically Perfect In Every Way.' As we passed Ealing Common, the sun pushed the sullen clouds aside and cast a May morning sparkle on everything. Including me.

Maybe it had the makings of a reasonable day, after all. Belinda was going to look like a dream, Maggie's nose was going to be seriously out of joint, and Mum's cup was therefore going to run right over into the saucer, and probably on to the carpet, too.

Nothing could possibly go wrong.

THREE

At least, that's what I was still telling myself for the next thirty seconds.

'I gather I'm a merchant banker,' he went on. 'Which outfit, and exactly what do I do in it?'

I'd been shoving this uncomfortable question at the back of the cupboard, so to speak, with everything else I preferred not to tackle, like coming-down hems. 'I've never been specific, but you're off to Kuala Lumpur tomorrow for a top-level meeting.'

To give him credit, he made no strangled noises. 'A top-level meeting on what, or didn't you specify that, either?'

'Er, not specifically, no.'

He made that strangled noise after all. It sounded a bit like 'Jesus'.

'I'm sorry, but I had to think of something! My mother was expecting us to stay over so I had to find an excuse. You've got to work tomorrow morning, too; finalise your presentation, or whatever.'

In the seconds before he spoke, I had a feeling he was quietly counting to ten. 'Forgive me if I seem hyper-awkward here, but what do I say if anyone asks who I actually work for?'

'You'll just have to fob them off. Look pained, say you never talk shop, and change the subject. If you

start saying, "Oh, I'm a fattish cat at Megabucks Inc.",
and one of the bridegroom's lot happens to be on the
board, we're going to look just a bit silly.'

The glance he shot me might have said, *For crying out
loud – if she's thought this through, I'm the Archangel
Gabriel*. But he didn't say it, which was just as well, as it
wouldn't have taken much for me to opt for dodgy-
oyster-gut after all. He could nip out at the next set of
lights, get a cab home, and congratulate himself on
getting a sizeable fee for doing sweet FA.

'Is it nerves?' he asked. 'Or do you always grip the
steering wheel as if you'd like to kill it?'

'I'm just a bit wound up.'

I was also making a decision, if you could call
throwing the ball into Fate's court a decision. Another
set of lights was coming up. If it turned red by the
time I reached it, he had oyster-gut. If not, the farce
continued even unto Act III, when some drunken
prat would appear, three feet from Mum and Maggie
Freeman, e.g. 'Josh, me old mate! How's it going
down at Rent-a-Stud? Any passable totty, or do you
just grit the old todger and think of the dosh?'
Whereupon Maggie would smirk and that cake-
cutting knife would come in handy after all. I could
even see the headline: *WEDDING GUEST
SKEWERED TO BUFFET TABLE. 'The bitch had it
coming,' says defiant killer Susan Metcalfe*.

The wretched light turned amber just as I was going
through. Trust Fate to mess up something so simple;
if Mum got life for Maggicide, it wouldn't be my fault.

'If you don't mind my saying so,' Josh said, as I

overtook a milk float, 'I don't quite understand your strategy.'

Could he really be that thick? He didn't *look* thick, but dopey men could be brilliant at covering up.

'If you told me what you didn't understand, maybe I'd be able to put you straight.'

'Put it this way: if everything goes to plan and your mother gushes approval of Dominic Walsh-Poppins, she might put even more pressure on you to bring him home.'

'Do you really imagine I hadn't thought of that? She probably will.'

'And then you'll be stuck in this situation all over again.'

'No, I won't. I'll just tell her I've dumped him.'

'On what grounds?'

'I'll think of something.'

'I could save you the trouble. If I were – say – to get mildly drunk, flirt with the bridesmaids and refer to one of your aged aunts as an old trout, your mother will tell you firmly that I'm not quite the thing and it's high time you got shot of me.'

Of course, it had always been a vain hope that any man likely to impress both Mum *and* Maggie Freeman would just take the money, sit back meekly and not imagine he could organise everything better himself. 'Now why didn't I think of that? Perhaps you could pick your nose as well and offer my granny a spliff. Weren't you *listening*? The whole object of the exercise is for my mother to approve of you. Wildly. The second object is to brown off Maggie Freeman.'

'Ah, yes. I was forgetting the Freeman factor.'

What else was he going to forget? Needing a fix, I scrabbled in the door compartment for the wine gums. 'Could you open them and pass me one? And help yourself, if you want.'

'It's a bit early in the day for me.'

Well, of course. Normal people don't stuff wine gums at barely nine o'clock. Even I wouldn't normally fancy them much before half-past. I held out my hand, to save him having to put it directly in my mouth. There's something distinctly intimate about a man putting sweets directly into your mouth and I didn't want him thinking I was contriving such intimacies.

Despite the worms, you see, my bloke-sussing antennae were still functioning. 'Excuse us,' they were saying roughly, 'but he's actually rather fanciable, in case you hadn't noticed.'

I didn't want to notice. Fancying a bloke I was paying was out of the question. He'd sense it and think I was desperate, after all. On the other hand, a fanciable man had his advantages. If this act was going to convince anybody there would have to be the odd arm around my waist, the odd little pat.

At least I wouldn't have to steel myself.

'Suppose you tell me what you *do* know about me,' he said. 'Let's kick off with the easy stuff. Are my folks still alive, for a start?'

Trying to remember all those lies was a nightmare. 'I think I said they'd retired to the Scottish Borders. You hardly ever see them, anyway.'

Here I thought a little confession was in order. 'To

59

be honest, you've become such an incubus round my neck, I've gone right off you. All I can see, when I picture you, is a thrilled-with-himself, self-important prat who irritates the daylights out of me.'

'No wonder you're going to dump me, then.'

'It'll be a relief, I can tell you. By the way, you had mumps a few weeks ago, which is why you couldn't make it to my folks' anniversary do.'

Out of the corner of my eye, I saw him wince. 'If it had to be mumps, I hope it stayed north of the neck.'

'I didn't go into gory detail. I was going to invent a poor old granny with Alzheimer's and kidney failure, but thought that might be a bit of a cliché. And on the last occasion, which was nothing special, just Mum thinking it was high time you showed your face, you suddenly remembered a lunch date with an old friend. You'd completely forgotten about it, but the old friend phoned you in a terrible state because his wife had just left him and you couldn't possibly let him down.'

'You have a very lively imagination.'

'That's what you think. I'll have you know I racked my brain for those excuses. I'll have another wine gum, please.'

He popped me a red one.

We were now hitting the Hanger Lane Gyratory. In case you're not familiar with this, it's a massive, multi-lane roundabout that gives nervous drivers heart failure. I'm not nervous but I hadn't been concentrating and was in the wrong lane. Eventually I nipped in front of a red BMW, whose driver was not pleased. He hooted long and hard behind me. I thought of giving him a V sign but thought better of it. Road rage was all I needed.

'Where exactly are we going?' Josh asked. 'I was told Lancashire, but—'

'It's a little hotel, out in the sticks. Very pretty, apparently. They were lucky to get a cancellation. They only got engaged a few months ago – it's all been a bit of a rush.'

From nowhere, Belinda's wobbly voice came back to haunt me. What if she hadn't been working herself up over nothing? What if she really had sensed a chilling of feet? The mere thought was enough to kick-start my worms. They were going forth and multiplying even faster than bacteria on the dirty dishes under Ace's bed. I had a hideous vision of rows of guests, all glancing over their shoulders and whispering, 'Running a bit late, aren't they? What's going on?'

'Relax, will you?' Josh said. 'You're doing the white-knuckle bit again.'

I put hideous visions out of my head. It was my own nerves rubbing off.

'If it's all been "a bit of a rush", does that mean she's only known him five minutes?' he went on.

I appreciated his polite interest, even if it was 'polite' rather than 'interested'. 'No, it started well before Christmas. October, I think . . .'

She'd met him at a club, having been dragged there by a friend who'd known the two-timer Marc and Melanie were almost certainly going to be there. 'You've got to see them sometime,' the friend had said. 'Tart yourself up to the nines and pull the best-looking bloke right under bloody Marc's nose.'

In the event, Paul had pulled *her* right under her bloody Marc's nose, and Belinda had still been floating three days later. 'Can you believe he sent me a huge bunch of flowers the very next *day*?' she'd told me over the phone. 'Mum hardly had enough vases to put them in.' There had been more flowers, expensive presents, and no sign of the cooling-off Belinda had constantly expected. Remembering, I hoped the cooling-off wasn't just about to happen.

Josh said, 'What's your sister's name? And the groom's, while you're at it.'

'Belinda and Paul. I've only met Paul a couple of times. He's very good-looking, and Belinda's absolutely gorgeous, so they'll make a lovely couple,' I thought I might as well tell him. 'Poor Belinda was in a bit of a state a week or so ago. I'm sure she thought Paul was going to leave her at the altar, so to speak.'

'Why would she think that?'

Where did you start? 'Well, most of her relationships have ended in tears – *her* tears. Plus, she's one of those sweet, unassertive types who always expect to get walked all over.'

'And consequently often are.'

'You said it. She always tends to expect the worst; I sometimes think it can turn into a self-fulfilling thing. And I'm afraid my mother's been fussing her to death with wedding this-and-that for weeks. So, when you add all that together . . .'

'You have the perfect basis for Grade A jitters?'

'A plus, if you ask me. I'll have another wine gum, please.'

He passed me a black one. 'Maybe he's thinking exactly the same about her. I've only been best man once but I never want to go through that again. He'd convinced himself she wasn't going to turn up. It was like babysitting a fifteen-stone jellied rabbit.'

Whoever was 'babysitting' Paul, I doubted very much that he'd have that problem. I couldn't see him ever resembling a jellied anything.

'If you're really that wound up, I'll drive, if you like,' he offered, a moment later. 'You might be more relaxed as a passenger.'

'I prefer to drive myself, thanks all the same.' God knows why I said that – I love being driven. Of all the company perks I'd really love, a chauffeur would even beat a business-wardrobe account at Harvey Nicks.

'If you told me exactly what you're worried about, we could prepare our defences,' he said, in practical tones.

From the mass of premonitions in my head I extracted just one: 'What if you bump into somebody you know?'

'That's a pretty remote possibility.'

'Yes, but *if* ?'

'I guess I'd just fire the first shot.'

'How do you mean?'

Briefly he considered. 'For the sake of argument let's say it was Mike, who currently does something in the property management line. In that case I'd say,

"Good God, Freddie, me old son! How's the used-car trade treating you?" I think he'd catch on,' he added drily.

'As long as he didn't see you first.'

'No chance – I've got eyes in my backside. Relax, will you? I can handle it.'

Confidence is all very well, but I've often found that overconfidence, particularly when unjustified, is a peculiarly male trait. Give them a *Teach Yourself Sailing* video and the next thing you know, they're saying Cape Horn'd be a doddle, as long as your halyards are starboard to your mizzens, and your rowlocks are three sheets to the wind.

'If it's not a sexist question,' he went on, 'wouldn't your self-important Dominic expect to drive you himself?'

'I told my mother I'd drive, so you wouldn't be too shattered for your flight tomorrow.'

He made a noise of faint contempt. 'If I shatter that easily, should I really be going all the way to Kuala Lumpur without my mummy?'

'I had to say something! Would you rather I'd said you drive like a boy-racer lunatic and you've just wrapped your Ferrari Testosterone around a couple of old ladies?'

I was half expecting him to say, 'Don't you mean "Testarossa"?' so I could reply, 'No, I used the word advisedly', and feel smugly one up.

But he just said, 'I guess not.'

Once we hit Staples Corner and the M1, I could put my foot down and begin to relax, if you can call absence of acute panic relaxing. The sun was following us north; lambs went hoppity-skip in the fields and the hedges were creamy with hawthorn blossom. For the first few miles of motorway I told him every lie I could remember. There hadn't been too many; Mum hadn't actually asked the names of all his assorted relations or whether he'd ever had to sit on the Naughty Seat at school. Together, we worked out the things she might ask, siblings, for example. He only had a sister, so that was easy: just stick with her.

'I've forgotten what you do,' he said, as we passed Scratchwood Services. 'Recruitment, was it?'

The sight of those services took my mind momentarily off nightmares. Despite being awake since five thirty, I'd been in far too much of a state to eat, which just goes to show how serious a state it was. My stomach was reminding me that it had been given nothing but a couple of wine gums since last night, and quite frankly, it was getting pretty browned off with the situation.

'You haven't forgotten, then, I manage the Fulham branch of Aristos, if that rings a bell.' Since Julia had volunteered nothing but the ex-Marine bit, this was the point at which I should have asked, 'And what do you do, apart from escorting man-less women?'

But since I already had a shrewd idea, I didn't ask. In my line of work I'd come across a few ex-servicemen, either slung out in Defence Cuts or feeling like a change, and finding the outside world tough. I didn't want to make him say, 'The square root of sod-all, if you want to know.'

'Any ongoing office dramas I should know about?' he asked. 'Any cut-throat rows over whose turn it is to buy the coffee?'

'Nothing so tedious but, since you ask, we do have a minor ongoing drama.' I went on to tell him about the character-building week and Jess, who might have calmed down by now if not for Neil from the estate agents next door. Neil often popped in, usually to avoid some irate vendor/purchaser, but also because he fancied Harriet, who had four-foot legs and was very attractive in an off-beat way. By some malicious quirk of Sod's law, Neil's previous employers had sent him on precisely this same course, so in between chatting up Harriet he was winding up Jess something rotten. He delighted in giving her every hair-raising detail, especially of the abseiling, and of the woman who'd wet herself from sheer terror. Already sentenced to go in July, poor Jess was now wetting herself at the mere thought and stocking up with Winged Things, just in case.

Not that I told Josh this bit. 'To tell the truth, I'm not relishing the thought, either,' I said. 'I don't mind heights or capsizing canoes, but potholing's given me the shudders since I saw some horrific thing on *999*.'

'I'm sure they won't make you do it,' he said.

'You're supposed to make your*self* do it, that's the whole point. To make yourself do things you hate.'

'You never know, you might even enjoy it. How long have you worked for this outfit?'

'Two years. I was in Human Resources before I side-stepped. In my last HR job, the company was downsizing ruthlessly and I'm much better at placing people than firing them, especially when it's just before Christmas and they've got mortgages and kids. You don't get commission in HR, either.' I was hoping to move up into big-league head-hunting soon, but I didn't say so. If he was out of work, it might be insensitive.

'How long have you lived in London?' he asked.

'Five years. I was working in Manchester before.'

'And living at home?'

'God, no. Not that I don't get on with them or anything, but I'd go crackers.' I sometimes wondered how Belinda hadn't gone crackers still living at home, but she'd seemed generally happy until the wedding-witters. Money had also been a factor, since she'd never earned very much.

Thoughts of earning and money brought my mind back to more immediate matters. 'Josh, would you get my bag off the back seat?'

He got it.

'If you'll look inside the front pocket, there's an envelope with some money. It'll save us having to work out your expenses later. You might have to pay for the odd drink; my parents are old-fashioned enough to expect the man to put his hand in his pocket.'

After a minute's hesitation, he tucked it in his breast pocket. 'It's Dominic, remember? If you get in the habit of Joshing me, you'll give the game away.'

Something in his tone shattered my precarious cool. There was a definite hint of, *This is strictly business, remember? So don't let's get too matey.*

I cast him a sneaky glance. He was looking out of the side window, almost as if trying to avoid me.

I don't know how it is that at the age of thirty you can suddenly feel as awkward as a fourteen-year-old in the wrong clothes, but I did. What the hell *had* the agency told him? Had they given him a bonus for taking on a case of neurotic desperation? Was he having visions of me suddenly making a dive for his zip – *'Oh God oh God oh God – quick – please please please . . . ?*

Suddenly he turned to me. 'I only threw down half a cup of coffee before leaving. Any chance of stopping for a sandwich?'

After the initial 'phew' I made a mental note to get a grip. At this rate I was well on the way to being sectioned for Dangerous Delusional Paranoia. 'We're making pretty good time so far – we could stop for twenty minutes at the next services.'

'I thought you'd never ask. I've been having quiet fantasies about an Uncle-Tom-Cobbleigh-and-all breakfast.'

I wasn't quite with it. 'Sorry?'

'The works,' he said. 'I haven't had one in months: bacon, sausage, hash browns . . .'

The mere thought of it practically made me shudder. And I'm sorry to disappoint you if you're the organic muesli type, but it wasn't a disgusted, no thanks shudder; more the multiple orgasmic type. It was ages since I'd indulged in anything so calculated to earn you a stiff reprimand from the health police; a low-fat Greek yoghurt constituted a mega-breakfast nowadays. The fact that I frequently topped it up mid-morning with half a packet of Hob-nobs was entirely beside the point.

I would definitely have to watch my antennae; there's something rather attractive about a man who shares your secret vices. I thought about asking whether he ever bought Rowntree's Blackcurrant Jellies and devoured half the cubes before he even got to the checkout, but thought better of it.

'How long have we been an item?' he asked.

'Since just before Christmas. Long enough for me to start going right off you by next Tuesday lunchtime.'

'Point taken, but if it's been that long I guess the odd term of endearment is in order. Love, sweetheart, darling – which do you prefer?'

Asking a total stranger to call you 'darling' was positively embarrassing.

'Honey-pie?' he continued. 'Piglet?'

I tried not to bristle; in the circumstances, I didn't begrudge him a morsel of fun. 'No piglets, please. Unless you'd like me to call you Bunnikins.'

This only produced another little twitch. 'That'd be a new one. I'll stick to the odd "darling", if that's all right with you. Safe and inoffensive.'

I began to wonder whether I should 'darling' him, too, or stick to 'Dominic'. I practised in my head. *Darling, would you get me . . .? Dominic, be a love and get me another double V&T, would you?*

If only. It'd have to be straight tonic. Or Perrier. A clear head was mandatory, what with the driving and the lies. God, what a nightmare.

The sun was getting positively hot. Making a mental

note that my next car was going to have an air conditioner, I wound the window down and pushed in an old Queen CD to drown out the noise. The wind played hell with my hair, but what the hell? The hairdresser might even still be there, if we were early enough. Mum had booked her for both of them. Since the Inn was over an hour from home they were changing there, to save creases.

'Have I contributed towards the present?' he asked. 'And what is it, just so I don't look blank if I get a thank you for the lovely whatever-it-is?'

The list had all been very practical and tasteful but since most of it would probably have worn out or got broken in the end, I'd opted for something more enduring. Having dithered shamefully over the card, I'd eventually written, . . . *and Dominic*, and loathed myself for doing it.

'I got them something beautiful and useless: a little antique Indian silver box, with tiny Hindu gods all over it. At least it'll still be there when all the dinner plates are broken.'

'I hope you're not implying that they're going to be chucking plates at each other.'

'I hope not. Not Minton ones, anyway, at twenty-five pounds a throw.'

The thought of plate-chucking led my jittering thoughts back to that tiff. However, the honeymoon was all sorted. Since cancellations had obligingly appeared they were off on that five-star safari after all. I told Josh about it, adding Belinda's wiggly-thing to give him a laugh, and he duly chuckled.

'So I hope Paul's got a sensitive attitude where wigglies are concerned,' I went on. 'She always says, ". . . but don't kill it!"'

'No crunching of cockroaches underfoot, then. Probably just as well. The big ones can make a hell of a mess.'

For the next few miles I filled him in on family and friends: who was good fun, who was most likely to ask awkward questions and therefore best avoided like the plague. All of which only made me more aware of possible perils and got my worms going again. By the time we pulled in at the next services I was more or less back to pristine nervous-wreck condition.

As I switched the ignition off, Josh gave an exasperated 'tut'. 'You've made a pig's ear of that, haven't you?'

I gaped at him. 'What?'

'Just look how you've parked.'

I'd driven in front first, and if it was half a degree off the parallel with the cars on either side, that was all. 'Would you kindly keep your nit-picking to yourself? I can do without it!'

'Darling, you *never* park straight.' He added a noble, patient sigh. '*How* many times have I told you to reverse into a space?'

I was so desperate for light relief, I almost laughed. 'Oh, I get it. Now we're playing games.'

'Dress rehearsal.' He added a little wink. 'Like all good actors, I'm getting into my role well before the first performance.'

'The only performance.' I exited and locked the

door. 'And you're playing the wrong part. Dominic doesn't back-seat park.'

'Of course he does. He's a thrilled-with-himself, self-important prat who irritates the daylights out of you.'

'Not today, he isn't. He's a paragon. Practically perfect in every way, just like this wedding's going to be.'

'I admire your optimism.' As we strolled into the building, through a dither of the curly-perm-and-white-cardie brigade, he added, 'In my limited experience, weddings are the worst sources of stress known to man. They cause divorces, if you ask me.'

We followed that lovely, foody smell up the stairs to the restaurant. Now and then that fried-junk smell can turn my stomach, but just now, like our dog, Benjy, when he's hoping for a morsel of your toasted cheese sandwich, I was positively salivating. To be perfectly frank, Benjy's tongue is not the only bit of him that hangs out on such occasions; his brain gets a trifle muddled between food-lust and the other sort. My mother has been extremely embarrassed when she's just given some easily shocked guest a nice cup of tea and a piece of cake. 'Poor Miss Peabody just didn't know where to *look*,' she told me once. 'She never even had a boyfriend, poor old thing.'

As we arrived at Foodie Heaven, Josh handed me a tray. 'Everything but the egg, please,' I told the girl. They always do them with jelly-white on top and it makes me heave.

'I'll have her egg,' Josh said. 'Just give me two.'

After his patronising boyfriend bit, I thought I'd

even up the score with a still-prickly girlfriend. 'One egg's enough for anyone! Why do you always have to be such a *pig*?'

The girl gave me a hopeful glance, as if a good fight might liven up her morning.

'Let's not argue about it, darling.' Playing along like a lamb, he slipped an arm around my waist. 'Give me a smile and tell me how much you love me.'

Seeing the girl's expression – *We've got a right pair here*, more or less – I tried not to laugh. 'Stop trying to get round me, will you?' I nearly shook Josh's arm off but let's be honest, it felt nice and I thought I might as well enjoy it. He felt hunkily firm and a good deal larger than me, which is always a plus when you're feeling the effects of sofa-vegging rather than the gym, and pots of Nutella eaten with a spoon. 'I'm going off you at the speed of light,' I added.

'You loved me this morning.' With this he contrived a wonderfully hurt expression. 'When I brought you a nice cup of coffee in bed and ran your bath for you.'

Since the girl was now following the exchange with unashamed interest, I couldn't resist a bit more. 'I didn't want coffee. I wanted tea, only you never remember I like tea first thing.'

'Everything, please,' he told the girl. 'I thought it very noble of me to bring you anything at all,' he said to me, in hurt tones. 'Especially since you had a "headache" last night and made me sleep on the sofa.'

The girl perked up even further. 'D'you want two eggs or not?'

'Not,' he replied. 'I'm in enough trouble as it is.'

73

'It was your own fault,' I retorted. 'For telling me I was putting weight on and making me feel like a fat cow.'

His hurt look turned to cut-to-the-quick. 'Darling, don't twist my words. What I actually said was that I *prefer* cuddly women who enjoy their food.'

I barely needed to act any more. 'If you call me "cuddly" again, you'll be sleeping on the sofa for ever.' Torn between laughter and miffed-ness, I made for the tea and coffee bit. I knew I shouldn't be miffed. If he continued to act like that we'd pull if off, no problem. On the other hand, weren't arm-and-a-leg escorts supposed to flatter you, lie through their teeth and make you feel all warm and special?

As we sat down I said, 'If you want a tip at the end of this, don't call me "cuddly" again,' and regretted it instantly. It sounded patronising, as if I were trying to put him in his place. I'd never have dreamt of offering a tip in any case.

Not that he seemed in the least put out. 'Tipping's strictly against the rules,' he said, pouring coffee from a dribbly pot. 'They're very professional at Just For Tonight. Escorts shall not expect or accept gratuities, neither shall they drink to excess, belch at the table or tell off-colour jokes. The agency shall pay promptly, shall do its best not to pair escorts with grudge-bearing Bobbits, and shall furthermore undertake not to dish out addresses or phone numbers.'

If that was a hint, I didn't need it, thank you very much. Still, I could see the necessity. I could imagine a client requesting someone a second time and a third,

the agency finally saying tactfully that he wasn't
available any more . . .

With Josh sitting directly opposite, it wasn't so easy
keeping my antennae firmly 'off'. Now and then they
tapped me on the shoulder with comments like, *Lovely
eyes*.

I was trying not to look, which was a bit difficult.

*And that crookedy little smile should come with a health
warning.*

Give it a rest, will you?

In a tick. Have you noticed his hands?

I was trying not to. I've got a thing about hands.
Even if the rest of a chap's quite passable, damp, white
crawly hands turn me right off.

*Nice, aren't they? Imagine one of them sliding a bra strap
off your shoulder.*

For God's sake! Go back to sleep, will you?

'Have I got time for that wet shave?' he asked, when
we'd nearly finished.

'I'd rather get on, if you don't mind. There might
be time when we get there, if you really feel the
need.'

Full of bacon, beans and sausage, we diverted to the
shop, where he bought shaving things and I bought a
packet of Silk Cut, purely for insurance purposes. If I
had some, there would be absolutely no disaster to
make me think I'd kill for one.

With dodgy job questions particularly in mind, I
thought I might ask, after all. 'You don't happen to be
employed in the financial sector, do you?' I asked as
we returned to the car. 'It would make it easier.'

75

'I'm afraid not, but I can bullshit, if necessary. I've got a degree in bullshitting.'

Just as I was about to say, 'If it's not a nosy question, what *do* you do?' he said, 'I gather you invented me in the wake of somebody else. Am I supposed to know, in case anybody mentions him?'

'His name was Kit. And to save you asking, yes, he dumped *me*.'

As the miles passed I filled him in on details of my CV and his, in between chatting about inconsequential things. As men go he was a good chatter, able to talk amusing rubbish for hours, which was exactly what I needed.

It was only the last few miles where I needed directing. The industrial heartland was far behind us. Dry-stone walls divided fields where lambs played by their mothers; just the occasional stone farmhouse was dotted on a hillside. Teeming London might have been at the other end of eternity.

The Inn was signposted from a little crossroads. We saw it long before we got there: an old stone building that looked as if it had grown out of the valley. A little stream sparkled close by, straddled by a little humpty-back bridge. The gardens around the Inn were bright with flowers – and still the sun shone.

Despite all this perfection, I was jittering for England.

This was It.

Dad's elderly but beloved and polished-to-death Jag was in the car park. In about half a minute . . . 'Are you sure you're up to this?' I muttered, grabbing my things

76

with DT-type hands. 'Because I'm not sure I am. I feel sick.'

'Relax,' he soothed.

What is about men telling you to relax that makes you want to thump them? I mean, I've known men who'd tell you to relax even if the *Nine o'Clock News* had just told us that a massive meteorite was going to wipe us all out during tomorrow morning's rush hour.

I was bursting for the loo.

Reception was bright and welcoming, bowls of flowers on the polished counter. Dad was there, talking to some man I knew vaguely.

Glueing on a bright smile, I went up. 'Hi, Dad! This is Dominic.'

Josh did me proud. 'How do you do?' he said, with a perfect, father-meeting smile.

'Ted Metcalfe. Nice to meet you at last, but I've been better, if you want the truth.'

I suddenly realised that he wore a hunted, harassed look. 'Is everything all right? Where's Mum?'

'Upstairs, with Belinda.' He nodded heavily towards the staircase. 'Room eight. All hell's broken loose, love. You'd better go up.'

FOUR

How I didn't throw up that mega-breakfast all over the Axminster, I will never know.

Shoving all my things at Josh, I charged for the staircase. I turned halfway and at the top I found myself in a maze of eccentric, ancient corridors and little trippety sets of three stairs which led to room twelve, when I'd only just passed seven and was naturally expecting eight. I finally ran eight to earth down another trippety pair of stairs and wrenched the door open.

' . . . really *too* bad,' my mother was saying fretfully. 'I really could absolutely *murder*— Sophy!' She charged up with a singular lack of let-loose hell. 'We weren't expecting you just yet, dear,' Kiss, kiss. 'I do hope the traffic wasn't too bad.'

I began to wonder whether I was on the tail end of a nightmare. No gnashed-out teeth littered the carpet. Belinda wasn't prostrate on the bed, clutching a note that said, *Sorry, Sweetheart – just can't do it*. Wrapped in her ancient navy bathrobe, she was sitting at the dressing table while the hairdresser fiddled with her hair. 'Hiya,' she called.

'Mum, what's wrong?' I gaped. 'Dad looked as if he were about to have a heart attack!'

'I'm not surprised,' Belinda said, with a slight edge

to her voice. 'Mum was throwing a fit because Maggie Freeman turned up ten minutes ago, wearing Mum's suit.'

I might have known. At the age of sixty-two my dear father still enjoyed winding people up.

'It's really absolutely *typical* of Maggie,' Mum said crossly. 'Just because she's only a size twelve and wants to show me up . . .'

Mum's a size sixteen, you see.

The hairdresser was doing her best not to laugh and in the mirror I saw Belinda raise her eyes to heaven. 'Mum, I'm sure she had no idea. You go to the same shops – it's just coincidence.'

'I doubt it, dear. She'll have found out somehow.'

I was feeling quite tottery with relief. 'Even if she had, imitation is the sincerest form of flattery, you know,' I pointed out. 'Anyway, she never carries clothes as well as you do. She's too hunched up.'

'Well, at least she hasn't got my hat. And why did she have to come so early in the first place? Just to have a good nose around and find fault, I suppose.'

Belinda repeated the eye lift. 'Mum, if you say one more word about Maggie—'

'I'm sorry, dear – I know I shouldn't go on, but it's really so infuriating . . .'

Actually, Mum's not a bad advertisement for size sixteen. Her hair's tinted back to its original dark brown and there's absolutely nothing of the frumpy old dear about her. She was already dressed in a very elegant suit of French navy, with fuchsia touches. I could see why Maggie had gone for it, too.

'Where's Dominic?' she asked.

'I left him downstairs with Dad.'

Her eyes widened. 'Then I'll just pop down and say hello. By the way, dear, I did book that room, so you can both get changed in comfort.'

Halfway to the door, she turned, her eyes wide. 'Goodness, I nearly forgot. You'll never *believe* who's coming – Sonia phoned last night and said he was staying a couple of days and could she possibly bring him, as Katie Smith's not well, poor girl, flu or something, and there'll be a gap at the table otherwise.'

As so often, her train of thought had lost me three stops back. 'Mum, *who?*'

'Kit, dear! Remember? He's Sonia's cousin or something – isn't that where you first met him? At Sonia's?'

'*Kit?*' I gaped.

'Well, I did think it was a bit of a nerve but I could hardly say no – he dropped in to see the family and Sonia didn't like to leave him on his own all day – her parents are away, you see – I do hope you don't mind, dear, but it's not as if you haven't got anybody else.'

'It's not "a bit of a nerve" – it's a bloody cheek.'

This was Belinda, indignant enough for a faint flush to colour her cheeks. 'Sonia's so unbe*liev*ably tactless. She knows he dumped you. She should never have asked.'

'Maybe he won't come, after all,' Mum soothed. 'But it's not as if Sophy's still pining over him, are you, dear?'

'Of course not!' I sat on the bed, thinking of all the

times I'd seen the back of a dark blond head in the street or on a crowded Underground platform, the sudden heart-leap and the lonely little ache when I'd realised it wasn't him at all. I hadn't seen him once since the bust-up. How would I feel?

'If he *does* turn up, dear, be cool but gracious,' Mum said. 'Let him see what he's missing. Smile a lot at Dominic, just to rub it in. And talking of Dominic, I'll just pop down and say hello . . .'

Once she'd gone, the edge to Belinda's voice was more marked. 'Gone to check him out. I hope he's up to it, poor man.'

'Oh, he'll be fine,' I said, in what I hoped was a breezy manner.

'Yes, but don't *you* think Sonia's got a colossal cheek? And what about Kit? I don't know how he can even think of swanning in, after what he did.'

The hairdresser said apologetically, 'Sorry, but could you just keep your head still a minute?'

I have to say Belinda's fierce loyalty touched me. Made me feel bad, too, after I'd been bitching about her to Alix. Still, she hadn't particularly liked Kit even before the bust-up. 'He thinks I'm a bimbo,' she'd said once, and I hadn't liked to say she might be right, although Kit would never have actually said it. 'I honestly don't care. He only dumped me, after all – he didn't beat me up and steal my cash cards. What's he doing at Sonia's anyway?'

'Called in on his way back from seeing friends in Scotland or somewhere. He should just push off back to bloody Barnstaple, if you ask me.'

This was not news to me: I'd heard through some vague mutual acquaintance that he'd left St Thingy's and taken up a post in Devon. It was just Sod's law that he should pick this weekend to see his cousin.

Sonia was an old friend of Belinda's, dating back to nursery school days. When I was eighteen and had just passed my driving test (third go) I'd popped round one Saturday morning to pick up Belinda after a sleepover. I'd felt unbelievably cool, swanning in with Mum's car keys so nonchalantly jingling and new, cool sunglasses pushed carelessly back over my hair. Just-out-of-bed Sonia had mumbled something about Belinda being still asleep but if I went through to the kitchen her cousin might make me a coffee – the olds were out shopping.

For some reason I'd expected a female cousin, so the boy sitting in just a pair of tracksuit bottoms at the kitchen table had been a bit of a turn-up. Hideously embarrassed but trying not to show it, he'd put his chemistry book aside, made me a Nescafé with too much milk, and we'd chatted politely for the twenty minutes it took Belinda to sort herself out. His name was Christopher, but everybody called him Kit. Like me, he was about to take his A levels. He was hoping to do medicine at Bristol but was worried about his chemistry; he'd only got a C in his mock. He'd been packed off for the Easter holidays to his aunt and uncle because his parents were going through a bad patch, rowing all the time, and he needed peace and quiet to revise. He was glad to be out of it and couldn't wait to go to university.

His couldn't-give-a-toss tones wouldn't have fooled a flea. Something inside me had sort of twisted; I'd wanted to give him a cuddle, take him home and give him one of Mum's lovely dinners – I knew from Belinda that Sonia's mother specialised in lumpy mince and stuck-together pasta. I'd badly wanted him to ask me out but although I'd chauffeured Belinda several times more before term started, I hadn't seen him again. Either he'd been in the garden, revising, or upstairs, revising.

And that had been that, until one Saturday afternoon when some regular from the local pub had dragged Alix and me to a charity football match for St Thingy's. Someone dressed as Daffy Duck had been in goal for the first half and then come round with a bucket, collecting money. I'd said, 'Have they sacked you?' and he'd said, 'Yep – out for a duck,' and I'd laughed, and looked at the face under the duck, and twigged. He'd smiled the kind of blue-eyed smile that student nurses fall in love with and said, 'I'm sure we've met somewhere but I can't place it. I must have been seriously hammered.'

And that was it, until Jocasta.

For the first time I was almost glad of Dominic. If I had to see Kit, far better to do it with somebody presentable on my arm.

I suddenly realised that Belinda was talking and I hadn't been listening. '. . . and I left my "something blue" at home so she was wittering on about that, and then wretched Maggie . . .'

The hairdresser shot me a look that said, *Don't worry – I've seen it all before*. What she actually said was, 'Excuse me. Must just pop to the loo—'

Once we were alone, Belinda did not erupt into a full-scale bitch, but merely gave a tense, up-to-here sigh. 'Sorry, but I was nearly hitting the mini-bar ten minutes ago. If you ever get married, for heaven's sake just slope off somewhere and do it quietly.'

In the circumstances I thought the mini-bar might not be a bad idea. 'Have a drink, then,' I said, already checking the contents. 'Look, there's a Drambuie. You like Drambuie.'

'Go on, then. Just half.'

I poured, wishing to God I could have the other half, but liqueurs in particular get my tongue into top gear while my brain is still in reverse. Before half an hour had passed I'd be gaily saying, 'Josh, come and meet—' and have to kill myself instantly. Besides, I needed the loo before any more liquid entered the system.

After a fairish swig Belinda nodded towards a plastic-swathed creation hanging on the wardrobe door. 'Mum doesn't like my dress much; it's sort of Grecian-Regency – my hair's supposed to match. She thinks the empire line makes it look as if I'm trying to hide a five-month pregnancy.'

'Well, are you?'

'Are you kidding? You know perfectly well that Mum would have sussed out a five-*week* pregnancy even before I had.'

True. 'Your dress looks gorgeous to me, anyway,' I

soothed. 'And it'll look even more gorgeous with you in it. You'd look gorgeous even if Benjy had chewed your dress up and Mum draped you in a Grecian-Regency old sheet from the back of the airing cupboard.'

'Poor Benjy, I wanted him to come,' she said fretfully, stroking base coat on her nails. 'I was going to put a ribbon round his neck and let him be a page-dog. The manager said "no problem", but Mum thought he might get overexcited with all the food, and disgrace us. So he's in the kennels until tomorrow, and you know how he hates the kennels.'

'He'll be fine,' I assured her. 'He can bark his head off all day and nobody'll tell him to shut up.'

As she carried on doing her nails I wandered around the room. It was a lot bigger than I'd have expected, smothered in the kind of tiny English-floral curtains and covers that might have been a bit much if they weren't so pretty. A large, low window looked out over the smooth, green valley with stark moors beyond.

I eyed the bathroom door. Whatever was the woman *doing*? Having a bad case of dodgy-something runs, or tactfully leaving us to natter?

Muttering an irritable curse, Belinda applied a pad of remover to her little finger and started again.

'Not still nervous, are you?' I asked.

'Only about Mum and Maggie having a row.' She started blowing on her now sparkly nails. 'Or Dad being embarrassing. I should go and rescue Dominic, if I were you. Mum's been dying to meet him. Just before you turned up she was still wittering on: "I do so hope he's a *nice type* – she does seem to be so *unlucky* with men . . ."'

Her passable mimicry made me laugh, albeit a very hollow effort. 'You couldn't call Kit a not-nice type, but that didn't stop him dumping me.'

Mum had actually pronounced him a 'lovely boy', not that I'd ever taken him home. Aware of a young hospital doctor's workload, even she hadn't pushed it. They'd met him just once, on a weekend trip to see some West End Show. I'd taken him to their hotel for a quick drink beforehand.

Helping myself to a Nice biscuit from the tea and coffee tray, I headed for the door. 'I'll go to the rescue. See you later . . .'

'Wish me luck, then.'

We're not a pair of your huggy-feely siblings, gushing. 'I love you, hon' three times a day after meals, but since it was a special occasion, and feeling a bit bad for not doing it before, I went back and gave her a squeezy hug. 'Good luck, not that you need it. You'll look so gorgeous even I'll be weepy.'

For a second she held me tight and then drew back. 'Push off quick, before *I* go all weepy.' She was half laughing, but her voice was wobbly, her eyes bright with incipient leaks.

And so, all of a sudden, were mine. 'I must be getting old,' I said, wiping an eye with a fingertip. 'Going all daft and sentimental . . .'

She passed me a tissue and wiped her own eyes, too. 'Push off then, you old hag. Go and rescue your toy boy before Mum wears him to a shred.'

'Don't you call me an old hag, you hideous trollop.' I half ran downstairs, dying to divert to the loo but fearing to leave Josh unaided any longer.

He was in the bar with Dad, and my pulse settled the instant I saw them. Evidently getting on like matches in a paper shop, they were propping up the bar, chuckling about something in a blokey kind of way.

I was no longer bent on parricide, but I marched up, trying to look cross while grinning with relief. 'Dad, why did you wind me up like that? I thought something catastrophic had happened!'

'It was catastrophic to your mother.'

He had lost the hunted look and was back to his normal jolly self. He was nearly as tall as Josh and getting a trifle portly, but not fat. His hair was grey but still thick. When he put his mind to it he could look a bit like a somewhat distinguished but very cuddly teddy, with a baritone rumble to match. With a dark grey suit and white buttonhole, he wore a rather dashing patterned silk waistcoat.

I parked myself on a bar stool, wishing to heaven I could order half a pint of vodka and a straw. Josh, however, looked perfectly relaxed. The bar was typically English oldy-worldy pub style, with hunting prints, horse brasses and a plethora of pewter mugs. 'Listen, aged parent,' I said, in ominous tones. 'Positively *no* embarrassing stories about what Belinda did in the bath, OK?'

Josh choked on his lager.

'I wouldn't dream of it, love,' said Dad.

'Yes, you would. If you dare say anything remotely embarrassing, I'll tell everyone it's your Viagra pills affecting your discretion.'

That might do it. He put on the chastened teddy look he used to get round Mum.

'So where's Maggie?' I asked.

'Polishing her broomstick, I expect. Or wandering the gardens with David and Zoe.'

David was Mr Freeman. Sarah wasn't coming. She and James had long-standing booked guests at their Yorkshire country seat and couldn't make it. I was sorry about this because Sarah was the only Freeman I really liked.

Just as I was wondering whether to indulge in a titchy vodka after all, Mum bustled up like a beaming battleship.

'Oh, there you are, dear – your room's all ready – you might as well use it for changing now I've booked it.' As I'd fully expected, she drew me a little aside. 'I must say, dear, he seems *very* charming,' she whispered. 'Such a pity you can't stay the night but I suppose it can't be helped.'

While I pocketed the room key she went on. 'What do you think of Belinda's dress? It's very pretty, of course, but I do wish she'd chosen something more *fitted* – such a shame not to make the most of a lovely little waist.'

Before I could answer, an anxious frown creased her forehead and she turned to 'Dominic'. 'Dear me, I forgot to ask after your poor friend. Terrible thing, his wife just walking out like that. How is he now?'

My heart shot to my tonsils, but it needn't have bothered.

'Fine, thanks.' He produced another of those perfectly judged smiles. 'They're back together. It was all due to a glitch on a credit card statement – some hotel bill that had been added by mistake.'

'Isn't that just typical?' my mother tutted.

I was almost dumbstruck with admiration. For brilliant off-the-cuff fibs he was almost better than me. Still, quit while you're ahead. I shot him a perfectly judged smile of my own. 'If you've finished your beer, don't you think we'd better go and get changed?'

He didn't twitch so much as an eyelash. 'Whenever you're ready.'

While he drained his glass I gathered up my things. So far, so good.

'Such a pity you can't stay the night,' Mum said to him. 'Still, the room's there if you change your minds. It'd be so nice if you could stay for dinner, at least – there's never time to chat properly at these big dos.'

Before she could develop this dangerous theme, I grabbed Josh's arm. 'Come on, darling, we have to go.'

It felt weird calling him 'darling'. I'd never been a darlingy type; an affectionate, 'Shift yourself, Warthog' was more my style. 'I hope they weren't giving you the third degree,' I muttered, as we headed for the stairs.

'Nothing I couldn't handle.' Halfway up he added drily, 'Your mama's obviously not one of those mothers who know you're up to no good but like to pretend you're not.'

'Are you kidding? After nearly five months, she's bound to assume we're more than just good friends.'

Still, I could see why he'd said it. Alix's parents were still unbelievably sniffy about this 'not under our roof' business. On the one occasion she'd taken Simon her ex, home, her mother had said, 'I don't care what you get up to at home, but that bed creaks and it'll make your father feel uncomfortable.'

We found room five down a couple of trippety steps at the end of a low-ceilinged mini-passage where Josh had to duck his head. Furnished in the same rampant little florals as Belinda's but only half the size, it held rather crammed twin beds.

'What did Belinda do in the bath, or shouldn't I ask?' he enquired.

'She poohed and told the whole street, but she was only two.' I grabbed my sponge bag. 'Excuse me, but I need the loo.'

Bursting though I was, I'm ashamed to say a ridiculous adolescent angst overcame me here. Through the locked door I could hear him quite clearly shutting the wardrobe, which meant he'd probably be able to hear me and I didn't want him thinking Niagara Falls had suddenly diverted to Lancashire. After padding the bowl with Bumdrex, I recalled taking exactly this precaution on a school exchange trip to France. At fifteen I'd rather have killed myself than have Marie-Louise's incredibly gorgeous seventeen-year-old brother hear what I was up to. I nearly did kill myself when I had to tell her *papa* that I'd *blocéed le* bog.

However, Lancashire plumbing was made of sterner stuff. I did my teeth and fiercely told my reflection to calm down. Everything was going fine, so far.

Feeling better, I emerged and hung up my things. Since the room was barely hamster-swinging size and the beds took up most of it, I was doubly glad of the bathroom. I wouldn't have enjoyed stripping down to basics with Josh within eyeshot; I was wearing tacky, Christmas-present knickers that said, *Hi, Big Boy!* and my thighs were not quite at their best.

He had crisped up in a way that said there would be no more jokes about 'headaches' or anything else that could possibly be misconstrued. 'Do you want to change in the bathroom, or shall I?'

'You have it. And by the way . . .'

He turned at the door.

'My ex might be coming,' I said. 'Kit. So if you could do your best to look besotted, I'd be grateful.' Briefly I explained the situation.

He raised an eyebrow. 'Bit of a nerve, isn't it?'

'Yes, I suppose, but he probably won't come anyway. I really don't care one way or the other.'

With another raised eyebrow he took his things to the bathroom and locked the door behind him.

After about twenty minutes he tapped on the door. 'Are you decent?'

'I'm just about ready.'

Still at the dressing table, I blotted a second coat of Hot Berry while he shoved his discarded clothes back in the carrier. Then I swivelled on my stool and had a proper look.

'Will I do?' he asked, with a trace of sarcasm.

'Do' was not actually quite the word. He wore a light grey suit, one of those white shirts with a sort of self-stripe in them and a navy tie with little white spots. From the end of a sleeve I could just see a gold cuff link.

Everything was obviously 'good', but you didn't notice any of them in particular. What you noticed was the whole package. He really looked quite remarkably edible, as Alix sometimes puts it.

'Very appropriate,' I said. 'I hope it'll be a comfort to you in your old age to know you kept my mother's end up with Maggie Freeman.'

'I can't wait to meet this woman,' he said drily. 'Your old man told me he calls her Winnie Vinegar-Bottle on the quiet.'

They must have been getting on well if Dad had told him a thing like that already.

Trying to sound as if I didn't care one way or the other, I stood up. 'Will I do, do you think?'

I hadn't been too sure about that suit. I'd have preferred something darkly slimming but you can hardly wear black to a wedding, and I wore grey and navy all the time for work. It was a delicate, spring-like primrose, with a slim skirt and an edge-to-edge jacket long enough to cover the worst. The cut was very flattering, but it bloody well ought to be – that's what you pay arms and legs for. With it I wore a silk camisole of a lovely blue somewhere between Greek Island and light navy. I'd shoved my hair up in a soft but mildly sexy look, which had turned out more or less right, for once.

I thought I looked pretty damn good, actually.

'Very appropriate,' he pronounced.

Gee, thanks.

'I might even go so far as to say mildly fetching,' he went on. 'What should I do if anyone starts paying you inappropriate attention? Ignore it, or do the *clear off, she's mine* bit?'

'I'm much more likely to be collared by some dreadful old bore and they're always impossible to get rid of without being downright rude. In which case I'd appreciate rescuing.'

I gave myself a good misting of Aqua di Gió. 'There – I think that's it. Shall we go down?'

'You're the boss.'

Just as I grabbed my bag, I remembered the necklace. 'Oh Lord, I nearly forgot . . .' From a holdall pocket I retrieved a three-strand rope of lapis lazuli and freshwater pearls, bestowed by Mum and Dad two Christmases back.

In normal circumstances I might have managed the fiddly little fastening in under thirty seconds. As it was . . .

'May I?' he said.

'If you don't mind . . .' I bent my head a little, to give him better access.

At this point I knew that keeping my antennae switched off for the duration was going to be a tall order. There was nothing whatever in his brief about interfering with my secondary erogenous zones, yet here he was, delicately teasing the nape of my neck as

93

if he had a Ph.D. in it. Still, I was entitled to a little flutter, after shelling out an arm and a leg.

Once we were back in that duck-your-head passage, another tidal wave of worms (sorry to mix metaphors here but that's how it felt) rose up and nearly drowned me. 'I feel sick,' I confessed. 'I can't get rid of this ghastly premonition of disaster.'

'Like what?'

Like (just for a laugh) what if the real Dominic turned out to be a cousin of Paul's? What if someone said, 'That's funny – I've just met another Dominic Walsh,' and then the *real* D.W. came over and said, 'Christ, aren't you that woman who got completely bollocksed and wrote your phone number on my arm?'

But I confined myself to more likely horrors. 'What if someone puts you on the spot about your job? Asks really awkward questions?'

'Relax,' he soothed. 'It'll be fine.'

'Can I have that in writing?'

'Sophy, calm down. If you go down like this, in a state of obvious tension, you'll make people think there's something wrong. Slap a smile on. Slip into some brazen confidence.'

'It's all right for you!'

'Relax! Faint heart never got away with blue murder, believe you me.'

'Are you speaking from experience?'

'What do you think?'

This was an interesting question, but I never got a chance to reply. Since there were family voices in the corridor, I stiffened the jelly that passed for a spine. 'Let's just go, before I chicken out completely.'

Pre-ceremony mingling went as well as it could, given my latent panic. I didn't see Kit, not that I was craning my neck in the throng; he was the least of my worries. The wedding hall possessed timber vaulting and old stone, so that it almost felt like a church, minus the mouldering hymn book smell; whole nurseries of flowers scented the air. We parked ourselves on rows of chairs upholstered in dark red velvet and a polite, expectant buzz went up until someone at an organ started playing 'Here Comes the Bride'.

I craned my neck to see her, and saw Kit first. He was sitting right at the back, next to the aisle, and our eyes met for about half a second. Some internal organ did rouse itself and shift slightly, but nothing alarming. So I thought, Phew, and managed a cool-but-gracious smile just before Belinda entered on Dad's arm.

That dress would have looked lovely on just about anybody, but on Belinda it was amazing. A mix of simplicity and ravishing prettiness, it fell in cream silk folds from a pintucked little bodice, with just the odd touch of lace. Well, I did feel a bit weepy. Mum used several tissues and I dare say even hardened cynics would have pretended they had a sudden dose of hay fever from all those flowers.

I don't know what it is about morning suits, but they can make even ordinary blokes look passable, and since Paul was far from ordinary I was beginning to understand Belinda's jitters. If that had been me, I might have indulged in a pair of silver-plated handcuffs, in case of lurking predators. To the Jocastas of this world pinching a bloke at his own wedding reception would be a piquant little challenge and earn them fifty extra points.

The ceremony was simple and dignified, and when vows and rings had been exchanged I breathed a private little sigh of relief.

As we decanted ourselves into the adjoining room Josh murmured, 'So is he here?'

'Yes, but I can't see him in this lot . . .' Just then, as heads moved, I gave him a nudge. 'Over there, next to the girl in the red dress . . .'

I was glad Kit was so presentable. Only slightly less tall than Josh, he wore a navy jacket and a tie that I guessed was borrowed from Sonia's dad's wardrobe. He had a slight tan, and the dark blond hair was sun-streaked, making me wonder whether his move to Barnstaple had anything to do with his passion for surfing. I'd once spent a March weekend shivering on a North Devon beach, wondering whether he was mad, like the rest of them courting hypothermia in the breakers.

Josh murmured, 'What does he do?'

Why is that the first thing they always ask? 'He's a doctor.' Jocasta had been a colleague, which is probably why I'd hated watching *ER* afterwards. It was too close to home: all those pulsating passions over the electric-shock thingy while some poor person snuffed it.

Red-dressed Sonia caught my eye and buzzed up

just as we grabbed our bubbly. After a quick, 'Hi,' she drew me a little aside.

'You didn't mind me bringing Kit, did you?' she whispered. 'He said "No way" at first – said he'd feel really awkward – but I told him nobody'd give a toss and practically dragged him along.'

'No, that's fine,' I said, in warm-but-gracious tones. 'It's all water under the whatsit.'

'Well, thank God for that. I'll go and tell him you're not about to thump him. Doesn't Belinda look lovely? As for Paul, I'm sick as a pig. Why don't I ever get blokes like that? I don't get *any* blokes lately.' And she buzzed off again.

As we circulated with flutes of champagne, I caught Kit's eye again. He smiled, very awkwardly, I gave another cool-but-gracious back, and instantly wished I'd given a warmer one. God knows why, but I'd actually started feeling sorry for his obvious awkward- ness. This was probably because I'd just realised that no flames were about to whoosh up from remaining embers. Any remaining embers did not feel like the whooshing variety. In fact, I felt rather as if I'd just seen an old friend I'd had a flaming row with and wished we hadn't fallen out.

Still, I hoped he was noting my beloved, who was rubbing it in like an Oscar winner. Now and then, as we moved, his hand would rest lightly on my waist or on the back of my jacket, dead centre just below the nape of my neck.

It was a sinful waste. There I was, within fluttering distance of the most attractive man I'd seen in ages,

97

and too wound up to enjoy it. I felt more and more like someone who's smuggling ten kilos of crack through customs and fully expecting a heavy hand on the shoulder at any moment.

For security reasons, I tried to keep Josh right away from unknown male guests who'd instantly ask what he did. I tried to steer him towards female guests I knew well enough to control the conversation. If he got bored with constant 'Doesn't Belinda look lovely?' it was just tough.

Eventually we fought our way to the happy couple. Belinda seemed on some sort of beautiful high. She'd never stopped smiling.

'Here's Dominic – I thought I'd better let you check him out,' I said, and she laughed and gave him a kiss. 'Dominic' shook hands with Paul and said, 'Congratulations – you're a very lucky man,' with a very appropriate smile, and Paul said, 'Thanks, but you don't have to tell me.'

I said, 'I suppose you couldn't stick me in your suitcase, could you? I've always had a yen for Africa.'

Paul half laughed. 'I'm sure you could work on Dominic. After a hint like that—' His eyes suddenly shifted to somewhere beyond my left shoulder. 'Brian! Glad you could make it. Why haven't you got a drink? Jane, I do hope Saskia's feeling better.' He moved sideways to talk to these two, who were forty-ish and very smart.

With an apologetic little *moue*, Belinda whispered, 'Sorry – it's his boss and his wife. Their daughter fell off her horse last week and broke something. He didn't think they'd come.'

After a minute we moved on. In a dry murmur Josh said, 'Boss or no boss, he could have given you another two seconds before fawning over him.'

'For heaven's sake,' I said irritably, partly because I agreed with him.

'Sorry, but I didn't care for it. Nobody should oblige his wife of half an hour to apologise for his behaviour.'

'It didn't bother me,' I lied.

We circulated to Maggie Freeman, Zoe, and Oliver, who wasn't quite as chinless as Mum had said, but certainly nothing to write home about.

Maggie had once been blonde and her hairdresser ensured she still was. Her skin bore the marks of many expensive holidays in the sun and judging from her expression, she wasn't pleased to have Mum's braggings borne out by the reality. Which was fifty points to me. She'd had a dig at me at Christmas, at the traditional Christmas Eve drinks *chez* Freeman. First I'd had, 'I hear you've found a new chap *at last*,' followed swiftly by, 'Dear me, you get more like your mother every time I see you.' Maggie-speak for, *My God, you've put some weight on*. And Mum had overheard and been loyally indignant on my behalf. 'At least you look healthy. Zoe's getting positively anorexic, if you ask me,' she'd huffed. 'And these mince pies are *awful*. If Maggie really can't manage a bit of shortcrust pasty she should admit defeat and get Just-rol.'

Zoe wasn't quite anorexic. Elegantly thin rather than scraggy, she had short blonde hair in an elegant bob and wore a taupe linen suit. I'd never been overkeen on Zoe. She'd been a little cow to Belinda when they were kids, so I was pleased to see her glued-on, sick-as-a-pig smile when I swanned up with a big smile and my besotted Dominic on my arm.

'We've heard all about you,' Maggie said, in her carefully modulated but rather scratchy voice. 'Susan tells us you're a merchant banker.'

With an easy smile, he shook her hand. 'Yes, for my sins. It was either that or the priesthood.'

This jerked the Freeman eyes wide open. 'No! Really?'

'No, not really,' he confessed.

The rather raucous laugh that greeted this came not from any Freeman mouth, but from my old chum Tamara, who'd just joined us, and was absolutely the last person I was expecting to give me heart failure.

After shaking hands quite decorously with 'Dominic', she said, 'I hope you haven't been feeling uncomfortable, because I've been staring at you on and off for the past half-hour. You remind me of someone, but I can't quite put my finger on it.'

My God. Hara-kiri time already.

Josh produced only an amused little smile. 'If I've got a lookalike, I trust he behaved himself.'

'When I remember, I'll tell you,' she grinned back.

With what I hope was an insouciant little hoot of laughter, I took Josh's arm. 'That's blown it, darling. I knew you'd end up on *Crimewatch*. You should have kept your balaclava on, like I said.'

'It was itchy,' he said. 'Besides, I couldn't resist sticking two fingers up at the security cameras.'

'It's really bugging me,' Tamara said. 'Mind you, I've met so many zillions of people.'

'Tamara's a resort rep, on and off,' Zoe said. 'Ski-repping in the winter, beach-repping in the summer. Maybe you bumped into her on the Costa del Piña Colada.' She added a little titter to dilute the down-market dig, but Tamara ignored it.

'It'll come to me,' she grinned.

I changed the subject sharpish. 'What a shame Sarah couldn't make it. I was looking forward to seeing her. How is she?'

Maggie was only too happy to talk on this subject. 'Very happy, thank you. We went up for New Year. She was very busy with masses of guests, but it is a very *large* house, mainly sixteenth century, you know, and of course there was a shoot on New Year's Day. James has quite extensive shooting, you know. There were about thirty for lunch so Sarah was very busy supervising the staff.'

'Sarah's a Cordon Bleu cook,' I explained to 'Dominic'. 'She used to run a very swanky restaurant in Manchester.'

'And just as well,' Maggie tutted. 'James's cook hadn't a clue what to do with a truffle. You can't give these shooting types just anything. Tamara went up for the weekend a couple of weeks ago, didn't you, Tamara?'

'Certainly did,' she said cheerfully. 'It's a gorgeous house – makes you quite green-eyed with envy.'

Having thus reinforced Sarah's status, Maggie turned to 'Dominic'. 'James frequently has City types up for the shooting. You might know some of them. Do you shoot at all?'

'I used to, but no pheasants. Potting the heads off the buttercups was about my limit. I tried the wheels of the postman's bicycle, but only scored once. Moving targets are a bit trickier with an air rifle.'

Even Zoe laughed but Maggie didn't. 'I don't think that's in the least funny,' the vinegary old hag said stiffly.

'Sorry.' He shot her a smile to neutralise the most acidic vinegar in creation. 'Can I get you another glass of champagne?'

A minute later I moved him on before Maggie returned to City types and related, probing questions. I felt I was stepping in a minefield, with booby traps at every turn. 'Where the hell has Tamara met you?' I hissed.

'Nowhere, as far as I know. I'd remember.'

I dare say he would. She was certainly attractive enough to be memorable.

'It's a case of mistaken ID,' he went on firmly. 'Relax, will you?' The hand resting lightly on my waist gave me a tweaky little squeeze.

'Will you please not do that?' I hissed. 'It tickles!'

One possible unmasking had been quite enough to make my insides churn. What if there was another? I'd never had a panic attack, but just then I felt I might. I was hot, suddenly desperate for oxygen, and equally desperate not to let it show. 'I'm going to the loo,' I gabbled. 'You could go and talk to my father. He looks as if he could do with some light relief. He's heavily into cricket so you could ask what he thinks of the Aussie spin bowlers. That'll keep him talking all afternoon.'

I fought my way out to reception, which was mercifully quiet and cool, and found a quiet little hidey-place just off the lobby, where one of those mainly-for-decoration little armchairs sat. Right next to it was a little mahogany table with flowers and an ashtray.

Well, what were those emergency fags *for*? I scrabbled in my bag for five seconds and cursed myself. I'd only left them upstairs, in my travelling-up bag. Cursing myself again, I sat back and closed my eyes.

And opened them again pretty fast.

'Sophy! Are you all right?'

'Kit!' For a moment I thought he'd sussed me out. It had been Kit who'd made me give up, but not through nagging. On the contrary, his not-nagging when I knew he hated it had been far more effective, but I'd sometimes slunk off for a crafty one, as he'd known perfectly well.

'Are you all right?' he repeated, rather awkwardly.

'Fine – I was just hot.'

In a half-embarrassed gesture I remembered all too well, he ran a hand through his hair. 'I saw these on the way in.' He nodded at the wall behind him. 'I felt bad for not bringing a present. D'you think one of these might do?'

The wall was actually a mini gallery of paintings by local artists, so I got up and took a look. Shoulder to shoulder we gazed at accomplished watercolours of land- and sky-scapes, all tastefully framed, with discreet little stickers.

The prices gave me a bit of a jolt. 'It's really not necessary. I don't suppose you even knew she was getting married till you got to Sonia's, did you?'

He shook his head. 'I had no idea.'

'Well, then.'

We continued our pretence of watercolour gazing, as the atmosphere thickened with murky things unsaid. Eventually he said awkwardly, 'So how have you been?'

'Fine. How about you?'

'Not bad.' He paused. 'Your Whatshisname looks a nice guy.'

'He'll do.' I'd never have gushed, as he'd know perfectly well. 'How's Jocasta?' I added lightly.

'I wouldn't know. I haven't seen her in ages.'

Well, it was nice to know. 'Did she come out in nipple warts?'

He turned to me, startled.

'That's what I wished on her,' I explained. 'I won't tell you what I wished on you.' I said this in a light, jokey tone, intended to ease the atmosphere, but only succeeded in making him look more ill-at-ease.

In a low voice he said, 'I never wanted to hurt you.'

I dare say I should have said something soothing to stop him feeling bad, but I couldn't, quite. 'I'm not going to pretend you didn't but it's all ancient history now, so let's just forget it, shall we?'

He wouldn't look me in the eye. 'I should never have come.'

'Then why did you?' Quite frankly, I was getting just a tad exasperated. 'But since you *are* here, could you try not to look as if you're undergoing some subtle form of torture? This is a wedding, for God's sake, not a wake! Get pissed! Have a laugh! If you can't, then go home and stop trying to make *me* feel bad!'

Leaving him to stew, I flounced off through reception. Wondering whether to nip upstairs for a fag after all, I almost collided with Tamara, coming the other way. 'Where are you going?'

'To the loo. The ones back there are packed.' She gave me a curious little glance. 'You haven't rowed with Dominic, have you? I thought you seemed a bit tense, back there.'

Had it been that obvious? 'No, I just sneaked off for a fag and he's said he'll dump me if ever touch the evil weed again. Only I've left them upstairs.'

'Have one of mine, then.'

Thank God for fellow sinners. I followed her to the deserted loos, where she handed me smokes before disappearing.

'I met your ex,' she called from the loo. 'I couldn't believe it when Sonia introduced me. Bit insensitive, carting him along, wasn't it? Were you gobsmacked?'

'You could say that.' The first drag tasted vile, of course, but I was prepared to suffer for my pleasures.

'Not still holding candles, are you?'

'Not now. I was just talking to him in the foyer. He's obviously wishing he hadn't come.'

105

'Yes, that's the impression I got. He looks quite sweet, though – not a bit like I'd imagined. What does your other half think about him showing up?'

'He's not bothered. Why should he be?'

'No, I suppose not . . .'

While she exited I drowned my fag in the loo and flushed it. Two loathsome lungfuls were quite enough; I was going light-headed already.

'It was really bugging me, who he reminded me of,' Tamara went on, washing her hands. 'But it came back to me. I think it was his crack about the air rifle that did it.'

Naturally I was wrenched between dying to know and dying to change the subject.

Before I could say anything she went on, 'It was ages ago, but it's some mannerism or other, something about his eyes . . . He hasn't got a twin, has he?'

'Not unless he's dead.' Despite myself, I had to ask. 'What was his name?'

'Josh.'

Oh, God. 'Can't possibly be him, then.'

'Not that he'd remember me even it if *was* him.' Giggling slightly, she fluffed up her hair in the mirror.

I had to ask. 'Don't tell me – a holiday fling in Newquay when you were seventeen.'

'Not even that.' Giggling more, she went on, 'If I tell you, will you promise not to laugh?'

It would have taken a much sterner will than mine to stop it there. 'Of course I won't!'

'OK, then. He was my first love.'

FIVE

My first reaction was disbelief. I'd known Tamara since she was ten and there'd never been a Josh that I'd heard of. My second was that I was going to kill him. If he had connections in the area and hadn't told me . . .

'Not that anything ever happened. I don't think he even knew,' she went on. 'He was at school with Jerry. If I met him three times that was it – when we went down for school plays and so on.'

Phew. Jerry was Tamara's elder brother and had gone to boarding school miles away, much to Tamara's relief, as he'd been an utter pain.

She perched on the pink vanity unit thing and lit a Marlboro Light. 'I was only about thirteen. I had those hideous braces on my teeth and was still desperately trying to fill a 32 double A bra, remember?'

'Just about.' Tamara now had the figure I'd had aeons ago – between a ten and a twelve.

'It started after a rugby match,' she went on. 'Mum and Dad took us all out for steak and chips. A couple of Jerry's friends came too, as they were all permanently starving and their folks hadn't come. Josh's parents were abroad. I remember that as Mum felt sorry for him and said she'd send him some tuck. Anyway, there he was at this Beefeater table, right opposite me, and he winked at me and pinched a couple of my chips. That was it – I was utterly smitten.'

She started giggling helplessly. 'Jerry was hideously embarrassed. I was gaping at Josh like a braced drip and it was terrible for his image – Josh was the king of cool among them at the time. He'd nearly been expelled for pinching the caretaker's motorbike or something but they didn't actually kick him out because of his folks being abroad. I couldn't take my eyes off him. I'd have given him all my chips if he'd asked. I fell over on a gravel path on purpose afterwards and really hurt myself, just so he'd pick me up. I knew Jerry never would.'

I could empathise with this. 'I did something like that once, only it was Stuart Dangerfield from the riding stables. It must have been so obvious.'

'I suppose this was. Jerry was such a little shit – he said, "Christ, she's such a spastic," but Josh just told him to shut up, so of course that made me love him even more.'

Well, it would.

She gave a rosy, reminiscent little giggle. 'I filled pages of a diary about him – one of those locking ones. I drew pink hearts on every page and had sweet little fantasies about him: we'd be marooned in a snowbound cottage and he'd have pneumonia and I'd nurse him tenderly – my braces would have come off by then, of course – and when he was better he'd suddenly look at me and say huskily, "My God, Tamara, but you're beautiful . . ." And then there'd be one chaste kiss. God, I was so innocent then . . . Didn't last long, did it?'

I had to join in her giggles. Lord knows, I needed some light relief, but it lasted only until she went on, 'If he hasn't got a twin maybe it's a cousin. Sod it – I'm going to ask him.'

'No!'

As her startled look turned to sparking curiosity, I knew my cover was loose, if not entirely blown. 'Look, it probably *is* him. If I tell you something will you swear not to breathe a word?'

She was bursting with agog-type mischief. 'Sophy, *what*?'

It took half a minute to give her the gist, and of course she cracked up; Tamara would. After Alix's constant forecasts of disaster, it was a colossal relief to see someone giggling helplessly. 'My God, I thought you were slightly twitchy but I'd never, ever have imagined—'

'Let's just hope nobody else has. I was dreading him bumping into someone he knew. Thank God it was only you.'

'Don't worry! I won't tell a soul. *Escorting*, though! I suppose I shouldn't say it, but it's a bit sleazy, isn't it? It's quite spoilt my innocent little fantasies. I had him going to be a vet, like I was supposed to be if I'd been any good at science, and we'd live in a dear little cottage in the country and save poor little animals together.'

'He was in the forces. Ex-Marines.'

'Well, maybe that figures more than the vet bit. Now I come to think of it I could imagine him crawling

109

behind enemy lines to blow up tanks. What's he doing now?'

'I didn't like to ask. At a guess I'd say not very much, that's why he wants the money.'

'How much do they charge?'

I told her.

'Fuck a duck! I'm damned if I'd shell out all that. Why ever did you?'

I told her about Maggie and the brag factor. 'Maggie rubbed Mum's nose in it so much over Sarah – she was positively gloating for months and now it's Zoe's wonderful Oliver as well, so it was ninety per cent keeping Mum's end up and ten per cent mine. I never liked the old hag anyway.'

'She might not be gloating much longer, if you ask me.' She glanced at the door, but still nobody was desperate enough to join us. 'I dare say Sarah keeps up the façade when her folks go up, but when I went the other week she was up to here. I don't think they're actually going to split up, but they were at each other like something off *Jerry Springer*. Practically chucking heirlooms.'

I was all guilty ears.

'I'm only telling you because I know you won't pass it on,' she continued. 'I hope to God it hasn't got around already. I made the mistake of telling Mum, as she was sick of Maggie's gloating as well. I made her swear not to pass it on, but you know what they're like.'

I'd really liked James at the wedding: quietish, but with a very dry sense of humour. 'They seemed so good together! What went wrong?'

For a couple of minutes she enumerated cracks in the supposedly perfect country lifestyle. Heavily mortgaged estates, of which Sarah had known but not told her parents. An old house that ate money and cost a bomb to heat. Sarah slaving her guts out for shooting and fishing weekends, up-market bed and breakfast, etc. James similarly slaving. No proper holiday since the honeymoon. Both of them too knackered for sex and the bedroom too freezing anyway. James's Ma still expecting to live like some pre-war Lady Muck. James's idle younger brother refusing to lift a finger, snorting money up his nose and writing Sarah's car off while stoned. James and Ma refusing to see that money was going up his nose, Ma constantly giving idle brother more. James then having to subsidise Ma, as bank manager was getting stroppy. James refusing to take a stand. Etc.

'God,' I said at last. 'Poor Sarah.'

Any residual envy I'd felt was vanishing like snow in May. Because I *had* envied her, just a bit. Who wouldn't? The house was one of those noble-looking stone piles that might have grown there. You could imagine it looking down its nose at some upstart Georgian residence and saying, 'Dear me, how frightfully nouveau.'

'I dare say they'll work it out,' Tamara shrugged. 'But if Maggie finds out . . . Still, serve the old bag right for gloating.'

My worms, banished for five minutes by all this other stuff, were back in droves. Or squirms, perhaps.

111

'I'd better get back to the zoo, in case anybody's asking my beloved awkward questions.'

'Hang on a tick – these pants are right up my crack again . . .' Having adjusted, she went on. 'I must say, I think it's very noble of you. I'm damned if I'd shell out all that just to keep my mother's end up. I hope he doesn't think you're desperate.'

'He probably does, not that it matters. I'm never going to see him again.'

'Yes, but you don't want any bloke thinking you're desperate, let alone someone like him. Maybe you should have said you *did* have a bloke, but he's far too unsuitable to tell your old dears about, which is why you had to make up somebody suitable.'

Why hadn't I thought of that? 'Like who?' I said, hastily reapplying Hot Berry.

'I don't know . . . Someone who's just done time for GBH? Some rabid, Jurassic-Labour Trotskyite?'

'It's a bit late now.'

On the way out she said, 'Will you tell him I've sussed him out?'

'Then I'd have to tell him I'd filled you in.'

'Doesn't matter, does it? Only please don't remind him about my daft little crush – if he was ever aware of it, that is. I don't suppose Jerry ever said anything. He'd have been too embarrassed. You only admitted to sisters if they were shaggable, with tits.'

It took me a minute to find Josh and when I did, a fresh wave of killer worms hit me. He was talking to a male trio of Paul's crowd, all of whom looked the types to get on to 'shop' after twenty seconds.

Pinning on a bright smile I eased him away. 'Why didn't you go and talk to my father, like I said?' I hissed.

'He was surrounded.'

'I know he was! By a load of old ladies! Which is exactly why he'd have loved an interruption!'

'If you disappear for twenty minutes, what do you expect me to do?' he muttered. 'Stand around like the proverbial spare prick?'

'Look, I'm sorry. I was talking to Kit in the foyer. He felt really bad.'

'That's his problem. If you ask me, he should never have come in the first place.'

Although this was precisely the thing a besotted beloved should say, he did not utter it in the required tone of righteous indignation. It had more of a *just-about-up-to-here-already, why-did-I-ever-get-myself-into-this?* flavour.

'What were you doing in the foyer, anyway?' he muttered.

'Having a panic attack, if you really want to know.' Like him, I was muttering through smiling fangs, in case anybody thought we were rowing.

'I'm not surprised. Before you shot off, you felt like the last stages of rigor mortis.' He replaced a hand on my waist. 'You still do. For crying out loud, relax.'

Re-forming my tense, Hot Berry lips into something I hoped was spontaneous, I hissed through them. 'Darling, I'm in quite enough of a state already, so just put a sock in it, will you?'

Briefly he raised his eyes to the marquee roof. 'Why did I ever get myself into this?' he muttered.

'Nobody made you do it!' I hissed, through smiling fangs. 'If you can't cope, just say so and we can have a row now and be done with it!'

'Fine,' he muttered. 'I'll give you a good shove into those flowers and accuse you, in good, carrying tones, of cheating on me. With another woman might be good – less of a tedious cliché. Then you can give me an outraged slap and we can finish this farce now. You obviously aren't up to this, and if you're going to twitch non-stop like a nervous rabbit, neither am I.'

In a casual, loverish manner that would have fooled anybody, he leant closer. 'And by the way, Piglet, you've got lipstick on your teeth.'

'Then why didn't you *say* so?' I scrabbled in my bag for a tissue, wiped, and bared my fangs. 'Is it off?'

'Yes.'

'Look, if I'm really driving you crackers you can go and lie down upstairs and watch Sky Sport. I'll tell everyone you've got a stinking headache. Or suffering from executive stress, if you prefer.'

'My "stress" would disappear instantly if you'd only stop twitching and get a grip. If you spin brazen lies you should be brazen enough to carry them through.'

'I didn't do it for *me*! I did it for Mum, to stop her fretting about me!' It wasn't easy, whispering like this whilst still baring my fangs in a Hot Berry smile in case anybody was watching. And they were: Mrs Gardner, for a start, who'd lived six doors away from my folks for about three hundred years.

114

'Hello, Mrs Gardner,' I said gaily, over my shoulder. 'Lovely hat!'

Josh followed my gaze. 'Lovely hat?' he muttered. 'It's a bloody awful hat. It makes her look like a superannuated gorgon.'

'She looks like a superannuated gorgon anyway! I was trying to be nice!'

'It might be more to the point if you tried being nice to me.' Mrs Gardner's hat had eased the tension, however, I could sense his tether lengthening again, like one of those extending dog leads. 'Take a deep breath and force yourself,' he added drily.

I gathered the shreds of my cool. 'No force will be necessary, darling. Come and meet some of the more human members of the clan.'

I led him to Auntie Barbara and Diana, who were about as safe as you could get. Diana was three years younger than me and two stone slimmer, with long, glossy dark hair, and a mischievous, mobile mouth. 'I do wish you'd stay over,' she pouted. 'I could do with the company. It's going to be all boring old people otherwise.'

'Thank you, dear,' said Auntie Barbara, placidly enough.

'I didn't mean *you*, Mother.'

'We really can't,' I said apologetically. 'Dominic's off to Malaysia tomorrow.'

'Bit of a pain,' he said, with a smile that would have convinced anybody.

At this point Mum bustled up. 'We're doing the photos in the garden – can you all come?'

115

Diana and her mother drifted off and suddenly it was relatively quiet. 'None of those suits asked any awkward questions, did they?' I asked Josh.

'Nothing I couldn't handle, though you might have told me we were "practically engaged".'

'Who the hell told you that?'

'Some gushing woman in a pink hat. Caught me in passing, said she'd heard we were "practically engaged – how *lovely*", and gushed off.'

'Well, we're not!'

'Whatever you say, darling.'

I wanted to mutter, 'And stop laughing, will you?' but desisted. If he was deriving cynical amusement from all this at least he'd look chilled out, which was more than I was. Pink Hat was probably Trudi from the golf club, who I gathered, wanted strangling at the best of times.

We followed everybody else out on to sunny lawns, where female guests looked like so many brilliant butterflies with their more soberly dressed mates. Photos were taken on the old stone terrace, or on the lawns, against a background of pink rhododendrons and green velvet grass. I was dragged up for family shots, and inevitably, 'Dominic' was dragged up, too.

'I thought it'd be nice to have you two with Paul and Belinda,' Mum beamed. 'Over there, on the terrace.'

She'd had a few glasses of fizz by then – it was showing in a rosy flush on her cheeks – but even for Mum it was a bit obvious: the two happy couples together. If he'd been for real, I'd have been as mortified as I was at the age of seven, when she'd tripped and shown her knickers in the school sports day mothers' race. I knew Josh was silently cracking up; he couldn't quite hide a flicker at the corners of his mouth.

I could just see him a day or so hence, having his friends in fits. 'Christ, no wonder she had to hire someone. Her mother'd frighten any normal guy off in five minutes – obviously desperate to get her hitched.'

Certain he was thinking on these lines, or something considerably ruder, I stuck on a plastic grin and felt a complete prat, squashed up against him while the photographer fussed and re-posed us, taking endless shots.

Only Tamara, grinning conspiratorially from across the lawn, relaxed me and made me smile for real. Poor old Mum couldn't be quite that bad. She hadn't frightened Paul off.

Once that was over we were summoned to a marquee, where more pink and cream flowers drowned us all in scent. White cloths, silver and glasses all sparkled, unlike me, unsparklingly bracing myself for ticklish questions over lunch.

Josh was placed almost opposite me at the round table. Now and then, as we ate poached salmon, he shot me the tiniest wink. Still, I wish Mum hadn't put him next to Auntie Rosemary, who'd recently got divorced from Uncle George after not speaking to him for two years. Rosemary was not a restful type. Her eyes darted over everybody like demented calculators, sizing up their earning power, family backgrounds,

117

and so on. She worked at an estate agent's in Cobham, and this led to the next subject.

'You really should persuade Sophy to buy her own place,' she said to Josh, in a carrying, advisory voice. 'It's quite ridiculous, paying rent at her age when she's earning good money.'

'It's her choice,' he said.

'That's right – you tell her,' said Granny Metcalfe, who was sitting on my right. It had not perhaps been perfect planning to put these two together. Rosemary was Mum's elder sister, and although I'd love to say that both sides of the family got on like The Waltons at a church social, I'd be lying.

There's a good old north-south divide in our family. Mum came from Hampshire, where her father had been a civil servant, all very middle-class and respectable in the not-much-money-but-trying-to-look-as-if-you-have kind of way. Her mother, Granny Simons, had come from the kind of family where the word 'common' was used a good deal, and had continued this noble tradition.

Dad's family, on the other hand, had been blue-collar. Ma and Pa Simons had therefore been appalled when their daughter had met Dad on a weekend in the Dales and shortly afterwards announced her intention of marrying him.

At the time he'd been working in a small engineering business, getting his hands dirty. Granny Simons, who'd intended Mum to land an ear, nose and throat consultant at least, had pleaded with her not to throw herself away. She'd never quite forgiven Dad for subsequently taking over the business, doing extremely well, and providing Mum with a better home and lifestyle than any of her other children had managed. He wasn't *supposed* to. Mum was supposed to have ended up with five grubby kids and a husband downing pints of ale every night. She was supposed to be going out charring to stop the bailiffs taking the telly away and crying 'Oh, Mother, why didn't I listen to you?'

Granny Metcalfe, naturally enough, sensed all this. She didn't care much for Rosemary either, who she looked on as another anti-oop-north snob in her mother's image. 'I can't think why you had to go to London in the first place, love,' she said. 'I'd not go back there if you paid me.'

She'd been to London just once, twenty years back. Some sniffy salesgirl in a West End shop had looked down her nose at her and she'd never forgiven it.

'I wanted a change,' I said, as the starters were cleared away. 'And the people aren't all Satan's little helpers, you know.'

'Hmm. Mind you, I quite like your new lad.' Here she took another good look at Josh. 'How long have you been courting, again?'

'About five months,' I said.

'And not living together? I thought they all lived together these days. Saves on the bills.'

Auntie Rosemary put on her pursed-up, *dear me – the peasantry* look. 'Really, Mrs Metcalfe, I think that's their business.'

Granny M enjoyed stirring her up. 'I only asked. Sophy doesn't mind, do you, love?'

119

The main course arrived: new Welsh lamb with rosemary and weeny new potatoes. 'Of course not,' I said, wondering how to change the subject before it got even more ticklish. 'We've just never discussed it.'

'I think Sophy prefers to keep her independence,' said Josh, still as chilled out as vichyssoise.

'Well, I suppose she's right there,' said Granny Metcalfe. 'Takes away the mystery, living with a man. They only end up skivvying for them, ironing their shirts and so on. Plenty of time for that when you're wed. Dear me, this lamb's very underdone. Just look at that! Pink! Turns my stomach.'

This gave Rosemary the perfect opportunity to put her down. 'It's *supposed* to be like that, Mrs Metcalfe. They do it the French way.'

'What's wrong with the good old English way? I can't do with underdone lamb.'

'I'll ask them to change it,' I said.

'Don't bother, love. I'll just eat the vegetables.' In a whisper she added, 'I don't want some waitress thinking I don't know what's what.'

Unaware of the whisper, Josh beckoned to a waiter. There was no comment, not even a 'look', but poor old Granny M was still a trifle embarrassed. 'I didn't want to be a nuisance.'

'Of course you're not a nuisance,' I said. 'I'm sure they've got some well done somewhere. You can have whatever you like.'

Across the table, Josh shot her a little wink. 'And if anybody doesn't like it, stuff them.'

'Of course, well-done lamb *can* be a delicacy,' said Rosemary, evidently thinking she'd gone a bit far. 'In Cyprus they cook it in bread ovens till it falls apart. They call it *kleftiko*.'

'But I suppose it's not a delicacy if it's done in my gas oven in Bolton,' Granny M retorted. 'Things have to be foreign to be delicacies, I suppose. Coriander. They put coriander in everything on the television. If I put coriander on my poached eggs I dare say they'd be a delicacy. Delia Smith'd write it up in one of her books.'

I sensed a safe route here; once roused on a pet topic she could rabbit on for ages. If I could just get her on to the EU (wretched Germans telling us we couldn't have smoky bacon crisps, what did we fight the war for? etc.) I'd be safe till coffee.

Just as they were clearing the plates, Sonia appeared and half knelt beside me. 'You didn't say anything to Kit, did you? Only he's sloped off – left a present for Paul and Belinda, called a cab and went.'

Instantly I felt bad and wondered why the hell I should. 'I only spoke to him for two minutes,' I said, a tad irritably. 'If you ask me, he didn't feel very comfortable being here at all.'

'That's what he said. Oh dear, I suppose it was all my fault for dragging him along.'

She went back to her own table, leaving me feeling even badder for being irritable. She meant well, poor girl, and if she possessed the tact and diplomacy of a bullfrog it wasn't her fault.

At least there were no Dominic disasters; by the coffee and *petits fours* stage I was beginning to think we

121

were going to pull it off with gold stars and laugh all the way home.

'Mind you, Rosemary's right,' Granny M whispered, as we left the table at last. 'No sense putting money in a landlord's pocket. Get your own bricks and mortar. And don't live with him, love, not if you really want him. Better to keep him keen.'

Stringing her along felt almost worse than deceiving Mum and Dad, and all this wild approval was going to make it hellishly awkward to dump him. However was I going to justify it?

The afternoon went so panic-freely, I almost started enjoying myself. With fewer nerves to contend with, another little problem quickly presented itself. Josh would keep putting his hand on my waist, and my antennae, which had been taking a little nap for the past hour, were waking up again and having a field day. Still, I could handle it. All flutterings were strictly under control: a passing, sensual pleasure to savour in guilty secret, like a whole packet of those fat-free biscuits that make you thin if you only eat enough of them. Once he even patted my bottom, in an uncalled-for and grossly overfamiliar fashion, I hissed, 'Don't *do* that!' and he didn't repeat it, damn him.

Before I knew it Belinda was going upstairs to change. I'd hardly spoken to her all afternoon. She'd been constantly surrounded, laughing a lot, and, I suspected, getting moderately ratso. And had only looked the more gorgeous for it, which was exceedingly unfair, if you ask me.

As Josh wandered off to inspect the plumbing, I sat on the terrace steps in the sun. With her characteristically wicked-innocent expression, Tamara came up and parked herself beside me. 'I was just talking to Sonia. She thinks Kit still fancies you and that's why he sloped off like that.'

I gaped at her. 'She does realise *he* dumped *me*?'

'Yes, but she thinks that other woman – what was her name?'

'Bitch-face.'

'Well, she thinks maybe Bitch-face was just a rampant passing thing. She thinks he couldn't bear seeing you all lovey-dovey with "Dominic" and he's gone off to cry into a pint of Boddies.'

'More likely some hideous old geriatric found out he was a doctor and asked him to take a look at his varicose ulcer. Even more likely, he just felt bad, as well he might.'

'Yes, that's what I said.'

'You're not *supposed* to say that,' I said, somewhat miffed. 'You're supposed to massage my pathetic little ego and agree with her totally.'

Tamara's expression underwent a not-so-subtle change. 'You're not telling me you *do* still want him?'

'No! I'd just appreciate the poetic justice of it! Or perhaps poetic irony, in the circumstances. Wouldn't you?'

'Yes, but I wouldn't call it poetic anything. I'd just say it'd serve the bugger right.'

We started giggling so helplessly, some passing elderly guest who looked half cut already gave a roguish wink and said, 'Dear, dear, all these pretty young things who can't take their bubbly – makes an old man feel quite perky.'

'Gruesome old fart,' Tamara whispered, as he tottered off. 'Probably having fantasies about the pair of us whipping him with his surgical truss.'

We erupted again.

'Mind you, Sonia could just be right,' she went on, as the giggles wore off. 'Josh is exactly the sort of bloke to have on your arm if you wanted to make an ex realise what he's missing.'

For the first time, part of me began to wonder whether it was really so impossible. And, I have to confess, it glowed with a certain gratification.

'As Sonia said . . .' she went on, '"She really looks quite nice when she's all done up, doesn't she? I just hope I look as good when I hit thirty."'

More ego fodder. 'Dear, sweet girl,' I sighed.

Tamara was giggling again. 'I nearly forgot – just before Belinda went up to change I heard your mother say, "Don't forget to throw your bouquet before you leave, dear. And I don't have to tell you where to aim it."'

'If you ask me, she's already pencilling in June Saturdays for next year. Thank God he's not for real.'

'Pity poor old Belinda didn't know that. She said, "For heaven's sake, do you want to put the poor man off for life?"'

I hoped she hadn't upset Mum, but I didn't have much time to think about it. Josh was back and a buzz was summoning us to the forecourt, where the newlyweds were about to depart. They hadn't appeared yet, but seconds after we'd joined the expectant throng Mum drew me from Josh's side, all agog. 'You'll never *believe* what Jane Dixon told me, not half an hour ago.'

Tamara was right, then. 'What?' I asked, as required.

She lowered her voice. 'She told me that Sarah Freeman's – sorry, *Lambert's* – marriage isn't turning out well at all. They row all the time. He's got a drink problem, apparently. She's even thinking of leaving him.'

'Mum, I'm sure that's not true.'

'I'm only saying what Jane told me, dear. The estate's heavily mortgaged, apparently, which is why he has to have all those shooting parties for incredibly wealthy people who can pay through the nose. And the awful thing is, Maggie hasn't a clue. Jane heard it from Tamara, who had it from Sarah herself when she went up.'

Before I could say anything, she was off again. 'Poor Maggie.' She shot me a defensive glance. 'Yes, I know what you're thinking, dear, but I'm not gloating. I can't help feeling just a bit sorry for her.'

That was a turn-up, but I suppose it's easier to love your enemy if you can feel really sorry for her first. 'Look, Tamara did tell me something but it's really not that bad, so for heaven's sake don't go telling anybody else.'

'Sophy, you know I hardly *ever*— Here they come!'

Instantly the air was filled with a cacophony of well-oiled voices, wishing them well. Wearing something cream and stunning, Belinda threw her bouquet in the rough direction of blokeless Sonia and a really raucous cheer went up.

Just before they left, I managed a final farewell.

'Take care,' Belinda whispered, holding me tight. 'And don't let Mum frighten him off. You look great together.'

By now I was right up Guilt Creek without a paddle. 'Don't worry, I know when I'm on to a good thing. Have fun, and give my love to all the dear little heffalumps.'

As the car finally departed, trailing an old boot or two, Tamara came up, looking as if she'd just had a really good laugh. 'They nearly had something less boring than wellies,' she giggled. 'Sonia had a massive blow-up willy from a joke shop, but it punctured the second we tried to tie it to the car.'

She wandered off, leaving me laughing and extra-ordinarily mellow, in the circumstances. 'Just as well it punctured. Mum would have had a pink fit,' I said to Josh, who was also still laughing. I checked my watch. 'Another hour and we can push off. You must be dying to go.'

'It hasn't been that bad.'

'You don't have to be polite. Other people's families are always a nightmare, especially all afternoon, *en masse*.' Half the guests were drifting off, the rest were wandering back to the marquee, where afternoon tea had just been laid.

Nobly ignoring the *pâtisserie*, I semi-perched on a

table and helped myself to a smoked salmon sandwich. 'Might as well stock up now, otherwise we'll have to stop at the services and I'll stuff myself with more junk.'

Josh semi-perched alongside and took a sandwich. Now we were nearly out of the woods and nobody was within earshot, I thought a little thank you would not be tempting fate.

'You're a brilliant liar. That story about your friend and the credit card deserved an Oscar.'

'Like I told you, I'd handle it.'

'I didn't think you'd handle it that well.'

'Oh, thee of little faith.' He passed me the sandwiches. 'Chew on one of those.'

I took another. 'I've been imagining every worst-case scenario for days,' I went on. 'I must have had at least forty-eight litters of kittens in the past twenty-four hours, and a few baby elephants as well. If you only knew all the pitfalls I'd imagin . . .'

'Exactly. They were imaginary. You got all wound up for nothing.'

What did I say about unjustified overconfidence? 'They weren't, as a matter of fact,' I said, a trifle acidly. 'Tamara *had* met you before.'

He turned to me with evident disbelief. 'When?'

'Were you at school with a Jerry Dixon?'

'*Jerry?*' Dawning incredulity washed his face. 'Christ, is she his sister?'

'Hole in one.'

'Jesus.'

For a moment I saw ancient memories fight their

127

way to the surface. 'She was going to ask whether you had a cousin or something, so I more or less had to confess.'

'You *told* her? I thought the whole point was not to tell anybody! What if she passed it on?'

'She wouldn't!' He was still looking vaguely stunned.

'She remembers you because you pinched some of her chips,' I said. 'She was most put out.'

'I'd never have recognised her.' As the stunned look wore off, a tiny quiver at the corner of his mouth told me he was maybe remembering more than the chips.

'What?' I said.

'Jerry's folks were good for a dinner out.' He passed me the sandwiches again.

'No, thanks.' I glanced over my shoulder at the doilyed dishes. 'I do wish somebody'd take those éclairs away before I make a complete pig of myself.'

'A piglet wouldn't hurt.' Before I could blink, he was brandishing one right under my nose. Smothered with chocolate, it was fatly stuffed with whipped cream. 'Open wide.'

It would have been ungracious to refuse. I opened, he stuffed. 'I was trying to give them up,' I said.

'Don't talk with your mouth full.' He stood up crisply. 'I'm going to make a phone call.'

Well.

I ate another sandwich, wondering who he was phoning and whether he was giving a progress report. I could just imagine it.

'How's it going, sweetie?'

'As expected, pretty bloody dire.'

'What's she like?'

'Overweight and neurotic. I just shoved an éclair in her mouth to shut her up and she still kept talking.'

Wallowing in these happy thoughts, I ate another smoked salmon sandwich. I might have indulged in another éclair, too, but people were leaving and I went to say goodbye to Tamara.

'I might phone Jerry and see whether he's still in touch with Josh,' she said. 'It's intriguing me why someone like that goes escorting. In fact I'm going to see Jerry in a couple of weeks. He's just moved into some really old place near Cambridge. He's working for some software company now.'

Jerry had done some horrific computer science degree at Cambridge, stayed in the area ever since and married above five years back. 'I suppose he's mortgaged and babied by now.'

'Mortgaged but not babied. The only happy event they're expecting is a divorce on the grounds that it was a disaster practically from day one. He's having a massive housewarming-cum-thank-God-I'm-on-the-loose-again party. He's only invited me because he fancies this girl Charlotte I work with and he wants me to bring her too, plus any other hot totty I can rake up, as he so delicately put it. Brothers are the pits, I can tell you.' Her eyes widened. 'Why don't you come? Jerry might be a bit of a pain but he does throw a good party.'

I made a face. 'No thanks. Sounds too much like a meat market and I'm right off meat markets.'

'Don't tell me. I'm only going because he's got an Italian friend who looks just like David Ginola. Jerry brought him up a few weeks ago to see Man U play at home. That's when he met Charlotte. Just his accent makes me go weak at the knees. Didn't some dead white male write a poem about Latin bastards?'

'Bastard *Latin. That soft bastard Latin, that sounds as if 'twere writ on satin*, or something. Bryon, I think.'

'Well, he said it, though Latin bastard's probably spot-on, too.'

I saw Tamara off and by the time I returned all the éclairs were gone.

Half an hour later Josh and I escaped upstairs to gather up our things. However, you can never just disappear from a do like that. You have to spend twenty minutes cooing 'Byeee – lovely to see you' to all the ghastly people you're hoping not to see for the next ten years.

For our final farewells we made for the bar. It extended on to the terrace, where most of the remaining guests had taken themselves. The evening sun washed stone and lawns with gold, and from somewhere in the distance came the bleating of lambs. The scene was so peacefully enticing, I suddenly longed to be able to sit down in the sun, order a large double anything with a straw, and not have to get into that car and drive for hours.

After a moment it dawned on me that the atmosphere wasn't quite as relaxed as it should have been. There were undercurrents to the conversation, tuttings and shakings of heads.

As we stood on the threshold, Auntie Barbara saw

me. 'Your mother's looking for you. I'm afraid she in a bit of a tizz,' she said, in . . . *so brace yourself* tones.

Right beside her, Diana was wearing a wicked grin. 'Poor old Sophy. The best laid plans, and all that . . . I should push off quick, if I were you.'

I went cold.

Tamara.

'Have we missed something?' said the idiot beside me.

'Oh dear, they haven't heard,' said Auntie Barbara.

'Heard what?' said the idiot.

'It was just on the news,' said a voice behind us. We spun round. The barman was wiping a cloth over the counter. 'Bomb scares on the motorways. I thought we'd done with all that carry-on. There's a sixteen-mile tailback on the M6 and the M1's closed. The other roads are murder already. The police message is, "Don't travel unless you have to."' He slung his cloth in the sink. 'Can I get anyone a drink?'

Since this was the closest I had ever come to passing out with sheer relief, I could have murdered one. In the three seconds before he'd elaborated, my brain had been making wild stabs as to how in hell my secret had got on air. Whoever Tamara had told, he or she was a mate of the reporter who covered weddings for the local rag, who was a mate of someone on local radio . . . I'd almost imagined a further mate on *The News of the World*, about to offer ten grand for exclusive rights to my *FAKE LOVE SHOCK* story.

It's amazing what your brain can come up with

when you think you're going to have to kill yourself in three minutes.

Trying to look merely browned off, I sank to a handy bar stool. 'God, I can't face it. We won't be home till midnight, crawling along heaving roads . . .'

'If your mum's got anything to do with it, you won't be crawling anywhere,' Diana grinned. 'And yes, please. I'll have a pineapple Bacardi Breezer,' she added to the barman. 'Is it still a free bar, or are we paying?'

'Let me,' said Josh. 'Anything for you, Barbara? Sophy?'

'How can I?' I said irritably. 'I'm driving!'

'Oh, there you are, love.' It was Dad. 'I take it you've heard,' he added, seeing my face.

Now the blissful relief was subsiding, I *was* browned off. 'Yes, thank you. I could spit.'

Hot on Dad's heels came Mum, doing a fair impression of the cat that's had the goldfish and possibly the budgie, too. 'Oh, there you are, dear – I've been looking all over. Thank heaven I booked that room – you can't possibly drive back now.'

My inner cynic began to wonder whether she'd engineered this on purpose; nipping off for a little hoax call in between cups of tea would have been a doddle. 'Well, I'm very sorry for the inconvenience but I couldn't let a perfectly good hotel room go to waste,' I imaged her saying to Detective Chief Inspector Slammer. 'Sophy can be very stubborn, you know. She takes after her father – you wouldn't believe the trouble I had to get him to go to the doctor about his piles.'

'What do you mean, *can't*?' I demanded. 'It might take a couple of hours longer—'

'And the rest, dear. The traffic'll be terrible. Still, you might as well make the best of it – have a nice, relaxed evening with the family.'

'It's just tough. A traffic jam won't kill me.'

'*Please*, dear, don't say things like that!' She put on an anguished voice. 'You'll be exhausted! I'll be worried to death in case you nod off at the wheel!'

Emotional blackmail, just for a change. 'No, I won't. J— Just to stop you worrying. I'll let Dominic drive halfway.' My heart was doing a black flip. I'd so nearly said 'Josh'.

'I can't,' he pointed out. 'I've been drinking.'

I could have thumped him. Couldn't the moron see I was looking for excuses?

As always Mum turned plaintively to Dad for backup. 'You tell her, Ted. You know I'll be a nervous wreck otherwise.'

'It might be more sensible, love,' he said.

'Dad, we *can't*.' I said desperately. 'I told you, Dominic has to get back.'

'What time does he have to be back?'

'One-ish,' Josh replied. 'Half-one would do.'

I couldn't believe he'd said it. 'Your *flight's* at half-one, isn't it?'

'No, darling, what's when I've got to leave.'

'Yes, but—'

'There you are then love,' Dad said. 'If you left really early, you'd be in plenty of time. Even if the motorways are still closed, the other roads'll be clear first thing.'

133

I turned to Josh for support. 'It's entirely up to you,' he said, in the placid, reasonable tones of the placid, reasonable, pain-in-the-arse Dominic.

'There you are, dear,' said Mum triumphantly. 'You can't argue with that, can you?'

Oh, yes I could. Just as I was about to escape undiscovered, I was not going to allow the door to slam in my face. 'I'd rather get back,' I said, very firmly. 'I've got things to do, too.' Like getting spectacularly pissed in my relief that it was over.

Well, that told her. Five minutes later we were off.

Off up the stairs again, to room five.

Six

'Why the hell did you say you had to *leave* at one thirty?' I fumed, ramming the key back in the door. 'And what about the work you were supposed to do tomorrow morning?'

'I'll do it on the plane. On my state-of-the-art, trusty executive laptop.'

'Oh, for God's *sake* . . .' I had a headache now, a throbbing cocktail of tension and fatigue. The very room was winding me up. Those busy little flowers were enough to give anybody a migraine.

'Well, what the hell was I supposed to say?' he demanded. 'You should have told me what time the flight was. You'd only just been moaning that you couldn't face crawling home for hours. I thought maybe you wanted to stay!'

I wasn't going to tell him it was only a post-panic cover. 'Well, I didn't! Wasn't it obvious?'

'I thought you might be concerned about inconveniencing *me*. Which was obviously a bloody stupid notion,' he added, shoving his things back in the wardrobe.

'I was! I'd have thought you'd run a mile!'

'Will you calm down?' With a very crisp edge to his voice, he shut the wardrobe door. 'It's the sensible thing to do, anyway. The traffic *would* have been murder, it *would* have been a hell of a long drive, and your mother probably *would* have been a nervous wreck.'

'That was just emotional blackmail!'

'Not entirely, I suspect.'

All right, not entirely. Mum always worried until she got that call to say, 'I'm home, OK?'

'At least you can have a drink now,' he pointed out. 'And if you ask me, you could do with it.'

'Are you kidding? Didn't you hear me nearly give the game away just now? If I start knocking back vodka—'

'I said nothing about "knocking back". I said "a drink". If you can't hold it, don't have one.'

'Oh—' Turning away, I muttered a rather less delicate version of *Go away*.

'I heard that,' he said.

Good.

'You think I want to stay here, in the back of the Lancashire beyond?' he demanded. 'I do, actually, have a lunch date tomorrow. Don't you think I'd rather have gone home and slept in my own bed?'

'Then why the hell didn't you back me up?' I hissed. I'd rather have yelled, but my head couldn't take it. 'I didn't stand a chance, what with Mum and Dad and wretched Auntie Barbara sticking her oar in . . .' If I'd continued to dig my heels in it would have looked suspicious. Already I'd seen Mum beginning to wonder whether we'd had a row.

'If you were really set on leaving, you should have made a stand!'

'How can you stand against half a dozen bulldozers?'

'You bulldoze back! Harder!'

'Will you please not start having a go at me? I've got a stinking headache – I'm exhausted – I was awake at half-past five with nerves—'

'Then it's just as well we're staying.'

From one point of view, maybe. I hadn't even got a T-shirt to sleep in and in case you're thinking *So what?* I should explain that I'm one of those messy sleepers who frequently kick the covers off in the night. Occasionally (I hate to admit this inelegant habit) I even adopt an infantile, face-in-the-pillow, bum-in-the-air attitude. A pre-Kit boyfriend had caught me like this, wakened me with a hefty slap and laughed, the bastard. 'Look, I'm sorry, but I just wasn't geared up for this, sharing a room and everything.'

'Neither was I.' He was leaning against the window sill, arms folded across his chest. 'But is it really such a big deal?'

I was beginning to realise I'd been overreacting. It was twin beds, after all, not a double; they must have run out of those, thank God. Maybe I could sleep tidily for once. Maybe he'd sleep like a log and not notice if I didn't. 'I guess not. But I talk in my sleep sometimes. I hope I won't wake you up.'

'No chance. I had a late night last night. I'll be out like a light and short of a minor earthquake, nothing wakes me.'

Thank God for that.

'Look,' he went on, in firm, practical tones, 'why don't you have a bath or a shower? It'll relax you. I'll bring you up a drink, if you like, and then clear off and leave you to it.'

It was so typical of men. Right after making you livid enough to want to punch them, they turned all kind and thoughtful and made you feel bad. 'Perhaps I will. A titchy vodka, double tonic.'

'I'll be right back.'

Kicking my shoes off, I flopped on to that bed. It was Sod's law, of course. Since the disasters I'd been dreading had failed to materialise, it followed that Fate would chuck in an unexpected one.

I groped in my bag for a couple of paracetamol, grabbed a glass of water, and rang home. Nobody was in, which was just as well. I couldn't have faced post mortems with Alix, especially since it wasn't 'post' yet. I left a message, flopped back and was just drifting off when Josh knocked on the door.

'Room service.'

I hadn't locked it, so he was evidently being polite in case I was prancing about in my knickers.

As if.

'There you go,' he said. 'Sorry – you weren't asleep, were you?'

Obviously I wore that dopey, coming-to look. 'Nearly,' I confessed.

'Well, enjoy your bath. I'll see you later.'

Just as he was about to open the door, my nerves got the better of me. 'Dominic!'

He turned. 'What?'

'What if I call you Josh by mistake? I nearly did, downstairs!'

He considered only a second. 'A nickname?'

'A *nick*name? How can you justify Josh from Dominic?'

He shrugged. 'It doesn't have to be connected. I used to play the trumpet so excruciatingly badly, they called me after the Joshua who trumpeted the walls of Jericho down.'

'It's a bit far-fetched.'

'Not really. I did play the trumpet excruciatingly badly. The neighbours labelled me a public nuisance.'

'Sounds a bit like me and my violin.' I managed an anaemic sort of smile, evidently sickly enough to make him rethink.

Semi-exasperated, he ran a hand through his hair. 'Look, if it's going to be such a major headache, we'll drive back now. I'll back you up.'

Now he said it. The mere thought of going through all the pros and cons again with Mum made me feel exhausted. Besides, with that lovely cold V&T in my hand . . . 'I'm not sure I can face driving back now. I was geared up before and now I'm not. But if you'd really rather go . . .'

'I wouldn't if you want the truth. What I'd like right now is a whisky, followed by dinner, followed by several hours of oblivion.'

Except for the whisky, snap. After the kind of day we'd had, that drive'd be a killer. 'Well, if you can stand sharing with me for a night, I can stand sharing with you.'

'Then we'll stick to plan A. I'll see you downstairs – enjoy your bath.' At the door he paused. 'Look on the

139

bright side. You've been expecting disaster all day. This is evidently it.'

Too right, matey.

Still, as the door closed behind him, I told myself we'd survived the worst. If I engaged brain carefully before every mouth-opening, we should survive the rest, but, oh dear, I was beginning to wish for nice, non-fanciable Colin, after all. I was going to be quite wound up enough without the added strain of spending a whole evening and night with a man I fancied the pants off while pretending I didn't (to him), while at the same time pretending I did (for the family) . . . if you follow me.

Not that it was going to be much fun for Josh either: more tedious hours of someone else's tedious relations, trying desperately to swallow your yawns . . . Poor bloke.

Even poor girlfriend, if he had one. I thought it very noble of me to feel sorry for the girlfriend of a bloke I fancied, but I did, just a bit. On acid wings, Alix's words were zooming back: 'Would you want to be involved with a man who did that from *choice*?'

Would you want to be involved with a man who did it at all, was more to the point. Maybe he was even now giving the poor girl a call.

'*Look, don't get mad, but I've got to stay over.*'

'*WHAT?*'

'*It's the motorways – you must have seen it on the news. Her mother's in a tizz about her having to drive for hours—*'

'*Oh, for God's sake!*'

Bang.

And he'd only just started. I imagined him still at it, weeks hence. I imagined her kissing him goodbye as he went off to 'work'.

'*If you dare fancy her, I'll kill you.*'

'*For God's sake – I* never *fancy them!*'

Bang.

If that were me, I'd be a nervous wreck all evening, picturing some Jocasta-cow all over him: *Go on, you know you want to. She'll never know . . .*

Then I'd be sniffing his clothes, hair, etc. the instant he came back.

'*You kissed her, didn't you?*'

'*No – she looked like a geriatric sow.*'

'*I bet you did, you lying bugger.*'

'*All right, so I did, but only a peck. I felt sorry for her.*'

'*Liar! Geriatric sows don't smell of Joop! You fancied her, didn't you? I bet you touched her tits, too! I'll tell that bloody agency and you'll get the sack! Why can't you get a proper job?*'

And whatever would you say to friends when they asked what he did?

'He's a, well, a sort of escort, but it's all strictly on the level and it's only temporary till he gets another incredibly high-powered job like he had before.'

I could just see the *Oh, yeah?* expressions.

No thanks. Give me Darcy and Clooney any day: steamy fantasies whenever you wanted them and you didn't even have to shave your legs. They never moaned if you wanted to watch *Animal Hospital* either.

On the way down I stopped at reception to ask for a wake-up call at six.

'Would you like breakfast before you go?' the girl asked. 'It would only be continental, I'm afraid, but it's no problem to arrange.'

No, thanks – I just want to get the fuck out.

Not that I actually said it; Josh would probably want sustenance. 'That would be lovely, thank you.'

Pre-dinner drinks were relaxed enough. Josh was extraordinarily skilled at deflecting conversation away from himself. The restaurant was Saturday-night packed. Furnished in comfortable, small country house style, it overlooked the terrace. The doors were open and it was unbelievably balmy for mid-May. In the fading, pink-dusky light, the gardens were beautifully peaceful. You could still hear the odd bird singing, until the music started. I hadn't even noticed the little dance floor until a perky young DJ began playing the corny golden oldies he imagined these decrepit over-twenty-fives might dance to.

Various couples shuffled on to the floor, in that vaguely embarrassed, I-hope-I'm-not-making-a-prat-of-myself way and gradually, as the floor filled, Mum started casting me expectant glances. However, since Josh was talking to Uncle Mike, Auntie Barbara's other half, and presumably unaware of what was expected of him, I pretended not to notice.

Now, in normal circumstances I'll be the first to admit that dancing with a man you fancy is one of life's more delicious experiences. Paying for his company and having to share a room with him later put rather a different complexion on things. Besides which, I'm no masochist. Why torment yourself by becoming addicted to something that would be history in under twenty-four hours?

I went and sat next to Granny Metcalfe, who whispered, 'Are you all right, love? I thought you seemed a big edgy earlier.'

Had it been that obvious? 'I was just a bit shattered. It's been a long day.'

'Just as well you're stopping, then.' After a moment she went on, 'I hope I didn't say the wrong thing earlier, you know, about living together. I wondered afterwards whether you might be upset because he *hadn't* suggested it.'

'Lord, no.' I did my best to produce an airy little laugh. 'He's far too tidy – he'd drive me crackers in a week.' I quickly changed the subject and wondered whether tidiness could be grounds for dumping him. Doubtful, if we weren't cohabiting. What, then? Non-specific annoyingness? Certain people annoyed me merely by the way they said, 'Morning!' or always lifted a corner of their lunchtime sandwich and sniffed it before taking a bite. I could get worked up to screaming pitch just waiting for them to do it. If I lived in LA I swear I'd have shot someone by now.

'. . . and what d'you think about this honeymoon?' Granny M was going on. 'Half of Africa, by the sounds of it. Costing a fortune, I dare say.'

'He can afford it.'

'Wants to spoil her, I suppose. If you ask me, it'd do her good not to be spoilt for a bit. Your mum and dad always spoilt her. Between you and me, love, I always thought you got a bit left out.'

143

'Oh, Granny, I didn't.'

'Not with *things*, love, but the way they were with her. Fussing her. Wrapping her in cotton wool.'

I almost laughed. 'But I didn't *want* wrapping in cotton wool! Mum needs someone to fuss over. I was glad Belinda was there to take the pressure off!'

With the dance floor filling fast, Mum could keep quiet no longer. 'Sophy, aren't you and Dominic going to have a little dance?'

Raising an eyebrow, as if to say *Well?* Josh glanced across at me.

I was prepared, apologetic smile and all. 'Afraid not, Mum; my feet are killing me. I knew it was a mistake to wear new shoes.' They were, but the soft Italian leather felt like a pair of kid gloves.

'Then take them off, dear.'

'I'll dance with him.' Never backwards in coming forwards, Diana gave a mischievous grin. 'On your feet, Dominic.'

He went with perfect grace and Mum did her best not to look miffed.

While listening to Granny Metcalfe, I half watched the dancers. No left feet: he looked as if he were enjoying it. Diana certainly was. The Metcalfe clan is very girl-heavy and it's not much fun dancing with your father.

When they came back, I just knew he was about to take up the attack. 'Come on, Sophy,' he said, in exactly the sort of teasingly coaxing tone a real boyfriend would have used. 'Work some of that dinner off.'

144

Well, I could manage a little banter for the sake of form. 'Get some of my fat off, you mean,' I retorted.

The look in his eye said, *Anything you can do* . . . 'If I wanted a stick insect, I'd find one.'

'That's right, you tell her,' Mum put in. 'She's got a lovely figure. I've told you often enough, dear, men don't *like* skinny girls.'

We really should have kept her off the liqueurs. After a few Cointreaus her embarrassment potential goes right off the scale.

'If you ask me, it's all these skinny models that make girls anorexic,' she went on, to Auntie Barbara. 'I can't think why they don't use *real* girls with a few curves.'

'Stands to reason, Susan.' Auntie B was as pinkly flushed as Mum. 'All the designers are gay. They don't want bosoms in their clothes, or bottoms either. Not proper, *girls'* bottoms.'

'If they want boy's bottoms, Barbara, they're welcome to them, that's what I say.' The pair of them started giggling like a couple of schoolgirls sharing a smutty joke at the back of the class.

'My God, you can't take them anywhere,' Diana grinned. 'Pissed as newts, the pair of them.'

Evidently doing his best not to crack up, Josh raised an eyebrow. 'Come on, Sophy. A couple of dances before I turn into a pumpkin.'

'If you won't dance with him, I will,' Diana grinned.

'Go on, then. I promise not to scratch your eyes out.' I shot a sweetly apologetic smile at Josh. 'Sorry, darling, but my feet really are killing me.'

Diana was only too pleased. After another energetic

145

number, the DJ put something slower on.

After watching for half a minute I whispered to Granny Metcalfe, 'I need some fresh air. I'm just going into the garden for a bit.'

Once over the terrace I took my shoes off anyway, since Mum was probably watching. The grass was soft and damp, the air scented with new-cut grass and summer. A soft breeze riffled my hair as I strolled towards a little stone bench by the beck.

I hoped Mum wouldn't think I was sulking because 'Dominic' was dancing with Diana.

Because I was.

Perversity is my middle name.

I sat and listened to the water playing sweetly over pebbles, wondering whether I was the silliest cow in creation. Across the warm, evening air the song still drifted to me. That wretched DJ had known what he was about. It was one of those slow, dreamily erotic ballads that can make a dance with a man who's already making you fluttery into an almost orgasmic experience.

And bloody Diana was dancing with him.

I recalled feeling a bit like this at a birthday party when I was about six. Having politely refused the last mini-jelly because I'd thought it might seem greedy to take it, I'd been green as a pea to see Emma Jenkins scoff it only seconds later.

On the other hand, maybe it was just as well. Covering up semi-orgasmic flutters while smoochy dancing is almost impossible. Only the thickest Neanderthal would fail to get the message and I didn't

146

want the poor man taking fright, thinking I'd pounce on him in the night.

It was quite nice out there, with the light going all soft and duskified. I could imagine it getting quite creepy later; already some eerie-sounding bird was crying like a lost soul over the moors. I started thinking of Heathcliff (I'd had fantasies about him once) and wondered whether the Inn was haunted. I imagined some poor kitchenmaid, seduced by the Young Master, turned out in her shift on a bleak January night. Huddled against a dry-stone wall she'd have frozen to death, vowing with her dying breath to haunt the evil Sir Deveril for always. And ever since, her pale, grave-cold spectre had drifted over the—

'Jesus!' My heart leapt to my tonsils. 'Don't *do* that!'

'Do what?'

'Creep up behind me!'

'I didn't creep,' he said. 'I walked, perfectly normally, on two well-shod feet.'

I didn't quite like to say I'd thought he was a pregnant kitchenmaid's ghost. 'I didn't hear you. You gave me a fright.'

'Sorry.' He stood a few feet away, minus jacket and tie, the top button of his shirt undone. Hot under the collar after dancing with Diana, no doubt. 'Are you all right?'

'Of course! Why wouldn't I be?'

'I don't know. Your mother was wondering.'

Might have known. 'So she sent you to check?'

'Not exactly. She said, "Do you think Sophy's all right, out there all on her own?"'

'I don't know what on earth she thought was going to happen to me.'

He sat on the bench, about a foot away. 'Killer minnows in the stream?'

I almost laughed. 'It's the beck. I shall have to teach you ancient Oop-Northish.'

'No thanks. I had enough trouble with Russian.'

Since I somehow wouldn't have had him down as a linguist, I wasn't surprised he'd had trouble. 'Was that school Russian?'

'Yes, but I barely scraped an O level. I only did it because I fancied joining MI5 and doing a James Bond. It was still Cold War, then.'

I had to laugh. 'I suppose you fancied all those clever little gadgets from Q – exploding lighters and cars with built-in ejector seats . . .'

'Don't forget the luscious female spies inveigling themselves into my bed,' he said, in mock lip-smacking tones. 'At sixteen or so, that was almost as enticing as the gadgets.' He glanced down. 'How are your feet?'

He'd fallen for that one, then. 'All right, now I've got my shoes off.' I wiggled my toes; the grass felt cool and dewy.

'Then why didn't you take them off and dance with me?'

I was beginning to wish he'd stayed inside. My flutterings were waking up again. 'I'd have laddered my tights.'

'That's the most pathetic excuse I ever heard. If I was willing to make the effort, you could have played along.'

Effort? It hadn't looked like 'effort' with Diana, damn him. 'I didn't feel like it, OK? Anyway, Diana was only too willing.'

'Yes, and your mother was a trifle miffed about that, if you ask me. She wanted to see you and me entwined on the floor, not me and Diana.'

'Then she'll just have to lump it, won't she? Besides, I didn't feel like getting entwined with you. Don't take this the wrong way, but I'm not too keen on your aftershave.'

'I'm not too keen on your perfume either, but I'd have suffered in a noble cause.'

'I'm very sorry. I had no idea you'd been holding your nose all day, metaphorically speaking.'

'It's not that bad.' Leaning fractionally closer, he gave a little sniff. 'It's mellowed.'

Since my flutterings were about to bounce right out of bed, I didn't really want him leaning closer. However, I thought of Emma Jenkins' jelly and made the most of it. The breeze picked up, riffling my hair, and that eerie-sounding bird did its lost soul bit again.

It made me shiver.

'Are you cold?' he asked.

'No – it's that bird. It sounds like a lost soul. Makes me think of *Wuthering Heights* and Heathcliff.'

He gave a little chuckle. 'It's probably hungry. I've been known to give a similar cry of anguish when I find only a solitary spring onion and a couple of beers in the fridge. If there aren't even any beers, than it's really serious.'

Just as I was girding myself up for being really nosy

and asking whether he lived alone, he nodded over his shoulder. 'Should I go and report back that you're not suffering from anything serious, or would that defeat the object of the exercise?'

The object being, of course, to separate him from Diana and get him out here with me. 'I'm sorry. Subtlety is not my mother's middle name, particularly after a few drinks. She can be really embarrassing.'

'She didn't embarrass me.'

'I don't suppose she did. Mothers embarrass their own children, not other people's.'

I glanced over my shoulder at the lit-up Inn. 'She's probably watching us this very minute.'

'Then perhaps we should play along.'

Subconsciously, I suppose I'd been hoping he'd say exactly this. I just hadn't been *expecting* it. 'How d'you mean?' I asked, all innocent.

'A little stroll, by the stream?' Standing up, he extended a hand. It was quite unnecessary, but since it was suitably gentlemanly and lover-ish for Mum's benefit, I took it anyway. Then he let it go and slid an arm round my waist, instead. Not a light, token arm, as he had during the reception, but a proper, strolling lover's arm that held you close and brought your hips together.

The temptation to slide a reciprocal arm round him almost overwhelming, but then there'd be nothing to stop my right 36C squashing against him and that might be pushing it.

'I thought Tamara had spilled the beans earlier,' I confessed. 'I could have died.'

'You shouldn't have spilled the beans in the first place. Beans once spilled are impossible to get back in the can.'

'I know, but it was a colossal relief to tell somebody, especially somebody like Tamara. She just thought it was hilarious.'

'Pity you didn't think it was hilarious instead of being a nervous wreck all day.'

'Hilarious?' I almost bristled here. 'It would have been really hilarious if we'd got found out right in the middle of the reception. I'd have wet myself laughing.'

'Relax! You're doing your spark-and-twitch bit again.' He gave my waist a tweaky little squeeze.

This was potentially addictive. 'Don't! I'm ticklish!'

He did it again. 'Then maybe I should tickle you. A good giggle might relax you for two minutes.'

'I am relaxed!'

'No, you're not. You're strung as tight as one of Pete Sampras's tennis rackets.'

His hand dropped from my waist. Instead he took my wrist and led me to a large beech tree that stood a yard or two from the beck.

God help me, now what?

'It's high time we went in,' I said, in what I hoped was a non-wobbly voice. 'My feet are soaking.'

'In a minute.' Leaning against the trunk he held me very lightly by the waist, my back to him. 'You need to take a tip from that stream. Go with the flow.'

'It's easy for you to say.'

I could hardly get the words out. The way he was holding me suddenly felt infinitely more erotic than anything in a *Lads' Weekly* article about 'How to Turn Your Bird On'.

Still, that wouldn't be difficult.

'Do you think your mother's still watching?' he mused.

I'd have put money on it. I could just see her giving Dad a little nudge.

'Just look at those two.'

'Stop spying on them, love.'

'I'm not spying, dear, just interested. Anyway, they can't possibly see me.'

'I wouldn't put it past her,' I said.

'Then it'd be a shame to disappoint her.'

At this point I felt like a bimbo butterfly on her first date. Not to put too fine a point upon it, I was woozing for England. 'How d'you mean?' I asked, like an idiot.

'Take a wild guess.'

I'd never thought he'd go this far; I could bet it was against agency rules. Still, if ever a girl deserved a little treat . . .

Slowly, he turned me round. With light hands on my waist, he drew me closer.

It was a bit late in the day, I admit, but that was when the bimbo butterfly vanished. I mean, I'm not that thick. You don't get to thirty without knowing when some wretched man's playing games with you.

Still, I'd always been good at games. Especially when you could play really dirty.

I knew exactly what he was going to do, and I was right. A slow, tantalising brushing of lips, just guaranteed to have me panting for more.

The trouble was, either I was too starved of this sort of thing or he was just too good at it. I suppose it was the combination of power and gentleness that finished me off; the firm arms round my waist said, *You can't get away* . . . but his lips said, . . . *even if you wanted to.*

Add to that the faint brushing of shaved chin and that elusive male scent and I nearly played right into his hands. After all, it was bloody months since I'd been within fluttering distance of anyone remotely yummy. I went so woozy, I nearly lost my nerve for the next bit.

Just as I'd known he would, after this tantalising little crumb he drew back. That was the idea, you see. To throw me a crumb, see how pathetically disappointed I was, and have a really good internal laugh.

I didn't give him a chance.

Going in for the kill, I put one arm round his neck, drew him sharply towards me and finished what he'd started. If you want the gory details, it was the kind of kiss I might have given someone I fancied like mad when I hadn't seen him for a month and was confidently expecting frantic shedding of clothes and rampant coupling in under two minutes.

And after the first second or two, I wasn't acting. Of course I felt his (literally) gobsmacked shock, but that was his problem. I went at it with a devouring thoroughness, exploring bits of his mouth he didn't even know he had. And after a few seconds, evidently thinking of nympho gift horses, he responded in kind. He held me suddenly tighter, crushing my

153

36Cs against his chest, and believe me, they weren't complaining. That weird, unnamed organ that only comes to life at such times was suddenly lurching alarmingly, all my hibernating instincts going wild. He devoured me back to such an extent that my inner primeval female was screaming, *Quick! Why do you think you were put on this earth?*

So you will appreciate that sticking to my original plan took more self-control than I normally possess. Breaking the lip-suction with a sucky kind of 'plop' I drew back. My heart was pounding, but I ignored it. 'All right, that'll do,' I said brightly. 'No need to overdo it.'

His expression was a picture. A whole faceful of male confusion, shaken *and* stirred.

Fifty points to me.

I put on my best bewildered innocence. 'What are you looking like that for? It was your idea!'

'Not like that, it wasn't!'

I added a put-out tone, too. 'If Mum was watching, we might as well give her something to watch. If you can play-act for five more minutes, we'll go back in. My feet really are soaking. Could you repeat that arm, please?' I added sweetly. 'Might look funny, otherwise.'

We weren't far from the stone bench, when I retrieved my shoes.

He said not a word.

My heart was still pounding all the way back. Once we were inside I said, 'I'm just going to the loo – could you get me something long and cool? A 7Up 'll do.'

'Will do.'

I needed a breathing space, and where better than a loo seat for private reflection?

Bastard.

I knew I hadn't imagined it. I wasn't quite that paranoid, but if I'd blinked I suppose I might have missed it. A tiny mouth twitch, a minute flicker in his eyes.

Laughing, or, to be more precise, patronising male amusement. *Poor cow*, or words to that effect. *Pathetically loveless for months, desperate for a little tender romancing, and therefore quivering in delicious anticipation of what I'm so graciously about to bestow.*

Obviously I'd been kidding myself about those flutters being firmly under wraps. How long had he been sensing them? All afternoon?

Still, I shouldn't have been surprised. I'd long suspected that flutters have a chemical component. Maybe we give off some come-and-get-me hormone and the bloke picks it up on his male hormone receptors, like the Great Horned Moth in the mating season. All a bit primeval, but then most blokes are largely primeval anyway. And because the come-and-get-me is only sensed by the primeval bit of their brains, blokes are quite unaware of the process. They think it's all down to their brilliance at shaggability spotting.

It took several minutes for my assorted systems to calm down. All those sensations he'd dragged out of months of hibernation (I'm not counting fantasies here) were moaning like hell at being cheated. 'Well?'

155

they complained. 'Have you got us all worked up for nothing?'

Worth it, though, to see his face. I even began to wonder whether he'd welcomed this 'sleepover', just so he could have a bit of fun.

Once my pulse had settled I returned to the dining room, feeling grimly one-up and pleased with myself. Now I came to think of it, that almost-concealed amusement had been rather like the look on his face when he'd suddenly recalled Tamara. *My God, that Tamara. The skinny little squirt who thought I was the greatest thing since Barbie's Ken.* Jerry must have said something, after all. Maybe they'd had a good laugh behind poor little Tamara's back.

Evidently recovered, he was talking to Uncle Mike. 'Darling, your drink.' He indicated a glass on the table.

'Thank you, darling.' With a sweet smile, I took it. 'I'll take it up with me. I'm really tired and we've got such an early start. I'll leave the door open. Don't crash around and wake me up, will you?'

I hoped my instructions were clear: *Don't come up just yet – I'd like to get ready for bed in privacy.*

I pecked him on the cheek, pecked Mum and Dad, forbade them utterly to get up to see us off, made my farewells, and went.

Josh gave me three-quarters of an hour. Very quietly, he opened the door. I'd left one bedside light on and a window open. Odd, plaintive bird cries came from the night outside, the curtains just shivering in the breeze.

Not that I could see anything. Still bra-ed and

156

knickered in case of cover-kicking, I lay motionless, my head half under the covers in case he saw my eyelids twitching.

Very quietly, he closed the door. He moved around the room as if on eggshells. As if petrified of waking me.

Maybe I'd shocked him more than I knew. Maybe he was petrified of this hitherto harmless-looking creature suddenly turning rampant again and pouncing on him in the night.

Within five minutes, he was in bed, the light off. I lay quite still, wishing to heaven he'd snore or something so I could relax and go to sleep, and the next thing I knew was the wake-up call.

Under the covers I pulled on the sweater I'd worn on the way up; I'd kept it on the floor by the bed for that very purpose.

With the curtains closed the room was nicely dim, so I wasn't about to open them. I nipped out of bed and gathered things up. Beginning to sit up, Josh was tousled, blinking, and looking as if he could have done with another four hours.

'I'm going to have a quick shower,' I said.

'Go ahead.'

I was out again in less than ten minutes. He was half dressed, in the trousers he'd worn on the way up, no shirt. Having opened the curtains, he was standing by the window, his hand on the wall.

The shirtless back was much as expected: olivey, muscly, edible-looking. I could have done with a few hideous spots – anything to put me off.

Twenty minutes later we were downstairs, having

exchanged fewer than ten words. Somebody had laid out croissants, butter, jam, etc. and some poor bleary-eyed person produced a pot of coffee.

'I'll give the AA a ring and check on the roads,' Josh said.

While he was on the phone, I poured a coffee and smeared a piece of croissant with low-fat spread. After that massive breakfast yesterday I'd have to under-indulge for a bit.

Josh came back. 'The M6 is still closed, but the M1's clear.'

'Could be worse, then.'

He devoured a whole croissant spread with black cherry jam, and then another. By the time he picked up the third, the sight of all those squillions of calories going down his throat was beginning to get to me.

'You're not going to eat them all, are you? I was hoping to be away by now!'

He cast a glance at the three-quarters of a croissant left on my plate. 'Sophy, if you want to starve yourself, that's fine. Just don't expect me to keep you company.'

'How did you sleep?' I asked, just to be polite.

'Fine, thank you.'

Just as we were about to leave, I heard Mum's voice on the stairs. Might have known.

'I *told* you not to get up,' I said, trying not to sound exasperated as both parents hurried up, having obviously just scrambled into their clothes. 'It's far too early.'

'Don't be silly, dear; of course we want to come and see you off.'

They followed us out into the still, early morning. When everything was loaded and we were about to depart, Mum said, 'By the way, dear, you know Paul and Belinda are staying with us the night they get back?'

I gaped at her. 'Their first *night*?'

She looked distinctly hurt. 'They'll be dying to see the photos, dear. We'll have them by then, so I asked if they'd like to come for dinner. It was Paul who suggested they stay over. He doesn't want to have to stick to mineral water all evening.'

In the Gospel according to Mum, the bloke always drives.

'But I was just thinking how nice it'd be if you came too,' she went on. 'I'm sure you'd like to see the photos and spend an evening together.'

I gave her a bright smile. 'Lovely, Mum. I'll give you a ring.'

That, of course, was not the end of it. With a tentative smile she turned to Josh, 'You too, Dominic, if you're free. It'll be quite casual, next Saturday fortnight, just the six of us, a nice little dinner at home . . .'

'He's probably busy, love,' said poor old Dad.

I had to hand it to Josh. His smile would have won first prize in any perfect-potential-son-in-law competition. 'It's very kind of you, Mrs Metcalfe. I'll have to check my diary. I have a couple more overseas meetings and things might run over but if not, I'd be delighted.'

Mum almost flushed with pleasure. 'We'll look

forward to seeing you. It's been so nice to meet you at last. Do have a good flight, won't you?'

Eventually we got away.

Half a mile down the lane I said, 'If you dare say, "I told you so", I'll kill you.'

'On the contrary, I'm looking forward to it. I'd lay odds on your mother being a thoroughly good cook.'

I gave him a sharp glance and saw, too late, that it was his feeble idea of a joke.

'Don't worry, I won't be asking you to repeat this little farce,' I said, in lemon-juice tones. 'It was the one-off to end them all.'

'I'm glad to hear it.' His tone was very blunt. 'It's gone quite far enough.'

'You can say that again.' I slowed down behind a tractor. Sheep grazed on either side and a lonely-looking pony hung his head over a dry-stone wall. If I'd been on my own I might have stopped for a chat.

I wasn't sure of the non-motorway route; you tended to forget there even was one. 'I'm going to need navigating. Could you check the road atlas, please?'

He grabbed it from the back seat. 'So what excuse are you going to make this time?'

'As I said, I'll tell her I've dumped you.'

'On what grounds?'

Funnily enough, I'd just had a minor brainwave on that very subject. 'I'm afraid you're not going to like this.' I said sweetly.

I was, though.

SEVEN

'Remember your bad case of mumps?'

He gave me a sharp glance.

'Unfortunately, there were complications,' I went on. 'And you've just found out you're infertile.'

'Well, thank you so much.'

Served him right for playing games with me. 'And of course, I'm terribly upset about it, as I haven't altogether ruled out kids one day.'

His tone became ever more sardonic. 'So I have to go, do I? Because I can't give you babies?'

'I'm afraid so.' Overtaking the tractor at last, I gave the driver a cheery wave. 'And Mum's going to be decidedly relieved I've got shot of you.'

'Oh, you reckon?' he said, in *Who are you trying to kid?* tones.

'I'm afraid so. She's going to tell me I did the right thing, dear, and she didn't really like you anyway, there was a hard streak in your eyes.'

'Will she hell.'

'She will.' I waited for a second before my *pièce de résistance*. 'Because you didn't mind a bit about being infertile. You were rather chuffed, as a matter of fact. You told me you never wanted kids anyway, they were nothing but an expensive nuisance and it'd save you all the trouble of a vasectomy.' By now my pet little devil was perching on my shoulder, egging me on. 'I hope you're not put out.'

'Why the hell should I be?'

'Because of your imminent infertility and the consequent slur on your manhood.'

'Sophy, if it'll make you happy, you can have me castrated. Turn right at the next junction.' His tone said: *If you really think I give a stuff what you tell anybody, you're flattering yourself.*

For the next mile or so I felt about one and a half worms high. Then, just as I was beginning to envisage arctic silence all the way home, he said, 'I get the impression that you're a trifle browned off with me.'

Since I wouldn't have thought he'd be bothered enough to mention it, I reflated a fraction. 'Whatever makes you say that, I wonder?'

'You've been browned off with me since last night.' He paused. 'Ever since a certain incident under a tree.'

At least he'd sussed that out. At the junction I slowed down, checking both ways. 'No more browned off than you are, because I beat you at your own game.'

'It wasn't a game.'

I was warming up nicely. 'Josh, please don't take me for a fool. I'm not some wide-eyed nineteen-year-old with nothing between the ears. I know exactly what you were doing.'

'Why don't you enlighten me?'

'Oh, come off it!' I knew I hadn't imagined it. I wasn't quite that paranoid. 'Do you really think I couldn't see it? You thought: Poor cow, she's obviously desperate, it might be amusing to give her a little thrill.'

162

'It wasn't like that!' His voice rose slightly, and fell again. 'You're getting this utterly out of proportion. It was going to be the merest token. It was an impulse.'

'Impulse my foot. You knew exactly what you were doing. You were amusing yourself at my expense. Or thought you would,' I added tartly.

'Rubbish.'

After a mile or two of very tense silence he said, 'You know what I think? I think you're paranoid. I think you're paranoid about people thinking you must be desperate.'

'You thought I was desperate, last night!'

'I – did – not!' He paused. 'But if you'll forgive me for saying so, if you go around eating people alive like you ate me last night, they will start thinking you're desperate.'

I fought down a furious flush. 'I wanted to wipe that smug grin off your face, that's all. And for your information, I'm not desperate for "eating", or anything else.'

'No, of course not,' he said sardonically. 'You obviously "eat" on a regular and satisfactory basis, which is why you had to go and pay for a let's-pretend meal from an escort agency.'

At this point I nearly stopped and slung him out, but almost immediately he went on, 'Look, I'm sorry. I shouldn't have said that.'

'Just shut up, will you? Unless you want to get out and walk.' I wasn't consciously thinking of what Tamara had said, but I suppose part of my brain was on autopilot. 'And for your information, I "eat" at home. On a regular and most satisfactory basis.'

The trouble with your brain doing this sort of thing is that you get quite a start when it comes out of your mouth.

It wasn't just me either. His disbelief was almost palpable. 'Are you telling me you're in a relationship?'

Bless you, Tamara, my child. 'Why the hell shouldn't I be?'

'You said you weren't!'

'I never said any such thing! I said I invented a "suitable" boyfriend to get my mother off my back!'

'Are you telling me you've got an unsuitable one?'

'Ten out of ten. You worked that out fast.'

'Don't tell me. He's a married bisexual with a criminal record.'

Again, I wasn't consciously creating, but my brain had found another template and embroidered him already. 'There's no need to be sarcastic. He's just unsuitable in my parents' eyes because he doesn't have a "nice" background or a brilliant job. He didn't have a job at all until recently. He was living rough on the streets.'

It was all clear to me now, in every last, fibbing detail.

For a moment he digested this in silence. Somehow, the tension had eased a little, as if I'd actually told him the truth. 'Does he live with you?'

'Yes – you might have seen him. He was with me at the window when you arrived yesterday.' I knew Ace wouldn't mind, not that I'd have to tell him.

'I saw someone.' After a moment he went on, 'If it's

not an intrusive question, how the hell did you come to meet a man like that?'

I had to 'borrow' somebody else now, but my brain had him all ready. 'He used to sell the *Big Issue* near where I work. I used to buy a copy now and then, and stop and chat for a minute. Sometimes I wondered whether he was really homeless. You can never be absolutely sure and he wasn't terribly scruffy, but I never asked. We went on like this for ages; he seemed like a permanent fixture on the pavement.'

I felt a bit bad here. This chap actually had existed and this much was true. 'I saw him as usual the day before last Christmas Eve. We'd had a couple of drinks at work and I was feeling mellow. I took him a can of beer and a packet of crisps, slipped him a tenner and went and got my train.' This was true, too. 'I went home the next day to the usual family Christmas – log fires, half the turkey going to the dog, masses of boxes of chocolates that everybody was too full to eat, the usual over-indulgence. And I couldn't help thinking about him, wondering what sort of Christmas he was having.'

Since Josh wasn't uttering, I carried on. 'When I went back to work, he wasn't there. The weather was vile – wet and sleety and freezing at night – so I wondered whether he was keeping warm somewhere.'

Still true, in case you're wondering. I'd worried quite a bit about that chap. I'd wondered what I'd do if he turned up again on a freezing night, with an imminent-pneumonia cough and looking really ill.

This was the point at which I really had to lie, but it

was only what I'd told myself I'd do if it had actually happened. 'He turned up about a week later. It was colder than ever. He still seemed cheerful enough but he looked awful. He was shivering and he had a bad cough. I just couldn't leave him there in the cold. I grabbed a taxi, shoved him in, and took him home with me.'

By now you will be relieved to know that I felt as guilty as hell for making myself sound like some noble, earnest, do-gooding pain. Because although I *had* told myself I'd take him home, I'd known I'd chicken out when it came to the point, in case he turned out to be a schizo with a penchant for kitchen knives, or a crackhead who'd nick anything saleable the minute my back was turned.

In the event, I hadn't had to make a decision; I'd never seen him again. Someone else had started selling the *Big Issue* on that pitch. When I'd asked, 'Where's Mick?' he'd shrugged. 'Dunno – think he might have got a place in a hostel.'

So I'd sent a cheque to St Mungo's and felt guilty for not doing it before.

It had started to rain. Tiny drops spattered the windscreen, just enough to warrant intermittent wipers.

At last he spoke. 'And he stayed?'

I nodded. 'He got better quite quickly but the weather was so cold, I knew he'd only get ill again if he went back. And he was thin. He needed what my mother calls "building up".' Might as well make it sound good.

'And it went on from there?'

'Yes.' I thought I might tell Ace, after all. He'd crack up, which would lessen my guilt. I'd never tell Alix. She wouldn't mind her brother turning into a homeless waif-and-stray, but she might think I secretly fancied him, God forbid.

The traffic was thickening by the minute. The tension between us, on the other hand, had thinned out. In its place was a certain gobsmacked silence. I could absolutely feel him wondering what the hell I was going to come out with next: a confession of murder, perhaps, or just the fact that I was being treated for mild paranoid schizophrenia.

'How old is he?' he asked.

'Twenty-six.' Not quite cradle-snatching: perfectly acceptable.

'How did you explain me? Did you tell him?'

On reflection, he'd hardly relish a Dominic on the scene. 'He hasn't a clue about Dominic. He'd have a fit. I just said you were an old friend of the bridegroom's, temporarily without wheels, and I was giving you a lift.'

I was getting positively brilliant at this fibbing business. 'I said my folks can be a bit funny, so I couldn't tell them about him. Even if I had, he'd never have come. A do like that would have been Ace's idea of a nightmare.'

'*Ace*? What kind of a name's that?'

'A nickname, what d'you think? It's his initials.'

'And you've kept him quiet from your folks all this time?'

'Not exactly, but I had to say something in case he ever answered the phone. I just told them we'd got a male flatmate for a change – my other sharer's brother. Even if I wasn't involved I could never go into his history. Dad would have a pink fit. He'd think he was a petty criminal or a drug user at the very least.'

'How do you know he never was a drug user? How do you know he never shared dirty needles?'

'I know, OK? He only ever used puff, he told me. And millions of people use puff.' (Ace did the odd E as well, but puff was his drug of choice.)

Eventually Josh said, 'Why didn't you tell me all this yesterday?'

Good question. 'There was absolutely no need for you to know. It was better that you didn't. You might not have acted so well if you'd thought I had somebody else at home.'

He could hardly argue with this.

The rain had stopped but it was still dull and miserable. I overtook a camper-van, hoping the poor occupants were heading for the ferries and southern sun.

'Did "Dominic" come before or after Ace?' he asked. 'Just so I can get fact sorted out from fiction.' This had a sardonic edge, which hardly surprised me.

'Just before. So naturally, I kept him going.'

'Naturally.'

For a long time there was silence, except for dishing out directions.

'Why was he on the streets in the first place?' he asked eventually.

'Just the usual. Broken home, abusive stepfather, disrupted education. He'd been put in care and run away, so lack of qualifications didn't help him in the job market.'

'Has he got a job now?'

'Oh, yes. In a music superstore.' Just like the real Ace, funnily enough.

I was rather startled at how easy it was to spin massive tissues of fibs and have people believe you so utterly. Still, I'd had plenty of practice lately. Maybe I should have started a Rent-a-Fib agency.

We were coming up to the M1 at last. Some light conversation was called for but my brain had exhausted itself with fibs. It refused to come up with anything. As my eyes flitted over not-very-interesting countryside, I scraped barrels. 'See those sort of corrugated fields? Somebody once told me they date back to the Middle Ages.'

He gave the rippled meadow a cursory glance.

'It's the remains of strip farming,' I went on. 'They used to farm in furrows. A furrow of this, a furrow of that . . .'

'Really?' He covered a yawn.

At least I was trying. 'That's where we got "furlong" from,' I went on. 'A "furrow-long".'

He stifled another yawn. 'I'll remember that. It might come up in a crossword.'

'You never know. Useless information can have its uses.'

I put the radio on. The news told us that the police had found a small explosive device in a culvert and two obsessive environmentalists with a grudge against the internal combustion engine were 'helping them with their inquiries.' They were linking the suspects to a previous incident at a multi-storey car park.

I thought of all the browned off motorists hoping they'd get twenty years, but at least they'd made one person's day. Mum'd probably send a nice cake to them, care of Her Majesty's Nick.

'Nutters,' Josh grunted.

'It might be extreme, but they're right,' I said, in a pious tone I hoped would get right up his nose.

'Oh, so you'd like to go back to stagecoaches, would you?'

'Don't be stupid. There are these things called trains.'

'Then why didn't we take one?'

'Because two tickets and taxis both ends would have cost a bomb.'

'So what point are you trying to make, exactly?'

'I'm not trying to make *any* point! I'm just being awkward, OK?'

'All right, all right.' After a moment he added, 'Any particular reason, or shouldn't I ask?'

'I should have thought you could work that one out.'

'Yes, well, you made your point.'

After another mile or two he said, 'Mind if I put my seat back and sleep for a bit?'

'Feel free.'

'I'm not sure I can last through this lunch otherwise,' he went on, easing his seat back. 'A hostess dishing out three soporific courses, a host sloshing out soporific wine, both of them expecting three hours' non-soporific conversation . . .'

At least he wouldn't be short of something to talk about. 'You don't sound very keen. Why don't you just make an excuse?'

'Because they're friends of mine.'

That put me nicely in my place. 'Where do you want dropping off, in case you're still asleep when we get there?'

'Anywhere near a tube station. Ealing'll do.'

I still didn't know where he lived and I certainly wasn't going to ask.

Within minutes he was either asleep or doing a fair impression of it. Maybe he didn't want to have to talk, which would hardly be grounds for wonder. Or maybe he *was* tired. Maybe he'd been tossing and fidgeting half the night. Maybe he'd had a nightmare about escorting some normal-looking woman to a wedding and suddenly finding *he* was the bridegroom. Even Cilla might be in on it: '*Surprise, surprise!*' Mum would be showering him with confetti, Sonia brandishing a massive blow-up willy . . . Enough to make anybody wake up in a cold sweat.

I wouldn't have been surprised if he now suffered further nightmares, about bestowing a casual kiss on some harmless-looking woman who subsequently turned into a female spider and ate him.

I woke him shortly before Ealing Broadway, and by the time I pulled in at the Underground, the sun was out again.

Full circle.

He still looked half asleep. 'Thanks for everything,' I said crisply. 'Take care.'

'You too.'

I thought that was it but, with his hand on the door handle, he paused. 'Look, I'm sorry about last night. You were right – it did amuse me, in a way.'

I couldn't believe he'd admitted it.

'But with your mother watching, and all that . . .' he went on.

And me quivering with anticipation . . . He'd never admit that, of course, and I hardly expected him to. It was just mortifying that it had been so obvious. 'Well, maybe I did overreact. Sorry about the overtime. I know it was a pain.'

'At least the dinner was good.' He produced that dry little half-smile that should have come with a health warning.

I wished he hadn't. 'Well, I owe you one. If you ever need a favour, you know where to find me.'

'I'll call you next time I need a convincing lie to get me out of some tedious dinner party.'

'Very funny.'

'I was deadly serious.' At last he got out, grabbing his things from the back seat. 'Take care.' He nodded down the road, at an approaching traffic warden. 'You'd better go, before the parking sharks get you.'

''Bye, then. I hope you won't have to wait too long for a train.'

In the mirror I saw him wave. For a couple more

172

seconds he was there on the pavement, and then his back view disappeared into the Underground.

Well, I was glad to see the back of him.

I just preferred the front, that's all.

Still, count the pluses. No real disasters. I'd got through it without even ripping the Cellophane off the emergency fags. Surely this called for a pat on the back and a Mars bar? I stopped at the Pop-In for the purpose.

When I finally got home, only Ace was there to greet me. He was actually up, if not dressed, and making pasta with grated cheese. Given half a chance, Ace would have lived off pasta with grated cheese.

'You didn't have to kill yourself, then?' he grinned. 'Is your old lady still speaking to you?'

'She loves me. He went down like a dream. If you ask me, she's already pencilling in June Saturdays for next year.' I dumped my things on the floor. 'Where's Alix?'

'Gay Paree, with what's-his-face.'

'*What?*'

'Quick trip on Eurostar. It was a last-minute thing.'

Even if she was at the rhubarb crumble stage, it was a bit much – off on impulsive lovers' weekends while I was having litters of baby elephants. 'Great,' I grunted, putting the kettle on.

'You proved her wrong, anyway,' he said, draining a mini-mountain of macaroni. 'She was convinced there'd be a foul-up. She was crapping ostrich eggs.'

I stuck a tea bag in a cup. 'Don't you mean laying them?'

173

'You know what I mean. Getting her knickers in a twist.'

I should hope so.

'Want some of this?' he asked, grating mature Cheddar over the pasta. 'There's loads.'

I could have murdered some – mountains of calories and not a health-giving vitamin in sight. 'No, thanks,' I said nobly. 'I'm not that hungry.' I was overdue for a diet now the bikini season was coming up. Not the habitual starting-tomorrow diet, but starting right now.

'Suit yourself.' He dumped the grater in the sink. 'She almost didn't go in case you phoned in a state because he'd got sussed out. She phoned this morning, to check you hadn't killed yourself.'

In that case, I might just forgive her.

'I thought he *looked* all right,' he went on. 'Not like a total plonker, anyway. Did you get on OK?'

With Alix safely out of the way, I just had to tell him. 'It was what you might call a perfect disaster. You'll never believe what I did.'

While he shovelled pasta I told him the whole thing, except for the fact that I'd fancied Josh like mad.

True to expectations, he nearly choked on his pasta. 'Pity you didn't bring him in for a beer,' he grinned. 'If you'd given me a bell from the services and filled me in, I'd have done you proud.' Putting on a GBH-type scowl, he jabbed an aggressive finger at the fridge. 'I hope you kept your filfy 'ands off of 'er. I'm going over 'er tonight wiv a microscope. One fingerprint on 'er tits and I'll send some of me mates round to rearrange yer face.'

174

I had to laugh, but it had an edge to it. 'Don't tell Alix, for God's sake.'

'She'll think it's just a laugh!'

'*Please*, Ace. This is strictly between you and me. I feel daft enough as it is.'

'OK – don't fret.'

'And don't tell Tina, either,' I went on. Tina was his girlfriend. 'Especially Tina. She'll think I'm some sad, pathetic old cow.' I'm sure she thought I was a sad old cow anyway. She was twenty-one, looked seventeen, and frequently made me feel forty-three and a half.

Ace didn't contradict me, which was honest, but did sod-all for the feeling-good-and-loving-myself factor. 'You're not safe to be let loose,' he grinned. 'You need a minder, if you ask me.'

I picked at a morsel or two of his pasta. 'I know it sounds daft now, but I was so infuriated. I could see exactly what was going through his mind – thinking he'd give me a little thrill . . .'

'Sounds like a right pain.'

'Well, yes. But he half admitted it in the car. He even apologised. It was partly because we were playing along for Mum, after all.'

His dawning-light expression reminded me that Ace is not as daft as he frequently appears. 'You fancied him, didn't you?'

Now he'd sussed it out, I didn't mind admitting it. 'Well, yes. A bit.'

'Only a bit?' he grinned.

'Well, quite a bit. I suppose that's why I was so mad,

because he sensed it. I told you, didn't I? I told you they'd think I was desperate.'

He wiped some melted cheese off his plate with his finger and licked it. 'Fancying someone doesn't make you desperate,' he scoffed. 'You're getting paranoid.'

He was dead right there.

Alix and Calum came home around eleven, laden with shopping. They wore that pink, pleased-with-themselves look you only get from delicious over-indulgence in food and wine, plus lots of inventive shenanigans in unfamiliar hotel rooms, showers, etc. What a shame people have stopped talking about 'dirty weekends'. 'Weekend break' never sounds half so much fun.

'I'm not speaking to you two,' I said, all mock sulks. 'Buggering off to play French mummies and daddies while I might have been committing ritual suicide.'

'I nearly didn't go!' Alix protested. 'Calum'd got the tickets as a surprise!'

'All my fault, as usual,' he said apologetically.

'I was kidding, dopey.' I gave them both a kiss. 'I'm just jealous. It was fine.'

'What was he like?' Alix demanded.

'Made for the part. Mum loved him, anyway.' I peeked into all the bags. '*Food?* Only food? I thought you'd at least have bought yourself a pair of knickers from Galeries Lafayette.'

'She didn't get a chance,' Calum grinned. 'I was too busy drooling over juicy French tarts.'

They'd brought some back: *tarte aux pommes*, *tarte aux abricots*, both begging to be eaten there and then.

While they were cutting one up, scuffly laughter wafted from the kitchen. It sounded as if Calum had gone off French tarts and wanted something fruitily English instead. Alix sounded half cut. Her giggles had a decidedly *Stop it, I like it* flavour.

Not for the first time, I felt a pang of envy. It wasn't on account of the dirty half-hour they were obviously going to enjoy before they were very much older, or even their dirty weekend, though I wouldn't have said no if Darcy or Clooney had turned up with tickets. It was the easy intimacy they shared. The having-a-laugh-together stuff.

They came from the kitchen bearing acres of French tart and glasses of wine and I put the diet back on hold, where it went just about every time anything yummy was on the menu.

I told them about Kit, and Alix was suitably indignant. I also told them about Sonia's conjectures and Alix, who by then was three-quarters cut, said, 'Well, she might be right. Maybe you should have let him think you still wanted him, so he'd come – hic – crawling back and you could tell him – hic – to sod off.'

Satisfying, in theory, but I had a feeling I could never be really bitchy to Kit. Not because I'm incapable of being a bitch, you understand; being a thorough-going bitch to a crawling-back bastard of an ex would perk me up no end. However, you could never call Kit a bastard, just helpless prey for the Jocastas of this world. Bastard exes never come crawling back, anyway. And, to be honest, I didn't think Kit would either. I had my own theory as to why

177

he'd let Sonia drag him along. It had been an opportunity to see me in a civilised, crowded setting, where he could make civilised peace with me and go away feeling relieved. And I'd screwed it all up.

I wished I hadn't now, but it was just tough.

Over the next couple of days, far from relieved at having the ordeal over, I felt restless and irritable. Sooner or later Mum was going to ring and make hopeful noises about that weekend and the whole thing would start all over again. The mumps story was far too over the top to use but I couldn't think of anything that would sound plausible without making Dominic utterly unpleasant.

However, inspiration struck on Wednesday evening, while I was having a quick drink with Alix and Calum at the Rat and Ferret. A soppy Old English sheepdog was trying to be friendly to some man who didn't want to know. He licked his arm and the man went mad: on and on about hygiene and how dogs shouldn't be allowed in pubs, etc. He was an utter pain, but I was grateful for the inspiration.

Dominic, I had just found out, didn't like dogs one bit. He could see the point of guide dogs, police dogs, etc, but the rest were barely one up from vermin. I'd become so devious at this fibbing business, I worked out every tiny detail. It had all started at the kitchen sink, while I'd been attacking an encrusted lasagne dish. 'Pity Benjy's not here,' I'd said. 'He'd have had this sparkly clean in no time. He's almost as good as a Brillo pad.'

At this, Dominic had gaped with genuine disgust. Surely we didn't let our dog lick human dishes? 'Well, of course,' I'd replied. 'That's his job. And they go in the dishwasher afterwards – hot enough to kill any germs. People have germs, for God's sake.'

This argument had gone nowhere. Dogs lick their backsides, he'd said. And their dicks. At which I had retorted that he was just jealous because he couldn't lick his. (I might not tell Mum this bit.) A major row had ensued, almost to the point of throwing things. To me it had naturally been a revelation, as if he'd said he belonged to the Flat Earth Society or joined the National Front.

Thank God Benjy hadn't been a page-dog at Belinda's wedding, after all. He's a very polite sort of animal; he'd have given his paw to Josh and that excuse would have gone right down the drain. Unless he actually *did* dislike dogs, of course. You never knew.

I was ratty at work, too. The weather was still hot and sunny, which made me even more restless and dissatisfied. The air conditioner wasn't working properly, one of the plants was dying on me, and Sandie, our trainee consultant and general dogsbody, kept slurping her Cokes. Added to that, Neil was popping in every other day, trying to get Harriet to go with him to the Met Bar or wherever. And the more she said no, the more he persisted. 'It's because I'm an estate agent, isn't it?' he eventually asked, all pathetic.

'No, Neil,' she said. 'It's because you're a bit of an arse and you fancy yourself rotten. Will you please get off my desk?'

'Everybody hates us,' he went on pathetically, regardless. 'We're a persecuted minority. Somebody's got to make a killing out of the property boom, for God's sake. Somebody's got to dream up all those brilliant lies on the handouts.'

Maybe I was in the wrong job, I thought, but I was in the middle of typing a long and complicated e-mail. 'Then go and dream some up, will you?' I said testily. 'Some of us have got work to do.'

He strolled over to the coffee tray instead, and pinched one of my hazelnut cookies. 'Maybe I should have stuck to marketing.'

'Then why didn't you?' Sandie asked.

'Too much like hard work, sweetheart.' With a sudden grin, he turned to me. 'Heard from Dominic lately?'

After a freaky double-take, I caught on. 'Who?'

'Dominic Walsh, from our Wimbledon branch! You gave him your phone number at Jess's bash, remember?'

'Gosh, did you?' said Jess. 'Was he the one who looked a bit like Tom Cruise, only taller?'

There are times when I swear I'll never touch alcohol again, but they soon pass. 'He might have looked like Freddie Kruger for all I remember,' I lied. 'I was just a tad *pizzicato*.'

'You were completely rat-arsed,' Neil grinned. 'He remembers you, anyway. Found your number the other day – said he might give you a call. I said, "Go for it, my son. She's not half as scary as she looks."'

'How sweet of him to think of me after all this time,'

180

I said in acid tones. 'But I'm a bit tied up lately, what with my counted cross-stitch class and my "Junk the booze for Jesus" group.'

'I'll tell him you're still up for it, then,' he grinned. Hands in pockets, he strolled over to Jess. 'How are you, my lambkin? All psyched up for your jolly jaunt in Wales?'

'Don't,' she almost shuddered. 'I had a nightmare last night. They were going to make me abseil down the Empire State Building. I said, "I *can't*!" and they said if I didn't do it, they'd send a Rottweiler round to eat poor Alice.'

Alice was her cat.

Sandie snorted and Neil shot her a wink I wasn't supposed to see. 'Abseiling's the least of your worries,' he said, patting Jess's shoulder. 'What you've really got to worry about is all those sex-crazed, ex-SAS hunks ambushing you in the woods. One of the women on my course said it wasn't too bad, if you were into sixteen stone of raw muscle rogering you senseless on a bed of sheep droppings.'

Jess said, 'Honestly!', Sandie snorted again, and I said, 'Neil, will you please get the hell out of here?'

'God, I love you when you're angry,' he grinned, but exited before I could throw anything.

Harriet said, 'He really is an arse,' and Jess said, '*Honestly*, the things he *says* . . .'

'I bet there *are* some hunky blokes,' Sandie giggled. 'I wouldn't fancy the sheep droppings, though.'

'Bluebells would be nicer,' Jess agreed. 'A bed of bluebells, in the woods . . .'

Harriet and I exchanged startled glances. 'There won't be any bluebells in July,' I pointed out.

'I know! In theory, I meant.' She went a bit pink and flustered, and started arranging papers on her desk.

Harriet and I exchanged *Blimey* glances.

I looked at Jess with new eyes after that. More than once since then I'd seen her gazing dreamily into the distance, going all pink and sheepish when I had to wake her up.

Well, it takes a fantasist to know one. Jess was working on something Mills and Boony, I suspected, on the lines of, *'You can't fool me,' he smouldered gratingly. 'Under that prim façade, your body's burning for me.'*

'No, honestly. My nipples always go like this when I'm—'

'You talk too much. Take your clothes off, before I rip them from your quivering flesh.'

'Oh, go on then . . .'

I confess to a titchy *frisson* just from this vicarious fantasy, which depressed me intensely. I saw myself six years hence, getting as desperate as Jess and sending off for Plain Cover King Size vibrators.

On the Wednesday evening, Mum phoned.

'Have you heard from Belinda?' I asked, hoping to forestall the inevitable.

'Yes, dear – just a quick call – they'd just come back from a game drive and seen a lioness make a kill. A poor zebra, she said – I think she was bit upset. I suppose it's only nature but you know what she's like.'

Since I was bracing myself for shattering her cosy little dream, it was a bit of a turn-up when she went on,

'I do hope you don't mind, dear, but your bedroom's turned into a storeroom for a few weeks – Trudi's still dithering and she asked if we could have a few of her things till she makes her mind up.'

Trudi, as you may remember, was Pink Hat from the wedding. Twice divorced, she had recently sold her house and was dithering between a) living in Marbella with a chap fifteen years her junior, and b) finding a nice little retirement flat in Harrogate. As Dad had said, they must have been diluting her HRT with Horlicks.

'In fact I'm a bit put out because she said a *few*, and there are *mountains* of boxes – your room's crammed full,' she went on. 'And Daddy was *really* put out, not least because she expected him to do most of the to-ing and fro-ing and carting up the stairs – she didn't want it going in the garage as there have been a few break-ins lately. As Daddy said, if she can afford to have her bosoms lifted she can afford proper storage and a navvy to do the humping. And then he said, "And probably the other kind of humping, too, knowing Trudi," and I said, "Really, dear, don't be so *coarse*," but I couldn't help laughing.'

Since this was obviously going to be just the usual ramble about not very much, I tittered politely and settled myself for the duration.

'But I do hope you don't mind, dear,' she went on.

'Not in the least,' I said brightly. 'As long as she doesn't store her toy boy there too, and exercise him on my bed.'

'Well, I really would draw the line there, dear. But

183

it's not as if it matters much – if you come up next weekend you can sleep in Belinda's room and I'll put Dominic in the torture chamber, as Daddy *will* call it. I'll have to give Paul and Belinda the double bed, of course.'

I was almost dumbfounded with the sheer cunning of it: lulling me into a sense of false security before sneaking up behind me, like a Border collie with a hapless sheep. The torture chamber, in case you're wondering, was the smaller spare room, containing a single bed, an exercise bike and a rowing machine, neither of which would ever wear out from over-use.

Again I braced myself for dream-shattering, but already she was off again.

'I do hope he'll be able to come, dear.'

'I'm not so sure. The thing is—'

'Oh, go on, dear. Persuade him. It'd be lovely to have the four of you – the photos are due in a day or so – I'm sure there'll be some lovely ones of you two.'

I had to stop shilly-shallying and just *do* it. 'Mum, will you listen a minute?'

'I am listening, dear. I haven't heard any more about Sarah, by the way – I haven't said a word to anybody. I saw Maggie yesterday – she obviously hasn't a clue – I can't help feeling a bit sorry for her, though I can't think why – if it was the other way round I don't suppose she'd feel sorry for *me* – I told her you were probably coming up with Dominic and she said, "Oh, yes?" – you know, as if she wasn't the least bit interested—'

'Mum—'

184

'And I saw Jane Dixon this morning – she thought him very charming, by the way – everybody thought you made a really lovely—'

'For heaven's sake!' I don't know quite what came over me here but something exploded in my brain. 'Don't you realise how obvious you are? You might as well play the flaming "Wedding March" when he walks in the door!'

The instant I'd said it I could have cut my tongue out. There was a horrible silence.

'I'm sorry, Mum, I didn't mean it,' I said weakly. 'I've just had a bad day.'

More silence.

'I know you were only trying to be friendly,' I went on desperately. 'He thought you were really nice. He said so in the car. He said he'd lay odds on your being a brilliant cook, too.'

When she finally spoke, Mum had adopted the small, dignified voice she used when dreadfully hurt, bitterly wounded, or mortally offended. In this case, all three.

'I'm very sorry. I won't say another word about it. If you can manage to come we'll be very pleased to see you, but only if you can spare the time. I must go, I've got a casserole in the oven.'

'Mum, *please*—'

Click.

I stared at the receiver in despair.

I'd really done it now.

'She'll come round,' Alix soothed. 'Tell her you were feeling lousy. Tell her you were upset because you'd just rowed with him over the dog thing. Then you can give it another few days, dump him, and bingo, problem solved.'

'What about *this* problem? She hardly ever gets sniffy like that. I feel awful.'

'She'll come round,' she soothed.

I still hadn't told Alix about the kiss or the Ace lie – just that Josh had gone down fine. All this lying was beginning to get to me. It's a terrible strain trying to remember who you've told which fib to.

I tried phoning Mum the following evening and wished I hadn't. She was still very off with me and made some excuse after twenty seconds about having left the iron on upstairs.

On the Saturday morning, Tamara phoned. 'You wouldn't fancy this party at Jerry's after all, would you? It's next weekend.'

'Not really, thanks. I'm getting past the meat-market bit.' I felt a trifle meaty, too. Despite sticking to the diet for two and a half whole days I'd put on a pound. Still, it was probably only fluid. The weather had turned even hotter and I'd been drinking masses of water, diet vodka, etc.

'God, anyone would think you were *old*,' she scoffed. 'By the way, I phoned Jerry. He hasn't seen Josh in ages, but he thought it was bloody hilarious that he'd gone escorting—'

'You didn't say it was me?'

'Of course not. Not that it'd matter – he hardly ever comes home. I just said it was an *extremely* attractive woman whose bloke couldn't make it, so she'd hired

186

someone to fend off the drunks and gropers you invariably get at all the best weddings. OK?'

'Brilliant. By the way, the bastard did think I was desperate. We ended up staying over because of the roads, and it was obvious later on.'

'He didn't come on to you?'

I wasn't going into detail. 'Not exactly, but I could tell. So I came up with an "unsuitable" boyfriend after all so Josh thinks I'm unavailable rather than gagging for it.'

She started laughing, 'GBH or Trotsky?'

'Neither,' I told her briefly about Ace. 'And that wiped the grin off his face, I can tell you.'

'I bet it did,' she giggled. 'By the way, Jerry thinks Josh has got his own business, or at least he had, but he can't remember what. I said it couldn't be doing very well if he had to top it up with escorting, and Jerry just chortled and said get real, and good on him – he had half a mind to do it himself.'

Since the following morning promised to be even hotter, I thought I'd go and sunbathe on the common. All my bikinis had somehow shrunk since last summer, but at least it meant more acreage would get the sun. I rammed towel, book and bottle of water into a bag and unearthed my sunglasses. Alix was at Calum's yet again; Ace was still in the shower.

'Ace!' I yelled. 'I'm going to the common. If you want a job, the sitting room needs fumigating.'

'OK,' he called back. 'If I can borrow your Immac for my bum hair. Tina thinks it's gross.'

'Use hers, then!'

Just before leaving I remembered the Swiss cheese plant in the living-room window. Bought as a relative tiddler for five pounds, it had already outgrown two pots; in this weather it needed watering practically every day. While I was giving it a good slurp of Baby Bio the phone rang, but since we often leave it in pretending-to-be-out mode, in case it's someone we can't be bothered to talk to, the answerphone cut straight in. An exasperated female voice said, 'Andrew, if you're there will you *please* pick up the telephone?' (I still couldn't get over anyone calling Ace 'Andrew'.)

There followed an even more exasperated 'tut'. 'I'm just sick to death of all those bits of motorbike in the garage. If you don't come and get rid of them by next weekend your father's going to take them to the tip.'

'OK, Ma, chill out.' He had just wandered in, clad in one of my towels.

Retrieving a couple of fag ends from the cheese plant compost, I had some sympathy for his mother. 'Will you *please* stop using my plant as a bloody ashtray?'

'You can talk. It's cruel, keeping it cooped up in a pot like that. It should be in the jungle. I was talking to it last night – it said you never talk to it. It said you only value it as a plant object, not for itself. I gave it half a flat beer to cheer it up.'

'Oh go and do your bum hair.' Shoving the fag ends at him, I headed for the common. It wasn't far away: a green, tree-lined oasis, brightened with many seasonal varieties of *Cola Can Discardus*, *Crisp-packetus-cheese-and-onionus*, and the occasional, fragrant dog turd underfoot.

I found a secluded little spot near a tree, slathered myself with factor eight and lay on my back with my book, trying not to notice how the cruel sun made my lotioned acres gleam like a lake of white blancmange.

Still, a couple of people were baring far grosser blancmange than mine. They lay like blubbery whales, giving not a damn. I was grateful to them for making me look good by comparison. On the other hand, revoltingly slim people were flaked out on the grass, too. To add insult to injury, one or two of them were already respectably tanned. This was perfectly acceptable if they were male, of course. It enhanced the environment.

The book wasn't bad but inevitably I started people-watching instead; you can have a good old gawp behind the cover of sunglasses. About thirty paces away some revoltingly brown cow was constantly standing up to oil herself and show everybody else up. Her bikini bottoms were hardly more than a thong and the bottom they flaunted could have been an advertisement for one of those anti-cellulite creams that gullible idiots shell out small fortunes for, in the vain hope that they'll work. (OK, even I did, once.) Every passing bloke had a good old gawp.

I returned to my book, but with the sun beating on my head the complexities of some crime involving dodgy lawyers were eluding me. I put the book down and checked on Thong. There she was, up again, smoothing oil sensuously into her shoulders. Did she really *have* to stand up to do that? Or was she hoping some passable bloke would take the hint and offer to do it for her? She paused to coo at a couple of babies in a buggy, pushed by some New Man Daddy in shorts and an unbuttoned shirt. And of course, he stopped and chatted back. She was still lazily oiling as she spoke; any minute New Man Daddy was surely going to say, 'Like me to do your back?' He looked quite passable, actually, in fact, he looked just like . . .

I couldn't believe it.

Two babies! Twins!

Half paralysed with shock, I lay quite still, watching behind my sunglasses. Thong was cootchy-cooing at the babies again, but he didn't start anointing her. After another twenty seconds, he moved on.

Right in my direction.

EIGHT

By the time I'd gone into panic-freeze for a few seconds it was too late for my preferred option, i.e. pulling my clothes on and legging it. Of course, he might veer off and fail to see me anyway, and even if he did he might pretend he hadn't, but with all that pork hanging out I wasn't taking any risks. What kind of contrast was I going to make with Thong, damn her?

With sunglasses it's easy to pretend you're asleep; you don't have to worry about keeping your eyelids still. Consciously I relaxed everything and started breathing in that slow, rhythmic way that says you're out for the count. For good measure I left my mouth open just a fraction.

Even with sunglasses I didn't dare keep my eyes open, so it was nerve-racking, waiting for what seemed ages. In fact I'd nearly written if off as a false alarm when I heard what sounded like the squeak of buggy wheels close by.

The squeaking stopped. So did my heart, just about. 'Sophy?'

It was tentative, as if he wasn't sure. I concentrated on my breathing and lay quite still.

The next thing I heard was footfalls on the grass, and a shadow fell over me. Then, from a vague rustle of clothing and minute squeak of shoe leather, I knew he was kneeling down to take a closer look. 'Sophy?'

Well, I can be very resourceful when cornered. Moving my head and arm slightly, as if in a restless dream, I said in a dopey burble, 'No, I got the prawns from Safeways . . .' I let my voice trail off and left my mouth fractionally more open, as if I were about to start snoring, too.

For a moment there was no movement of that shadow, no sound. Then one of the babies started the kind of turning-up whinge that says they're going to be screaming any minute.

'All *right*, Katie,' he said, somewhere between a soothe and a mutter. 'We're going.'

Only he didn't, immediately. The next thing I heard was, 'Jesus, Ben, not *again*. What's your mummy been feeding you?'

'Ba ba ba ba ba,' said an infant voice.

'I'll give you *ba ba ba*, you filthy, stinking little sod.' He said this in reasonably affectionate tones, however, and the next thing I heard was squeaking buggy wheels, squeaking off into the distance.

It was at least a minute before I dared open my eyes.

Twins! And presumably a Mrs Josh putting her feet up, or at least a Ms Partner. Still, at least I wouldn't waste any more fantasy-time on a lost cause. (Yes, of course I had.) If I'm fantasising about someone I actually know, I prefer him to be theoretically available. Speaking as one well versed in the art, I can tell you it adds a certain edge.

I went home two hours later with a vague headache from the sun and much of my blancmange nicely pink, and found Ace sprawled on the sofa watching the football. The living room looked marginally cleaner than before – at least a couple of Hula Hoops had disappeared from the hideous brown carpet. Instead it was decorated with the *News of the World* and the glass coffee table was littered with two empty beer cans, an empty Pot Noodle tub and an apple core. 'God, why are you such a slob?' I asked, as if I were as house-worky as Jess.

'Genes, Sophe. Go *on*!' This last was directed at the screen, where a massive roar was going up. Ace clasped his hands to his head in despair. 'Wanker! Even my mum could have got that one in!'

'Who's thrashing poor old Tossers, then?' I asked. 'Thessalonika under-thirteen girls again?'

'Very funny, ha ha.' He turned his head slightly. 'Did Rent-a-Stud find you?'

I felt as if a large and violent jelly had hit me in the stomach. 'What?'

'Whatshisface from the wedding! He came here looking for you half an hour after you left. Said you'd promised to do him a favour and since he was minding a pair of sproglets for his sister—'

'His *sister*? I thought they were his!'

His brow creased. 'You did see him, them. I'd have thought he might have said they weren't his own work.'

'I didn't *speak* to him, dopey! I saw him coming and pretended to be asleep!'

193

He gaped at me and actually turned the TV down. 'Why?'

'Why d'you think? All my flab was hanging out and I thought he was sodding well married!' I stomped to the kitchen and helped myself to a glass of Cape White from the box in the fridge. Ace followed. 'What the hell was I supposed to think, seeing him with a couple of babies in a buggy? What was he doing babysitting anyway?' I downed half the glass in one go.

'Said they were doing his sister's head in. He'd got them till lunchtime to give her a break. *Did* you say you'd do him a favour?'

'Yes, but I never thought he'd take me up on it!'

But I suppose I'd subconsciously hoped, that's why I'd said it. Yes, all right, there was nothing *sub* about it. I'd said it in the same way you buy a lottery ticket, with hardly a hope in hell of the right balls popping up.

Ace helped himself to another beer. 'The sproglets were just an excuse, if you ask me. He fancies you and he came to check out the opposition.'

Another jelly hit me, but not for that reason. 'You're supposed to be my bloke!'

'I know, thicko! I was a bit gobsmacked, but I acted like a dream.' Grinning at the recollection, he immediately adopted a scowl instead. 'I went, "What d'*you* want?" – like this.' Re-enacting it, he said it in vaguely aggressive tones, matching it with belligerent hands on his hips. 'And he said who he was, and *I* said . . .' he repeated the scowl and the stance, ". . . I know who you are, mate. I saw you arrive the other week. I was checking you out from the window."'

I have to say he did it very well – just aggressive enough to be convincing.

'And he sort of went like this . . .' He raised an eyebrow in a vaguely sardonic fashion, '. . . and said why he'd come, and *I* said, "Well, she's not here, is she?" So he said where were you, and *I* said, on the common, sunbathing. Well, I thought you'd want to see him, didn't I? So he said he'd go and see whether you were up to that favour, and *I* said . . .' he repeated the scowl, ". . . it'd better just be a favour, mate, that's all." And he pushed off. Why the hell didn't you speak to him?'

'What was the point? I thought he was married! Or partnered, anyway.'

'If you ask me, he fancies you and he came to check me out.'

'Yeah, right.' Hardly daring to entertain this heart-stopping possibility, I downed another mouthful of plonk.

'OK, he didn't.' Ace put on his best *up to here* look. 'He just needed a mug and thought you'd be a soft touch. There I was, acting my bollocks off to egg him on—'

'How on earth would it egg him on?'

'God, Sophe, you can be really thick sometimes. I was acting like a total prat— shit, I forgot the best bit. Just as he was going I yelled after him, "And if you see her ask her what the fuck she's done with my black T-shirt. I put it in the wash days ago." A challenge, see? Make him think: What the hell does she see in a bloke like him? And start doing something about it, right?'

'He'll just think I'm a complete headcase, putting up with someone like that!'

'I thought you'd be grateful!' he said, in hurt tones.

'I'm sorry, OK? I'm sure you did it beautifully, but how was I to know?'

'Blimey, I nearly forgot,' he went on. 'You'll never believe who phoned while he was at the door. Yours truly has a rival from your murky past and I'm a bit hacked off, I can tell you.'

Instantly I thought of Sonia. 'Don't tell me it was Kit?'

'Not *him* – Dominic Mark One. I left it to ring in case it was Mum having a go again, so the answerphone kicked in. The volume was still right up so I know he heard.'

'Ace, if you're having me on . . .' I raced to the machine and turned it to play. 'Hi, it's Dominic,' said a voice of smooth, drawly confidence. 'Dominic Walsh, for Sophy. Look, sorry I didn't call before but I was itemed at the time and then I lost your number. If you're still up for dinner or whatever, give me a call on—'

'Bugger off!' I switched him off, cursing both Sod's law and Neil, who'd doubtless urged him on. '*Now* he rings? After bloody *months*? Just when Josh is at the door?'

'S'pose it's like buses, Sophe. You wait hours and two turn up at once.'

'It's not like buses! What sort of nutter must he think I am?'

'Not that much of a nutter, if he's after a date.'

'Not *him*, you dope! Josh!'

'Oh, right,' he said. 'I gather you didn't tell him there was a Mark I.'

'Of course I didn't!'

'Still, at least he can't still be thinking you're desperate.'

'No, just screwed up! Did you say anything?'

'Well, I was a bit gobsmacked, and so was he by the looks of it, but I reckon I was great.' Grinning at the recollection, he went on, 'I should be on *EastEnders*, if you ask me.' He put that scowl back on. 'I went, "I don't know who that wanker is, but I'm wiping him right off."'

And this was my beloved. 'Oh God . . .' I sank to the sofa and put my head in my hands.

'Well, what did you *want* me to say?' he demanded, all hurt. 'That he was welcome to you, I was sick of a fat old tart who couldn't even get my washing sorted?'

'Thanks a lot! I think I'll just go and kill myself now.'

But I had another glass of wine first, and Ace's last thing of Pot Noodles, by which time my head was throbbing nicely and I wasn't up to suicide. I lay on the bed instead, and sulked. It was all Thong's fault, for deliberately planting herself right in his path and showing me up.

I must have nodded off, and woke feeling dry-mouthed and horrible. Everybody was out. I played wretched Dominic's message again, just to check that I hadn't imagined the smooth confidence of a man who doesn't even know how to spell 'rejection'. 'If you're still up for dinner or whatever . . .' Bloke-speak for,

You'll be up for a shag, at any rate. I wiped him off, hating myself for pandering to his ego in the first place.

Ace came back around seven-thirty with Tina and a takeaway Chinese for two. I said, 'Thanks for getting me some,' and they both looked awkward and made me feel bad. I said, 'Oh, forget it, I'd rather have a Greek anyway.' I stomped up the road to the Kouzina and tried to be nice when I got back, especially to Tina, as she often irritated me and I had a feeling it showed. She had a tendency to titter, said, 'basically' every other sentence, and was constantly wittering on about whether it'd really, really hurt to get her navel pierced.

She left an hour after I got back. Once the door had closed behind her I said to Ace, 'You didn't tell her about Josh, did you?'

'No!'

'I bet you did, you little toad. If you dare tell Alix, I swear I'll kill you. It's bad enough thinking I'm screwed up and neurotic myself. I don't want her thinking it, too.'

'I know the feeling,' he sighed. 'Not that she thinks *I'm* screwed up and neurotic. She just thinks I'm a dickhead.'

When she finally came back with Calum, Alix depressed me even further. They'd been to Brighton for lunch in The Lanes followed by a laze on the beach, where her Thong-type thighs had acquired a tan worthy of a week in Antigua. It was the perfect end to a pile-of-pooh day. Wondering what one earth I'd done in my previous life to deserve it, I took my own pink blancmange body to bed.

All the following week there was ominous silence from Mum. Several times I tried to psych myself up for ringing and saying I'd finished with Dominic, but the only time I actually phoned there was no reply.

On the Thursday evening, Tamara rang me. 'I do wish you'd come to this party. I'm sure Charlotte's going to let me down. She's doing some Open University course and she's got an assignment due. I honestly wouldn't bother going, only I can't stop thinking about Paolo.'

'He might not even be there.'

'He will – Jerry said. And you'll never believe what he said about me. He said I looked like "a leetle Botticelli angel". If that isn't Italian for "promising pull scenario" I don't know what is. Come on. You haven't got anything else on, have you?'

'Not apart from *Blind Date*,' I had to admit.

'Go on, then. It should be good for a laugh. And even if it isn't, we'll just get pissed and bitch about everybody. Jerry's booked some rooms in the local pub. It's staggering distance up the road. Some of them are staying with him but the house is still a tip – bathroom out of the ark, apparently, so the stray blokes can have that. I'll fax you directions. Shall I see you at the pub around eight?'

I still hadn't spoken to Mum by Saturday afternoon and since she was preying on my mind I was glad of a distraction. I arrived at ten past eight. The Blue Boar was one of those low, rambling places, ancient, but not quaint or chocolate-boxy. If it had been one of its own customers, it would have been a weather-beaten farm-worker, saying he didn't hold with any poncy nonsense – he just wanted a good old-fashioned jar, out of the wind. Around it were flat fields and the odd, non-quaint farm cottage. It was still warm, but not as warm as London. I imagined the place in winter, with the wind coming straight from Siberia.

I was shown straight up to a passable room overlooking a field. Tamara was half dressed, wielding a hot brush. Charlotte had come after all, but was still in shorts.

'She only decided at the last minute,' Tamara said. 'I mean, even one of Jerry's dos beats psychology assignments.'

When she wasn't studying, Charlotte worked for some market research company where Tamara was currently temping until she got bored and took off again. Slightly shorter than Tamara, she had a similar figure and golden-brown hair in a shoulder-length bob. She was very attractive in an unusual way, but looked on the shy side, making me think she was the follower to Tamara's lead.

'I'm afraid we're all in the same room,' Tamara said, indicating the Z-bed thing shoved beside twins. 'Jerry had even more take-up than he expected. And the bathroom's down the landing, so it's not exactly five star. I'll have to go in a tick. I promised Jerry I'd give him a hand with the food.'

She buzzed off fifteen minutes later in a little dress of silky bright jade that set off her hair and made her look as stunning as she ever would.

Charlotte and I looked at each other. 'I didn't really want to come, but she went on and on,' she confessed. 'I rather think she's hoping we'll be company for each other if Paolo comes off.'

Not daft, then. 'I rather thought she wanted me to be company for her if he *didn't* come off.'

We laughed, and an instant ally-relationship was born. 'But I did quite like Jerry,' she went on. 'I know she says she can't stand him, but I'm sure it's all talk.'

I wasn't quite so sure about that. 'Either that or she's had a brainstorm. I'd have thought she'd tell him to get some other mug to help with the food.'

'Oh, that. She's only gone because she wants to be on the spot in case Paolo turns up early.'

'Hopeless strategy,' I tutted. 'She must have got it really bad.'

'We don't have to rush over, do we?' she asked. 'I'd rather let it warm up first and I need a shower. It was so hot in the car.'

She was still in the bathroom when Tamara came charging back about forty minutes later. 'Look, I thought I better warn you – Josh is there.'

'*What?*'

'Well, I didn't know, did I? Jerry apparently phoned him the other day and said if he felt like coming feel free, but he never told *me*. Still, I got him on his own for a minute and said for God's sake not to let on it was you he was escorting, just in case of jungle telegraphs. He'd known I was coming but you obviously came as a bit of a turn-up. He said was your other half coming too – thank God you warned me – so I just said, "Oh, him – well, he's been a bit of a pain lately, so she's left him to stew."'

At least this tied in with Ace's act. 'What did he say?'

'Nothing, but listen to the best bit. I remembered what you'd said about him thinking you were desperate and I had a brainwave. I said, "Anyway, I don't think he's going to last much longer – her old ex wants her back. He was at the wedding." Brilliant, wasn't it? So now you're positively fighting them off.'

Trying to look both tickled and grateful for solidarity in the face of the enemy was not easy, but I think I managed. I even produced a little hoot of mirth. 'I'd better not get too pissed or I'll be tripping over all the lies.'

If I hadn't drowned in a sea of them first.

What had Josh said about spilt beans? Not only could you never get them back in the can, they got trodden all over the carpet, too. I made an instant decision not to update Tamara with the not-quite-meeting-on-the-common bit. She might embroider that with the wrong stitches and I'd look more of a prat than ever.

'Anyway, you look really nice,' she said.

'Thanks.' I'd chosen some slinky black trousers and a black top that covered my hips. Most of it was thin silk jersey, but the sleeves and the top of the bodice were as filmy as ten-denier black tights, revealing just an inch of cleavage. It had been expensive, and looked it.

'I'm sure you'll be fighting off a few more,' she said. 'And that'll wipe the remaining grin off his face.'

She shot back to Jerry's, and Charlotte and I

wandered over shortly afterwards. My stomach was in a bugger's muddle of knots, with a whole rain forest of butterflies added. At the back of my mind still lurked Ace's, 'He fancies you . . .', but it made even less sense now. If he did, why hadn't he come back for that favour? Instead he'd come to this mainly singles bash with not a clue that I might be present.

As Tamara had said, Jerry's place was within staggering distance. It was a low, rambling farm-housey dwelling in a large, encircling garden that consisted mainly of rough grass where masses of cars were spilling over from a gravel drive. They ranged from a Mercedes sports to a beat-up Golf, and I wondered which was Josh's. The whole place was totally unprettified; I guessed it had belonged to somebody old and broke who'd spent nothing on it for fifty years, but it obviously had massive potential if you had a hundred thousand to spare.

Inside it would have been very bare, if not for dozens of people already well past the warm-up stage. A bare, stone-flagged hall led to a huge square room, and off that was a huge farmhouse kitchen with beams and a massive pine table serving as the bar.

Looking decidedly browned off, Tamara was unloading cheese and pâté from a massive new Westinghouse fridge – the only post-sixties item in the room, by the look of it.

'Can you believe Paolo's going to some other do first?' she muttered. 'I'm sick as a pig. I bet he won't turn up after all. I could kill Jerry. He just said. "Oh, didn't I tell you?" Take these, will you?' She passed

203

bowls of various *crudités* and dips. 'God knows why I'm doing this. I was chopping up bloody carrot and celery sticks for hours. I should have been getting pissed on that rum punch instead. It's authentic West Indian – guaranteed to blow your head off. If you ask me, Jerry's hoping some poor girl's going to pass out on it and save him the trouble of his customary twenty seconds' foreplay.'

Charlotte and I exchanged glances. Following Tamara, we carried the eats to a large spare room, where a pine refectory table stood against the wall. Baguettes were already plonked there, with bread-boards for cheese and pâté. Wallpaper-type jazz was coming out of a massive CD player and Tamara made a face at that, too. 'I *hate* that stuff. I should have brought my old 'Agadoo' tape, just to piss him off.'

Charlotte and I exchanged glances again.

I didn't have to stop myself scanning the room for you know who, as only half a dozen people were in there. Old-fashioned French windows opened on to the garden, where already forty-odd people were clustered on the grass. I still couldn't see Josh. Beyond a far hedge was a field with cows. It was getting dusk, but lights had been rigged up somewhere.

Two minutes later, armed with a wimping-out spritzer (I had to keep a clear head), I wandered with Tamara and Charlotte into the garden. Tamara had already downed one and a half rum punches.

'Right, now who can we bitch about?' she said, scanning the company. 'I'm just in the mood. He'll do, for a start.' She indicated a red-bearded chap in a

204

mustard corduroy shirt. 'Just look at that shirt – no dress sense. He's got wet-fish hands, too. Jerry introduced me earlier. An academic, wouldn't you know it? Jerry's still got mates at the university. Doctor of nerdology or something. He carted her along, too. That six-foot job in the cream skirt.'

I could only see a back view. She had long blonde hair and legs obviously up to her armpits, though she wore a mid-calf cream skirt, slit up the back. Slim and willowy, she was also, in heels, nearly as tall as Josh, who was right beside her and listening intently to whatever the cow was saying. (Yes, I know I'm a bitch, but only a humanoid would not have felt that instant contraction of the stomach that spells pure, green-eyed stuff.)

Also flanking this vision were Jerry and Red Beard. 'She's called Svetlana,' Tamara went on. 'A research student from St Petersburg. Well, if she's doing an in-depth study of the intrinsic pratology of the Anglo-Saxon male, she's come to the right place. Just look at Jerry, all over her.'

'Looking for clues,' said a bloke who'd just appeared at Tamara's elbow. In amused tones he went on, 'Jerry and his mates have got bets on her being a honey-trap industrial spy, trying to bed her way into their microelectronics developments.'

'In their dreams,' Tamara said scathingly. 'Roger, this is Charlotte and Sophy.'

After ritual handshakings I was still gut-knottingly watching Josh, and suddenly he turned his head a fraction and saw me. He raised his eyebrows in subtle acknowledgement, and added half a smile. My stomach contracted again – at this rate it was going to end up a tenth of its usual size – and I gave a casual one back. However, since Roger was asking whether the M11 had been a pain, I had to focus on him. A former colleague of Jerry's, he was nice enough, but sparkly small talk was a hell of an effort so it was a relief when he went for a refill a couple of minutes later. Trying to sound as if any mingle-fodder would do, I said, 'Shall we go and mingle?'

'You bet we will,' said Tamara. 'Let's go and wreck Jerry's chat-up. I could do with a laugh.'

And so it was, dear reader, that ten seconds later I found myself separated from Josh by only a body (Tamara's) and all my butterflies going forth and multiplying like rabbits.

I hadn't seen Jerry in ages but he hadn't changed much. He was a slim six-foot-ish blond of the golden, Scandinavian type, and undeniably good-looking with a hint of *and don't I know it*.

He said, 'Hi, Charlotte – nice to see you.' Tamara said, 'I suppose you remember Sophy?' and he said, 'Just about. How are you doing?'

We were introduced to Svetlana and Red Beard, whose name eludes me. Tamara said to Josh, 'This is Charlotte, I think you met Sophy at the wedding.'

A lazy spark flickered in his eyes, but he just said, 'Yes, how's it going?' and I said, 'Fine, thanks.'

Svetlana could have been any age between twenty-five and thirty-five and until I actually saw her face I'd naturally been hoping it'd be ordinary, if not actually hideous. So it served me right when she proved to be almost in Belinda's league. Despite Nordic blond hair and blue eyes, she had vaguely Slavic cheekbones and the eyes had a sickeningly attractive slant. In short, she was the last woman you wanted to see two inches away from the man who was haunting your fantasies. Given her looks, I could almost understand that daft male joke about honey-trap spies. In logical, gut-knotting turn, I naturally recalled Josh's adolescent James Bond fantasies and wondered whether he was even now rehashing them in relation to this leggy vision.

Still, I did my best to be nice. 'How long are you here for?' I asked politely. I can tell you, it was very off-putting to have to look up to someone like that. Since I'm usually the tallest woman in any given group, I wasn't used to feeling like a stumpy midget.

She sounded very Russian, with all those heavily stressed ls. 'Seex months, but I do not stay alll ze time in Cambridge. I have many friends at ozzer univer-sities here. Is it good allso to see ze country and meet ze people.'

'As long as you're selective,' Tamara said, in a sweetly mischievous tone that might have fooled anyone who didn't know her. 'Don't listen to anything this lot are telling you. English men are all appalling liars and sexist pigs, too.'

This brought a faint smile from Svetlana. 'Russian men are allso sexist peegs,' she said. 'Allso zey are llazy. It is ze women who do ze work. Allso zey drink alll ze time too much vordka and beat on zeir wives.'

207

'My ex used to beat on me,' said Jerry, 'She was a fruit cake.'

'Excuse me?' Svetlana raised an elegant Russian eyebrow.

'Crazy.' He tapped his forehead. 'Hysterical.'

Tamara downed more of her head-blowing punch. 'She was nothing of the sort,' she retorted. 'If I had to live with you, I'd beat on you, too. He has some disgusting personal habits,' she added sweetly to Svetlana.

Watching Jerry's reaction distracted me from Josh. Any fool could have seen that Jerry was intensely irritated with Tamara for muscling in. Equally, it was obvious that whether he'd fancied Charlotte or not, he now fancied Svetlana a hell of a lot more, so I hoped Charlotte wasn't upset. Her casual 'I quite liked Jerry' had hinted at rather more.

And since Tamara had sussed all this out and resented his chatting up Svetlana on Charlotte's behalf, her pet little devil was urging her on. 'The vast majority of Englishmen are unfortunately both anal and puerile,' she went on sweetly. 'They only laugh at jokes about farts.'

'Excuse me?' Svetlana said, while Jerry was clearly dying to strangle his sister forthwith.

'Farts,' Tamara said sweetly. 'Like this.' She made a graphic fart noise that didn't altogether go with that Botticelli-angel face.

Svetlana gave the kind of little laugh foreigners give when they're privately thinking English people are not only mad, but also dangerous. To Jerry she said, 'I sink I must go to ze bassroom. Where eez eet, please?'

'I'll show you,' he said, clearly glad of an excuse to get Svetlana away from Tamara.

'He'll go in with her if she's not careful,' Tamara said, watching them go. 'Probably tell her it's an olde-English custom for hosts to accompany lady guests to the loo in case of rats coming up from the sewers.' She looked down at her empty glass. 'I don't know about anybody else, but I could do with another one of those.'

Charlotte went with her, Red Beard evaporated, and suddenly I was left with my rain forest of butterflies and Josh, who was watching Tamara go.

'Do I gather that she's a trifle hacked off with Jerry?' he said.

'Just a trifle.'

'Why?'

I wasn't going to betray her Paolo thing. 'Just ancient sibling stuff,' I shrugged. 'They've always snapped and snarled like a pair of wolf cubs.'

'Then why did she come?'

'It's not *serious* – just a habit, if you ask me.'

Tamara disappeared inside, and Josh turned to me. In case you're interested, he now had a bit of tan that made him look more horribly attractive than ever, and a can of beer in his hand. He was wearing a black, short-sleeved shirt and jeans. I wouldn't have thought they'd suit him, which just goes to show how thick I must be in such matters.

Now he was looking straight at me, I wasn't sure what to make of the look in his eye. I detected a trace of private amusement, on the lines of, *Obviously semi-mad, and therefore good for a laugh.*

'How's your friend?' he asked. 'The one with abseil-phobia?'

'Still phobic,' I said. 'But trying to take the wider view. See the positive aspects, and all that.'

His mouth gave a little twitch. 'How about you? Still freaking out about potholing?'

'Good Lord, no.' I said briskly. 'I've got to set an example to my team. I've convinced myself that I can handle anything they throw at me. Ritual humiliation can be rollocking fun, you know, and I dare say the sadists all come from broken homes, bless them.'

'Sounds as if that guy's been winding you up, too,' he said. 'I'd take it all with a couple of barrels of salt, if I were you.'

'If you say so. How many bookings have you had since me?' I went on quickly, before he got on to ticklish subjects, like Dominic. 'I hope none of them was quite such a nightmare.'

'I haven't had any, as a matter of fact.'

'*What?* Not even one?'

'Not too good for the ego,' he confessed. 'Julia Wright thinks maybe I look too conventional. A lot of clients go for the long-haired type.'

There had been a high proportion of those, all looking like resting male models, but if you ask me any client who preferred them wanted certifying.

'Talking of long-haired types, I met your other half,' he went on.

Oh Lord. 'Yes, I gathered.'

'I hope he didn't give you a hard time,' he went on. 'Stroppy little sod, if you'll forgive me for saying so. Evidently thought I had a hidden agenda.'

I was dying to say, 'Well, did you?' but miserable spritzers don't give you that kind of nerve. 'I have to make allowances,' I shrugged. 'He's a little bit insecure, you see. After all, the situation could look suspicious. You might have thought I wouldn't be able to resist a poor helpless bloke with two dear little babies, and then you'd proceed with your dastardly agenda.'

Cue for him to say, 'Well, that was the general idea.'

Fat chance.

'Then why did he tell me where you were?'

He nearly had me there, but I was quick. 'Because he knew I'd never play ball,' I said sweetly. 'I'm useless with babies. I haven't a clue how to work them. I only have to look at them and they start crying.'

'I'm no great shakes either.'

'Then why were you babysitting in the first place?'

'Fiona was tearing her hair,' he said. 'Her other half's away. She'd locked herself out of the house the night before and I went round with a spare key. And since I owe her a few favours, I said I'd take them for a couple of hours in the morning and let her get some kip. She only lives about a mile and a half from you, so I thought I'd push them over the common and see whether you were up to that favour you promised.'

'Then I'm sorry I couldn't oblige.'

'So was I. I was knackered after three hours. I won't be offering again until they're at the stage when you

211

can take them to McDonald's and shove them in front of the video afterwards.'

Useless though I am, I almost felt I'd have done it if I'd only been there and decorously covered. 'Wasn't there anybody else you could have asked to give you a hand?'

'I did phone a couple of friends. The first said very apologetically that she was busy. The second was more honest and said she'd sooner indulge in a spot of do-it-yourself female circumcision, thank you very much.'

I almost felt sorry for him now. After all, how many men would offer to babysit twins? This heart-touched soppiness I suddenly felt had nothing whatever to do with the fact that the golden brown fuzz on his arm was within shivering distance of my own arm, of course. Neither did it have anything to do with the scents wafting so tantalisingly under my nostrils, i.e. a heady cocktail of clean shirt, shaving stuff, and warm, male body. 'But you thought I'd be a soft touch?'

'No, but it was worth a try.' His eyes were following a blonde girl who might have been Thong in slinky white trousers with apparently no knickers under-neath, or maybe it was another thong, which was probably what he was trying to work out, damn him.

Having evidently done so, he turned to me again. 'In fact I found you on the common, but you were asleep.'

'You're kidding!' I produced what I hoped was a suitable startled expression. 'I hope I wasn't snoring like a pig. Why didn't you wake me up?' This was crafty, I felt.

'I thought you'd give me a mouthful. One of the bratlets had just crapped for the second time, so on reflection I thought you'd rather snore.'

'I do hope I wasn't,' I said, in what I hoped were half-embarrassed tones.

'No, but you were mumbling in your sleep.'

'Nothing to make me blush, I hope.'

'Not unless garbage makes you blush.' Very lightly taking my arm, he moved me out of the path of a chap approaching with a precariously laden tray of drinks. I'd seen him coming but pretended not to in the hope that Josh would do exactly this, so you can tell to what depths I'd sunk.

He let go almost at once and I asked my next question with the utmost casualness. 'Are you staying over at the pub?'

'No, I'll either crash here or drive back.'

Since I'd just invented a piquant little fantasy about colliding with him in the corridor in the middle of the night, this bashed it right on the head before I'd even got to the good bit.

'Have you dumped me yet?' he went on.

'Not exactly, though I thought of a brilliant reason the other day.'

'Not the mumps, then?'

'No.' I told him about our doggy row, which seemed to amuse him well enough. 'Only I haven't actually used it,' I confessed. 'I sort of bottled out when it came to the point.'

'How do you mean?'

'I told Mum she was too pushy and obvious and

would frighten poor old Dominic off,' I explained.

He made a wincy sort of face. 'Oh Lord.'

'You may well say "Oh Lord". She's got a sort of face on in her voice, if you know what I mean.'

'I can imagine.'

'She's barely speaking to me. I hardly dare phone again and say I've dumped you. In fact I might just have to hire you again, just to keep her happy, and *then* give you the elbow.'

Naturally, I hadn't meant to say this. I haven't a clue why I did, except maybe to see whether he'd blanch and run a mile.

The tantalising little flicker he produced could have meant anything. 'I'm not sure I could stand another session with you twitching non-stop like a nervous rabbit.'

'Oh, I'd give you a hefty bonus,' I said gaily. 'You'd need it, for all the oohing and aahing over wedding photos. Only I'm not sure I could face that agency again. It was embarrassing enough the first time. It'd have to be a private arrangement.'

His mouth did more than flicker then. 'You wicked woman – you'll get me sacked.'

If you ask me, men like him should not be allowed to look at women like me in that fashion, on the grounds that it makes us feel like doing daft things, e.g. suddenly pretending to faint, so they'd have to scoop you up in their powerful, muscly, etc. etc.

'Oh well, it was an amusing notion. If Mum doesn't speak to me till Christmas, I suppose it might be a relief.' I also wanted to say a number of other things,

214

e.g. *'I made Ace up, dickhead. Can't you see I fancy the pants off you? And why do you have to have greeny-browny eyes like a river with the sun on it?'*

He said, 'Why don't you just tell her you dumped me and take your ex instead? I gather he's back on the agenda.'

Although half of me wanted to put him straight, the other half was applying bloke-psychology to the situation. A stroppy little sod like Ace pretended to be was one thing; Kit was quite another.

'I gather Ace is consequently due for the chop,' he added.

'I'm not sure I want either of them,' I said lightly. Inspired brilliance, I thought. It was hardly even a lie. 'Maybe I'd like to be on the loose for a bit.' Even more inspired. Cue for him to say. *'In that case, what are you doing on Tuesday night?'*

However, just as I said it, Jerry came back, looking like Thor the God of Thunder on a bad day. 'I don't know what's up with Tamara, but I'm itching to give her a good slap,' he muttered. 'Svetlana actually asked me whether she had "pseekological" problems.'

'Come on, she wasn't that bad,' Josh said, in easy, indulgent tones.

'She bloody well was.' To me he went on: 'He's got a soft spot for her, if you ask me. She used to have a thing about him when she was barely out of Barbie dolls. Used to write all this stuff about him in her—'

'Jerry, don't drag all that up,' Josh said, with a half-amused 'tut'. 'She was just a kid. I'd never have recognised her.'

215

If there had been anything left in my glass, I might have contrived an 'accidental' spill all over Jerry's nice clean trousers. Adolescent crushes are not the kind of thing a sensitive sibling brings up.

'You're amazed she's turned out halfway passable, you mean,' Jerry said. 'In strictly aesthetic terms, I mean. She can still be a total pain, so I wouldn't harbour any ideas in that direction, old son. Especially if Paolo eventually shows his face.'

Josh raised an eyebrow. 'Who?'

'Paolo. Italian mate of mine she's got the hots for. You didn't think she came all this way to see *me*?'

The breeze was back, giving me a perfect excuse to get away. 'I'm going in. I need a fill-up and it's getting chilly out here.'

On the way in I passed Svetlana coming out, and some low-life bloke a few feet behind her said to another, ditto, 'Christ, imagine those legs wrapped around you.'

It was enough to make you puke, but I wasn't worried about her any more.

NINE

Well, that's a lie – I was. In fact I was worried about any halfway attractive woman within a three-mile radius, but one was suddenly looming larger than the rest.

I must have been utterly thick not see this angle before. Josh might not have known I was coming, but he'd known someone else was coming.

'*Where the hell has Tamara met you?*'

'*Nowhere . . . I'd remember.*'

Looking back, it had sounded more like, '*Believe me, I'd hardly forget.*' The fact that she was totally focused on Paolo was beside the point.

Beginning to wish I'd stuck with *Blind Date*, I slapped on a having-a-brilliant-time smile and went in search of Tamara and Charlotte.

For the next hour or so faking a brilliant time proved not so difficult, after all. There were some really good fun people among the horde, including a couple of passable blokes who flirted with me in a feel-good (rather than shudder-making) way, and had a store of the kind of jokes that make you thankful for laugh-till-you-cry-proof mascara.

At some point Josh strolled up and joined us, but since one of the joke-blokes was paying me lots of flattering attention, I concentrated on him. For a while he talked to both Tamara and Charlotte, but after a while he wandered off again. This partly eased my horrible green-eyed stuff, but then again, maybe he was just playing it ultra-cool.

It was only later that I spoke to him again. By then I'd ditched miserable spritzers and gone on to that rum punch. And since it was lethally moreish, I thought it wise to make a second assault on the remains of the food. While I was hacking myself some baguette Josh appeared beside me and took one of the few remaining celery sticks.

'I was wanting a quiet little word with you,' he murmured.

This sounded vaguely ominous. 'Oh, really?' I said brightly. 'Have some of this salmon and prawn pâté. It's really nice.'

He broke off a baguette end and dolloped a spoonful on top. 'Why didn't you tell me Dominic was real?'

Since I was prepared, it was easy. 'He wasn't!' I scoffed.

'He sounded real enough to me.'

'Oh, the phone call.' I gave what I considered a perfect little shrug and added a couple of celery sticks to my paper plate. 'Yes, Ace was a bit put out.' After all the lies, a little truth might not come amiss. 'If you really want to know, I met him at a party, got completely pissed, and wrote my phone number on his arm.' I added a couple of cherry tomatoes, too. 'So when Mum phoned a few days later he made a convenient sort of template. My imagination's not up to concocting blokes entirely out of thin air.' I added a bright smile. 'Satisfied?'

218

'I guess.' He dipped a celery stick into what was left of the hummus. 'What's that anaemic-looking pink stuff?'

'Taramasalata.'

He stuck another celery stick into that. 'So when are you going to do the evil deed and dump me?'

'After next weekend, always assuming I actually go. If Mum's still upset with me there'll be an atmosphere and I wouldn't want that with Paul and Belinda there.'

'If there's one thing worse than family rows, it's atmospheres,' he agreed.

'On the other hand, if I *don't* go, she'll be even more upset with me.'

'Looks like you're in a no-win situation.' He paused to watch Svetlana stroll past, with Jerry at her elbow.

'Obviously smitten,' I said. 'Him with her, I mean.'

'I'm not so sure it's reciprocated,' he mused, still watching.

I was beginning to wonder whether he'd given up on Tamara and had other ideas. Alternatively, maybe he'd never had designs on Tamara in the first place and it was just my paranoia going into overdrive. I nearly said, '*I suppose you fancy her yourself,*' but changed it to, 'She's very attractive,' hoping he'd come back with, '*Yes, but not my type.*'

He said, 'And interesting, in that peculiarly Russian fashion. Who was it who talked about riddles wrapped in mysteries wrapped in enigmas?'

'Churchill, but he was talking politically.'

From the crowd I'd left came shrieks of the laughter you only get from a really good joke. I looked over and saw joke-bloke shoot me a wink, which was gratifying. I smiled back and hoped Josh had clocked it, too, but maybe not, since his mind was still on enigmas.

'It's all the same thing,' he said. 'A nation's character is innately bound up with its politics. Look at Italy.'

'And look at Russia,' I said, cross that I wasn't riddly and enigmatic and mysterious, too. 'It's in a right old mess, so what does that tell you?'

'I'll have to come back to you on that one,' he said, which served me right, but at least he'd turned his attention back to the food.

'I should have got stuck in earlier,' he tutted, scooping the remains of a coarse pork pâté out of a ceramic dish with a crust of bread. 'All the carnivorous stuff's gone down the gannets' throats. I might take you up on that oohing and aahing after all,' he added sardonically. 'At least I'd get fed. Your mother looks like the good old roast type. I haven't had a proper roast in months.'

Mum fancied herself at the *couscous* and rocket stuff lately, but since the basic description was sound I couldn't resist playing along, if only to delay his pursuit of mysterious Russians. 'It's usually a nice pink sirloin from the organic butcher in the village. Or else a leg of lamb, with far more crispy roast potatoes than anybody can possibly eat, and cauliflower cheese—'

'Stop it,' he groaned, putting the last, forlorn radish in his mouth.

'And roasted onions, if it's lamb, and lots of meat-juice gravy, half of which goes to the dog, who always licks the roasting tin out, too, so you'd have to look really disgusted about that, in view of our barney. On the other hand . . .' I was really getting into creative gear now. 'I've just had a much better idea. Remember what you said to Winnie Vinegar-Bottle about the priesthood?'

It was satisfying to see him do a double take. 'For crying out loud . . .'

'Yes, but you know what they say about true words spoken in jest,' I moved slightly to let someone else get at the taramasalata. 'You're sick of all this sordid money-grubbing and have re-discovered your long-suppressed vocation.'

Eminently pleased with this, I took one of the last two cherry tomatoes. 'Brilliant, isn't it? I never liked the dog thing much. Of course, I could always invest you with pervy penchants for lacy knickers—' I very nearly put my foot in it here with '—*as Ace suggested*', but engaged brain just in time. 'Or rubber, if you prefer.'

'I think I prefer the mumps,' he said, in a tone as dry as James Bond's Martinis.

'Suit yourself, darling,' I added a mischievous little smile, also perfected in the bathroom mirror at sixteen. 'Only we'd better get it sorted before I phone and tell my mother you're positively salivating for a roast, and she goes straight round to Winnie Vinegar-Bottle to score a few more points. Of course, I could always just say you've turned into a complete pain in the bum.'

Again came a maddening little flicker that could have meant laughing *at*, or *with*, 'I'll leave it up to you. What should I take her? Flowers or chocolates?'

'Flowers; she's always on a diet.'

'Any particular variety?'

Something in his tone jolted me like a cattle prod. 'Josh, I was joking!'

'So was I.' He took the last cherry tomato from the dish. 'Do you think there's any more of that pâté in the kitchen?'

I felt such a prat that if I'd been the blushing type I'd have gone pinker than Barbara Cartland's frocks. 'Why don't you go and look?'

Just as I said it, joke-bloke came up and grabbed my arm. 'Sophy, I need you to settle an argument.'

Bless his little heart. 'Excuse me,' I said sweetly, and let him drag me off.

Half an hour later Paolo still hadn't shown up and Tamara's party-animal mask was beginning to crack. Nearly in tears but pretending to be merely mad, she dragged me to a quiet corner.

'Bastard,' she muttered. 'I only came and chopped up all those sodding vegetables because I thought he might come early and think how sweet and domesticated I was. I'd never do it for an English bloke. They only make those puerile jokes about women having little feet so they'll fit under the cooker, but Italians are different, aren't they?'

'Probably not,' I said. 'But satin-Latin sexism sounds better. Think of some complete yob yelling. "Show us yer tits" and imagine *that* in Italian.'

'I suppose . . .' She was doing her best, but I could tell she'd have liked to sit down on the floor like a three-year-old and wail that she wasn't playing any more. 'But if Jerry thinks I'm going to help with clearing up, he's got another think. Just look at him with Svetlana. It's embarrassing. You can tell a mile off she's only being polite. If you ask me, it's Josh she's after.'

I had already noted the Svetlana-cluster of five or so, with both Josh and Jerry in attendance, but had tried not to look. Now I did, and it was fairly clear if you observed for more than ten seconds that her conversation was addressed mainly at Josh, while Jerry was doing his best to divert it to himself.

'Jerry's hoping to get his disgusting end away, if you ask me,' she muttered. 'I've got a good mind to tell him to stop making a prat of himself.'

'I wouldn't if I were you.'

But not long afterwards I saw her mutter something to Jerry, who did not look best pleased, but still he didn't leave Svetlana. I suppose it was about ten minutes later that our two groups somehow converged, so that there were about ten of us suddenly arguing the toss about whether at Wimbledon the women players should be paid as much as the men.

And suddenly, like a miracle to put the smile back on Tamara's face, there was Paolo. Apologising profusely in an accent satiny enough to have even me going weak at the knees, he was at her side almost at once. Well, I could see her point, though I didn't usually go for long hair. Not only was he fantastically good-looking, he looked nice, too: a combination that should be put on the Endangered Species list.

Jerry, however, was still miffed enough to shoot

poisoned arrows. 'Thank God you showed up,' he said, in jokey tones that might have fooled some people. 'She's been like a bag of cats.'

Tamara flashed him a warning look, but he flashed one back that said, *You asked for it*.

'Actually, she used to have a thing about my old mate Josh here,' he went on, in jokey-sounding tones loud enough to get everybody's attention. 'She used to have this little diary and write stuff like, *Dear Jesus, if you make Josh love me I'll never bite my nails again, and please,* please *let me have 34B boobs like Suzy Clarke's.*'

I couldn't believe he'd said it in front of everybody, but Tamara was laughing, like just about everybody else, except for Charlotte, who'd gone almost white, and another girl who looked appalled.

Josh said, 'Jerry, for crying out loud . . .'

'You're just jealous because nobody had a thing about you,' Tamara giggled. 'How did you find my diary key, anyway? I used to hide it under the hamster cage.'

'Which was the first place I looked,' he grinned back, as if it were all as good-natured as you like.

Just about everybody laughed again, and Tamara giggled. 'Yes, but that's not nearly as funny as when I walked in on Jerry in the bathroom when he was sixteen.'

From the flash in Jerry's eyes I could tell the gloves were really coming off now.

'What was he doing in the bathroom?' said a girl who looked on the dopey side.

Since I vaguely recalled Tamara once telling me

something really gross about Jerry's clandestine bath-room activities, I held my breath.

Tamara was really cracking up now. 'He wasn't too happy with his measurements, either,' she giggled. 'He was sizing himself up with my little *Hello Kitty* ruler. I said, "Yuck! Get that off your willy!" and he said, "Fuck off, Squirt. If you dare tell Mum I'll crucify the hamster."'

More gales followed and even Jerry was laughing, possibly out of relief that it hadn't been worse.

As it was all dying down, Tamara said brightly, 'Anyone fancy a coffee? I'll go and put some on.'

Seconds later I followed and found her dissolving into furious tears in the deserted kitchen, '*Arse*hole,' she wept. 'How could he embarrass me like that, in front of Paolo?'

'You laughed it off brilliantly,' I soothed. 'And you got your own back even better.'

'He doesn't care,' she wept. 'Bastard! I hate him so much, I should have told everyone about that time I caught him wanking into the washbasin.'

'I thought you were going to,' I confessed. 'Didn't you ever have locks on the bathroom at your house?'

'The screws were always falling out – Dad was so useless at fixing things,' she sniffed, grabbing a piece of kitchen roll. 'Not that Jerry'd have cared even if I *had* said it. He'd only have smirked and thought what a Jack-the-little-lad he was.'

Just then, Josh came in.

'I suppose you've come for another good laugh,' she sniffed miserably.

Anyone could see he hadn't. He wore an expression I could read all too well. 'I had a feeling it was an act,' he said. 'You're not leaking, are you?'

This was enough to set Tamara off again. 'Why did I have to have a brother like him?' she wept. 'Why couldn't I have had one like you?'

I stood aside, helpless, as he took her in his arms and let her mop her leaks on his shirt. Feeling sick with guilty jealousy, and hating myself at the same time, I slipped out and nearly collided with Dopey.

'I was looking for you. Your friend's not feeling very well,' she said. 'Charlotte, is it?'

It hadn't been Jerry's poisoned arrows that had made her go so pale. I found her in the bathroom, doing lovely technicolour yawns down the pan. 'Probably the rum punch,' I said, as she straightened up, looking dreadfully pale and shaky. I filled a handy glass with water and passed it to her.

'I don't think it's the rum. I had a prawn sandwich on the motorway on the way down. It didn't taste very nice but I didn't think—'

She decorated the pan again.

'I'll take you back to the pub,' I said.

'No, really – I'll go by myself. I don't want to drag you away . . .'

'It's fine. To be honest, I've had enough.'

Dopey was hovering anxiously outside, asking whether she could do anything. I shouldn't call her that, she was really very nice, but her name eludes me. 'I'm going to take her back to the pub. Would you quietly make our excuses after we've gone?'

Charlotte threw up again on the way back, under a hedge. She fretted tearfully about how disgusting it was, like lager louts in Tenerife, but that seemed to be that in the puke department, which was just as well, with the bathroom down the landing. 'And I don't know how I could ever have liked Jerry,' she went on miserably. 'I thought he was really mean to say that in front of everybody. I should have stayed at home and got on with my horrible assignment.'

Half an hour after we got back she was tucked up in bed and already asleep, while I lay in bed with the television on as low as it would go, to take my mind off other things. A tap at the door announced Tamara, wide-eyed. 'Is she all right?'

'More or less.'

'I feel awful. I didn't realise you were both gone till ten minutes ago. You go back if you want. I'll stay with her.'

'No, I really don't mind.' I added a yawn for good measure. 'I'm a bit tired, to tell you the truth.'

Anxiously she said, 'You did enjoy it, though?'

'Oh, yes – it was a brilliant laugh.'

'Thank God for that. I'd have felt awful if you'd come for nothing.' She suppressed a mischievous little smile. 'What do you think of Paolo?'

'Tasty,' I said. 'I take it you're feeling better?'

'You could say that.' The smile was no longer suppressed. 'I felt such a prat, crying all over Josh. He was really sweet, wasn't he? But a minute later Paolo came after me, too. He thought it was so cute that I'd had a crush on Josh. He kept saying, "Poor leetle

227

Tamara", like that, and stroking my hair, so I was almost glad Jerry had said it in the end. Paolo's waiting downstairs, so if you're sure you're OK, I'll get back.'

At least she was happy.

I lay awake for hours, watching some rubbish film but not taking it in. I almost knew now that Josh's comforting of Tamara had just been 'niceness', which somehow only made me more forlorn. If he'd callously cracked up with Jerry at least I'd have had a perfect basis for going off him.

Just to torture myself further, I indulged in a fantasy involving my car conveniently breaking down in the pouring rain, a hundred yards from wherever he lived. It had to be a hundred yards so I'd be soaked to the skin by the time he happened to look out of the window and see me scurrying to the phone box, since I'd conveniently have forgotten to charge my mobile. There would then be the offer of a hot shower and his bathrobe afterwards. I'll leave the rest to your imagination.

I eventually fell asleep around three thirty and was woken again by Tamara coming in at ten past six.

'Sorry,' she whispered. 'I didn't mean to wake you up. Has Charlotte been all right?'

'Fine. Did you have a wild time?'

'Brilliant. We've just had hooligan soup and bacon butties in the kitchen.'

'*What* soup?'

'Hooligan. One tub of vanilla ice cream, one pot of runny honey and a bottle of brandy, all sloshed together in a washing-up bowl.'

'Sounds disgusting.' I could have murdered a bacon butty, though; to add to everything else, I now felt ravenous, too.

'Paolo's coming up to see me the weekend after next,' she went on. 'Which is very convenient, since the old dears are off to Vienna for their anniversary.'

Why was everybody having dirty weekends except me?

Just after getting into bed she whispered, 'And I was right about Svetlana. Not long after you left she went off with Josh. He speaks a bit of Russian, apparently, not that I think they'll be doing much talking. Serves Jerry right for being such an arsehole. Night-night.'

Brilliant. I lay there until around seven, when I got up as quietly as possible, left some money for my share of the bill with a note saying I had stuff to do, and went off to kill myself.

The following evening, just as I'd got out of the shower, the phone rang. Alix called, 'It's your father,' which in itself was enough to send my stomach into uneasy knots. He never phoned. He often spoke to me, but only after Mum had said, 'Daddy's here – he'd like a little word . . .'

'Is everything all right?' I asked at once.

'More or less. Your mother's at her computer class, or I wouldn't be ringing.' He hesitated in a way that told me exactly what was coming. 'The thing is, love . . .'

My throat constricted. 'I know I upset her. I didn't mean to, but she was going on and on – you know what she can be like – and I was worn out anyway and it just came out . . .'

'I know, love, but she's taken it very much to heart. She didn't tell me till last night. I knew there was something wrong but she wouldn't say. I started thinking she must have found a lump, so last night I asked if that was it, and she burst into tears.'

I felt like forty-eight guilt-ridden piles of pooh. 'I'm really sorry,' I said unsteadily. 'I didn't mean it. I honestly never thought she'd take it like that.'

'I know, love, but she's got it into her head that she embarrasses you, and that's why you didn't bring Dominic home before.'

I felt so awful, I nearly confessed there and then.

'I hate to push it, love, but I suppose there's no chance that he could come?' he went on. 'It'd mean a lot to her. She had something planned for Sunday as well – just a little lunch, but it's Pud's eighty-fifth birthday – I don't know whether you remember – and she'd set her heart on a nice little do at the Old Windmill.'

'Pud' was what he called Granny Metcalfe; the Old Windmill was a lovely restaurant about five miles away.

'I know Mum mentioned it, but have you said anything since?' he went on. 'I mean, if Dominic's really not keen the last thing I want is for you to pressure him.'

Just how awful can you feel? 'As a matter of fact, I did mention it the other day,' I said, which was only the truth. 'But the phone rang or something and we

forgot about it. I will ask him, but please don't
anything yet. I have a feeling he's got something lined
up so I can't promise.'

Once you start, lies just pop up like tissues from a
box. You take one, and there's the next one waiting.
'I'll give her a ring anyway tomorrow evening,' I went
on.

'Don't say I phoned, will you?'

'Of course not!'

'Thank you, love.' He sounded so relieved, I felt
double awful. 'I know she can be a bit over the top
sometimes, but all she's ever wanted is for you to be
happy.'

Correction: triple awful. 'I know.'

''Bye, then, love. Look after yourself.'

Five minutes after hanging up, I was in tears of
miserable guilt.

Alix brought me a large V&T. 'It's a bit drastic but I
suppose you could always take him home again and
"dump" him afterwards.'

I could hardly believe she'd voiced what I hadn't
dare voice myself, in case she had me certified
instantly. 'I'm not sure I could face that agency again.
I'm sure they were having a good laugh the instant I
walked out the door.'

'Maybe you wouldn't have to. If he was at that party,
whatshername's brother will probably have his number.'

Naturally, I'd already thought of that.

'Sooner you than me, though,' she went on. 'What if
he thinks you fancy him and you're just using this as
an excuse?'

That was it. I could never tell her now. I knew Mum wasn't the only reason I was contemplating this next charade. He was obsessing me, haunting my dreams. Even if he had half a dozen Svetlanas on the go, I had to see him again. Already I was fluttering, just at the thought. 'Of course he won't.'

'I wouldn't bet on it. Any bloke who goes escorting has to have a sexual ego the size of the Millennium Dome.'

If I leapt to his defence she'd suss me out instantly. 'What does it matter as long as I sort Mum out?'

'I suppose it'll be easier the second time,' she went on. 'All that money, though! It grieves me to death. Think how you could splash out with that!'

When I phoned, Tamara wasn't in, but her mother was. I explained that I needed Jerry's number as I wanted to contact a guest from the party. Mrs Dixon said, 'Yes, I heard you'd gone. So nice for you all to keep in touch, I think. Did you take Dominic, too? Tamara didn't say.'

All these lies were getting like wafer-thin ice. Whatever I said, she was bound to report it back to Mum. 'No, he had to go away for a couple of days, so I was at a loose end.'

I wasn't looking forward to phoning Jerry. He was bound to make some remark. Evidently in a hurry, however, he dished out Josh's number with barely a word.

It was a BT line, not a mobile. 'I'd phone him straight away, if I were you,' Alix said. 'He might already be tied up, whether socially or professionally.

Still, presumably he's not seeing anyone or he'd have taken her to that do.'

In that horribly familiar green-eyed fashion, my stomach constricted. 'I hope he isn't. He apparently left with some Russian woman who looked like the front cover of *Vogue*.'

Alix gave a little snort. 'I hoped she watched herself, that's all. God knows what she might catch. I bet you those blokes are all putting it about like tomcats.'

'He wasn't like that!'

'No, because you weren't begging for it,' she said, unrepentant. 'I'm sure they can *seem* OK. They'd have to, or they'd never get taken on in the first place. *Shit*, that pasta, it'll be soggy as hell . . .'

She went to check the *penne* we'd put on twenty minutes back. In a state of nervous flutter just at the thought, I was glad to be able to phone Josh without an audience. Hardly expecting him to be in, I pushed buttons rapidly.

'Carmichael,' he said crisply, after only two rings.

'Josh, it's Sophy.' Almost seeing his taken-aback state, I carried on before he had time to utter. 'I got your number from Jerry. I'm really sorry to bother you but I'd like to take you up on the oohing and aahing, after all. I'd never ask, but I evidently upset my mother far more than I realised. I just had my father on the phone – she's been crying her eyes out, thinking she embarrasses me and that's why I never took you home before.'

'Oh Lord,' he said.

'You can say that again.' I was practically in guilty

tears again. 'She wouldn't tell Dad what was wrong for days. He thought she'd found a lump or something – he was really worried. He made her tell him last night, and she burst into tears. She'd planned something special for Sunday as well. I'd completely forgotten but it's my granny's eighty-fifth the following week so she'd booked a surprise lunch out, just the immediate family, but it was supposed to be a lovely weekend and now she feels awful.'

'Oh Christ.' He paused. 'The thing is, I've fixed something for next weekend.'

My heart sank. 'Never mind, then – forget it – sorry for bothering you – bye-bye.' I hung up, shrugged my shoulders, and pretended it was just a minor irritation in the scheme of things.

The *penne* were soggy but we ate them anyway, with tomato and fresh basil sauce, though even that didn't lift my mood one bit.

'You could always tell your mother he dumped you but you hadn't liked to say, and that's why you were so ratty the other day,' Alix suggested.

'Yes, but then she'll just think she's frightened him off. God, why did I ever say it?'

Half exasperatedly she said, 'Well, why did you?'

I could hardly say, '*Because I fancy the pants off him and was consequently cringing to think how her over-eagerness would have looked if he* had *been for real.*' 'I don't know! She was getting on my nerves!'

'Tell her he dumped you,' she said firmly. 'Then at least she'll feel sorry for you. She can always tell Maggie it was the other way around.'

I had almost decided on this course when the phone rang, around twenty minutes after I'd hung up.

'Sophy? It's Josh.'

My heart and stomach did a drunken little *pas de deux* together. I tried to say, 'Oh, hi,' as if I were nonchalantly examining my nails, but had a feeling it didn't quite come off.

'Look, maybe we can work something out,' he went on. 'I'm going on Friday night to see someone in Durham—'

'*Durham?* That's miles!'

'Yes, but I wasn't planning to stay all weekend anyway. What time do you have to get to your folks' on the Saturday?'

'Seven-ish, latest.'

'OK, then. What if you met me at Manchester Piccadilly at six? Would that do?'

'The station? Aren't you driving?'

'Not to Durham on a Friday night, thanks. The train takes half the time. Can you do Piccadilly at six?'

My head was in a right old spin. 'Yes, but don't you want to check train times first?'

'They shouldn't be a problem. I'll see you at six. OK?'

Crisp as an iceberg lettuce.

'I suppose he wants the money,' Alix said. 'Pay his train fare. It'd probably be as much as an air fare, come to that.'

It struck me then that we hadn't mentioned sordid business matters. 'I didn't say anything about money!

235

God, how embarrassing. Should I ring him back?'

'I wouldn't bother. He'll assume it's the same rate as before. Just take your cheque book or a load of cash – I bet they prefer cash. Stick it in an envelope and hand it over at the end.'

But I'd do something else first.

I was going to do what I should have done at the party, i.e. be brave enough to tell him Ace was a daft lie and I still owed him that favour, so if he fancied dinner out in the next week or two . . .

And if I saw an *Oh, shit* expression cross his face, and he started politely explaining that he was going to be busy for the next fourteen years, I'd smile and say, 'Never mind, it was just a thought.'

'What about dumping him afterwards?' Alix asked later. 'Is he going to give Benjy a good kick?'

'Are you kidding? He might just be heading for the priesthood.'

'*What?*'

I explained about the seed he'd planted with Maggie.

Alix was not impressed. 'Why don't you go the whole hog and make him gay as well? I mean, half of them are gay. No wonder they wear those long black frock things.'

I mentally filed that idea under dire emergencies/ last resorts.

The following evening I phoned Mum. After delivering the glad tidings I spent the next two minutes saying how sorry I was, I'd been exhausted and not very well, I hadn't meant any of it, I didn't know what had come over me.

More fibs for the collection.

It made me feel a bit better when she fibbed, too. 'I really *never* meant to be off-putting, dear. And as for wedding marches, I never thought any such thing. You know I've never been one of those mothers who are desperate to get their daughters married. Of course Daddy and I'd be only too pleased to see you settle down with somebody nice, but you know perfectly well I've never said a *word*.'

Just before she hung up, I delivered my final peace offering. 'By the way, he's hoping you'll do a roast. He said you looked the really good home-cooked roast type and he hasn't had one in ages.'

If that didn't mend fences, nothing would.

Half an hour later, Tamara phoned. Mrs Dixon had naturally passed on every detail of my call and Tamara was mystified. 'Did you hit it off with somebody after all?'

'I wish. I was going to phone you anyway. There have been developments on the Dominic front.' I went on to explain the basics. 'So if you hear I'm bringing him up again on Saturday, don't look gobsmacked, will you?'

'You mean he's agreed to do it?'

Something in her tone made me uneasy. 'Why wouldn't he?'

'No reason, I suppose. Only Jerry was apparently kidding him about the escorting and he said he'd only done it the once, for a bet. Still, maybe he's embarrassed to admit he needs the money, not that I said that. Jerry reckons the bet was whether he'd get his end away, but he would.'

She was doing a great job of cheering me up lately.

I left at half-past one on the Saturday, which should have left ample time, but the traffic was a crawly nightmare and I was jittering non-stop, thinking I'd be late. I crawled along in coned-off lanes, having visions of Josh exasperatedly looking at his watch and saying, *'Oh, to hell – I'm going.'*

Who was this person he'd gone to see, anyway?

Naturally my brain had already been working on this. It had asked questions like:

What is there at Durham?

Castle and university.

And what do we find at universities?

Drunken students. Stoned students.

And what else?

Er, research students?

Would you care to elaborate?

Er, visiting research students from St Petersburg?

Yes, this is a distinct possibility.

So no prizes for guessing how my imagination was working. Svetlana wouldn't be wearing that long skirt, of course; if anything it'd be a satin teddy or maybe just a velvet ribbon around her neck, like that blonde spy in *From Russia with Love*. She'd be pouting like something out a blue movie, too. *'Dahlleeng, do you 'ave to go? Can't ze mad beetch find some ozzer cup?'*

'Mug, *Svetlana, my sweet*.' And he'd kiss her with

besotted tenderness. '*God, I hate to leave you, but it's money for old rope. Say something poetic in Russian to keep me warm. Say you'll writhe on my dickski all night, on the golden road to Samarkand.*'

'*I say fock ze mad beetch, dahlleeng. Stay here veez me and I put caviar and sour cream alll over your deeckski and leeck it off teelll you scream.*'

I ate a half packet of wine gums, just theenking about it.

Unlike last time, we'd have less than an hour in the car. How was I going to play it? All nice and matey? Cool and casual? Mild and pleasant, like the weather we were supposed to be having, but weren't? The heat wave was over; we were back to March-like damp and chill. Summer was definitely here.

In the event I was twenty minutes early. All the parking spaces were gone, as usual, so I had to drive round and round in the drizzle, cursing. I made it back at one minute to six, and he was actually there, armed with two bunches of flowers. 'Thought I'd better get one for your grandmother, as well,' he explained, shoving everything on the back seat.

It was grossly unfair, going all sweet and considerate when I was desperately looking for reasons to go off him. I nearly said, '*Give me the bill and I'll add it to your expenses,*' so he could say, '*OK – and the train fare from Durham was forty-five quid,*' and make me feel better. Or worse.

Instead I said, 'You really needn't have bothered. I've brought a present.' I still had to wrap it up: the latest Catherine Cookson and a huge box of Thornton's.

'How's the situation with your mother?' he asked.

'Just about back to normal, so thank you for pitching in. I hope the weekend won't be too much of a nightmare.'

'Put it this way – I've survived the fire, so the frying pan should be a doss. How's Charlotte?'

'Fine, apparently. I think it was something she'd eaten.' Casually I added, 'How was Durham?'

'I didn't see much of it. You know how it is.'

Yes, thank you very much, I could just about remember how It was, if It was what he'd been doing. At this rate nice and matey was going to be a tall order, especially in the type of traffic that makes me road rage-ish at the best of times.

Consciously I calmed myself. After all, whatever he might or might not have been up to, it was absolutely none of my business. The fact that he'd cut it short to come and assist in my hour of need might even mean that he'd never expected it to be very great shakes in the first place.

Nominally perked up by this notion I pulled up at a pelican crossing, where an elderly lady was waiting to cross. The little green man must have been perfectly visible by then but still she hesitated.

'Come along, dear,' Josh tutted. 'One foot in front of the other, that's it, easy does it . . .'

As she eventually dithered over he went on, 'They all do it – peer suspiciously from lights to car and back again. I swear they think it's some sort of monstrous trick devised by the splat-a-wrinkly brigade.'

I had to bite my lips. 'Poor old thing. Don't be so

rotten. And they don't *all* do it.'

'You're quite right,' he agreed. 'They don't all. It's usually the woolly hatted ones. There must be something about woolly hats. When added to old ladies they produce an infuriating excess of dither.'

'What about old *men*? Little old men in cars, in those little-old-men hats? They dither worse than any old ladies.'

'It would make an interesting topic of reseach,' he mused. 'The dither-properties of hats when applied to pensionable heads. Would it come under applied textiles or applied psychology?'

'Under applied piss-taking, I should think.'

From then on, it was nice and matey all the way. How can you stay cool with a man who makes you laugh?

'Have you driven me all the way?' he asked.

'It might be simpler.' I hesitated over the next question, in case the answer was going to make me sick. 'I hope your friend wasn't put out that you had to shoot off.'

'Shouldn't think so. Why are you driving me again? Won't it look just a tad odd?'

I wanted to say, '*Before I answer that, could you please answer my previous question more specifically, e.g. "He didn't give a stuff?"*' Instead I said, 'I don't see why. You like being driven. You find it relaxing.'

He didn't contradict me. 'When did the newlyweds get back?'

'They were landing this morning, early. Then they'll have taken the shuttle to Manchester and gone back to

Paul's. Well, Paul and Belinda's, now. He's got a place in Altrincham, about ten miles from my folks.'

'It's been a long honeymoon. Kenya, wasn't it?'

'And Tanzania, I think.'

'Did Belinda have any hairy encounters with the wildlife?'

'I don't know, but on a five-star jolly like that they ought to be guaranteed close encounters with everything from elephants to *Tyrannosaurus rex*.'

'I meant the *dudus*, not the big stuff.'

'The *what*?'

'The *dudus* – it's Swahili for wigglies.'

As I laughed he went on, 'I spent some time in East Africa, as a kid.'

'Really? Where?'

'Zambia first, then Kenya. My old man worked there for years. He was an engineer and moved around a fair bit, so we were packed off to boarding school from ten to eleven.'

Which tied in with what Tamara had told me. 'Have you ever been back?'

'No, but my folks have. My mother was very disillusioned, especially with Nairobi. Said she'd hardly recognised it.'

'Paul and Belinda were spending a couple of nights in Nairobi. Some really smart hotel. Paul insisted on *the* places to stay.'

'Probably the Norfolk,' he said. 'It's got a lot of character – dates back to ox-cart days. My old man told me how there was once a swamp right opposite, complete with lions. There was some apocryphal story

242

about a Lord Delamere shooting a lion in the bar. I thought how incredibly cool it'd be to stroll around with a rifle permanently on your shoulder, order a beer, and calmly dispatch some ravening beast that was about to pounce on the steward. After which you'd return to your beer with a cool, "Don't know what the damned place is coming to. They'll be letting women in next."'

'You sexist little beast!'

'I guess I was. Or at least still at the uncomplicated, twelve-year-old stage of failing to understand what the hell anybody sees in girls.'

Given my current state, this was a vaguely unsettling remark. Mile by mile, Sophal-warming had progressed to dangerous levels. Once again I might have downed a couple of vodkas with ice, lemon, and a good dash of sexual ambrosia. Blood pumped just that bit faster. Nerve-endings tingled. The mere scent of his shaving stuff was enough to make me go very slightly woozy.

Still, I'm sure you know the feeling.

I was glad he'd opened up: it meant I could ask a few questions without seeming intrusively nosy. 'Julia Whatshername said you were in the Forces – the Marines, wasn't it?'

'Yes, I went in at eighteen. As the careers master said, it was marginally better than jail, which was where I'd end up otherwise.'

My expression made him laugh again.

'You're winding me up,' I said.

'Not entirely. Let's just say if I ever have a son like I

243

was, it'll serve me right. But I wanted to join up. I fancied myself at the parachute and pop-gun bit.'

'Perhaps more accessible than MI5,' I agreed. 'When did you come out?'

'Several years ago.'

'Had you had enough?'

'Partly. I wanted to do something else.'

I couldn't leave it there. 'Like what?'

'Like starting my own business. Well, not quite my own. I've got a partner. Makes it easier when I want to slope off for a few days – he can mind the shop. And when there's a cock-up, I can blame it all on him.'

I laughed, partly out of relief that he'd qualified 'partner' with 'he'. It had taken only half a second for my brain to come up with some Thong-type cow with an accountancy degree who did the books and shagged him senseless every night, too.

I was glad he wasn't unemployed, but half a business hardly guaranteed wodges of readies either, especially half a small business of the chilled-out variety, which was what it sounded like. Chilled-out small businesses do not generally equal satisfied bank managers.

Which led my thoughts on to that bet, but I wasn't going to ask. As Tamara had said, maybe it had just been a ploy because he was embarrassed to admit he needed the money. On the other hand, he hardly struck me as the type to be embarrassed by anything.

I was just about to ask what sort of business it was when I nearly killed the pair of us, instead. We were on a quiet road and I suppose I wasn't concentrating as well as I should have, but two boys of eleven or

244

twelve, flat out on bikes, suddenly shot out of a side lane nearly into the middle of the road. Swerving violently, I ended up in an emergency stop on the other side of the road.

'Jesus.' My heart was pounding.

Josh exhaled deeply. 'Are you all right?'

'Just about.'

Neither boy had even fallen off his bike. Evidently shaken, however, they were gaping at the car.

'Brainless little sods,' Josh muttered. 'I've seen more road sense in a cat. Hang on a tick . . .'

I was about to say, 'You might as well save your breath,' but he was already out of the car and banging the door. He strode over to them and their shaken expressions instantly turned to the up-yours defiance that makes me thank God I never went in for teaching.

Since the windows were up I couldn't hear what he said, but it was obvious from his back-view body language that he was tearing them off a strip, as Dad used to say.

After half a minute he strode back, looking grim, and the boys sped off. He got back in the car and shut the door with rather more force than necessary. 'Well, I exerted my undoubted authority.'

'I could see that.'

'And naturally, they were suitably chastened. One told me to fuck off, the other told me I'd better not get any nearer, his mum had told him about dirty old gits like me.'

I bit my lips but it wasn't really necessary, as an exceedingly wry little smile was flickering his mouth, too. 'I'll probably end up with one like that,' he sighed. 'As I said, the wages of being a little sod yourself are having an even worse little sod of your own.'

I moved off again. 'You might even have a pair of them, if twins run in the family.'

'Christ, don't.'

As I overtook the boys they both stuck fingers up, grinning like monkeys. 'It wouldn't be a bad excuse for dumping you, if you're going to have delinquent kids,' I said. 'Maybe you've just been genetically tested for the delinquent-kid gene and come up positive.'

'Have we got to the kid-planning stage, then?'

'No!' Was I giving myself away here? I mean, I had a vague idea of kids one day, but I certainly wasn't at the stage of panicking about my biological clock. Not often, anyway. Only about once a month, when I got all miserable and hormonal and imagined myself at forty-three, going to car maintenance classes and pretending to be interested in spark plugs, in case some halfway passable bloke might fancy me. And I'd be Auntie Sophy to Belinda's kids and Alix's kids, and Poor Old Sophy to Belinda and Alix, and Alix'd be saying to Calum, *'How about that Ken bloke at work? I know he's a bit of an anorak, but he's quite sweet, isn't he?'* And Mum'd still be ringing every Tuesday night, saying, *'Anything nice happened lately, dear?'*

Pushing this recurrent nightmare aside, I said casually, 'Actually, I don't think I'm going to make any particular excuse. I'll just say it's amicably fizzled out.'

Which meant I'd better find myself a real bloke sharpish, or I'd be back to square one.

Josh made no comment. As home came closer I wondered whether Winne had found out about Sarah's marital problems, and if so, whether she had also found out that Mum had found out first. It would add to her mortification considerably. In fact, I doubted whether normal cold-war relations would ever be resumed. It would probably be hot war for a bit, with poison gas thrown in.

I told Josh about it. 'I feel awful for Sarah. I haven't seen her since just after the honeymoon, but we were friends for years.'

'There's a lot of it about,' he said. 'At least half my married friends are either divorced or separated. One girl I knew took a fancy to a guest at her own wedding and ran off with him straight after the honeymoon.'

'God.'

'But the bridegroom was a smug sort of bastard,' he added. 'It wiped that grin off his face for a bit.'

Half a mile on, we were nearly there. 'I hope you're starving,' I said, 'because Mum tends to assume that all men have the appetites of ravening adolescent boys. She invariably over-caters and if you don't want second helpings she thinks there's something wrong with it. There hardly ever is, but she'll still apologise for everything as it goes on the table. The meat'll be over- or underdone, the potatoes will be either too crispy or not crispy enough, the gravy'll be too thick or too thin, you name it.'

He laughed. 'They're all the same.'

The village consisted of one picturesque little street that still had a few cobblestones. It was lined with tubs

247

of flowers and little shops, many still bowfronted, which had once been greengrocers, ironmongers, and so on. In the past twenty years most had been taken over by the kind of specialist shop that can do well in affluent, semi-rural areas. Riding and outdoor gear. Arm-and-a-leg Italian leather. Lately there was that organic butcher who specialised in venison (low cholesterol) and would prepare anything with surgical precision.

From this street meandered a couple of green winding lanes with wide, grass verges. All half hidden in well-established gardens, the houses had all been built since the turn of the century in an eclectic mix of styles from mock-Gothic to mock-villa-in-Marbella. Ours was what an estate agent would describe as *a substantial family home in the mock-Tudor style*. In my teens I'd gone through a stage of despising it as unbelievably boring. Now I just saw it for what it was: comfortable, safe and traditional, like everything else about my parents.

'How long have they lived here?' he asked, as I turned into the gravel drive.

'They bought it when I was five. It was in a bit of a state. They've been doing it up ever since.' I parked next to a shiny black Porsche. 'Paul's' I added. 'I expect they've been here an hour or so. I just hope Belinda's not too sickeningly brown. And this is Benjy.' He came bounding from round the side of the house, woofing joyously and leaping up to lick my face.

'Part retriever?' Josh asked, giving him a fondle.

Benjy was sort of tan, with a white bit on his chest.

248

'We think so. The rest is anybody's guess. He came from a shelter at six months.'

We were still yards from the front door when Dad opened it. 'Sophy, love, thank God you're here.'

He wasn't going to catch me again. 'Don't tell me – Benjy's scoffed the joint, Mum's throwing a fit in the kitchen, and you're being sent out for a takeaway.'

'I only wish it were that.'

From nowhere a cold, horrible lump had formed in my stomach. It wasn't an act. He looked suddenly old.

TEN

'Dad, for God's sake, what is it?'

'It's Belinda. She's gone missing.'

'*What?* What d'you mean, missing?'

He shrugged helplessly. 'Just what I say. She left a note for Paul and disappeared. On their last day. Just hours before the flight.'

I felt suddenly numb and crawly-skinned, as if I were about to pass out. 'You mean she's left him?'

He only nodded.

My mouth had gone dry. Stupidly I said, 'How is he?'

'Not so good. Your mother's not taking it very well either.' To Josh he added, 'I'm sorry. Looks as if you haven't picked a very good weekend to come.'

Josh touched my arm. 'Standing out here won't do any good.'

Unrooting myself, I walked numbly through the apricot-carpeted hall where little antique pieces gleamed with polish. Dumping all our things on the floor, we went through open double doors to the sitting room.

Having half expected to find Mum either crying or running around like a chicken with its head cut off, what I found was almost worse. She was sitting quite still in an armchair. Like Dad, she looked utterly bewildered, utterly confused, and suddenly much older. She turned her head, her lip trembling. 'Oh, Sophy . . .'

Apart from slipping an arm around her, there was nothing I could do. 'Oh, Mum, try not to worry.'

It sounded trite and pathetic, but I couldn't think what else to say. I was still numb, partly because a belated penny the size of a meteorite had just dropped from the ceiling and nearly knocked me out.

'We didn't know anything till Paul arrived, half an hour ago,' Mum said, in a trembly voice I hardly recognised. 'He thought she might have gone to the Altrincham house after all, or at least rung him there, but there hasn't been a word. He thinks she might ring here.'

Paul was standing with his back to us, at the window. Tentatively I asked, 'Paul, are you OK?'

'Of course I'm not OK. Would you be OK?'

He turned round, running a tense, irritable hand through his hair. 'What's she playing at?' he demanded of nobody in particular. 'I mean, what the bloody hell is she *playing* at?'

'Sit down, Dominic,' Dad murmured. 'Let me get you a drink. What'll it be?'

'A malt whisky, if you have one. Straight.'

'Get Mum a brandy, Dad,' I said. 'I think she could do with it. So could I, come to that.'

As Dad departed, numb, awful silence filled the room. It felt as if there had just been a death in the family. 'What did her note say?' I asked at last.

Without a word, he handed me a sheet of hotel paper.

Dear Paul,

I'm so terribly sorry, but I've made an awful mistake – it just doesn't feel right any more. I'm taking an earlier flight home and I'll stay with friends for a bit. I'm terribly sorry – it's not your fault, so please don't blame yourself in any way. Please tell Mum and Dad not to worry. I'll contact them very soon. I'm so terribly sorry.

Love, Belinda.

I felt sick. 'I'm so sorry, Paul. I just don't know what to say.'

'I know what to say,' he muttered.

I couldn't blame him. He was hurt and angry.

I wanted to show it to Josh but he was still sitting several feet away on the end of a sofa and Paul didn't need his humiliation shared with virtual strangers. I was glad Josh was sensitive enough not to ask me to read it out, or come and read it over my shoulder.

Dad returned with the drinks. With a sip of firewater inside me, I reread the note. 'What does she mean, *an earlier flight*? How come she was on her own long enough to organise all this?'

'I was playing golf.' He sat heavily on the other end of the sofa from Josh. 'We were back in Nairobi for our last day and I wanted to play golf at the country club. I think I was entitled to play golf for a couple of days of a nearly three-week honeymoon, for God's sake.'

I picked this up at once. 'Had you had a row?'

'No!' He said it almost angrily. 'Well, not what I'd call a row. She didn't particularly want me to go, but there wasn't much else to do. She said she'd do some shopping and lie by the pool.'

'And you came back and found her gone?'

'What do you think?' He took a sip from the glass in his hand. 'I couldn't believe it.'

After a long, awful pause, his voice rose angrily. 'How could she *do* this to me? What the hell got into her?'

Nobody answered.

'I was in shock,' he went on. 'It must have been twenty minutes before I even checked the airport. I might have well not have bothered. The earlier flight had already left.'

In a tentative voice I asked, 'So what did you do?'

'What do you think?' His voice took on a sarcastic, bitter note. 'I sat and availed myself of the mini-bar. I nearly missed my own bloody flight.'

Mum tearfully said, 'I'm so worried – what if she's been abducted?'

'Of course she hasn't, love,' Dad soothed.

'She might have been. They might have made her write a note to make it look as if—'

'Of course she hasn't!' Paul's voice rose with tension. 'People who've been abducted don't tidily pack their every last possession right down to their bloody nail polish! They don't spin reception some line about ". . . meeting my husband later, but I'll just pay the extras on the room before I go"!'

After a moment's silence, Dad said quietly, 'I know you're upset, lad, but there's no need to speak to Sue like that.'

'Sorry,' he muttered.

Mum rose unsteadily to her feet. 'I'll go and check the dinner . . .' Her voice was unsteady too, on the verge of cracking.

I followed her to the vast kitchen that had been redone two years ago in antique pine.

'And now the dinner's ruined,' she said tearfully, opening the oven to check the roast. 'It was more or less ready – I meant to turn the oven down but I forgot in all the upset and now look at this beef – all dried up . . .'

'Nobody'll notice,' I said. 'I don't think anybody's really hungry any more.'

'And the potatoes are overdone . . .' Tearfully she jabbed at one with a fork. 'All ruined . . .'

Josh had just slipped in behind us. 'I like them like that.'

'Nobody else will,' Mum said tearfully. 'I might as well give the whole lot to the dog . . . I'd better make some gravy anyway – and the horseradish – I forgot the horseradish . . .' She began an agitated search of the vegetable rack. 'Where is it – I know I bought some fresh horseradish . . .'

'I'll find it,' I soothed. 'And I'll make the gravy. You sit down and get that brandy down you.'

Suddenly her fragile self-control cracked. With a deep, indrawn sob she put her hands to her face. 'It's all my fault,' she wept.

Appalled, I steered her to the pine table and sat her down. With an aghast glance at Josh, I put an arm around her. 'How can it possibly be your fault?'

'It's a judgement on me.' Through her sobs, she could hardly get the words out. 'Because I was gloating about Sarah Freeman. Only a tiny bit, but I was. I couldn't help it, after Maggie had been so smug. There's a word for it, some horrible long German one . . .'

Schadenfreude. And to someone like Mum, indulging in even a smidgeon of *schadenfreude* wasn't nice. It produced an overdose of good old one-syllable Guilt.

'Even if you were, how could it possibly have had anything to do with it?' I grabbed a piece of kitchen roll for eye-wiping. 'It's *not* your fault. You must get that right out of your head now.'

Gradually she got herself partly under control. 'If she wasn't sure, why didn't she *say* something?' she pleaded, through sniffs and eye-wipings. 'She could have told me – I'm her mother!'

If I'd given an honest answer to that one, she'd have felt fifty times worse.

'I had a feeling she wasn't quite herself, a week or two before the wedding,' she went on fretfully. 'But I never once imagined . . . I thought maybe it was me, getting on her nerves . . . She was so jumpy – kept saying, "Mum, do stop *fussing* . . ." I know I do fuss sometimes, but it was only because I wanted everything to be absolutely . . .'

Her voice dissolved again, into tears.

I felt awful. 'You weren't to know. How could you? You're not a mind-reader.'

But I should have known. God help me, I should have seen this coming. As if it had been taped in my brain, that phone call with Belinda was going through my head. There had been cold feet, all right, but they hadn't been Paul's. Why the hell hadn't I twigged? How had I got the wrong end of the stick so spectacularly?

Then I thought back to her engagement-party glow, and wondered why the hell I should feel remotely guilty. She *had* been besotted – what on earth had happened in the interim?

But I couldn't say any of this to Mum. Her eyes shot to Benjy and the tears began afresh. 'The poor little boy, I completely forgot – nobody's fed him . . .'

Benjy was sitting mournfully by his empty dish. He hadn't uttered so much as a small, polite woof, but then he could see that things were a bit fraught.

'I'll feed him,' I soothed. 'You go upstairs and wash your face. I'll sort everything out down here.'

Once the door had closed behind her, I started ransacking cupboards for dog food. Since the new kitchen had been installed I could never remember where anything went, but I was glad of the activity. 'I could kick myself. I knew she was worried but I got it totally arse-about-face . . . Where *is* this bloody dog food?'

Josh was leaning against the worktop, arms folded. 'You thought she was worried about him chickening out.'

'Yes, because it never once occurred to me that *she*'d have cold feet!' I found a can of Tripe and Chicken, and rifled drawers for a can opener. 'I didn't listen. I got irritated and ridiculed her. I was too wound up in my own stupid mess . . .'

As I opened the can, Benjy's paws and quivering nose were up on the worktop, checking which variety was on the menu. I put the dish on the floor, where he proceeded to push it around and suck up the contents at the same time, like an animated vacuum cleaner.

'I don't see why you should blame yourself in the slightest,' he said. 'How old is she?'

'Twenty-seven.'

'Then she's old enough to know her own mind.'

'But she obviously didn't, did she?'

Benjy had pushed his dish into the corner, where it would keep still for a final lick and polish.

How nice to be a dog. No complicated relationships; a warm bed and a smelly canned dinner were all there was to heaven.

Josh was watching him, too.

'I'm really sorry, landing you in all this,' I said.

'It doesn't matter.'

'It does. And dried-up roast beef, too.'

'I've eaten far worse than dried-up beef.'

I tried to make a wan joke of it. 'At least you won't have to ooh and aah over endless wedding photos.'

'I almost wish I did.'

Putting his empty glass on the draining board, he folded his arms and looked at me. 'I know it's a hideous cliché, but it really isn't the end of the world.'

257

He was standing at least ten feet away, with a substantial pine table between us, but the eye contact still played merry hell with my insides. Which only racked up my guilt by another fifty points. In the circumstances I had no business to be fluttering; it was like telling dirty jokes at a funeral.

Turning away, I searched the veggie rack for the horseradish. 'It *is* the end of the world, for my mother.'

'If she's really made a mistake, it's surely better to admit it now,' he pointed out. 'Better than five years down the line, when there might be a couple of kids to think of.'

When I'm in a state of guilt and tension, it takes only a minor irritation to spark me into anger. And I had one: I couldn't find the horseradish. He was right; why the hell should I be blaming myself? 'I could kill her. Why did she have to make such a bloody drama of it? If she really couldn't live with him, why couldn't she just give it a few months for the sake of form and quietly leave him?'

'Why did she go through with it at all, is more to the point.'

'I can guess,' I was about to elaborate but Dad was back, bearing a glass.

'Paul wants a fill-up,' he said heavily, heading for the fridge. 'He's in a bad way, poor lad, I feel so helpless . . .'

Helpless? Never once had I heard him utter the word. I wouldn't have thought he even knew the meaning of it. I couldn't bear to see him like this.

Shocked, numb, he'd aged ten years.

He took ice from the fridge. 'Where's your mother, love?'

'I sent her upstairs to wash her face. She was in a bit of a state.'

'Poor Sue,' he said. 'She's going to take this very hard . . . Will you see to the dinner?'

'Dad, need you ask?'

'That's good, then. Thank the Lord you're here, love. The table's done. I suppose I'd better open the wine . . .'

'I can do that,' Josh offered.

'No, lad, I need something to do. You stay with Sophy. I'll get this back to Paul and go up to see Sue . . .'

As he was halfway out, practicalities hit me. 'Dad, is there a starter?'

He nodded in the vague direction of the fridge. 'I think so, love, avocado or something . . .'

It was actually asparagus, tied in neat bundles for the pan. There was Hollandaise sauce, too, in a covered dish, and a large meringue, presumably intended for the Pavlova that was one of Belinda's favourites. I found prepared raspberries and straw-berries in a glass dish, and another dish of whipped cream, ready for decoration.

All ready for a lovely family dinner. All lovingly prepared for two daughters and their respective beloveds.

I could have wept.

Instead I ransacked cupboards like a demented

burglar. 'For God's sake, there must be some ready-made horseradish somewhere, unless it's in the fridge.' I found a pot with a bare teaspoonful left. 'Stuff it, then, we'll just have to have mustard. Get the mustard out of that cupboard, will you? I've got to put the vegetables on. God, I don't even know what bloody vegetables we're supposed to be having . . .' I rummaged through the fridge bottom drawer and found broccoli and a lump of horseradish.

'Looks like it's under control. Take a look.' At the cooker, Josh was lifting lids off various pans. 'Cauliflower and carrots. I'm not sure what this is.'

I dipped a finger in and licked it. 'Cheese sauce. For the cauliflower. Well, thank God that's done.'

The carrots were cut into fingers, the cauliflower divided into florets, waiting patiently in their cold, salt-water baths. I slung the horseradish into the veggie rack. 'I can't be bothered to grate horseradish. Find that mustard, will you? I've got to get this asparagus on, never mind the gravy . . .'

As I filled a suitable pan with water, Josh produced a jar from the cupboard. 'Not *Dijon*!' I exploded. '*English!* Dad'll never eat French mustard with roast beef!'

Without a word, he put it back.

'I'm sorry,' I said unsteadily, fumbling into oven gloves. 'I shouldn't be taking it out on you.' Yanking the oven open, I made a grab at the roasting tin, burnt my wrist on the shelf and cursed violently.

Josh came to inspect the damage. 'Stick it under the cold tap.'

I was too irritable to take advice. 'It's fine – I'm not going to die of it.'

While I worked with irritable speed he withdrew to a safe distance, sat at the table and fondled Benjy's ears. 'I don't want to get in the way, but if I can do anything, just bleep.'

This only made me feel worse for flying off the handle. 'I can manage, thanks anyway. Would you like another drink?'

'No, I'm fine.'

Still trying to make sense of it all, I stirred the gravy. 'She was mad about him! I just don't understand what went wrong, unless . . .'

'Unless what?'

I hesitated. 'There was obviously an intensely physical buzz between them. If that was wearing off and she'd somehow mistaken it for something more . . .'

'Possible,' he said. 'What did her note say?'

I told him.

After a moment he said, 'What were you going to say, just before your father came in?'

I turned round. Benjy was still sitting quietly at his side. 'I couldn't have said it in front of Dad, but I think she'd have gone through with it even if she'd just found out he had three bigamous wives in the closet. It would have taken a very hard nut to burst Mum's bubble and Belinda's no hard nut. Mum had talked of nothing but the wedding for weeks. It must have felt like being on some sort of rollercoaster. The more it gathered momentum, the more she couldn't get off.'

He stared at me.

'And I bet Dad's thinking exactly the same thing,' I went on. 'Only he'll never say it, not to Mum. She'll work it out for herself sooner or later and feel even worse than she does already.'

Afraid of overcooking it, I whipped the cauliflower off the gas and tested it with a knife. If anything it was underdone but if I put it back I was bound to forget it. The asparagus was coming to the boil; I never knew how long you were supposed to cook the wretched stuff for. Three minutes? Four?

I put the cauliflower into a colander to drain, chopped parsley for the carrots. I worked mechanically, my mind elsewhere. So many things were belatedly clicking: her irritability on the morning; even the way she'd drunk more than usual and laughed uncharacteristically loudly. 'She knew she was making a mistake but she went through with it because she couldn't face the alternative.'

'Then she's a damn good actress. Nobody would have dreamt there was anything wrong.'

'I know, but – oh, *bugger* it, the asparagus . . .' I'd forgotten it now and it *was* overdone.

Muttering curses, I drained it. 'Mum was right – we should have given this lot to Benjy and sent out for an Indian. How am I supposed to keep my mind on asparagus, for God's sake? I could kill Belinda, I really could. Look at this! It's only fit for the waste disposal.'

Over my shoulder, Josh looked. 'Nobody's going to notice. Is everything else ready?'

'As ready as it'll ever be. Go and tell Dad, will you?

Then he can sheepdog everybody to the table for the dinner from hell. The asparagus is disintegrating, the gravy's lumpy and the cauliflower's so *al dente*, it's practically raw.'

With no comment he departed, leaving me to realise that I'd just been sounding exactly like my mother. Unless I dropped the gravy *en route* to the dining room, things couldn't possibly get any worse.

It was the direst dinner I've ever sat through. And I've sat through a dinner where some couple bitched at each other continuously until she told him to bog off, and he bogged. Having tipped the entire table over first, lemon zabaglione and all.

But even that gave us a laugh afterwards. I couldn't see us ever laughing over this.

The table had been laid hours previously and nobody had thought to remove the redundant place setting. I whipped it away – not that it made the slightest difference. Belinda hovered over us like a cloud of noxious gas.

I could never remember our dining room feeling quite like this, even when both grannies were squaring up for battle over Christmas dinner. It was a lovely room, with crimson walls and warm-toned Liberty curtains, but more suited to winter cosiness and candle-light. That night, with the curtains open, the damp, chilly garden seemed to seep through the glass. The actual room temperature had nothing to do with it. Because of the March-like weather the heating was on; a faint, painty scent of hot radiator mingled with roast.

The asparagus wasn't too bad, but might have been turnip sticks for all the pleasure anybody took in it. And later, as Dad carved, Mum fretted. 'I knew I should have done a casserole – a casserole wouldn't have spoilt . . .'

'It's fine,' I soothed.

It was far from her usual pinkly perfect sirloin but Josh, bless his little heart, had seconds. Paul ate little and spoke less, but his glass was refilled more than anybody's. I was afraid of Mum fretting about his low food intake and irritating him beyond endurance. Now and then she could turn into a bit of a Yiddisher momma where food was concerned: '*Eat, eat!*' Tonight, however, she could see that a nice boiled egg wouldn't make anyone feel better.

Even Benjy caught the atmosphere. Not once did he put a paw on anyone's knee, hoping they'd slip him a morsel. He curled up quietly under the table, hoping we'd drop something, instead.

'Why doesn't she *phone*?' Mum fretted, more than once. 'Doesn't she realise how worried we all are?'

Nobody answered. You could hardly say, '*Of course she won't phone yet. She'll be dreading speaking to any of us.*'

Josh was sitting opposite me and I was colossally glad of an ally. Now and then he caught my eye and, just once, gave me an almost imperceptible wink. It wasn't unsuitably jokey, just a 'cheer up, it's not the end of the world' gesture that made me feel marginally better. From Paul, sitting on my left, tension prickled like electric icicles.

Just as we'd nearly finished the main course, Mum

264

framed a tentative question. 'I wonder if it'd be worth phoning any of her friends?'

Paul's tension cracked into irritation. 'How can I? How can I phone her friends and ask if they know where my wife is?'

Mum's lip trembled and poor Dad tried to smooth things. 'I wouldn't think she'd have gone to any friends around here, love.'

'But nearly all her friends are around here,' Mum said plaintively. 'Unless she's gone to any of those girls she met in London. I suppose she might have done that. There was some Trish she got friendly with at that agency . . .'

This was the agency Belinda had worked for during those post-Marc months with me.

She turned to me. 'Do you think she might have done that?'

It was possible. In the circumstances, she'd hardly have gone to anyone round the corner. However . . .

'I don't think she was ever that close to anyone at the agency,' I said, 'and even if she were, I wouldn't have a clue where any of them lived. Lots of her old local friends have moved on. She might have gone to one of them.'

More knife-cutting silence.

When it was time to clear, I hoped for five minutes' respite. 'Let me – I'll see to it.'

Dad, however, was already on his feet. 'No, love, you stay here. I'll give Mum a hand.'

Once the door had closed behind them Paul ran a tense hand through his hair. 'For Christ's sake, how could she *do* this to me? What the hell are people going to think?'

I was glad he was angry; it was easier to cope with than white-faced shock or weepiness. 'They'll just think she's off her head.'

'You reckon?' He re-ran that hand through his hair. 'I don't. They'll think it's me. They'll think I've done something. Or not done something.'

'Of course they won't,' I soothed.

'What do you mean, "of course"?' He turned to me with a savage irritation that almost made me flinch. 'There's no "of course" about it! They'll think it's my fault!'

Josh said, 'There's no need to bite her head off.'

Instantly I felt Paul bristle. I realised then that to him, Josh's mere presence felt like a taunt. *My woman's here – my women don't run off and make me look like a dick.*

If only he knew. I felt awful.

'I'm very sorry,' he said, with sarcastic grit, 'but it may have escaped your notice that I'm not quite my sunny little self this evening. Maybe it wouldn't bother you if your wife ran off and left you after a mere three weeks of marriage, but I'm afraid it bothers me just a bit. It bothers the fuck out of me. It bothers the fuck out of me that people are going to think it's my fault.'

Evenly Josh said, 'If I were in your position, worrying what people were going to think would not be my prime concern.'

I could have kicked him. I tried, missed, and glared, instead. 'Dominic, *please*! You're not helping!'

Paul was positively sparking and I couldn't blame

him. 'Who the hell asked you? I don't need you sticking your smug oar in!'

It was almost a relief when Mum and Dad returned with the Pavlova that nobody could face eating. After that came cheese, that only Dad and Josh touched.

Just as we'd nearly finished, the phone cut the silence like an electric shock. Before anybody else could move, Mum raced to answer it.

We sat on pins.

After less than half a minute she returned, looking hopeless with defeat. 'It was Dorothy Clark, about the day centre coffee rota. I told her I'd ring back on Monday morning.' Again her lip trembled. 'What am I going to tell people?'

She looked so woebegone, I could have cried. As for Dad, he looked as if he'd like to lie down quietly somewhere and die.

'Maybe it'll all sort itself out,' she went on, with a pathetic attempt at optimism. 'Maybe she was just confused.'

'Confused about what?' Paul asked irritably.

She looked down at her plate. 'I don't know, dear.'

I'm sure even the Last Supper must have been more of a laugh than this. Once it was over, I 'volunteered' Josh to help me clear and get the coffee on. With the others safely being miserable in the sitting room, I shut the kitchen door behind us.

'For God's sake, did you have to speak to Paul like that?' I hissed. 'How could you have been so insensitive?'

'He had no call to bite your head off like that!'

267

'He was angry and upset! How the hell would you feel?'

'All right, so I wouldn't like it. But I hope I wouldn't bite heads off, especially not your mother's. She's upset enough as it is.'

'You still should have kept your mouth shut. He feels desperately humiliated already without you making it worse. It's that business at the wedding, isn't it? You just don't like him.'

'I didn't care for him, no. I thought he was bloody rude.'

'He wasn't rude to you, so I don't know why you give a toss.'

Irritably I spooned coffee into the filter and started loading the dishwasher. Benjy sat politely by, hoping his services would be called on. I put the roasting tin on the floor and emptied the leftover gravy into it. This would keep him happily occupied for at least twenty minutes. Benjy believed in doing a thorough job. He'd hold the tin down with one paw and keep at it till only the worst burnt-on bits remained.

Josh passed me plates for loading. 'They'd evidently had a row. If you ask me, he's feeling guilty.'

'I'm sure plenty of people row on their honey-moons. It was more than that. She knew she'd made a mistake.'

'Then why, as you said, make such a drama of it? If you want my opinion, it was a pretty bad row. Bad enough to make her think she had to get away.'

Shocked, I straightened up. 'What are you trying to say?'

'What do you think?'

I felt my colour drain away. 'You don't think he was knocking her about?'

'It might explain it. Why else would he be so worried about what people are going to think?'

It took only seconds for me to get this into perspective. 'For God's sake, you've really got it in for him, haven't you? Just because he was slightly ill-mannered – OK, he *was* – it doesn't mean he's knocking her about!' I carried on dish-loading, 'It's ludicrous.'

'How do you know?' He passed me the gravy boat. 'By your own admission you hardly know him. You said yourself you'd only met him a couple of times before the wedding.'

'It *is* ludicrous.' I straightened up. 'If he'd been knocking her about, she'd have had the perfect excuse for calling it off. Nobody would have blamed her. She must have realised he just wasn't "right", and you can't define not-rightness. She'd have had to say she'd gone off him and then everybody would have got exasperated and asked why the hell she'd got engaged in the first place. Pass me those side plates, please.'

He passed.

'Anyway, she said in her note that it wasn't his fault,' I went on. 'She said he wasn't to blame himself in any way.'

'That means nothing. They say a certain type of woman often blames herself if a man starts using her as a punch-bag. I knew one once; she took it for years and told herself it was her fault, she got on his nerves.

And I'm afraid your sister's got the look of the type of woman who attracts that sort of guy.'

I stared at him. 'What do you mean?'

'I don't quite know.' He paused, his eyes straying to Benjy. 'It's a combination of vulnerability and a certain type of looks.'

A certain type of beauty.

I hated myself for the sharp, green-tipped needle that pierced me. Belinda had 'got' him, too. She had that effect on some men. She appealed to the corny old white knight in them. No wonder he liked to cast Paul as the black Sir Roger de Dastardly.

'You said yourself she's unassertive. You said yourself she expects to get walked on.' He folded his arms and faced me. 'As I said, I've seen the type before. Their very submissiveness attracts bullies. Their willingness to take it can almost make you want to shake them.'

Some tiny trace in his voice told me it wasn't a friend he was talking about, or even a sister, but someone he'd loved in vain. For a moment I saw some fragile, tearful girl with huge eyes, one of them black. *'It's no use, Josh – I love him . . .'*

And, cow that I am, I hated the silly bitch in case he still loved her. I wanted to think of him saying, *'Well, sod you, then. I'm off.'*

But I was supposed to be thinking about someone else. 'Belinda might be unassertive, but she's not a masochist. She'd never take violence.'

Belatedly I remembered the two bunches of flowers Josh had bought, still dumped with everything else in

270

the hall, and shoved them into a bucket of water in the utility room. The coffee was ready, which meant we now had to join the gloom and despondency in the sitting room. 'I don't know how we're going to get through the evening. I can hardly suggest a nice game of Monopoly to pass the time.'

He produced that lethal little half-smile I could have done without. In fact, that was another thing I'd ban if I were a dictator. Men you fancied rotten would be banned from smiling at you like that unless they fancied you back even rottener. Or 'more rottenly', if you insist.

'Cluedo might be more apt,' he said. 'A Bolting Bride version. *I suggest that Belinda bolted to Birmingham, with Bob the Banker*. Sorry,' he added, seeing my face. 'It's no laughing matter.'

It wasn't that. I'd just had an awful thought. Well, two.

Namely, Marc and Rebound.

ELEVEN

But I could hardly discuss them in front of Paul.

If dinner was bad, post-dinner was worse. We sat uncomfortably in the sitting room, Paul resembling a morose stone. I wondered why he didn't just go home but he'd drunk far too much to drive, which would mean a taxi, and they weren't exactly ten a penny on Saturday nights. Besides, he thought Belinda was going to phone and wanted to be on the spot when she did.

No wonder she hadn't. He was hardly going to say, '*Never mind, Sweetheart, no hard feelings.*'

The room, like the hall, was carpeted in soft apricot, and furnished with squashy, comfortable sofas. It was brilliant for big parties, of which they threw plenty, but far too big for five miserable people. The house had been greatly extended when I was sixteen. The sitting room had been made into a huge L shape, and off the short bit of the L was a massive conservatory full of Mum's jungle-sized plants and a fair-sized pool.

The garden went right round the house: lots of lovingly tended lawn and roses, old apple and plum trees at the far end, where wasps had driven us mad during the summer. Near the house was a paved area with built-in barbie. Dad fancied himself at the barbie; it was more his style than formal dinners. He liked a good dozen people, all getting merrily ratso. He liked cooking far more spare ribs and sausages than anybody could possibly eat.

Dad put the television news on, which at least made you realise that things could be worse. There was some dreadful item about three little children dying in a fire. I glanced at Mum and saw her wipe an eye. She'd be feeling guilty, now, to think of some other mother suffering a million times worse than she was.

Benjy paced restlessly from Mum to Dad, sitting at their feet with a polite, hopeful expression, until Mum got the message, 'He wants his walk, poor little boy. Would you and Dominic mind taking him, Sophy?'

I thanked heaven for a minor mercy.

'Do put jackets on,' she called anxiously after us. 'It looks very chilly out.'

I grabbed a navy fleece from my bag, still dumped where I'd left it in the hall. Josh's jacket, a light, lineny thing, was lying over his own bag. 'Aren't you going to put it on?' He was wearing a khaki-ish short-sleeved shirt, no sweater.

He shook his head. 'I've got central heating.'

I didn't push it. I've known men who insist on going without jackets even when it's really freezing, just to prove how toughly macho they are.

On the way out, a thought struck me. 'I'm going to phone home. Belinda didn't know I was going to be here. She might just be trying to ring me.'

I charged upstairs and used my mobile but if she *had* been trying, I didn't find out. Nobody was in, which was not unusual for a Saturday night. I left a message:

273

'I can't explain now, but if Belinda should ring, get a number and phone me here at once. OK?'

God alone knew what Alix and Ace would make of it.

It was a colossal relief to escape. The sky was thick with cloud but there was no wind. The air hung damply around you but it was better than the atmosphere we'd just left.

Benjy charged off instantly, checking whether his Afghan lady friend had passed by lately, or that upstart poodle from down the road. If so, he obliterated his pathetic scent with a far superior one of his own.

'I guess I was a bit over the top with Paul,' Josh said, as we were passing the Freeman residence. 'All right, I don't care for him, but it wasn't very sympathetic in the circumstances. I'll have a word with him when we get back.'

'It might make matters worse. He can obviously sense that you don't like him and I don't think he's exactly in love with you, either. If he thinks you're feeling sorry for him, he'll hate it.'

'Then I'll keep quiet.'

In any case, I thought the damage had been done. '*Benjy*! Don't you *dare*!' I shooed him away from a very dead hedgehog he was about to roll in. 'I've been wondering whether there's an element of rebound here.' I went on to explain the Marc saga. 'Paul would have been precisely what her ego needed. He's exactly the type she used to fall for, who then used to dump her after three weeks.'

He raised an eyebrow.

The chill air snaked around my neck; I walked a

little faster. 'Don't get me wrong – she always had plenty of men after her. She sometimes ended up going out with men she didn't remotely fancy, just because she couldn't bring herself to hurt their feelings by saying no. It led to some awful situations. She wouldn't dare answer the phone because some chap would keep ringing and Mum would constantly have to say she was out, or asleep or whatever. The trouble was, when she *was* keen, she let it show. And then she wasn't a challenge any more. It gives a certain kind of man quite a kick to be able to boast that they dumped someone like Belinda.'

'Maybe it's a case of getting exactly what you want and then finding that you don't want it, after all.'

'Maybe.'

A few yards further on he said, 'Can we walk a bit faster? It's brass monkey stuff.'

I knew it. 'Why on earth didn't you put your jacket on?'

'If we can just stop ambling like a pair of dithery hats, I'll warm up fast enough.'

As he strode on in that blasted route-march fashion, I gave way to wistful thoughts. If he'd made a tiny move, I'd have cuddled up to him. I'd have slipped an arm around him and warmed him up that way.

But he didn't move, damn him.

We must have been half a mile from home when the rain started, just at the point where I'd have turned back. We stopped and looked dubiously up at the grey heavens.

'It's going to chuck it down any minute,' he said. 'Isn't there a pub round the corner?'

'Yes, but I haven't got any money. I didn't think I'd need any.'

'I haven't got much either. I left my wallet in my jacket pocket.' However, he found a few pounds in his trouser pocket and we headed pub-wards.

The Bear was four hundred years old, still untarted up by brewery chains. I half expected the odd vague acquaintance, but nothing to panic about. What I hadn't expected was to see Tamara, in a corner of the saloon bar with a man I didn't know. She saw us first, her eyes widening with agog-type mischief. 'Sophy! And Dominic! Well, blow me down with a feather.'

'We were walking Benjy and it started raining,' I explained.

'Grab a pew, then. This is Bill – Bill, Sophy and Dominic.'

'Hiya,' said Bill, already grabbing pews. He looked like a Bill: earthy, good-natured, and traditionally bloke-ish. The only thing he had remotely in common with Paolo was that they both looked nice. 'He's not much like satin-Latin,' I managed to whisper.

'He's just a friend,' she whispered back and added wickedly, 'I'm saving myself for next weekend.'

'Lucky cow. I wish I had someone to save myself for.'

Suppressing a giggle, she said at normal volume, 'So how are the newlyweds?'

'Fine.' While slipping my fleece off, I shot her a 'look' so pregnant, it might have had twins on the spot.

'Dominic, would you get me a V&T? I'm just off to the loo.'

Of course she followed – Tamara knew a 'look' when she saw it. We found a quiet little corner by the fag machine.

'What?' she whispered, even more agog. 'Josh hasn't got sussed, has he?'

'Even worse. Belinda's done a bunk.'

'*What?*'

I explained the gist and, for the first time in my life, saw Tamara seriously shaken.

'We can't talk here. Why don't you come back to my place?' she whispered. 'It's OK, the old dears are out, so there won't be any nosy ears. Bill's got his wheels so you won't even get wet.'

Within two minutes we were in Bill's beat-up old Land Rover. 'Can I tell him?' Tamara asked. 'I mean both items? He's not local so it won't matter and he'd never blab anyway, would you, Fart-face?'

'I wouldn't dare,' he said. 'Tell me what, anyway? Is it juicy?'

I glanced at Josh, unsure whether he'd want his status on the table.

He didn't seem to mind. 'It's up to you.'

By the time we arrived at Tamara's, Bill was fully filled in.

'Bugger me,' he said. 'Nearly as good as *Brookside*. All we need now is "mareder" and "droogs".'

'And that's a crap Scouse accent,' Tamara said, unlocking the front door.

We sat in the kitchen with Irish coffees – a lot more

277

Irish than coffee, I can tell you. The Dixon kitchen was bigger than ours, done a year later in pale green dragged oak. Mum and Maggie had gone to admire it together, and Maggie had been very effusive and obliquely implied that dragged oak was more up-market than antique pine. (The Freeman kitchen was dragged oak, too.) Mum had naturally been very miffed about this. 'Even if we'd wanted one, we couldn't possibly have had a painted finish,' she'd huffed afterwards. 'Just think what Benjy's claws would have done to it!'

'I still can't believe it,' Tamara said.

'I don't see why not,' Bill said. 'You weren't that struck with him.'

It was my turn to be shaken. 'Tamara! You never said!'

'I didn't *dis*like him,' she said defensively. 'I just wasn't over-keen.'

'You thought he was a prat,' said Bill.

'So did you!'

I was gaping from one to the other like a Wimbledon umpire.

'Well, I could hardly *say* anything,' she pointed out. 'I could hardly tell her I wasn't too keen on her fiancé. You don't, do you?' She shot Bill a glance. 'Bill met him just the once. We all had a drink together a few weeks before the wedding. He didn't do anything, exactly; it wasn't anything you could really put your finger on . . .'

Bill took over. 'He was just a bit patronising. To Belinda, I mean. Implied that she didn't know what she was talking about. She didn't say anything – just looked into her glass and shut up. I felt sorry for her.'

'So did I,' Tamara confessed. 'I know he's very good-looking and earning loads and all that, but I was never sure they were really suited.'

'Looks like you were right,' Bill said.

I explained the stick whose wrong end I'd grabbed so spectacularly.

Tamara said, 'You mustn't feel bad. I expect I'd have thought exactly the same.'

'That's what I told her,' Josh said. 'Belinda's not a kid.'

I dare say it's all very easy with hindsight, but for the past few hours I'd been looking back and picking up on tiny negatives I'd unconsciously registered about Paul. It wasn't just that incident at the wedding. An ounce too much confidence here, an ounce too little humour there, a *soupçon* of arrogance . . . I suppose I'd ignored them because I'd wanted to like him properly, for Belinda's sake. On the surface, after all, he'd been the man who had everything, and when a man like that's besotted with a sister who's apparently equally besotted, you don't look for pinpricks to bitch about.

After we'd discussed it some more, Tamara said, 'Talking of runaway wives, Sarah's done a bunk, too.'

'She hasn't!' I gaped.

'She has. Little brother apparently wanted a few thousand to start a business – one of those wonderful businesses where you get rich in three months without actually having to do any work. James was actually going to give it to him and Sarah went ape. She's gone off to some friend in Normandy while James sorts his priorities out.'

It wasn't *schadenfreude* exactly, as I really do like Sarah, but being nominally human I couldn't help thinking that at least this would stop Maggie looking so smug when Mum was eventually obliged to tell her about Belinda. If Maggie was in the picture, of course.

'Do her folks know?'

'Yes, and all hell broke loose, apparently. Sarah hadn't told James where she was going so he phoned Maggie, thinking she'd be there, and Maggie got in a right old tizz, wondering where the hell she was. So Zoe had to tell her what had been going on – she'd known all along, of course. And of course Maggie had hysterics and gave Zoe merry hell for not having told her before, and Zoe completely lost her rag and said why was she taking it out on *her*, and banged the phone down. She then phoned Sarah and gave *her* hell for landing her in it, and Sarah phoned last night and told me.'

'Like I said, *Brookside*'s got nothing on this place,' Bill said blithely. To Josh he added, 'Sooner you than me, that's all I can say. Do you get danger money for coming into a war zone?'

He gave a wry little smile. 'Not even a flak jacket.'

The mention of money made me feel awkward. 'He could have done with a flak jacket over dinner,' I said. 'He upset Paul. I thought he was going to thump him.'

'Don't exaggerate,' he said. 'He just wanted someone to take it out on.'

I glanced at him, and then at Tamara. 'Josh doesn't

like him. It was something at the wedding.'

'It wasn't just that. I didn't take to him.'

'Neither did I,' Bill said frankly. 'Right up his own, high-flying little arse, if you ask me.'

Tamara said, 'Honestly, I haven't heard one other person say a *thing*.'

'Well, they won't, will they?' Bill said. 'The women all think he's God's gift, and if the blokes say anything, it'll be to other blokes. If they said anything to women they'd just think they're jealous because he's good-looking and earning a bomb.'

'It's just the same with you lot,' she retorted. 'If a woman's really attractive but obviously a complete bitch, and we say anything to a bloke, he just thinks we're jealous. Blokes can never see through bitches.'

'Too right,' I said, thinking of Bitch-face who'd stolen Kit.

It was well past ten when we got back, but the atmosphere had eased a fraction, if only because Paul was absent. 'He's gone to bed,' Mum said. 'He must have been so tired, poor boy, never mind all the upset . . . You didn't get wet, did you?'

'No, we nipped into The Bear and some chap of Tamara's gave us a lift. It's all right,' I added, seeing her face, 'I didn't say a word.'

This lie failed to soothe her. 'Whatever am I going to tell people?' she fretted.

'The truth,' Dad said wearily. 'What else can you tell them?'

I sat on the sofa. Josh sat beside me and stretched his

281

arm along the back of it in such a way that his hand just brushed my hair. This was quite enough to get my flutters going, so I sat a little forward. In the circumstances I couldn't cope with it.

Mum lowered her voice. 'I couldn't say anything before, not with poor Paul here, but I've been wondering whether Marc's at the bottom of it.'

I wasn't surprised that the same Awful Thought had occurred to her. I'd only met Marc once but the negatives I'd registered about him had rather exceeded those about Paul. Still, if Belinda had left a reasonable bloke for a worse one, she'd only be about the squillionth woman in the history of this earth to do so.

'I never liked that Marc,' Mum went on. 'There was something about his eyes. He was two-timing her, you know, with that Melanie. I never liked her either. Too much make-up. I'd never have trusted that girl an inch.'

As if Paul were about to appear, she lowered her voice again. 'If you ask me, Marc's exactly the type to resent the fact that she was happy with somebody else. I wouldn't put it past him to try to spoil it for her. Dog in the manger, you know. He didn't want her, but he didn't want anybody else to have her either.'

'If she really *had* been happy with Paul, Marc wouldn't have been able to mess it up,' I pointed out. 'But if she'd already been having second thoughts . . .'

'I knew she was rushing it,' Dad said heavily. 'I thought it all along.'

'Ted!' Mum turned to him, bewildered. 'You never said a word!'

'How could I?' For the first time, he sounded irritable. 'Everybody else seemed happy as Larry. You were, Belinda apparently was, even Coral was.' Coral was the cleaning lady. 'Paul certainly was,' he went on. 'He was the one who rushed it, as far as I could see. I'm sure Belinda would have been happy to wait for a slot at St Luke's.'

'I thought you were glad she wasn't getting married at St Luke's! You don't like the vicar!' Mum turned to me. 'Daddy didn't like what he said at Fred Stevenson's funeral. Thought it was too much like sermonising.'

'I couldn't give a bugger about the vicar! I'd have been pleased for her to get married in McDonald's, as long as she was happy!' Obviously conscious of upsetting Mum further, he lowered his voice. 'I'm sorry, love, but it's no use fretting now.' He rose heavily to his feet. 'I'm off to bed. Good night, everybody.'

Once he'd gone, Mum's face reverted to its former anxiety and bewilderment. 'I do just wish Daddy had *said* something. I mean, I sometimes wondered whether they were rushing it, too. Once or twice I thought . . .' Her voice trailed off. 'Well, it hardly matters now.'

I had to ask. 'What did you think?'

She gave a deep sigh. 'I know it sounds silly now, but I did think she might be pregnant and didn't like to say anything beforehand. Older people can still be funny about these things. My mother would certainly have had something to say.'

Yes, she most certainly would.

'When she started getting tired and irritable I thought it might be her hormones,' she went on. 'It takes some people like that: I even said it to her in a jokey kind of way; even her dress seemed to confirm it.'

With evident effort she brisked herself up. 'Well, it's obviously not that, and just as well. Thank heaven I didn't say anything to anybody.'

Eventually the question I'd been dreading came up. 'I do hope it wasn't because of me,' she said plaintively. 'She might have thought I'd be terribly disappointed if it was all cancelled. You don't think it was because of me, do you?'

What could I say? 'Of course not. She probably thought it was just cold feet. She thought they'd warm up, only they just got colder.'

'But why doesn't she *phone*?' As if it could answer, she cast pleading eyes at the telephone on the side table. 'I suppose she's afraid to. What on earth is she going to say to Paul? I hope it's not Daddy she's afraid of, after all that money he spent. I know he can hardly be pleased, but he hasn't said a word. And the presents. All those presents'll have to go back . . .'

'I wouldn't worry about the presents,' Josh said. 'These things happen.'

Since she looked almost pathetically grateful for this I thought another crumb was in order. Briefly I related the Freeman saga but Mum's embryonic *schadenfreude* seemed to have disappeared as completely as Belinda.

284

'Maggie must be so worried but at least they know where she is,' she fretted. 'I do wish Belinda'd *ring* – I can't bear to think of her all alone somewhere and feeling too dreadful to pick up a phone . . .'

'She'll be with friends somewhere,' I soothed.

'Yes, but *who*?'

I tried to control an increasing sense of exasperation. 'I don't know, Mum. If I did, I'd be ringing them.' After a moment I added, 'What about Granny's lunch tomorrow?'

'Daddy cancelled the table. We weren't going to tell her till tomorrow morning anyway, so at least she won't be disappointed. Not about that, anyway.' She gave a deep sigh. 'I suppose I might as well go to bed. Will you lock up, dear?'

'Of course.'

'Night-night, then.'

As she came to bestow the usual kiss, Josh stood up. 'Good night, Mrs Metcalfe. I hope you get some sleep.'

After that, she just had to peck his check, too. 'I'm so glad you two are here – I don't know what we'd have done without you.'

I felt like Judas.

At the door she paused. 'Oh, by the way, I put Paul in the torture chamber – it seemed silly for him to have the double and in the circumstances I didn't quite like to put him in Belinda's room. All your things are up there – Daddy took them up while you were out.' For the first time since we'd arrived, she almost smiled. 'Nighty-night, then. Sleep tight.'

The door went 'click' behind her.

I gaped after her, appalled.

Josh was similarly gaping. 'What the hell does she mean, "torture chamber"?'

'That's what Dad calls it. It's a mini-gym with a bed.'

'Oh.' He looked decidedly relieved, which was more than I was.

'You don't get it, do you? She's put Paul in the torture chamber and us in the spare double. Double *bed*.'

I wouldn't say it was exactly horror on his face; it had more of an *Oh Christ, what have I done to deserve this?* flavour.

For want of anywhere better to put it – e.g. in the gas oven – I put my head in my hands. 'I might have *known* she'd do this. I just never *thought* . . .'

He was still upright, hands thrust in his pockets. 'I hope you're not one of those women who thrash around and hog the covers.'

Naturally I put him straight. 'There's no way we're sharing a bed! I'll sleep in Belinda's room and tell Mum I had to, you were snoring like a pig.'

'I'm not snoring just to be convenient!'

'Grinding your teeth, then!' I hissed. 'Does it matter?'

Two seconds later, the door opened again.

The atmosphere must have been hanging in the air like fag smoke. Mum stood uncertainly on the threshold, looking from me to Josh and back again. 'Is anything wrong, dear?'

I produced an inane little laugh. 'Of course not. He was just telling me to stop endlessly going on about my weight.'

'Thank heaven for that – I really couldn't bear it if you two fell out, too. I just came to say that there's only a thin summer duvet on that bed – it might not be enough now the weather's turned chilly but there are plenty of spare quilts in the ottoman.'

'Thanks, Mum, we'll be fine.'

Halfway to the door she stopped again. 'I'm sure I won't be able to get to sleep for hours and then Daddy'll start snoring and I'll never get off – I'll have to go and sleep in Belinda's room. I do wish he'd go and see someone about his sinuses. Anyway, no use worrying about that now – I'll go up. Night-night.'

For about thirty seconds after she'd left, we stared at the door. The way things were going she might pop back with an '*Oh, by the way, if you want the electric blanket . . .*'

In fact it was a very useful interlude. By the time our eyes swivelled back to each other my brain was back in working order. 'I've got it all under control.' I said, in my best matter-of-fact tones. 'I'll make a bed up on the floor with the spare quilts and she'll never know the difference.'

'Haven't you got an "old" room you can use?'

It was my turn to be stung. 'If you're afraid *I'm* going to snore and fart all night, I'll get the tent out of the loft and sleep in the garden!'

'Calm down,' he said, in that infuriating male way that only makes you more livid. 'I only asked.'

'My "old" room's full of junk,' I went on testily, and explained briefly about HRT/Horlicks and Trudi. 'So you'll just have to lump it.'

'Fine – whatever you like.' So saying, he sat down. Not beside me, where he'd sat before, but on the other sofa about three miles away.

Fine. Suit yourself.

I glanced at my watch, 'You go up, if you want. You can have the bed. I'm not going up yet. I'd never sleep.'

'Neither would I.'

Benjy slunk over to him in that deferential, I-hope-I'm-not-bothering-you way, and Josh obliged with an ear-fondle. I could have done with some ears to fondle. In certain circumstances dogs can perform the same function as a fag: calm you down and give you something to do with your hands. And I'd left my emergency fags at home, in the blithe confidence that they wouldn't be needed. Which just goes to prove that if you don't have insurance, something's bound to go wrong.

For the fiftieth time, I wondered where on earth Belinda was. 'Half of me could kill her for making all this trouble. The other half . . .'

He raised an eyebrow. 'What?'

'I don't know.' Restlessly I fidgeted in my chair. 'I hope she's not on her own, that's all. You know what it's like when you've done something really stupid and there's nobody to talk to. It seems like the end of the world.'

'Then let's hope she's holed up with a friend.'

'Yes.'

'And let's hope the friend gives her a minor rollocking and tells her she should have had the guts to call it off.'

I was glad he wasn't bending over backwards in poor-little-Belinda indulgence, but I wasn't going to say so. 'You've changed your tune, haven't you? A couple of hours ago you were accusing Paul of knocking her about.'

'I still wouldn't entirely rule out something of the sort, even if only in the future. He doesn't appreciate being made a fool of.'

This made me uneasy again, in case she was terrified of facing him. 'Maybe she couldn't face telling him she couldn't go through with it. Maybe she thought it was easier to disappear while they were away. If she knew he was going to be gone for hours, it gave her time to organise it. Though I still can't see her coolly phoning the airport and calling a cab. She's much more the type to agonise for hours and still do nothing at the end of it.' I glanced at the silent phone. 'No wonder she hasn't phoned. She must be dreading speaking to any of us.'

'She'll be waiting for the flak to clear.' He was still fondling Benjy, who was being thoroughly disloyal, gazing up at him as if he were the best thing since dried-tripe treats. Typical faithless male.

I pointed the remote at the television. 'I don't know about you, but I could do with some light relief. There must be something worth watching, preferably a really brainless comedy.'

After a minute's channel-hopping I found an old *Dracula*, just starting. 'This should be good for a laugh, not that I laughed the last time I saw it. It absolutely freaked me out – I couldn't sleep for a week. I had to wear my gold cross all night and sneak some garlic from the kitchen to smear around my bedroom door. I locked the windows, too, in case he sneaked in that way, as a bat.' I could almost have laughed, remembering it. 'Mum wondered why on earth my bedroom was suddenly smelling of garlic. I had to tell her in the end.' Catching Josh's eye, I added, 'I was only about ten, in case you're wondering. I'd seen it at a friend's house, on a sleepover.'

'I hope she didn't laugh.'

'She'd never have laughed at things like that – not in front of me, anyway.'

Trying to put Belinda out of my mind, I concentrated on *Dracula*. It was all so corny – the dark, creepy forest, the scary, Gothic castle . . .

Josh seemed less absorbed. After a couple of minutes he wandered to a side table, where assorted silver-framed photos sat. Me and Belinda, of course, at various stages from gap-toothed baby to school-uniformed eight-year-olds with new second teeth we had yet to grow into. Later, at just eighteen, we'd both been 'done' by a professional. I have to say that mine was my best photo ever. I'd been a lot slimmer then, even in the face. At the time Mum had said, 'Well, he's definitely caught something, though I'm not sure what.'

I'd known. I'd been immensely proud of it. Just beneath the innocence had been a whisper of wicked woman waiting to get out. Actually, she *had* got out; I'd just discovered what 'doing it' was like, with Malcolm Parker from the tennis club. I wouldn't say it was exactly sparks-and-fireworks stuff, but at least it had put me out of my wondering misery.

As Josh wandered round the corner of the L, I reabsorbed myself in *Dracula*. It was all coming back to me. A party of assorted upper-crusts was lost in the forest, with no transport. And what should happen along but a spare coach drawn by funereal black horses? Very handy.

Just as I was getting into the film, he returned. 'You didn't tell me there was a pool!'

'Why would I? You don't want to swim, do you?'

'I wouldn't mind, unless it's purely for decoration.'

'Of course it isn't. They both use it.'

'I could use some exercise.' He nodded at the television. 'I'm afraid I'm not into fangs and stakes through the heart.'

'Then feel free. That's what it's there for.'

Of course I hadn't mentioned the pool. I was long past the stage of thinking it anything special. Belinda and I had wanted an outdoor one but Dad had said it would be a waste of money, given the lousy weather. We'd have far more fun with an indoor one.

And he'd been right, but not perhaps in quite the way he'd imagined. In my wild and wicked teens I'd thrown some brilliant parties round that pool when Mum and Dad had been away. They'd have had to be away, I can tell you. Nobody had ever actually puked into the water, but there had been a couple of near misses and I'd always had to retrieve assorted fag ends from the plant pots, never mind beer cans and the odd bikini top from the bottom of the pool.

The way my sinful mind worked, it wasn't long before it started up-dating the wet-and-wild scenario. This was a purely hypothetical exercise, of course; I'd never have joined him, even if he'd asked. I didn't have a cozzie. I dare say there'd have been one somewhere: a too-small one of Belinda's which I'd have been bursting out of in all directions, looking even less gorgeously appetising than on the common.

Come to think of it, he wouldn't have a cozzie, either. Was he even now doing an *au naturel* front crawl? Or would he have kept his bottoms on, in case I came sneaking a look?

Trying to banish these unseemly thoughts, I concentrated on Count Dracula, who hadn't actually appeared yet. The sun had long gone down, which meant that somewhere in the mouldering cellars, something had recently roused from its coffinly slumbers, feeling a bit peckish.

The atmosphere was steadily building till I was having heart failure every time anyone rounded a corner in that creepy castle. As I recalled exactly what was about to happen, it started freaking me out all over again. It was freaking me out so much, I chickened out and changed channels.

It suddenly occurred to me that I hadn't given Josh a towel. Given that he might have stripped right off, should I take him one? Would it look like Peeping Tomette stuff, or would *not* taking it make me look like a prude who was terrified of catching Unseemly Glimpses?

Finally, why the hell was I tizzing in the first place?

I was beginning to remind myself of the heroine of some dopey Victorian novel: *Gentle reader, our sweet Sophia durst not venture thither. Her virgin heart trembled, lest the lordly Josh should have cast off his breeches.*

Oh, sod it.

I zapped the television, raced upstairs to the airing cupboard, and raced down again.

The conservatory looked almost tropically enticing. I'd forgotten to tell him where the pool light switches were, but he'd evidently found them; the water was as sparkly turquoise as anything in a holiday brochure. At the near end was a rattan table and chairs, where Mum and Dad often had their breakfast. Beyond the glass doors the garden looked black as Dracula's forest.

He was still swimming, a head-in-the-water front crawl, his head like a wet, brown seal. His clothes were flung over a chair, except for one item, which was white and still covering the basics. And just as well, since I wouldn't have been brazen enough to stand there gawping otherwise.

I waited till he stopped at the far end, shook the water from his head, and turned around.

'Sorry – I forgot to give you a towel,' I called, cool as lime sorbet.

'I'd have used my shirt.' So saying, he hauled himself out and walked around the side towards me.

While he was still three paces distant I tossed him the towel. 'There you go. I hope it was warm enough.'

'It was fine.' Slinging the towel around his neck, he held on to the ends. 'How's the film?'

'Rubbish – I switched it off. I wouldn't mind going

to bed now, only I have to wait for you so I can set the burglar alarm.'

'I'll be two minutes.'

'Would you like anything before we go up? Another malt? A nice cup of cocoa?'

'No, thanks.'

'Then I'll go and put Benjy to bed.'

I should have let him dry himself on his shirt. I don't know why wet fanciable men should stir the hormones more than dry ones, but I don't recommend an eyeful when you're trying to pretend he turns you on about as much as one of Benjy's rainy-day bones. I wouldn't say his white boxers were exactly transparent, but I don't think they'd have been a fit sight for Sweet Sophia.

I gave Benjy a Bonio (he always had to have a little bedtime snack) and he took himself to his basket. After this he expected a good-night kiss. If there were bedtime stories for dogs, he'd have had one of those, too. He'd have enjoyed a stirring tale about some valiant hound who did battle with the dreaded vacuum cleaner and actually killed it, instead of merely hiding behind a sofa and barking whenever it dared to come near.

As I was checking the back door, Josh entered. I set the alarm. The house was hushed. We crept upstairs, past another of Mum's monster plants on the landing. The guest double was at the back of the house, over-looking the garden. It had recently been re-vamped in blue and white, with a shower room added. At the end of the bed stood a white cane ottoman, containing the quilts. On the floor, neatly placed, were the bags we'd dumped in the hall.

'Right,' I said, all brisk and practical. 'If you want to use the bathroom, I'll make this bed up.'

By the time he emerged, I'd done a reasonable job with two cover-less duvets and an old eiderdown.

He inspected my handiwork. 'I'll sleep on the floor.'

'No, you won't.'

'Sophy, I—'

'Will you please stop *arguing*?' My latent tension erupted into a hiss. 'I'm going for a wash. Just go to bed, will you?'

I'd just had another thought that would have caused Sweet Sophia to call for the smelling salts. The nightie I'd brought was slinky, full-length chocolate satin, with tiny shoestring straps and a slashed-to-the-minimum bodice. In short, the kind of thing you might take on a 'clean' weekend in the hope of turning it really filthy. It had been a birthday present from Mum, not long after I'd 'met' Dominic. She had bought it, I swear, in order to encourage a healthy sex life with someone who might just ". . . *come to something, touch wood, because if she doesn't get a move on . . .*"

I'd only brought it so that she could see I was actually wearing it. And now I'd have to emerge from the bathroom with half my tits hanging out, whereupon Josh would think I was trying to drive him wild with lust, panic, throw himself out of the window, and kill himself.

However, help was at hand. Hanging behind the door was a dressing gown Mum had bought for her mother and then not bestowed. 'I think maybe it's a bit too old-dear-ish,' she'd said dubiously. 'What do you think? You know how she hates anything frumpy.'

I had thought it perhaps suitable for a one-hundred-and-three-year-old who was past caring. It was fleecy baby-blue, ankle length, with a high neck and long cuffed sleeves to trail in your Horlicks.

I emerged from the bathroom primly buttoned in baby-blue, but I needn't have bothered. Josh was already in bed, his head turned away from me.

I was under those duvets in three seconds. 'Could you turn that bedside light off, please?'

He clicked it. 'Good night.'

'Good night.'

Half an hour later I was beginning to have sympathy with that princess who had trouble with a pea under her twenty feather beds. Scores of fossilised prunes seemed to be lurking in the eiderdown. Besides which, I was wide awake. With such assorted thoughts to cope with, how could any brain switch off? Belinda. Paul. Mum worrying to death about where she was and what she was going to tell Maggie Freeman. Amongst all these darted two male visions. First, a wetly edible one in wet white boxers: second, a dark-cloaked one with chilling eyes, about to open his mouth . . .

I actually started wondering whether I'd left any windows open downstairs. A bat could crawl in anywhere and supernatural beings wouldn't set the burglar alarm off. Still, there was always Benjy. It was a well-known fact that dogs could sense evil presences and would bark their heads off. They sensed ghosts, anyway. On the other hand, maybe it didn't work for vampires. Maybe, like Crocodile Dundee, Dracula had power over animals. Maybe poor Benjy was even now lying bloodless in his basket, while the evil Undead was creeping up the stairs . . .

Funnily enough, my mind didn't dwell long on Undead Dracula. I wouldn't say he was thrashing around, exactly, but the evidently Unsleeping Josh was shifting restlessly under the covers. It was horribly unsettling for my imagination, which is ill-disciplined at the best of times. With touchy-feely special effects it kept re-running our rampant snog, wondering exactly how he'd slip a bra-strap off a shoulder, and having done so . . .

Such wriggly-making stuff was hardly conducive to restful sleep. In fact, I'd just got to a really good bit in that colliding-in-the-corridor fantasy when an exasperated voice wrecked it.

'Sophy! You're thrashing around like a hooked salmon!'

'I am not!'

'You are. Come on, change places. You're obviously not comfortable and more to the point, you're keeping me awake.'

If he hadn't said that, I might have given in. 'Tough! Count sheep! Or dithery old ladies in woolly hats. I'm not moving.' I turned away from him and wriggled myself back under the covers. 'And don't hiss at me like that again! I was just nodding off!'

*

After waking I lay for a moment in that dozy, uneasy consciousness of something awful having happened, but you can't quite remember what.

After Belinda a secondary nightmare hit me. Beds! What was I doing in the bed?

I peered over the side. He was quite still, his head, turned away from me. For a hideous moment I had visions of him lifting my dead weight in the middle of the night and suffering a heart attack as a result.

Thank God, I could just about see the duvet moving as he breathed.

Phew. On the other hand, there was an element of Sod's law here. A man I fancied the pants off had scooped my skimpily clad body into his arms in the middle of the night and I hadn't been awake to enjoy it.

Typical.

As I watched, he stirred slightly, shifted sleepily for a moment and opened his eyes. Just as mine had, they blinked dozily for a second or two before coming into focus.

He turned his head a fraction, saw me, and closed his eyes again. 'Oh Christ. It's coming back to me.'

Well, thank you so frightfully much. I raised myself further on my elbow. 'What the hell are you doing on the floor?'

'Trying to sleep.' With that, he turned on his side, away from me, and pulled the covers up to his chin.

I was incensed. 'Josh!'

'For God's sake, it's the middle of the night. Go back

to sleep.'

'It's ten past eight!'

'It's also Sunday morning.' This came in muffled tones from under the covers.

I was miffed enough to make a stinging retort. 'If you manhandled me in the middle of the night, I hope you've done your back in. Why didn't you do as you were told and stay put?'

'Because you were thrashing. And I didn't manhandle you.' He turned back towards me. 'I took your hand and said, "Come on, Sophy, into beddy-byes, there's a good girl." And up you got, like the sweet, obedient child you probably never were, and let me tuck you in. QED. And finally, I got some sleep.'

I eyed him boldly, in a refusing-to-believe-it manner. 'I don't believe a word of it.'

Propping himself on his elbow, Josh eyed me right back. 'You can believe what you like. I never do things the hard way, if there's an easy one.'

Somehow, I could believe this all too well.

'So I'm sorry to disappoint you,' he went on, 'but my back is still in perfect working order. Although I have to say . . .' his eyes dropped fleetingly from my face, '. . . I might just have managed to manhandle you without doing myself a mischief.'

'You want a bet?' I don't know why I said this. It was provocative, a challenge.

Well, that's a lie – I do know. Just before I'd said it, something had changed. I'd sensed it in the air between us, in the suddenly quivering line between my eyes and his. Only it had taken a moment for it to

299

register.

'Why?' he said. 'Do you?'

Once again, very fleetingly, his eyes dropped from my face. Suddenly I was acutely conscious of my body. Or to be precise, of my abundant left bosom, most of which was falling out of the side of my nightie.

He raised his eyes.

I don't know why hot flushes are supposed to be confined to the menopause. Just then I had the hot flush to end them all, only I don't think it actually showed on my face. I flooded with it.

In the circumstances, my voice came out reasonably normally. 'I'm going to get up.' I swung my legs out of bed and went to draw the curtains.

I opened a window wide. I needed the oxygen.

My legs felt most odd. One was saying to the other, 'I do a good jelly impression – can you do wet cotton wool?'

He hadn't moved, but he was still watching me; I could feel it. He was watching my every move.

I'd intended to charge straight into the bathroom, but I didn't. Perhaps I'd never really intended to at all. I just stood there, quivering with awareness and gazing almost unseeing over the dewy garden. I don't know where I found a voice, but it was more or less working. 'There's a squirrel. Digging a hole in the lawn.'

'Is there?'

'If Benjy sees it, he'll go mad.'

'Will he?'

I heard the rustle as he stood up. I heard his soft footfalls as he crossed the room. I felt him come to stand just behind me.

Like my legs, my voice was almost giving out. 'I'm sorry I kept you awake. I was probably having nightmares. About Dracula. The film started freaking me out again. That was why I switched it off.'

'You should have told me.'

Apart from tiny crisscross straps, the nightie was virtually backless. I could almost feel his body heat, right behind me. 'I didn't want you thinking I was a complete idiot.'

'I wouldn't have thought that.' Very softly, he blew on the hair at the back of my neck. 'I'm scared of the dark.'

I was woozing for England. 'Liar.'

'I am,' he said. 'Now and then.'

My heart was going boom-*boom*, boom-*boom*, like tribal drums. '"Scared" now and then, or "liar" now and then?'

'Both,' he said, very softly. 'Just like you.'

Like a fingertip whisper on my shoulder, he adjusted the left-hand strap of my nightie by a millimetre. 'It was about to slither down,' he murmured, in a voice that matched the touch exactly. 'Can't have that, can we?'

Never before had such an infinitesimal touch, or a voice, had such a powerfully erotic effect on me. As an old Irish friend once put it, "Jesus, Mary and Joseph, if ever I felt like having the arse shagged off me . . ."

301

'Perish the thought,' I said unsteadily. 'That's the trouble with satin. You've only got to breathe on it and it slithers right off.'

'Dangerous stuff,' he murmured. 'I should get shot of it, if I were you.'

My eyes closed. I wanted to scream, '*Go on!*'

TWELVE

It was just as well I didn't.

The tap at the door froze us both. 'Sophy? Are you awake, love?'

From somewhere I found a dozy, just-waking up voice. 'Yes, Dad, just about . . .'

'I'm just going down to make Mum a cup of tea. Would either of you like one?'

Tea. God help me. 'Yes, lovely – I'll be down in a minute.'

As he clumped off down the landing, neither of us moved. It was as if the electricity was hovering on the edge, waiting for a nudge. So I nudged it. I said, 'Would you actually like a cup of tea?'

Of course I didn't *mean* this to sound like, 'Would you actually like a cup of tea?' I was fully expecting a rough negative, followed by firm grabbings, slitherings of satin and rampant abuse of Mum's nice new John Lewis covers. Only unfortunately, it went wrong on the way out.

The effect was like a dose of Thrill-Kill spray.

'I'd rather have a coffee. Dark brown, no sugar.'

He said it in such nearly normal tones, I might even have imagined that oasis of electricity. I knew I hadn't, but I couldn't have shattered it better if I'd tried.

He melted away. I heard the bed creak as he got into it.

I don't know what I was expecting when I eventually turned around. If he'd been looking at me I might have seized the initiative after all, grabbed it by the balls, so to speak, but he wasn't. On the far side of the bed from where I'd been lying, he was semi-propped on an elbow, frowning as he tried to tune the radio on the bedside table. I'm afraid to say I instantly wondered whether this position was concealing evidence of mini-tents thrusting under the covers, but I suppose if things had got to that stage he'd have disappeared into the bathroom.

'Jesus,' he muttered, re-tuning rapidly as some hymn-singing Sunday service blared out.

Even if Benjy hadn't chosen that moment to pay his traditional morning call, I knew the moment had passed. There was a scratching at the door, followed by a sharp, '*Oi!*' type woof.

'Dad's let him out of the kitchen,' I said, like an idiot. 'He wants to come in for a cuddle.'

Still tuning, Josh wasn't looking at me. 'Well, don't mind me.'

Benjy bounded in, full of doggy beans, and greeted me with lavish, wet licks.

I went straight to the bathroom. When I emerged, re-buttoned in baby-blue, Benjy was flopped beside Josh, looking the picture of canine chilled-out-ness. He wore a lollopy grin that said. *Coming to join us? I do like being all cosy in the middle*.

If Josh was still suffering from *coitus frustratus*, my

304

novel attire took his mind off it. His mouth flickered with what I can only describe as cynical disbelief. 'That's not yours, is it?'

'Are you kidding? It's a spare.'

'It should go straight in the bin.'

'Waste not, want not,' I tutted. 'Come on Benjy, you horrible animal.'

As I padded downstairs in bare feet, with Benjy padding beside me, I didn't altogether regret that dose of Thrill-Kill, after all. There was still the little matter of his fat cash fee in my bag. How would I have felt afterwards, handing that over? And then there was Ace. I wouldn't have wanted Josh thinking I cheated on my men at the drop of a pair of knickers.

I'd have to come clean, sharpish.

Apart from all that, I'd have felt horribly guilty, doing anything so wickedly yummy with Belinda's disappearance hanging over us like a noxious cloud.

At least, that's what I was telling myself.

In pyjamas and dressing gown, Dad was busy with cups and so on, his back to me. Paul was up, too. In a silky, knee-length dressing gown, he was sitting at the table with the *Sunday Times*.

'How did you sleep?' I asked.

He barely raised his head. 'How do you think?'

'Sorry.' If I'd been thinking I'd never have asked such a stupid question, but my thoughts had been elsewhere. I'd like to say they were nobly concerned with the current family crisis, or even with how best to murder Belinda when she deigned to show up, but they weren't. They were on shivering touches and matters relating to tent-poles. Then again, they were also on enigmatic Russians and Jerry's 'bet' remarks.

Over his shoulder, Dad glanced at me. 'It's just about ready, love. How does he like it?'

'Actually, Dad, I'll put some coffee on – Josh prefers coffee.'

Until they both turned to me with *What?* type frowns, I didn't even realise I'd said it.

I could have died.

'It's just a daft nickname.' Thanking heaven for his foresight, I produced a bright smile. 'After the Jericho Joshua, remember? He used to play the trumpet and drive his family crackers.'

Dad gave me a smile that shot me through with guilt. 'A bit like you, love, and your violin.'

'You said it.'

I wasn't so sure Paul had bought it. Conscious of his suddenly narrowed eyes, I went to put the coffee on. 'Anything interesting in the paper?' I called, like an idiot.

'No.'

Dad fussed about for a few more minutes, looking for fat-free biscuits, tea cosy, and so on. When all was ready, he grabbed the *Mail on Sunday* and departed.

Left with Paul, I felt acutely uncomfortable. While waiting for the coffee, I heard him rise from the table. I knew he was standing against the worktop, watching me.

My mouth was suddenly desiccated. 'Like a coffee?'

'I've had one.' After a moment he went on, 'Josh is

rather a weird nickname for a Dominic, when you think about it.'

I grabbed a couple of mugs from the tree. 'It's not weird at all. In fact, I know a David who's commonly known as Chip. Don't ask me why.'

Please, please, go back to the paper.

'Where did you say he works?'

My mind went a complete, panicky blank. 'God, I don't know. I can never remember – he hardly ever talks shop . . .' I don't know where the name came from but it zoomed into the void and saved me. 'Price Waterhouse, that's it . . .'

With a harassed expression, Dad came back. 'I forgot the Sweetex. She's on a blasted diet again . . .'

While he searched and muttered I grabbed our mugs and legged it, my heart pounding like racehorse hoofs.

Halfway up the stairs I realised what I'd said.

I stopped dead, my eyes closing in sheer, God-awful realisation.

Shit. Shit-shit-shit-shit . . .

Josh was up, in just the trousers he'd come up in. I handed him the mug. 'I think I'm going to throw up. I just told Paul you worked for Price Waterhouse.'

'They're chartered accountants, for God's sake!'

'I *know*, for God's sake!'

Too late, I was thinking of Goldman Sachs. 'I couldn't think straight! I called you Josh by mistake. I used the Jericho bit and Dad bought it, but Paul started giving me really funny looks and asking questions.'

307

It took him only a moment to recover. 'Look, don't panic. If he brings it up we'll just say it was a slip of the tongue – you were still half asleep. I'll say Lazard, all right? He's hardly likely to check but if he does then I'm a fraud and you can dump me with a clear conscience.'

'OK, but I don't want any more questions. As soon as breakfast's over we're out of here. In fact, I'm not even going to wait for breakfast. I'll say I want to get home in case Belinda's trying to ring me. At least that won't be a total lie.'

At top speed I began cramming quilts back into the ottoman. How Mum had ever got them in there in the first place beat me, unless she'd borrowed an air-extraction machine; it was like trying to get several quarts into a pint pot. 'Do you want the shower first?'

He shook his head. 'Take your time.'

While doing my teeth, I rehearsed my excuse for leaving early: '*Just a piece of toast'll do. I feel I ought to get back in case she's trying to ring me. She didn't know I was going to be here, did she?*'

I turned the shower on and rummaged in a little basket for one of the shower caps Mum gleaned from hotels around the world. The box said *Old Winter Palace, Luxor*, and I'd have given a good deal to be at the Old Winter Palace and not here.

I don't know how it is that your antennae pick up impending disaster, but mine just had. Somewhere I'd heard Benjy barking in the quick, excited way he has when something's stirring. Benjy senses tension and the possibility of a scrap, and like any good, red-

308

blooded dog he likes to join in. He barks like this when Mum's just seen a tell-tale couple coming up the drive: 'Oh Lord, Ted, it's those Jehovah's Witnesses again.' Whereupon Dad says grimly, 'I'll get rid of them.'

Then I heard footsteps – quick, heavy footsteps on the landing. I heard a sharp knock on the bedroom door.

'Sophy! Open the door!'

I froze. My skin went cold and crawly; my stomach felt like a sick lump.

Josh sounded calm enough. 'She's in the shower, Mr Metcalfe.'

'Good! It's you I want to see. Open up!'

Too sick to move, I heard the door open.

'Do you mind telling me what the hell's going on?' This was Dad. 'What are these?'

What the hell . . . ? My heart was stuck fearfully under my tonsils.

Still Josh sounded relatively calm. 'May I ask how you came by those?'

'No, you may not! Just what kind of line have you been spinning my daughter? Are these yours, or have you stolen them?'

'Of course they're mine. Mr Metcalfe—'

'Don't Mr Metcalfe me! What the hell do you mean by coming into my house under an assumed name?'

Oh God. Having dragged that dressing gown back on, I opened the door.

The suddenly aged man of last night might never have been. I'd only ever seen him like this once before, years ago, when some maniac had nearly run Belinda over at a zebra crossing. Picture an enraged bull in a dressing gown and you'd just about have it.

In his right hand was a wallet. In his left were a couple of credit cards. 'What's he been telling you?' he demanded. 'What the hell's going on? Is he some sort of undercover criminal?'

'It's nothing of the kind,' Josh said. 'If you'll please just—'

'Shut – *up*!' Dad bellowed this at Benjy, who was barking his head off, but it only made him up the volume.

'Dad, *please* . . .' Just as I was gathering my courage for confession purposes, Mum appeared on the landing in her dressing gown.

Her bewildered face made me want to die.

'Whatever's going on?' she asked. 'Why is everybody shouting?'

Barely fifteen minutes later I left my parents' room and returned to Josh. I gaped around the empty guest room. His bag was gone. There was no sign that he'd ever been there at all.

Seized with panic, I fled downstairs to the kitchen. Only Paul was there.

'Has he gone?' I gasped.

He nodded towards the door. 'He's in the sitting room.'

My relief was indescribable. It was so profound, I almost spared a shred of sympathy for this picture of sullen defensiveness, standing with his arms folded over the dressing gown. 'Why did you do it?'

310

I despaired. 'Weren't things bad enough already?'

'How was I to know?' he demanded, with the aggressive self-justification that comes from being in the wrong. 'Your face was a dead giveaway. I knew there was something. He could have been anybody!'

'For God's sake, I'm not some dopey sixteen-year-old who needs protecting from herself! You should have minded your own business!'

'Well, what would you have done?' he demanded. 'What if you'd found some bloke X of Belinda's going around with a wallet full of bloke Y? Your mother's got some good jewellery! They've got some nice antiques!'

'I'd have asked her first! And I'd never have gone through his pockets!'

I left him and went to the sitting room. Josh was upright, phone clamped between neck and shoulder, the Yellow Pages open on the little table in front of him. His bag was dumped on the floor beside him. After a glance at me he checked his watch. 'Yes, that'll do fine,' he was saying. 'Thank you.' And he hung up.

He turned to me. His hair was damp from the shower but he hadn't shaved. 'There's a cab coming in ten minutes.'

Something inside me died a little death. 'You don't have to go.'

'Of course I do.' Even at a distance of several feet, I could feel his tension like fifteen stone of coiled steel spring, straining at the safety catch. 'What would you do in my position? Suggest a cosy lunch at the pub?'

There was no argument.

'Even without all this, the last thing a family crisis

311

needs is non-family getting in the way,' he went on. 'If you need a further reason, I have to get out of here before I ram that little shit's teeth right into his rectum.'

His gritted tone matched the words exactly.

I swallowed hard. 'You don't need a cab. I'll drive you to the station.'

'No. You need to stay here.' He picked up his grip. 'Where are your folks?'

'Still upstairs.'

'Give them my apologies, will you? I'll wait outside for the cab.'

'I'll just get dressed . . .' I fled upstairs, yanked my clothes on, dragged a brush through my hair and splashed my face. When I came down two minutes later he was standing halfway down the gravel drive, his bag at his feet.

Also at his feet was Benjy, dropping a manky red ball and wagging his tail. Josh picked it up and threw it so hard towards the back garden, I knew he was imagining Paul on the receiving end.

As Benjy bounded after it, I went up. 'I'm so sorry,' I said.

'So am I.' His tone was both short and tense. 'We should have quit while we were ahead.'

I made a pathetic attempt at optimism. 'Still, it could have been worse. It was a brilliant lie.'

'As I said, I've got a degree in bullshitting.'

Benjy trotted back with his ball, pausing to lift his leg and pee against the pristine right offside wheel of Paul's Porsche.

'Well done,' Josh muttered. 'Go and do the other three, will you?' But Benjy had found a sniff-trail into the shrubs that bordered the drive instead.

'I should have thought of it myself,' I said miserably. 'If I'd thought of it last week, at least there'd only have been one nightmare.'

'You should have thought of hitting this whole, ludicrous farce on the head months ago.'

The grit in his tone made me shrink inside, but he went on more gently, 'But there you go – a major fuck-up never did anyone any lasting harm. I've got a couple on my CV, I can tell you.'

I was so pathetically grateful for this my eyes misted up, but already the cab was crunching over the gravel. A chirpy middle-aged man in a white shirt and tie got out. 'Oakland cars?'

Benjy came bounding from wherever he'd been, doing a hound-from-hell impression that had the poor bloke shrinking to the side of his cab. I ran and grabbed his collar and said to the driver. 'It's all right – he's all talk.'

Josh said, 'I'll be one minute.'

Dragging the still-barking Benjy, we retreated several yards to the relative shelter of those shrubs. Josh said, 'Go back inside. You need to talk to them.'

I couldn't bear to see him go like this, but I knew there was no alternative. Since the driver had got back into the car, I let Benjy loose.

'Will you be all right?' he went on.

If he'd said it in a crisp and businesslike fashion, I could have handled it. But he didn't quite, and something inside me was dissolving like sugar in the rain. I'd have given anything to be able to do a Tamara here – i.e. throw myself into his arms and cry rivers all over his shirt. But I've never been much cop at the girly bit; I suppose it helps if you look like a leetle Botticelli angel, and not like a strapping lass who can take care of herself. 'Don't tha' worry about me,' I said. 'I'll be reet champion.' I meant this to sound sarcastic, at least like Doughty Northern Grit, but somehow it changed to stand-up comic on the way out.

The smile he produced was very wry, barely even there, but it still made me want to curl up and die. 'I'll be in touch.'

I'd heard that before. 'At least you can't say you've been bored out of your mind.' Nodding towards the cab, I pushed my hair back. 'Off you go, then, before he ups the fare.'

'Bye, then.'

I knew he was going to kiss me, and I knew exactly what sort of kiss it'd be. A brief, farewell brushing of lips on cheek, like he might have given an elderly aunt in her best hat. There was absolutely nothing wrong with it if you were an elderly aunt. He matched it with a little pat on my waist, like he might have given his sister. Both of them said, quite clearly, that whatever I'd longed for and thought I'd almost touched, there was now more chance of Benjy going veggie.

''Bye.' As he drew back I said casually, 'Just out of interest, what *was* that bet? Twenty to one on whether you'd get invited back for tea?'

It was my pet little devil again. I'd never meant to

314

say it, but neither had I expected the sudden flash of guilt he tried to hide.

It made me feel sick. 'Jerry told Tamara, so there's no need to look like that.'

'If he told her what I think he told her, it's a lie.'

'Then why did you just look as guilty as hell?'

He hesitated just a millisecond too long.

'I'm not sure Jerry's such a mate of yours any more,' I said. 'Did you pull Svetlana just to piss him off?'

I don't know what I was expecting, but it certainly wasn't what I got.

'Did I *what*?' Disbelief was written all over his face. 'I took her home! She'd had enough!'

The force in his voice shook me, but already he was going on. 'I sat up till four in the morning, listening to how bloody awful everything was in St Petersburg, and about her mother, who was "nuclear physicist at Chernobyl", and her father, who cleared off when she was six, and the poor old *babushkas* who have to beg in the streets because their ex-Soviet pensions barely buy a loaf of bread! All right?'

If I'd felt sick before, this was fifty times worse. 'I'm sorry – it was none of my business,' I said unsteadily.

'And while we're at it, can we get something else straight?' he went on. 'I came yesterday, against my better judgement, because although I thought you were a compulsive liar and possibly a raging headcase, too, I liked you, God help me, and I felt sorry for you because you were so upset about your mother. I barely slept all night, and not just because I so nobly slept on the floor. I'm now suffering from first-degree stress

315

because I want to flatten that jerk your sister married but I can't, because that's exactly what he wants me to do so he can sue me for assault. Added to that, I'm feeling like seven kinds of shit for having come here under false pretences and abused your folks' hospitality. For all this I cut short a visit to a very old friend I hadn't seen in four years. So if you'll forgive me I'll clear off now, before the dog pees on my shoes.'

And he picked up his bag and got into the cab.

I watched it disappear with only two thoughts in my head: a) Never in my entire life had I blown anything so spectacularly, and b) Please, please, let all this be a nightmare.

The journey home, which I embarked on an hour later, was the most lonely and miserable of my life. Tears of guilt and self-pity oozed constantly on to my cheeks and I didn't even have any tissues to wipe them with. I had to use my sleeve, and more than once caught an odd look from some passing passenger in the fast lane. One little kid positively gawped and I felt so ugly and miserable and hated myself so much, I stuck my tongue out. And then I hated myself even more, for being such a cow.

They were all there when I got home: Alix, Calum, Ace. My sole comfort was the absence of Tina.

Alix gaped at my face. 'Whatever's the matter? What's all this about Belinda? I tried to phone but they said you'd left. Your dad sounded a bit weird – he virtually hung up on me. What on earth's going on?'

It took me half a minute to explain the basics, by

which time all three of them were wide-eyed with shock.

'Blimey,' said Ace.

Alix had sunk, stunned, to the sofa. 'I thought she was mad about Paul!'

'So did everybody else. Mum thinks it's Marc at the bottom of it.' I related our conjectures and what Tamara and Bill had said.

'Maybe that's it,' Alix said. 'She got Paul on the rebound, started having doubts, and then bumped into Marc again. It would explain everything.'

'Paul must be feeling a right dick,' said Ace.

'Poor bloke,' said Calum. 'How's he taking it?'

'I couldn't give a stuff about Paul! He's a sneaky, devious little shit!' Surrounded by dumbstruck faces, I dissolved all over again.

Of course, it all came out. Well, not *all*. In between sniffs and eye-wipings I told the sorry, edited tale. If nothing else, it was livening up their Sunday afternoon. They sat silently, appalled and riveted in roughly equal measure.

'Blimey,' said Ace at last. 'I wouldn't have liked to see the state of your house after all that shit had hit the fan.'

Alix turned on him. 'For God's sake, it's not funny!'

'I'll get her a drink.' Calum said. 'Treble V&T, is it?'

'There's isn't any vodka,' Alix said. 'Get her some of that alcoholic blackcurrant stuff. Neat.'

None of them had uttered a word of reproof. None of them had said, 'Well I did warn you,' but I knew they were thinking it. I knew Alix was, and equally, I knew she'd never say it.

Calum came back with half a tumbler of *crème de cassis*. Why anybody adds champagne or anything else to this nectar, I'll never know. If you want an alcoholic comfort blanket, there's nothing to beat it.

'Still, it could have been worse,' Alix said. 'Imagine if you'd told them the truth!'

It didn't bear thinking about. Just as I'd been about to confess, with Dad ballistically demanding an explanation, Benjy barking his head off and Mum visibly paling at the edges, Josh had cut through it with a crisp, 'Will you please just *listen*?'

My heart had stopped. In the ensuing silence he'd said calmly, 'Dominic and Sophy split up just before the wedding. The only reason she didn't tell you was because she didn't want to cast a blight over everything and have everyone feeling sorry for her. I'm just a friend. She asked me to fill in.'

In the following dumbfounded silence my brain had got back into gear. 'I'm sorry,' I'd said lamely, 'but it seemed like a good idea at the time.'

Dad had recovered first. He had gaped from me to Josh, and then to the double bed in the room behind us. After years of relaxation, his native moral propriety had resurfaced. 'You slept in the same bed!'

'We didn't,' I'd said. 'Josh slept on the floor. I made up a bed with the spare quilts.'

Then it had been Mum's turn, and her white, devastated face had shot me through with guilt. 'Why didn't you tell me? I'm your mother!'

Keeping calm had been beyond me. 'Why d'you think?' I'd burst out. 'You were desperate for him to

318

come! You were desperate to keep your end up with bloody Maggie!'

She had looked as if I'd hit her. White-faced, she'd fled to her room, and after shooting me a look of despairing accusation, Dad had gone in pursuit.

After a few seconds' hideous silence Josh had said, 'For Christ's sake, did you have to say that?'

'It's the truth!' I'd burst out. 'What did you want me to say? That I'd done it for the sheer hell of it?' and I'd gone after Mum and Dad, trying to calm waters I knew would never be calmed by anything I could say.

Then I'd gone back to Josh, and you know the rest.

'What was Paul doing, while all this fertiliser was flying?' Calum asked. 'Having a good laugh on the sidelines?'

The comfort blanket wasn't working. 'He was downstairs but you can bet he was listening. I'm sure he hadn't suspected anything until I opened my stupid mouth. He just didn't like Josh, which was Josh's stupid fault for upsetting him the night before. He resented him. If he hadn't happened to go to the downstairs loo just afterwards . . .'

Our downstairs loo was massive, containing vacuum cleaner and three years' supply of loo rolls, as well as an antique coat-stand in the corner. And there had been Josh's jacket, complete with wallet, hung up tidily by Mum the night before.

Right under Paul's suspicious, resentful, little nose.

I knew it was unfair to put any blame on Josh, but I was so miserable I couldn't help it. 'If he hadn't left his bloody jacket lying around, nobody would have hung

319

it up in the first place. If he hadn't done that stupid, macho, too-tough-to-wrap-up-warm bit last night, it wouldn't have *been* lying around.'

'Dickhead,' Alix snorted.

'I'm surprised Paul had the nerve to go and show your dad,' Ace said.

'He'd have said he was already suspicious,' Calum pointed out. 'It must have looked a bit fishy, after all. You suddenly call the bloke by another name and look guilty as hell when you twig what you've said, and then you say he works for a bean-counting outfit when he's supposed to be something else . . .'

'He should never have gone nosing in the first place! I'm glad Belinda's left him. I hope she tells everybody he can't get it up any more. He actually had the nerve to pretend he was sorry, after Josh had gone – can you credit it?' Paul had departed about twenty minutes after Josh, leaving me in his perfectly stirred hornets' nest.

Once he'd gone, recriminations had begun all over again. Mum had been tearful, Dad grim, both voices bitter with reproach. How *could* I have done such a thing? Deceiving them like that, *twice*? They'd never, ever have believed . . .

And that's when my misery had turned to anger. I'd flipped: screamed at the pair of them. Why were they having a go at *me*? What had *I* done, except try to keep Mum happy? Did they think I actually *liked* deceiving them, just so Mum could score points off Maggie Freeman? Why weren't they having a go at Belinda, who'd wasted thousands of pounds worth of wedding because she hadn't got the guts to say she'd made a mistake? What did she have to do before they ever blamed her for anything? Disembowel somebody? No, not even that – it'd always, *always* be somebody else's fault. Did *I* get Mum to do my ironing, Dad to change my wheels? Did *I* live for peanuts at their expense? Well, stuff the pair of them. I was never, ever coming home again.

Exit furious Sophy upstairs for furious packing, followed by furious storming out, followed by collapse into misery ten minutes down the road.

I'd told them all this, of course.

As it all replayed in my head and I dissolved all over again, Alix patted my shoulder. 'Cheer up – it could have been a lot worse.'

That was just it; I couldn't tell them just how much worse it *had* been. At least, I could only tell them selected bits. 'He had such a go at me before he left,' I wept. 'He called me a compulsive liar . . .'

'Bastard!' Alix flared. 'How dared he?'

'But I am,' I wept. 'I've been lying for months . . .'

'So what if you have? Bastard hypocrite – wasn't he *act*ing a lie, for money?'

'Not this time. I didn't get round to paying him . . .'

'That's not the point! If he comes round asking for it, I'll shove it up his orifice. Mind you, I always said any bloke who goes escorting had to be basically a slime-ball.'

'He looked OK to me,' said Ace.

'You'd think Jack the Ripper looked OK!' she flared. 'Whose side are you on, anyway?'

321

I grabbed another tissue. 'And he said I was a raging headache . . .'

'Now that's not on,' Calum said indignantly.

'I am,' I wept. 'Normal women don't invent blokes –' sniff – 'and keep them going for' – sniff – 'months . . .'

'I don't see why not,' Calum said heartily. 'I used to invent women on a weekly basis. They all thought I was God's gift and they were up for it any time I liked, which was just as well, because I wasn't having much luck with real ones at the time.'

'Did you?' Ace grinned. 'I used to have this imaginary Chinese bird called Soo Li. She used to—'

'Oh, shut up, the pair of you!' Alix flared. 'Spare us your disgusting fantasies. Ace, go and get Sophy a fill-up.'

He took my glass but instead of going he perched on the arm of the chair and said, 'I know all this has been a bit of a nightmare, but *normal* escorting must be a doss.' He actually produced a grin. 'D'you reckon that agency'd take me on? For that kind of money I'd ponce about like Prince Charming – open doors for them, light their fags, talk bollocks all night, you name it.'

'For God's sake, they don't want anyone like *you*,' Alix said irritably. 'They want men who at least *look* at if they've got a bit of class. Not idiots who ask for HP Sauce just to see the waiter's face.'

'OK, keep your wig on.'

'Don't even think of it,' I despaired. 'You might get a nightmare like me.'

'There'd never be another nightmare like you, Sophe – you're a one-off.'

322

As he departed with a pat on my shoulder, I felt a rush of affection for him, despite the fact that the little toad had helped get me into this mess in the first place.

Except that he hadn't, not really. I had no one to blame but myself.

'How were your folks when you left?' Alix asked, in the semi-fearful tone of someone who already knows the answer.

'How d'you think?' I wiped my nose with the nth sodden tissue. 'God, I wish I was dead.'

Ace came back with my glass. 'You know what? All this reminds me of something I saw on the telly at Tina's. *Weddings From Hell* or something.'

'*We* saw that, and it was nothing like this,' Alix said irritably.

'OK, so she didn't actually go *through* with it. She got to the end of the road where the church was and told her dad to take her home again. She'd been having second thoughts for weeks, only she was too shit-scared to say so.'

I gaped at Alix, and then at Ace. Everything had gone horribly quiet.

'What?' he said.

'We missed that bit,' said Alix, in a voice as sick and hollow as I felt.

'Oh God . . .' I put my head in my hands.

Nobody spoke.

'Maybe she was trying to work up to it,' I despaired. 'I was so bloody patronising, assuming she was being hysterical over nothing . . .'

Nobody spoke.

'Arrogant, patronising cow,' I despaired. 'I hate myself so much . . .'

'I hate you too,' Alix said, in forced, jokey tones. 'You and your whopping great tits. Calum lusts after them non-stop, don't you, Bum-features?'

'All the time,' he said, all fakely hearty. 'If I give you a tenner, can I have a quick feel?'

Nothing on earth could have made me smile just then. Glass in hand, I stood up. 'I'm going to take this in the bath and drown myself.'

Downing cassis, I wallowed miserably in the bath. My Badedas was finished so there weren't even any bubbles. I looked at my thighs and wondered how I could ever have kidded myself they weren't gross. I squished them to make them even more dimply and cellulitey and disgusting, and thanked God Josh hadn't touched them, or he might be even now feeling sick at the mere thought. What if he'd told a friend about me, over a pint in a pub? *'Well, she was obviously panting for it, so I thought, Why not? Quite a goer, once she got going. Big hefty lass, though – walloping great arse. Yes, I will have another, mate, ta very much.'*

I knew he wouldn't talk like that but I had to torture myself.

I thought of Belinda and wondered why the hell I felt guilty for not reading her stupid, indecisive mind. I wanted to kill her for getting me in this mess in the first place. I wanted to kill her for being a mummy's and daddy's girl from birth. I hope she *had* gone off with Marc. I hoped he'd dump her all over again in three weeks and then she'd go crawling back to Paul and he'd tell her to bugger off.

And then I felt guilty all over again, for thinking it. I lay in a bath of guilt, wondering whether Ace had any Es stashed away and, if so, whether any illegal chemical was capable of drowning my misery. With a modicum of good fortune it might kill me instead.

Wrapped in a towel, I slunk back to my room. Just as I reached it, Ace put his head around the kitchen door. 'All right, Sophe?'

'Brilliant. You haven't got any Ecstasy, have you? I could do with a change from Agony.'

'No, but I could skin you up a quick spliff.'

'Maybe later.'

As I opened the door he came closer, looking vaguely awkward. 'Nothing else happened, did it? You and him, I mean.'

As I said before, not daft. 'No! In any case I was going off him even before we got there.'

He looked relieved rather than anything else. 'Well, that's OK, then. I was feeling a bit bad. I mean, it was me that encouraged you to hire him in the first place.'

It was almost enough to make me weepy again. 'For God's sake, it's not your fault. I'm old and daft enough to make my own mistakes.'

'And at least you hadn't paid him. Not this time, anyway.'

'No, not that it's any comfort.'

As I pushed my door open he was still there, still looking vaguely awkward. 'So you've still got all that dosh, then? It's not cash, is it?'

'Yes, as a matter of fact. Why?'

Awkwardly he kicked at the skirting board. 'The thing is, I'm a bit skint but I'd like to take Tina out tonight. She's been a bit fed up lately.'

Might have known he was after something. 'Why? Has one of her nail extensions come off?'

'Don't be like that, Sophe.' Awkwardly he kicked again at the skirting board. 'Her mum's not very well. She's got cancer.'

I was aghast with remorse. 'Oh God, I'm so sorry. Why didn't you say before?'

'She doesn't like talking about it. Says it depresses people.'

'Oh, I wish I'd known . . .' I was in my room, scrabbling in my bag almost before he'd blinked. 'Here – take it.' I shoved fifty quid of guilt money at him.

'God, Sophe – twenty'd be enough. I'll pay you back.'

'No, it's fine. Have a lovely time on me.'

In the past twenty-four hours I'd suffered enough guilt to keep half a dozen therapists busy for years. I need oblivion, preferably for a month. Still towelled, I got under the duvet and closed my eyes.

When I woke, feeling groggy and terrible, the flat was hushed and I felt more miserable still that they'd all gone out and deserted me. My hair had dried all messy and my face looked like something from a horror film. I dragged a brush through my hair and pulled on a grey tracksuit that made me look like a sack of particularly sexless potatoes. Later I would probably get through all my emergency fags and a bag of oven chips, too. I mean, if you're going to indulge in serious self-loathing, you might as well do it properly.

For non-food comfort I shoved Disney's *Sleeping Beauty* into the video. Alix had given me this the previous Christmas I'd given her *Cinderella*: a perfect swap for two hopeless addicts who felt too daft to buy them for themselves. Fifteen minutes into it, Alix emerged from her room.

'Thought you'd gone out,' I said.

'I'm working – I've got to finish that kids' camp brochure by Tuesday. Like a cup of tea?'

'Yes, please, with two spoonfuls of ground glass.'

I returned to *Sleeping Beauty*, beginning to have a certain sympathy for the witch. Princess Aurora was starting to remind me of Belinda, all annoyingly blonde and gorgeous, and beloved by the entire kingdom, even down to the fluffy little bunnies in the forest. It was enough to make you sick.

Alix came back with tea and a KitKat. 'Your father phoned earlier, but he said not to wake you up. He still sounded a bit funny, to be honest.' No wonder. 'He just said to tell you Belinda had phoned, but she didn't say where she was or anything – just that she felt awful but she was OK and not to worry.'

I could picture it exactly. Belinda would be all tearful while Dad said, *'It's all right, love, no use crying . . .'* Mum, equally tearful, would say, *'Ted,* please *let me speak to her—'* grab the receiver and cry, *'Darling, I've been so worried –* please *come home – nobody's cross with*

327

you—' And then Belinda would feel so awful she'd hang up, and they'd be in more of a state than ever.

'I could kill her,' I said, miserably sipping my tea. 'I wish a crocodile had eaten her on her honeymoon.'

'Yes, but she must be feeling awful.'

'She deserves to feel awful. Everybody else feels awful. *I* feel awful.'

'Oh, and that Josh bloke phoned.'

I nearly spilt my tea. 'When?'

'About an hour ago. I said you were asleep and I had no intention of waking you up.' With relish she went on, 'God, I had such a go at him. I said who the hell did he think he was, having a go at you like that, didn't he think you were upset enough already, and hadn't his mother taught him any manners, and if he was after his money he could come round right now and I'd shove it up his bum with the rough end of a pineapple.'

She turned to me with a pleased-with-herself-look that appalled me.

'What did he say?'

'Nothing! I didn't give him a chance. I just blasted him and hung up.' Her pleased-with-herself look was fading fast. 'What's the matter? You didn't want to speak to him, did you?'

'Oh God . . .' I put my head in my hands. 'Why the hell didn't you *tell* me?'

Thirteen

After that I could only come clean. And by the time I'd
finished narrating the sorry, unedited saga Alix felt so
bad I felt sorry for her, which made a change from
feeling sorry for myself.

'Why ever didn't you *tell* me?' she despaired for the
fiftieth time. 'I'm supposed to be your friend!'

'You'd have thought I was turning into some desperate headcase, like Muriel out of *Muriel's Wedding*!'

'I wouldn't! Well, I might have thought you were
getting just a teensy bit *paranoid*, but—'

'A *bit*? You might have thought I secretly fancied
Ace, too.'

'Sophy, do me a favour.' Her hurt expression
reminded me of Benjy when someone's told him to go
away, he smells. 'How could you have told him all that,
and not me?'

'I didn't tell him everything! I haven't said a word
since that fiasco on the common!' I'd told her not only
that but everything else, even down to Dad's untimely
offer of room service. Restlessly I went on, 'He said
he'd be in touch, but even before I had that go at him
I never thought he would. I thought he was just saying
it.'

'For heaven's sake phone him,' Alix pressed. 'Tell
him I'd got it all wrong.'

A number would be helpful first. I knew without looking that I hadn't put it in my address book. I'd scribbled on the nearest available thing. After a moment's blankness I gaped around the suspiciously tidy room. 'Please don't tell me you've taken all those papers to the paper bank?'

It took her only a moment to catch on. 'Don't tell me you wrote his number on a bloody *news*paper?'

'It was the nearest thing! *Have* you taken them?'

She winced. 'Calum took them yesterday. Why on earth didn't you put it in your address book?'

'I don't know! It's usually me who goes to the paper bank! Has anyone else phoned since?'

'My mother, wouldn't you know it.'

So 1471 wouldn't work, even if he hadn't phoned from a mobile. It meant phoning Jerry again, but first I had to ring the Dixons for his number and the only reply was the message on the answerphone.

'The phone book?' Alix suggested.

'I haven't even got his address!' I tried anyway. There were three J. Carmichaels. Two were polite wrong numbers, the third implied that people who phone wrong numbers should be put in the stocks outside Safeways and pelted with ordure. I said tartly that I wasn't sorry after all for disturbing him. If I'd known he was such a miserable apology for a human being I'd have phoned anyway, on purpose.

Bang.

For a minute we watched Aurora's prince, now cruelly shackled by the evil old hag of a witch.

'Why ever did you say that about pineapples?' I

330

despaired, suddenly remembering.

'I'm sorry, OK? I had this picture of some smarmy, over-confident git, crawling to your folks!'

'He saved me from the worst of it! If he hadn't come up with that brilliant lie—'

'That only confirmed it! I thought a bloke who could come up with an off-the-cuff whopper, just like that – *ping* – just *had* to be an arsehole!'

You read what you want to read, I suppose. 'I'm only phoning to apologise for you. After he called me a liar and a headcase, I'm hardly going to ask him out for lunch at The Ivy.'

'You *have* been telling a few porkies lately,' she pointed out. 'But he obviously fancies you – he virtually said so, didn't he?'

'Maybe he was just saying it to justify the session we nearly had.'

She was beginning to sound exasperated, and I couldn't blame her. 'If he *hadn't* fancied you, you wouldn't have nearly *had* a session.'

'Yes, but there's fancying and fancying, isn't there? I was standing there with my tongue hanging out – he'd have had to be a saint. Besides, he still thinks I'm involved with Ace.'

'No wonder he thought you needed a good old session, then. Ace! I ask you.' She picked at a stray thread on a check cushion and sniffed it. 'These cushions are disgusting. Ace must have been putting his stinky feet on them.'

'No stinkier than Calum's, I bet. You're always putting Ace down. He'll end up psychologically damaged, if you ask me. If you had a brother like Tamara's, I could understand you bitching.'

The valiant prince was now hacking his way through the forest with his trusty sword of truth. 'Even if I hadn't screwed everything up, it would never have come to anything,' I said.

'Why the hell not?'

'Because he makes me go woozy just looking at him. Because his thighs are chunkier than mine. Because I *like* him, damn him. Any one of which is quite enough to ensure he'd last about four days finding someone else to fancy a hell of a lot more.'

'God, you're hopeless. Why are you so defeatist?'

'Bitter experience. Nobody I really want ever wants me any more.'

'Don't be daft.'

Prince Valiant was still hacking. 'I wish someone'd love me enough to hack his way through a forest,' I said forlornly. 'But even if he did, he'd turn out to be some nerd I didn't fancy in the first place. He'd wake me with a horrible wet kiss and I'd throw up.'

'No modern bloke'd even hack his way to the corner shop,' she snorted. 'They'd go for ten minutes with a Black & Decker and then say it needed a new wing nut and wander off to watch the footie.'

'I bet Calum'd hack for you.'

'Are you kidding? He'd be knackered after a couple of brambles and slope off to the pub.'

I knew she was only saying it.

'My mother thinks it's the Pill, going into the water,'

she went on. 'In fifty years their balls'll be even more rudimentary than their brains.'

Later, we wandered up the road to the Kouzina, where Alix liked to practise her minimal Greek. Stavros said I looked about as happy as a sheep at Greek Easter, and Alix said, 'She's feeling like *kaka*, that's why. We'll have two *mikro souvlakias, se parakalo*.'

'Is a guy?' Stavros asked.

I said, 'Not exactly,' and Alix said, 'Of course it bloody is.'

He shot me a wink and said, 'You tell me who is the son of a *putana* and I chop up his goolies for doner kebab.'

'So that's what you put in it,' I said. 'No wonder I never fancy it.'

We ate our *souvlakia* on a bench on the common. It was a lovely golden evening, which perked me up not at all, as every lovey-dovey couple in London seemed to be strolling right past us, holding hands, laughing, eating each other, or all three. 'At least you saved your money,' Alix said, through a mouthful of pork and salad. 'Go and lash out on a Nicole Farhi sweater.'

Or a bath of vodka to drown myself in.

On the way back she said, 'Don't you think you should phone your folks? They must be terribly upset after you had such a go at them.'

'They should have thought of that before having a go at *me*! It's always been the same. Belinda would do something really stupid and they'd hardly say a word. I used to say to Mum, "For heaven's sake, if I'd done

333

that you'd have gone mad!" And she'd say, "Yes, dear, but you're not *like* Belinda, are you?"'

'Well, you're not. You've got twice the sense and you're three times tougher.'

'I'm not! People just think I am!'

'You know what I mean. You can act tough and people believe it. They don't expect you to screw up.'

When we got back the message light was flashing on the answerphone and my heart almost stopped.

'God, what if it's Josh?' As I dithered, almost too sick with nerves to press 'play', Alix did it for me.

I suppose I was expecting a terse mouthful like he'd given me at our un-tender parting, but the voice was almost as awkward and apologetic as mine would have been if I'd been phoning *him*.

Only, unfortunately, it wasn't Josh.

'Sophy, it's Kit. Look, I . . .' There was a pause while he obviously struggled to find words. 'I have to talk to you – I'll call back later.'

Alix made her, *Oh God* face. 'Looks like whatshername was right. To be honest, I had a feeling she might be.'

After the initial shock, all I felt was a crushing sense of let-down. Whatever variety of mouthful he might have given me, there was only one voice I'd wanted to hear.

'Sounded pretty awkward, didn't he?' Alix went on. 'As if he'd been psyching himself up for ages. Mind you, he would – he's hardly the pushy, Jack-the-lad who'd expect you to have him back just like that.'

Hot on the heels of let-down came hatred for that

Bitch-Faced cow called Life. 'Why does he have to want me back *now*? Why don't the bastards ever want me when I want them? Look at sodding Dominic. Why does this always happen to me?'

'It's nothing like Dominic,' she pointed out. 'You really liked Kit. He must think there's a chance of resuscitating it. Though he'd hardly expect you to chuck your bloke just like that. Unless . . .' she paused, 'unless Tamara spilled the beans and he knows.'

I shook my head. 'She'd never had told Sonia, and Sonia's the only person who'd have passed it on. Anyway, she swore not to tell a soul.'

'If you were nervous at the wedding, he might have picked it up and misconstrued it,' she pointed out. 'Might have thought you and Dominic were cooling off.'

I thought back to my casual '*He'll do.*' Why hadn't I gushed a bit, for once?

Alix went on, 'He must be coming back to London or there wouldn't be much point. Don't they do six-month stints or something?'

'Something like that.'

'What are you going to say when he phones back?'

'What d'you think?' Suddenly I was almost in tears at the unfairness of it all. 'Why couldn't the dickhead have wanted me back when I was miserable as bloody sin? I'll tell him to get lost!'

'Will you hell. You'll end up feeling sorry for him because he'll be all awkward and stumbly, and you'll think back to how sweet he could be, like when you had that really stinking cold and horrific runs at the

335

same time, and you'll tell yourself it was all Bitch-Face's fault because he was too "nice" to see through her, and then you'll feel bad, and wish you *did* want him back, and probably end up agreeing to see him just once.'

This was a depressing prediction, but undeniably possible. 'Then I'll leave the thing on "set" and pretend to be out.'

'What if Josh phones? If he phones from a mobile and doesn't leave a message . . .'

'He won't. I bet you any money he won't.'

'He might. If I were him, *I'd* bloody well phone. I'd want to know what the hell you'd been saying to make your friend slag me off like that.'

Alix went back to her kids' camp brochure. I sat with one eye on the television and the other on what bits of golden evening I could glimpse from our urban jungle window. It aroused in me an unbearable, aching longing for I knew not what.

Except that I did. Why was I sitting here like a lovesick fifteen-year-old, agonising over a phone that wasn't going to ring? Why couldn't I just shrug my shoulders and not give a stuff? Why didn't I jack my job in and travel around Oz for a year? Why couldn't Belinda turn up on the doorstep, so I could have a massive go at her for landing me in all this?

I tried the Dixons again at ten thirty, but since the only reply was that wretched answerphone it would have to wait. Kit didn't phone back.

At five to midnight, en route to bed, Alix said. 'Typically Kit-ish behaviour, if you ask me. Probably chickened out. Or went out for a few pints of Dutch courage and got waylaid by another Bitch-Face.'

'Probably. Useless bugger. If he phoned now, I really *would* give him a mouthful.'

After that siesta I slept badly and went to work feeling about thirty-eight per cent human. Just to cheer me up a bit more, there was an e-mail from personnel, saying I'd been booked with Sadists for September and a brochure was in the post.

The postman had already brought it. It detailed various jolly activities: e.g. constructing rafts out of moss and dead sheep, road-testing said craft in white-water rapids, and snaring frogs to eat raw for breakfast. If anyone chose not to participate in these character-building exercises, they were, of course, free to stay in their rooms watching *Sunset Beach* and nobody would imply that they were pathetic, spineless worms or in any way ridicule or humiliate them.

Jess said, 'Apparently, it's good to take a few Mars bars, in case you get lost up a mountain.'

Over coffee I consumed half a packet of Hobnobs and told them all about Belinda.

Jess was appalled. 'Why didn't she just call it off? The poor bridegroom! All that money!'

Harriet said, 'Better than dragging it out, if she's really made a mistake. It took my mother twenty-one years to admit poor old Dad was a mistake.'

Sandie said, 'God, my mum'd *kill* me.'

Jess said, 'Your poor parents! They must be in a terrible state.'

By lunchtime my poor parents were preying on my mind enough that I thought I'd give them a private ring on my mobile, only when I nipped out of the office for that purpose I hadn't got it. I realised I hadn't seen it since trying to ring Alix from home, which meant I'd probably left it on a chest of drawers a hundred and fifty miles away, where it was about as much use to me as size eight knickers. Since I could hardly talk with everyone pretending they weren't listening, I left it for later, which made two awkward calls to look forward to. Alix had hung up on Josh; would he hang up on me? I couldn't bear the thought of Mum crying down the phone either.

I never made either call. The moment I arrived home Alix said, 'Belinda phoned.'

A mini-surge of adrenaline went through me. 'When?'

'Around four-thirty, only I'd gone for a run. She left a message.'

Just as I'd expected, her voice was verging on tears. 'Sophy, it's me. I know you'll be at work just now – I'll ring later but please don't yell at me – I know everybody's mad with me but I've been so miserable. Please don't go out tonight and don't hang up on me. Bye.'

Alix said, 'I did 1471 and got a number.' She showed me the back of an envelope. 'I rang straight back – I had to. Only she didn't answer. It's some hotel in the New Forest.'

'*What?* What the hell's she doing there?'

'Search me. Give her a ring.'

I picked up the receiver and dialled. But instead of

asking for Belinda, I asked for the address and scribbled it down.

Alix was gaping. 'You're not going down?'

'Why not?'

'It's miles!'

'I don't think it's that far.' I nipped out to the car for the road atlas and checked. 'Look. It'll only take a couple of hours.'

'She probably doesn't want to see anybody!'

'I don't care what she wants! I need to see her! I need to have a go at her and it's not the same over the phone. She can hang up.'

Alix winced. 'Sophy, *don't*. She sounds in a terrible state.'

'So is everybody else!' Seeing her obvious concern, I toned myself down. 'Look, I'm not going to scream at her, but I need to know what's been going on and it's easier in person. And unless it's something really awful I have to say *some*thing. Somebody's got to make her see that this was unforgivable and Mum and Dad never will. She'll just cry and look beautiful and everybody'll say, "*There, there, never mind* . . ." Even Josh said she needed a minor rollocking.'

Suddenly filled with energy, I charged around, shoving the basics of an overnight stay in a bag.

'What about work, tomorrow?' Alix asked.

'If it comes to staying over, I'll leave at the crack.'

As I was going out she said, 'If it wasn't for this brochure I'd come with you but I'm going to be up half the night as it is. I'm dying to know what's been going on. Do you still think it might be Marc?'

'I think it's just Paul. She's hiding because she can't face him.'

While crawling to the M3 I thought maybe the New Forest wasn't such a wild choice of hiding place after all. As little kids we'd spent lovely holidays there with long-gone relatives of Mum's, illicitly fed the ponies bits of egg-sandwich picnic and paddled in streams. Maybe Belinda was going back to a sunlit, small-child idyll where the worst thing you could do was drip your Orange Maid lolly down your T-shirt and nobody was ever cross for more than two minutes.

Even with everything else on my mind, I spared half an eye for the passing countryside. It had been an iffy sort of day but the sun had eventually decided to show its face. With all the greens still fresh out of their wrappings and the evening sun adding a golden wash over them all, England didn't look too bad at all. It was the sort of evening to make you think of lovely old riverside pubs, a table in the sun, and a few ducks to throw your crisps at.

Of course there was one vital accessory to make such evenings perfect, and I don't mean a sweater for that inevitable point where the sun disappears behind a tree and you start saying, 'Gosh, it's getting a bit parky, isn't it?'

I did try not to think about vital accessories. I tried not to think about idyllic, rivery scenes: me bagging the best table in the sun while my perfect accessory went to the bar. I tried not to think how he'd look as he came back with V&T and a beer, making a face as he stepped in something iffy in the grass. '*Bloody duck shit all over the place – there you go – I know you're trying to give them up but I got you a packet of smoky bacon anyway.*'

I'm sorry if this sounds very unromantic but I never have the type of fantasy that involves Concorde trips to Barbados, or even single red roses and candlelit dinners. Give me the duck mess and smoky bacon any day – less of a come-down when it all goes pear-shaped. In this case, of course, it had never been round-shaped in the first place.

I tried to ignore that horrible, bereft ache you get in such circumstances. Fleet Services were coming up. Since I'd given the road atlas only a perfunctory check, I would now give it a proper perusal, with a coffee and a fat jam doughnut. There's always a crumb of comfort somewhere.

I missed the turning twice, mainly because the sign was partly obscured by trees. A quarter-mile avenue led to the kind of place you see on *Beautiful England* calendars. If I ever won a few million on the lottery and fancied being lady of the manor, this was exactly what I'd pick. It was a gloriously perfect hotchpotch of styles; bits stuck on here and there from the time of the Crusades till poor old George went potty. There were crookedy timbered bits, mellow Elizabethan brick bits, and later, statelier additions, all serene in the evening sun.

The inside was all wood-panelled, smelling of lavender polish and flowers, with a galleried landing and portraits of long-dead inhabitants adorning the walls. There was a fireplace you could have roasted

341

half an ox in, filled with a vast arrangement of flowers.

I engaged brain carefully before speaking to the receptionist; I didn't want anyone thinking I was pursuing unwilling prey. 'I've come down to see my sister. I wasn't able to contact her before I left. Belinda Metcalfe?' God, I wasn't thinking so carefully after all – she was Fairfax now, if she was using it.

Evidently not. The receptionist was young and efficient-looking, with a name badge that said 'Michael'. He checked the register. 'Room seventeen.' He glanced behind him at the pigeonholed keys. 'Only she's not in at the moment.'

Damn it. 'Do you happen to know when she went out?'

'Not since I came on, at five.'

'Have you got a room? Just for one night.' Minutes later I was following a porter up the wide staircase to the galleried landing. It was thickly carpeted, the panelling glowing with generations of polish. My room was just off the gallery, down a wide corridor. It was all beautifully done in country-house florals, but not the busy little type.

Having slipped the porter a tip, I did a quick accommodation check. Nice bathroom, tea and coffee tray, hairdryer, mini-bar with not only booze, but a couple of KitKats, too. A leaded light window that looked like an original looked out over the gardens. There was a Tudor-knot thing, assorted bits of statuary, and wrought-iron seating on the lawns, where guests sat in the sun and a waiter buzzed around with drinks.

I could do with one of those, never mind dinner. I went downstairs almost immediately. The dining room was full, but if I'd care to wait half an hour . . . I sat in a squashy chair near reception from where I could see the entrance, and asked a passing waiter for a large V&T.

Where the hell was she? I was beginning to feel like a lemon, all on my own without even a magazine to read. Reception was out of papers so I took a brochure from the desk.

The oldest part of the hotel dated from the late 1300s. It was not only on the English Heritage trail, but also on the – *what*? After a momentary freak-out, I read: . . . *on the Haunted Britain trail, though we hasten to reassure nervous guests that there have been no sightings since 1993*.

Thank God for that.

Interested guests could, however, read more on page 11.

No, thanks. If I ended up staying, I didn't want to read that the last sighting had been a see-through apparition at the end of my bed: *'Begone! 'Tis my deathbed you're sleeping on!'*

Michael called that the dining room now had a table. I asked him to let me know if Belinda came back, and he said, 'Will do,' and smiled nicely, poor chap, obviously envisaging a lovely, huggy-feely surprise.

The dining room was part-panelled and still busy. I was very good. I chose no starter, grilled lemon sole with salad and new potatoes, and a half carafe of house white plonk. And waited.

And waited. Had they gone to Bournemouth to catch that sole, or what?

Feeling like a lone-lemon all over again, I returned to that brochure, even page 11. I soon wished I hadn't. The story of the ghost was not a happy one. If there were a points score for candidates in the Haunting-the-Scene-of-my-Tragic-Death stakes, she'd win it, hands down.

I wasn't over-thrilled to overhear a conversation at a nearby table, either. Before long it dawned on me that this normal-looking party of sixty-ish people was on some sort of Saga-type hunt-a-spook break, to make a change from bridge. They were only planning a séance tonight, to summon her out of limbo.

Suddenly I didn't fancy that room at all, not on my own. Where the hell was Belinda? What if she'd come back and Michael had forgotten to send a message? Just as I was about to nip back and remind him, a voice behind me said, 'Mind if I join you?'

If I hadn't just put my glass down, I'd have spilt *vin de maison* all down the pale pink shirt and grey suit I hadn't bothered to change out of. 'Josh! How on earth . . .?'

'I called at the flat.' Now standing beside me, he was sending my assorted systems into a mix of nerves and flutter. He didn't exactly look grimly purposeful, as if having a go was his prime objective, but he didn't look exactly chilled out, either. 'I take it you haven't seen Belinda yet?'

'No. She's not in the hotel, but she hasn't checked

344

out. I asked them to let me know when she comes back . . .' As Granny Metcalfe would put it, I was all of a dither. 'Please, sit down . . .'

Crisply, he pulled the chair out, plonked car keys on the cloth and sat opposite. He was wearing some sort of khaki-ish trousers and a casual, olivey green shirt that 'matched' him so gorgeously I'd have bet fifty quid some woman had bought it for him.

'I met your friend,' he said, in only-just sardonic tones. 'The one with the novel idea about what to do with pineapples.'

Instantly I wished I'd got an apology in first, but I was still in a tizz at seeing him at all. Then again, I was in a secondary tizz about what Alix might have told him. Before I could un-tizz my tongue, he beckoned to a waitress. 'I'll have a menu, please.'

Just as I was about to say, 'Look, I'm really sorry—' he drew his chair closer and leant forward, his forearms folded on the table. 'Just what had you said?' he demanded, in a low but compelling voice. 'As a purely academic exercise I'd like to know why someone I've never met talks to me like that.'

He was still smarting and I couldn't blame him. I felt so bad, my throat constricted. 'I didn't say anything, exactly, but I was upset and said you'd had a go at me. She just inferred.'

'She evidently "inferred" that I was a jerk of the first order. You must have painted me in very flattering colours.'

Since the waitress was back, laying a place, I had to wait.

345

'It wasn't that!' I said, once she'd gone. 'I'd hardly mentioned you at all, but she'd built up some picture in her mind . . .'

'A picture of a jerk.' He sat back as if satisfied with this, and now smarting more sorely than ever. 'Well, at least I've sorted that one out.'

Conscious of nearby tables, I leant forward, too, and lowered my voice. 'Alix felt really bad afterwards. I'm sure she must have apologised.'

'Well, yes, she did,' he conceded.

'How long were you there?' I asked, with visions of Alix making him a coffee and saying, *'Look, don't for God's sake tell her I told you, but she's got the serious hots for you. Ace was just a load of rubbish because you thought she was desperate.'*

'Only a couple of minutes.'

No time for bean-spilling then, not that she would have anyway.

A tiny ember began to glow in that bloke-shaped void inside me. He'd hardly have come all this way just to have a go at me, not unless he'd got a flash new motor he wanted to boy-race out of London, and I really didn't see him as the type.

I carried on with damage limitation. 'I'm really sorry about the pineapple bit. I tried to phone you once I realised what she'd said but I couldn't find your number and I couldn't phone Jerry to get it, either – the Dixons weren't answering.'

'And then you went out.'

I suppose I gave a little start. 'You didn't phone again?'

346

'I came round. Maybe it's just as well you were out,' he added sardonically.

From this I gathered that he might not have comported himself precisely like an officer and a gentleman, not that I'd have cared. 'We only went to the Greek up the road. I wasn't out partying, if that's what you're thinking. I was feeling awful.'

'It wasn't the best fun day I've ever had either.' He picked up the menu, gave it a cursory scan and put it down again. 'The reason I phoned in the first place was to ask how you were and apologise for having a go at you.'

It was so unexpected, my throat constricted. 'We were both a bit stressed, what with one thing and another. And I had a go at you first.'

'Yes, but it was still over the top. I'm sorry.'

My eyes were pricking. 'I'm sorry, too.'

A tangible awkwardness fell over the table, as if neither of us knew quite where to go from here. He still seemed tense. Belatedly, I offered the carafe. 'Would you like some of this?'

'No, thanks.' He beckoned to a waiter. 'Bring me a half carafe of house red, please.'

'Wouldn't you like to see the wine list, sir?'

'The plonk'll do, as long as it's drinkable.'

This went down rather badly. In an offended tone the waiter said, 'We don't have "plonk", sir. Our house wine is very good quality.'

Josh produced a controlled little smile. 'Then would you be so good as to bring me a half carafe of your very good quality house wine?'

347

As the waiter departed, he said to me, 'Don't look at me like that.'

'I wasn't looking like anything!'

'Yes, you were. I'll leave him a good tip, all right?'

Before I could reply he went on, 'How are your folks?'

'I don't know. I haven't spoken to them since I left yesterday.'

He raised an eyebrow in a way that made me feel guiltier than ever.

'I suppose I should have told them I was off to see Belinda, but we didn't exactly part on sweetness-and-light terms and I couldn't face phoning.'

'Talking of phoning . . .' He delved in his jacket pocket and put a mobile on the table. 'Much like mine – I must have picked it up on Sunday morning. Normally I'd say sorry, how careless of me, but my mind was not entirely on the job.'

His sardonic tone made me feel terrible. 'I thought I'd left it at home.'

'Yes, I thought you might.'

My embers were dying right down again. An air of tense preoccupation hung around him, as if there were something else he wanted to say but couldn't quite work up to it. My first, depressing thought was his fee and I instantly wondered why I hadn't thought of this before. Maybe that was why he'd come round last night. Maybe he was working up to saying, *'Look, I don't want to appear mercenary, especially in the circumstances, but you seem to have forgotten that we had a business arrangement.'*

The waitress came back for his order. I got the impression that she was nosily interested in the situation, which hardly surprised me since anyone with half a functional antenna could have picked up tension. Josh gave the menu another cursory scan and ordered smoked trout and a rare sirloin steak.

The waitress said, 'Shall I bring the gentleman's starter first and the main courses together?'

I was starving. 'Yes, but I'll change my mind and have a starter too. Soup of the day'll do.' At least they wouldn't have to go and catch it.

As she departed, Josh sat back and gave me another look that only confirmed my ember-cooling fears, so I took the bull by the whatsits. 'Look, you didn't come all this way to return my mobile. I should have passed it over on Sunday morning. I'm afraid I haven't got it all in cash any more, but I can give you most of your fee now and a cheque for the —'

'My *fee*? Jesus Christ . . .' Looking briefly at the ceiling, he ran an exasperated hand over the back of his neck before looking me in the eye again. 'Sophy, I did mark two as a favour. I thought you'd sussed that much out.'

For once in my life it was a relief to have said entirely the wrong thing. My little ember started glowing again, especially when he went on, 'But you're right. I didn't just come to return your mobile. Or to apologise, either.'

Something in the way he said it made my heart turn over. I wasn't expecting anything Mills-and-Boony, of

349

course; more on the lines of, *Look, don't you think it's time we stopped messing about?*

Seeing him hesitate, as if he couldn't quite get it out, I said lightly, 'Don't tell me – you came for a buckshee dinner. I still owe you that favour, after all.'

'No, but I won't argue.' He gave an odd little smile, hesitated a moment longer and suddenly crisped up. 'As a matter of fact, I came to pick your brains. Are you any good at crosswords?'

'*Cross*words?' If I'd been floating on any Mills-and-Boony cloud, that would have shattered it. As it was, I felt as if I were in some surreal dream. Any minute I'd look down and realise I had no clothes on, and everyone would be pointing at me and cracking up.

'Some clue was eluding me,' he went on, frowning slightly, as if trying to recall. '*Earnestly request rent in order to secure food* – no, scrub that, I got it halfway down the M3. Ah, yes. *Amorous invention on a spectacularly imaginative scale*. Three letters, beginning with A.'

For cunning attack-strategy, you could scarcely beat it. I was, literally, dumbfounded.

The waitress came back, looking vaguely awkward. 'Er, is it separate bills or together?'

I found a voice. 'Put it on mine.' Indicating my room key, I tried to recover the shreds of my cool. 'I suppose Alix told you,' I said, once the girl had gone.

'No.'

That only left one suspect. I had no doubts that Alix would have filled Ace in. Ace would then have reasoned that a little wheel-oiling was called for. 'Ace, then. He's Alix's brother, in case you didn't know.'

Drily Josh said, 'He did drop me a word. He slipped out as I was leaving and said, "Look, mate . . ."'

Just as I'd thought.

My own complete-prat feeling was partly diluted by realising what a prat Josh must have felt. In which case it was no wonder he'd wanted to catch me unawares. If he'd thought I was a headcase before, God alone knew what he was thinking now. Probably wondering which specifically female psychiatric disorder I was suffering from. Nympho-by-proxy, perhaps, in which the sufferer gaily goes round telling people she's got blokes A to G on the go, when in fact the only person sharing her bed is a teddy like Mr Bean's.

Our starters arrived, and I was heartily glad of both sustenance and distraction. I fell on my cream of cauliflower like Benjy to his dish and Josh attacked his smoked trout with vigour and liberal amounts of horseradish.

The offended waiter brought his wine, but Josh said, 'Thank you,' with disarming politeness, and he went away looking rather as if he'd spat in it and now wished he hadn't.

After a couple of mouthfuls, I said, 'Well, I'm sorry, but you did rather ask for it.' Curiosity was also getting the better of me. 'What did Ace say?'

With a glance at the couple at the next table, who looked like 'Disgusted, Tunbridge Wells' types, he lowered his voice. 'He said, "Look mate, it was all a load of bollocks. Me and Sophe are just mates."'

Oh, to have been a fly on the wall. 'I won't ask what you said. I can imagine.'

351

'I doubt it, but have a go. Two words, one and four letters.'

Having already put money on four and two, of Anglo-Saxon origin, I went blank. 'One and four?'

'You're hopeless,' he tutted. 'Remind me not to phone you when I'm stuck with my *Times* cryptic.' After putting away the last of his trout, he went on, 'I said, "I know."'

Flabbered I was, and gasted. 'You never did!'

'Well, maybe not a hundred per cent. Let's say I had a fair idea. About a ninety-seven per cent fair idea.'

Since my gaping was eliciting interest from nearby tables, I lowered my voice. 'You're only saying that now because you felt a total prat! You drank it all in, in the car!'

'Oh, I believed it then. You did it very well. It was only later that I started having doubts. Almost as soon as you dropped me off at the Underground.'

So sad had I become, such a disgrace to my sex, that I felt a tiny glow of gratification, just to realise he'd been thinking about me.

The waitress cleared away the starters. Once she'd gone, he went on. 'I started thinking that if you'd invented one guy – who turned out not to be entirely invented, but forget that for now – you were quite capable of inventing another. Especially since you'd convinced yourself that I thought you were desperate.'

'You did think I was desperate! You admitted it!'

'I did not. I admitted to mild amusement, which is not the same thing.'

It was almost worse. Our main courses arrived, and

my sole was worth waiting for. Fat, grilled to perfection, it was drizzled with lime butter. 'I suppose it was Ace's ham acting that gave it away.'

'No, he did it rather well at first; I even started thinking he was on the level, after all. It was only when I was leaving that he went over the top with his stroppy little sod act. I knew you'd never put up with someone like that.'

I didn't have to think long. '. . . *ask her what the fuck she's done with my black T-shirt . . .*' I almost felt sorry for Ace – he'd been so chuffed with it. 'How do you know what I'd put up with?' I asked, nevertheless.

He sliced into a steak that looked butter-tender and smeared mustard over it. 'I'd spent over twenty-four hours with you. It's enough to form a few opinions worth betting on.'

Well, he had me there.

Food was restoring me. I swear food tastes better when someone you fancy like mad is just across the table. All your sensual thingies are highlighted. The faintest scent of showered male body and clean shirt drifted to my nostrils, and I couldn't keep my eyes off his hands. They were wielding knife and fork in a very businesslike fashion, but all I could think of was that fingertip whisper on my shoulder. Above all, I was aware of his eyes on me whenever they weren't on his food. I got the distinct, ember-kindling impression that there was a good deal more he wanted to say but he was going to make me sweat, to pay me back for Ace.

Seeing the ghost-hunters rise from their table,

I changed the subject. 'Did you know this place is haunted?'

'Haunted my backside.'

'It is!' Since the brochure was still on the table, I turned back to page 11. 'A Mary Fanshawe – lived here in the 1540s. The owner of the place was some foul-mouthed wenching drunkard called Thomas Cranleigh. She was supposed to be a poor relation but rumour had it that she was his by-blow. Anyway, he brought her here as an unpaid servant and the next thing you know, she's trying to fasten her stays over a tummy full of baby.'

He seemed cynically amused. 'Don't tell me – it was the foul-mouthed drunkard wot dunnit.'

'So rumour had it. She managed to keep it a secret until three days after it was actually born – makes me shudder just to think of it. But Thomas found out and sent it away to a wet-nurse. Or so he *said*, but rumour was at it again, whispering that he'd murdered it and buried it in the grounds. That's what poor Mary thought, anyway. Thinking she could hear her poor little dead baby crying for her, she went mad, threw herself over the gallery and broke her neck.'

He raised an eyebrow. 'I wonder how much the management paid someone to dream that up? All right, possibly she existed,' he conceded, seeing my face, 'but if she's ever been back, I'll sign up for that celibate priesthood.'

'Don't get carried away. There's a party of ghost-hunters here. I overheard them talking. They're having a séance tonight.'

. 'What did I tell you?' he said. 'Brilliant for business.'

I wished I could share his healthy scepticism, but I'm afraid I'm one of those hopeless hypocrites where anything supernatural's concerned. I don't believe in any of it until it comes to the point. However broke I was, if you showed me a house that was said to be definitely haunted and offered me fifty grand to stay all night in it, alone, I'd run a mile.

And even if I'd been a real sceptic I'd still have argued for the sake of form. 'An old night porter saw her, only a few years ago,' I pointed out.

'I bet you fifty quid the only spirits he ever saw came out of a Johnnie Walker bottle. You surely don't believe in all that rubbish?'

'I do when I wake up at three o'clock in the morning in a creepy old place like this.'

Cue for him to say, *'Maybe you could do with some company, then. I'll give any marauding spooks short shrift.'*

But Life was being as bitch-faced as Jocasta tonight. 'I dare say Belinda'll take your mind off spooks.'

'If she deigns to turn up before I hit the hay. She must have friends in the area, not that I've got a clue who they might be. She might not have liked to go straight round. Maybe she phoned first and they said, 'For God's sake, come over.'

'Maybe.'

'In hindsight, perhaps I should have stayed at home. She might have phoned the flat by now and Alix will have told her I'm here. Maybe she can't face seeing me. She'll think I'm going to have a massive go at her, which *was* the general idea when I left. Friends are bound to be less judgemental; they haven't got a foot in the devastated-parent camp as well.'

'Whatever she did, I'm sure she had her reasons.'

'Yes – like going off Paul and not having the nerve to say so.'

'It must have been more than that. Look, Sophy—'

'What d'you mean, "Look, Sophy"? If you're starting to bend over backwards in poor-little-Belinda indulgence—'

'I'm not. All I'm trying to say—'

'I know what you're trying to say! "*Don't have a go at poor little Belinda – it can't possibly have been her fault.*" Nothing's ever her fault – I'm sick of it!'

He retreated into a wary silence that made me regret my outburst instantly, but I'd meant it. And I don't mind admitting that it had been partly due to a touch of pure, green-eyed stuff. If I'd looked like Belinda, all fragile and Aurora-ish, maybe he'd have been doing the poor-little-Sophy bit. In more moderate tones I went on, 'If she knew there was an unpleasant side to him she should have said so. And done something about it, before all the old dears had their best hats on and Dad was writing colossal cheques.'

The waitress brought pudding menus. I chose sticky-toffee pudding, Josh chose something called Chocolate Disgusting and I wished I'd ordered that instead. In fact, I wished I'd had the nerve to order both. Comfort food looked like the only comfort I was going to get tonight.

What was I going to do if Belinda didn't come back

by, say, eleven? Sit alone in that room with Mary hovering about? If I saw those ghost-hunters I'd have a massive go at them, too. Dead people should be left alone, not summoned to New Forest hotels to freak out people like me. With a bit of luck they'd get Thomas instead, and he'd give them a robust, Elizabethan mouthful and curse them all for meddling.

Cross with everybody, especially Josh, I topped up my glass. I'd have to stay now. I'd drunk far too much to drive, which meant I'd have to leave by six tomorrow morning to get home and change for work.

The waitress brought our puddings. 'Cream or custard?' she asked.

Sod it. Sod everything. 'Both,' I said. 'Please.'

Once she'd gone he said, 'I hadn't expected to see you at Jerry's do.'

I was glad of a change of subject. 'I hadn't expected to see you, either.'

'Not until Tamara nipped back and told you I was there.'

Such spot-on perception was unnerving, and I was duly unnerved.

'I gather you'd filled her in on your love life,' he went on drily. 'But I'm afraid she's not the world's best liar. She needs to eliminate that momentary blankness before her brain kicks in.'

This was getting hideously embarrassing, but since the dining room was emptying fast it was no longer necessary to keep our voices discreetly low. 'If you knew about Ace, why didn't you say something?' I demanded.

357

'Why didn't *I*? Why didn't you?' With a semi-exasperated gesture, he tossed his napkin on the table. 'You were evidently playing some sort of elaborate game and if you're still playing it, I'm afraid I've had enough of trying to suss out the rules. Your signals change with the wind. I'm beginning to think you and Belinda are two of a kind. Neither of you knows what you want. Or if you do, you make damned sure nobody else does.'

Almost before I'd grasped the implications of this, he went on, 'And there never was a bet. Any kind of bet. That was just what I told Jerry.'

I wasn't sure I could take much more of this. 'Then why were you doing it? For the money?'

'No,' he said.

'For laughs?'

'*Laughs?* Sophy, if I were that desperate for laughs I'd go and hang myself now from the nearest tree.' With a semi-exasperated sigh he went on, 'Look, I was never on the agency books. Julia Wright's a friend of mine. I happened to see her just after your original went sick. There was nobody else suitable and she didn't want to let you down.'

I couldn't believe it. 'Why the hell didn't you *say*?'

'How could I? She'd told you one thing – I could hardly tell you another. The agency's a fairly new venture; she didn't want you thinking she was just dragging anyone off the streets to fill in.'

'You said you hadn't had any more bookings!'

'Which was entirely true.'

358

'She told me you'd just registered with the agency!'

'I know, but she'd never have done it if you hadn't been desperate—'

'Great! I suppose she told you I was neurotic and screwed up, too.'

'Will you let me finish? Her exact words were, ". . . desperate to keep her mother happy". You'd invented a boyfriend and it had got out of hand.'

And then I'd invented another . . . 'At least I didn't make Kit up, and Tamara wasn't bullshitting about him either, if that's what you're thinking. He phoned last night while I was out and left a message. He's going to phone back – he sounded so awkward and psyched up—'

'I'm not surprised. Look, Sophy—'

'Yes, I know what you're thinking, but he was never an asshole – just the kind of helpless prey a certain type of bitch can't resist pinching, just to prove she can—'

'Sophy, will you shut up a minute?'

Somewhat startled, I shut.

He was looking straight at me. 'I should have told you earlier, but it wasn't easy.' Momentarily averting his eyes, he ran a hand awkwardly over the back of his neck. 'Alix was in a bit of state when I turned up. She'd just had a phone call.'

An iced claw gripped my heart. All I could think was: *Dad*. After the shocks he'd had . . . And I hadn't phoned. 'Please, not Dad?'

'No! It's nothing like that. It was Belinda.'

In my relief, my brain plucked at any other clue.

'She's pregnant after all, isn't she? And it's not Paul's, and she didn't dare tell him.'

'It's nothing like that!' Again he ran that hand over the back of his neck. 'There isn't an easy way to say this. Alix wanted to come and tell you herself.'

He looked me right in the eye. 'Kit phoned last night because he thought he should do the decent thing and break it to you himself.'

Even then I didn't get it. I must have been so thick.

'Belinda phoned tonight for the same reason,' he went on. 'She wanted to tell you herself.'

He paused minutely. 'She left Paul for Kit. She's with him now.'

FOURTEEN

Only for a moment did I think it was a sick joke. As old Mr Cliché first wrote, *And behold, ye scales did fall from her eyes.* Bits of a jigsaw I hadn't even realised existed were crashing from the ceiling and nearly knocking me out.

'I'm sorry,' he said. 'Alix was going to come and tell you herself. I think she'd had as big a shock as you – only she'd got some deadline to meet . . .'

'Her kids' camp brochure.' As I suppose one does when in a state of shock, I started talking rubbish in a weird voice that sounded as if it belonged to someone else. 'She always leaves everything till the last minute . . .'

'She'd told Belinda she was coming down. She said it'd be easier for you, if you knew first.' With a certain hesitancy, he reached across the table and took my hand. 'You could do with a shot of something. How about a Rémy Martin?'

'I don't want anything.' Feeling cold and detached, I drew my hand away. 'You knew, all along. All the time we were sitting here, you knew.'

'It wasn't the easiest thing to throw at you over soup of the day.'

I felt such a fool. Why in hell had I not *seen*? Why had I not picked up the one clue I saw now so clearly?

361

I thought of Alix, knowing what a fool I'd feel, feeling sorry for me, and telling Josh. I thought of myself, gaily telling Josh that Kit wanted me back. What had he thought? Poor, deluded cow . . . I thought of Alix telling Belinda that I'd thought Kit wanted me back, and of Belinda telling Kit, and Kit thinking: Poor, deluded cow . . .

In short, I found out what abject humiliation feels like.

My voice was still coming out in that weird, detached way. 'So what's been going on? Had she been seeing him behind my back? Was he screwing her as well as Jocasta?'

He looked blank.

'Jocasta. The woman he left me for.'

'Alix didn't mention her. Belinda apparently said nothing had happened before the wedding.'

'*Nothing?* How can "nothing" have happened? Have they been conducting some bloody virtual-reality relationship in cyberspace?'

'I only know what I've told you. I was only there a few minutes – as I said, Alix was in a state. She wanted you to know before they tell you themselves. Look, let me get you a brandy before—'

'I don't – want a bloody brandy!' It was a lie; I did. I wanted something else, too. 'I could kill for a cigarette.'

'I'll get you some.'

'I can't! It's non-smoking in here!'

'Then we'll go to the bar.' He beckoned to a waiter. 'Can we have the bill, please?'

He brought it seconds later, intending it for Josh,

who evidently intended it for him, too, but I was quick. 'As I said, I owe you one.'

And just as I was signing, Josh muttered, 'Oh Jesus . . .'

He was looking over my shoulder. Following his gaze I turned and saw Kit. Having just entered, he scanned the room, saw us, and stopped dead. Then, with a face I can only describe as tortured, he approached the table.

It was just as well the dining room was almost empty. Only the staff laying up for breakfast witnessed the cabaret. 'Clear off for fifteen minutes, will you?' Josh said in terse tones. 'I've only just told her.'

Suddenly, I felt weirdly controlled again. Controlled and detached, as if it was all happening to somebody else. 'It's all right. I'm fine.'

Two paces from the table, Kit stopped. Under that slight tan he looked haggard and strained. 'Sophy, I'm so sorry . . . It's all been such a bloody mess . . .'

'Where is she?' I asked.

He nodded towards the door. 'In her room. We just got back.'

'Where from?' I asked, in perfectly controlled tones. 'Have you been out for dinner?'

'No! Oh God . . .' Looking wretched, he ran a hand through his hair. 'Where's Alix? I thought she was coming.'

'She was busy,' I said. 'Josh kindly took it upon himself to come and give me the news.'

'*Josh*?' As he gaped from me to Josh, I realised what I'd said.

I suppose it was a minor comfort to drop a bombshell in return. 'There never was a Dominic. I made him up, to get Mum off my back. I hired Josh from an escort agency.'

Under his tan, more of Kit's colour drained away.

Oddly enough, it didn't make me feel better. Coolly I stood up. 'Let's go and see Belinda. And then perhaps the pair of you'll tell me what Love's Young Dream's been up to behind everybody's backs.'

I didn't quite stalk, but I walked crisply, with my head up, Josh and the obviously shell-shocked Kit behind me.

Once we were in the foyer, Josh said, 'Unless you want me to come, I'll wait here.'

His voice was practical and sympathetic, but my humiliation was still so raw, any hint of sympathy stung like lemon juice. I could think only of him thinking: Poor cow – how am I going to tell her?'

'There's really no need for you to hang around. It was kind of you to come but I'll be fine.'

After a brief, assessing look, he raised an eyebrow. 'If that's what you want.'

Of course it wasn't what I wanted. I wanted him to say. 'Of course you're not fine. I'm staying here, even if it takes till three o'clock in the morning. I'll be here when you're through with whatever they come up with, and then I'll take you up to your room and pour you a stiff drink and we'll talk, if you feel like talking. If not, we'll finally stop messing about and go to bed. And I'll still be there when you wake up.'

I wanted a valiant prince, you see. A man who'd

364

know without telling. But valiant princes have always been thin on the ground where I'm concerned. 'Good night, then,' I said. 'Thanks for coming.'

It wasn't me he replied to, but Kit. In crisp, almost pleasant tones he said, 'Appearances can be deceptive. You don't look like a shit, but something stinks round here. I need some fresh air.' Without another word he turned for the entrance.

Kit looked stricken, but I didn't feel sorry for him. On the contrary, I exulted in this crumb of prince-like behaviour. 'What the hell did you expect?' I asked tartly. 'For him to say, "Ta-ta, mate, sooner you than me?" For God's sake let's get moving. I've got to go to work tomorrow.'

He moved. I followed him around reception to a wide, lushly carpeted corridor, where he stopped outside a slightly open door.

Room seventeen. Belinda was standing by the bed, her face tear-stained and fearful. 'I'm so sorry . . . I wanted to tell you so badly . . .'

Typical. There she was, hiding in her nice, safe room while Prince Kit braved the evil witch Sophy in her lair. I've never pretended to be a saint and I wasn't about to start now. As I stared at her, something welled up inside me. 'You little cow – I trusted you!'

Predictably, she burst into tears.

I suppose it was about two when I finally returned, exhausted and emotionally drained, to my room. I felt still more exhausted to think of setting the alarm for five-thirty, so that I'd be at work more or less on time.

As I closed the door some yellow A4 flyer that had been pushed under it lay on the carpet, cheerily inviting me to a jolly Medieval Night on Friday, with troubadours, mead, and spit-roasted serf with elderflower sauce. Wondering how anyone could be thinking of medieval jollity, I told it to fuck off.

Of course I hardly slept, partly because of being afraid that I'd sleep through the alarm, and partly because of what was going endlessly around in my head. Had I been blind? I badly wanted to ring Alix, but if she was still up, frantically working to that deadline, she didn't need interruptions. If she wasn't, she'd be sleeping like the dead.

It might have been a comfort if I could still have felt livid with them, but even that was denied me. Melted by their tortured confessions, my lividness had lasted only about fifteen minutes. Kit had left around midnight, leaving me with Belinda and more agonised soul-searching. All I felt now was miserable, humiliated, and so lonely I could have died.

I wept a little into the pillow. The room was blacker than midnight, odd creaks and rustlings coming from dark corners. I knew it was stupid, but part of me was back in a childhood nightmare, hiding under the covers so the grey form materialising at the end of the bed wouldn't know I was there . . .

I did oversleep, but not by much. I arrived home, unshowered, shortly after seven, and for once Alix didn't complain about being cruelly torn from sleep.

We sat in the kitchen with freshly brewed Blue

Mountain. Alix was in one of Calum's rugby shirts, looking almost as haggard and pillow-tossed as me. 'If only you'd phoned,' she despaired. 'I was up till gone three – I would have phoned but I thought you'd be with them or with Josh, and I didn't want to interrupt anything . . .'

I gave a hollow little laugh.

'I was shattered when she told me,' she went on. 'All I could think was, *How?* They were never even alone together!'

'But they were, just that once. At least, that's their story and they're sticking to it. Knowing them, it's probably true.'

'She was nearly in tears even before she told me,' Alix continued. 'I said, "It's not Marc, is it?", thinking maybe she'd gone off with him and they'd rowed again already. But she said, "No! Oh God, is that what everybody's thinking?" and then she just came out with it.'

After a moment she went on awkwardly, 'Actually, I did think I caught vibes between them, just once.'

It felt like the worst kind of betrayal. 'Then why the hell didn't you tell me?'

'How could I? It was so fleeting and nothing actually happened. I knew Simon fancied her – he was always saying what a cracker she was – so I suppose that made me hyper-suspicious.'

But Kit never had. Not once.

'And then she went home and it was all a massive thing with Paul,' she went on. 'I never even thought about it again.'

Ace chose that moment to wander in, yawning and

scratching the bits that weren't covered by holey tracksuit bottoms, so I then had to go over the whole thing again, with another pot of coffee and bacon butties kindly thrown together by Ace.

Only then did I get round to Josh.

'I couldn't believe it when he said he'd sussed me out,' he said, sounding positively hurt. 'I thought my act was brilliant.'

'It was, but you overlooked the fact that I'm not a doormat. In any case, he already had a fair idea.'

'I can't believe he just left like that,' Alix said. 'I really thought there was something there – he said straightaway. "Look, I'll go," and I suppose I thought seeing him'd make you feel better.'

'I *told* him to leave,' I despaired. 'I felt such a fool, having gone on about Kit like that, saying he wanted me back . . .'

'Give him a ring,' Ace said blithely.

'I can't! I haven't even got his bloody number! In any case, if he'd really wanted to be with me he'd have said so. He thinks I'm a headcase and I don't blame him.' Wearily I glanced at my watch. 'I'd better get moving. I've got to have a shower and find stuff for work, and tonight and tomorrow morning. I'm sure there aren't any clean tights . . .'

'She's meeting Belinda after work,' Alix told Ace. 'She's going home with her for moral support. I'm damned if I would.'

I wasn't much cop at work, but I went through the motions. Of all the things Belinda had told me the previous night, one little thing somehow stood out. It was something I'd said at the engagement do, about the trip to Florence being right out of the romantic rule book.

Looking back with hideous hindsight, she'd said that's exactly how it had seemed. As if he'd picked up the phone and asked his secretary to check the 'proposals' section of the rule book and order him a gold-plated, top-of-the-range job, and by the way he was overdue for a coffee and where was the Dibson and Dobson report.

But I'm jumping the gun a bit.

The whole mess had started not long after Belinda had turned up to occupy our cupboard, all wounded and beautiful over Marc. She had barely remembered Kit from before and he'd recalled only some pubescent girl, invariably giggling with Sonia. Suspecting that it was about him, he had kept out of their way.

Years later, he'd been a different animal from the men she usually went for. For a start he barely seemed to notice her, not that he was at the flat very much in the first place. She couldn't even remember when it had hit her, but one day, when I'd said, 'Kit's coming round later,' something inside her had given a wobbly little lurch.

Being Belinda she'd been appalled, but covering up had been easy enough. Other than the polite, 'How's it going?' variety he'd barely given her a glance. For Kit it had been exactly the same, creeping up on him almost unawares. He'd pretended indifference and she'd barely given *him* a glance. So adept had they

369

been at hiding it, neither had had a clue how the other had felt.

Until Kit had played doctor.

It had been my own doing. She'd had an insect bite on her leg, scratched it to bits and it had got infected, red and angry-looking. I'd nagged her to go to the GP but she'd made endless excuses. Ever since breaking an arm at eleven she'd hated anything to do with doctors or hospitals. She'd kept saying irritably, 'I *will* go, OK?' Eventually I'd said to Alix, 'If she doesn't do something about it soon, she's going to get blood poisoning. I'll get Kit to look at it next time he comes.'

I'd hated asking when he was off duty, but I hadn't expected him to be so irritable about it. He'd had a massive go at her for neglecting it and Belinda had practically been in tears. I'd actually been upset with him. Eventually he'd said it needed an antibiotic dressing and sent me out with a prescription. It had taken me ages to find the twenty-four-hour chemist and then the pharmacist had made a fuss because it wasn't on a proper form and his BMA number wasn't legible. She'd phoned the flat, to check. I'd been gone over an hour. And all the while, behind closed doors, two people who'd been desperately trying to pretend that they were nothing more to each other than a pair of old dishcloths . . .

All too well I remembered my rushing-back return. Belinda had been pink-faced and tearful, Kit gruff and still irritable. The instant he'd finished she'd disappeared into her cupboard – and I'd had a go at him for upsetting her.

370

As for Bitch-face, well, I was feeling a bit bad about poor old Jocasta now. When I looked back, I remembered. When had he ever said it was Jocasta? *I* had accused him and he'd let me believe it, because it was easier than telling the truth. But it wasn't Belinda that had broken us up. Even before she'd come he'd felt we were getting to the end of the road. He just hadn't known how to tell me. Somehow that had been almost the most humiliating thing of all.

Being Kit and Belinda, both too nice for their own good, they didn't just say 'sod it' and start a wild affair. No, they couldn't possibly do that to poor old Sophy. They made a noble, self-sacrificing agreement to forget it – probably it would soon wear off, after all. But Kit had finished with me anyway because he couldn't go on, feeling as he did about Belinda. She'd gone home about three weeks after the bust-up, having bought me Nutella and doughnuts, and said Kit was a bastard, and she hoped they both got herpes.

And not once had I ever suspected a thing.

He eventually went out with other people – he even went out with Jocasta a couple of times – and Belinda had met Paul. At first she really had been swept right off her size five feet. He'd sort of wiped Kit out, she'd said. In any case, she'd thought he'd have met somebody else by then and forgotten all about her. And Kit, being Kit, had thought exactly the same.

Made for each other obviously.

Christmas came and went, and Belinda got engaged. Kit moved to the Barnstaple hospital and found more Other People to go out with. But as the weeks passed she was still there, niggling at the back of his mind. Eventually, about three weeks before the wedding, he wrote to her saying he had some leave due soon, might be in the area, and maybe he'd give her a ring.

Just that, no heavy stuff, but it had thrown Belinda into torment. Suddenly she'd looked at Paul and known what she'd been refusing to see: he just wasn't right. Of course, rushing the wedding had been his idea; he'd said there was no point in waiting. He'd taken her to the Inn by the Beck for lunch, and there'd been a wedding going on. Idly she'd remarked that it was a lovely place for a wedding, and during the meal he'd gone off, supposedly to the loo, but actually to check the bookings. He'd said, 'They've got a cancellation in May. Shall we go for it?' He'd hardly even waited for an answer and at that point she'd still been telling herself he was all she'd ever wanted.

It was only afterwards that subtle changes in his behaviour had become more marked. He'd started dominating her, telling her what to do, what to wear, even what to think. She'd started to feel like some sort of beautiful possession to make other men jealous, like his car or his Patek Philippe. She'd even begun to feel that the sex was like a cross between something out of a Harrods catalogue and Uncle Ben's rice: gold-plated, top-of-the-range, perfect results every time.

She'd thought of calling it off, but only in the darkest moments just before the dawn. She'd thought of Mum's devastation, of Paul's angry disbelief and terrible hurt. But being Belinda, she'd told herself it

372

was just cold feet. Hadn't her friends been sick as pigs, told her how lucky she was? She hadn't even replied to Kit's letter.

If he hadn't turned up at Sonia's the day before the wedding I dare say it would have been like so many other marriages, i.e., getting steadily worse for two or three years and eventually ending in the divorce courts. And, of course, he hadn't just called to see Sonia and the family. He'd been hoping he might see Belinda, give her a call . . . News of the wedding had come like a kick in the guts, but he'd let Sonia drag him along anyway. Maybe he'd been building up some besotted fantasy in his head. Maybe he'd think: well, nothing so special after all, and go away feeling relieved.

Belinda had nearly thrown up when she'd heard he was coming but, like him, she'd told herself she'd worked him up into some sort of idealised dream. If he still wanted her, why would he be coming to her wedding?

She'd acted so well, Kit had thought she was happy and gone off to get drunk and kill himself, in that order. But Belinda had seen it in his eyes and felt sick. She'd gone off on her nothing-but-the-best honeymoon, thought about Kit every single day of it, and hated herself. Paul had wanted her to dress up in designer stuff and jewellery every night, even at the game lodges. And she'd said it was tacky and out of place, and he'd got cross, so she'd done it anyway to keep the peace. She'd longed to wear a pair of tatty old shorts and be with someone who wanted to watch the fireflies and the sunsets, instead of standing at the bar checking out the other tourists in case they might be useful for networking. She'd locked herself in the loo, taken Kit's letter from its hiding place in her make-up bag, and wondered what the hell she'd done. But being Belinda, she'd told herself it was too late; she'd made her designer bed and would lie on it.

She was still telling herself this until their last morning, back in Nairobi. Over breakfast, expecting her to be over the moon, Paul had told her that she could give her notice in at the nursery, he'd fixed her up a half-share in a smart little business with the girlfriend of a friend of his. Up-market fashion, in an up-market area. Right up her street. Designer stuff'd just walk off the rails, especially with her modelling it in the shop.

She had been dumbfounded at first, and he'd been peeved that she wasn't over the moon. She had explained that, actually, it wasn't up her street. She liked the nursery; why else did he think she was doing it? Then he'd scoffed and said, Come on, you can't really prefer changing nappies and wiping snotty noses to a smart little business? And she'd said, yes, actually, she did. And then he'd turned abruptly dismissive, in a way she'd only seen him adopt with other people, and said it was menial, wiping noses and changing nappies, and he didn't want his wife doing a menial job, and anyway she earned peanuts, not that he cared about that. She'd tried to talk to him but he'd gone like a cold wall, as she put it, and said they'd discuss it later. He was off to play golf and would she do his packing – he might not be back until shortly before they had to leave for the airport.

For over two hours she had sat in the room, agonising. She had told herself she'd go back with him and maybe it'd all work out. But then she'd got Kit's letter out of her bag again and re-read it endlessly. What if she left Paul in six months and Kit had found someone else? For once in her life, was she going to have the guts to go for what she really wanted?

By the time she'd made up her mind it was nearly too late. She'd left the note and taken a taxi to the airport, but the earlier flight had already closed. By then she'd begun to wonder what on earth she'd done but hadn't dared go back to the hotel in case Paul had come back and found her note. So she'd checked into another hotel, a cheaper one, and phoned the Devon number on Kit's letter, but there had been no reply.

After a terrible night she'd flown back the next day, arrived early on Sunday morning and tried to phone Kit from Heathrow. This time the colleague he shared with had answered. Kit wasn't there; he'd gone to his parents as his father wasn't well – would she like the number? He'd given the address, as well. The New Forest, Hampshire.

She'd hired a car and driven straight down, hardly daring to contact him in case he was horrified and told her to go back to Paul. She'd checked into the hotel a couple of miles from the house, and agonised for another hour before picking up the phone.

Kit had answered. She'd said, 'It's me. I've left Paul.'

For a moment there had been a silence so

devastating, she'd nearly hung up. But then he'd said, 'Where are you?' and she'd told him, and he'd said, 'I'm coming over.'

It was sweet, really, except for his father. 'Not well' had been an understatement: he'd had two heart attacks and was hanging on by a thread. She'd gone with Kit to the hospital and back to the house, and he'd told his stepmother she was a girlfriend. The stepmother had said tearfully how nice of her to come at a time like this but she was sorry if things were bit upside down just now, and made Belinda feel terrible.

Kit had left the hotel at midnight because he'd had to get back to the hospital. They'd been there before coming to see me; his strained look had not just been down to me and Belinda. And naturally, that had made me feel guilty for taking him away from his father.

As you may remember, Kit's parents had been going through a bad patch when I'd first met him. They'd eventually divorced while he was still a student; his mother had remarried almost at once. His father had taken a bit longer. I'd met both him and the new wife once, at their home in Guildford, and if Belinda had gone to Guildford instead I might just have sussed something out earlier. But only two months before all this they'd bought a dear little place in the New Forest, perfect for retirement, and had been busily doing the garden. And while he was carrying a massive bag of peat from car to garden, Kit's father had had the first heart attack.

As Josh had said, Kit had phoned the flat because

he'd felt he should break it to me himself, but Belinda had told him not to ring back, *she* ought to do it. In the end, of course, it had been Kit who'd braved the witch's lair. If there had been a forest to hack, I dare say he'd have hacked that, too. When you look like Belinda, there's always a prince somewhere to save you from yourself.

I'd arranged to meet her at Euston. In my exhausted state driving up was out of the question and since meeting me in central London in her hire car was never going to be easy, she had given it back to Hertz.

I wasn't mad with her any more: helplessly exasperated would describe it better. And I did feel sorry for what she'd been though. After all, some sisters would pinch your bloke and not think twice. However, giving moral support wasn't just down to noble selflessness on my part. I had to go home sometime and she'd take the pressure off. She was now the guilty party and Mum and Dad would feel sorry for me and think how good I was to bring the prodigal home.

If this sounds a tad cynical, it was.

She was waiting at the platform like a Saudi prisoner waiting for the chop, and not just because of what she had to face at home. Kit's father had died at ten-thirty.

'Then you could hardly have come at a better time,' I said, trying to cut short her agonisings. 'Imagine if you were him and the one person you'd been dying to see for months turned up!'

'Yes, but if he'd just married someone else and left her for me, I'd feel like a pile of pooh, too.'

I gave up. You could offer Belinda the best silver lining, fifteen trillion pounds per square metre, and she'd always find a hole in it.

She'd phoned and said we were coming, but hadn't gone into tortured detail. 'I'm sure Mum and Dad are going to think it's awful,' she fretted, as we finally boarded the train. 'I mean, both of us involved with the same man . . .'

Calling a spade by its name had never been her forte. 'Both sleeping with the same man, you mean. I suppose you have by now?'

She only flushed and looked guilty, probably because they'd done it while his father was hovering at death's door.

I had to ask. 'Did nothing really happen before? When you were alone with him that time?'

She flushed again. 'I suppose there *was* a kiss, but we both felt so awful there was honestly nothing else. I'd never thought he felt anything for me till then. I'd thought it was just me. But suddenly he sort of looked at me and I just sort of knew, if you know what I mean.'

Yes, I sort of did.

'I still can't believe it, about Dominic,' she fretted. 'Why on earth didn't you *tell* me?'

'You might have let it out.'

'I wouldn't! And I'm sure Josh must be a *bit* keen, or he wouldn't have come all that way in the first place. Why don't you phone the agency and leave a message? He might have thought—'

'Belinda, just leave it, will you?' The train was just

pulling out. 'I'm exhausted – I'm going to have a zizz. Wake me up if I start snoring or my mouth's hanging open.'

We got a cab at the other end and arrived home to the predicted prodigal-daughter bit. And lo, there was weeping and tearing of hair. But there was forgiveness also, and talk of split milk, and fatted M&S salmon *en croûte* were shoved in the oven. And there was weeping also for the firstborn, who had vowed never to return to the hearth of the wrinklies, but had relented. And mother wept unto daughter, saying, 'We never meant to upset you, dear – you know we've always been so proud of you – I was only saying to Trudi the other day . . .'

While it was all simmering down I sat on the sidelines with Benjy. 'Honestly,' I told him silently, 'all these dramas because civilised man has to make elaborate rituals over what is basically just a mating instinct, only slightly less crude than yours, if you'll forgive me for saving so.'

'Don't knock it,' Benjy said, with a lollopy grin. 'I got my leg over that tasty little springer spaniel last week.'

Around midnight Dad and Belinda took him for his fourteen-pee walk and I was left with Mum in the kitchen.

'Well, I don't know, dear, I really don't,' she said, for the nth time. 'You're being very good about it, but doesn't it make you feel just a bit awkward?'

'A bit, I suppose, but it's been so long and it's not as if I'm still languishing over him.'

'Do you think it'll last?' she went on. 'I sometimes

379

wonder whether she'll ever really make up her mind about anything.' Restlessly she twisted a table napkin in her fingers. 'She'll have to write to everybody and send all those presents back. And she'll have to go and see Paul – if he *will* see her, that is. I still feel terribly sorry for him, but I must say it wasn't very nice to go nosing through pockets, even if he did think he was some sort of con man. Anyone could see he wasn't a con man. Con men don't look you in the eye.'

'Some do. If they all looked like con men, nobody'd be conned.'

'I dare say you're right . . .' After a moment she went on, 'It was a bit late in the day, but Daddy told me last night that he'd never been quite a *hundred* per cent keen on Paul, not that he'd ever said. It was nothing he could put his finger on – nothing he could justify. He thought he was being the over-possessive father, thinking nobody would ever be good enough.'

I had to ask. 'I know it's easy in hindsight, but were you quite a hundred per cent keen?'

'I was, at first.' Her voice took on a tone of retrospective *if only*. 'I mean, he seemed so keen on *her*, and that's always the main thing. And he was always so crisp and decisive . . . On the other hand I sometimes felt you never quite got beneath the surface. He was always perfectly polite but now and then I thought there was a lack of *warmth*, if you know what I mean. But I'd never have upset her by saying anything. It was just a feeling and I wasn't marrying him, after all.'

I probably wouldn't have said anything either. As Tamara had said, you don't, unless the bloke's obviously a complete arsehole and even then you think three times.

'After all, Granny and Grandpa tried to put me off marrying Daddy,' she went on. 'And all it did was upset me and make me even more determined.'

Exactly.

'I really don't know what I'm going to say to people, but I suppose it could be worse,' she sighed. 'Eileen Thomas told me last week that her sister's daughter left her husband for another *woman*! Two children too, poor little things . . .'

Absently she wiped some pastry crumbs off the table and into her hand. 'So that Josh came to the hotel to see you?'

Belinda had let this out but it was all far too complicated to go into and I certainly didn't want Mum getting Ideas. 'Yes, but only to drop off my mobile. He was in the area.'

'Well, that was very nice of him, in the circumstances.'

She'd been dry-eyed for an hour but the leaks were coming back. 'About what you said on the phone that time – I do hope it wasn't a case of the truth coming out. I really can't bear to think you might be afraid of bringing boyfriends home in case I put them off. I dare say I was a bit over-eager with that Josh, but he did strike me as such a nice type . . .' She dabbed at her eyes with the napkin. 'I suppose he was laughing at me behind my back . . .'

For the nineteenth time in the past few days I felt like a pile of pooh. 'He wasn't, I promise. He felt just as bad as I did, because you were both so nice.'

This seemed to console her. 'Well, I must say it was very kind of him to drop in specially, just to give back your phone.'

She hesitated delicately. 'I suppose it *was* just for that?'

Would she ever give up? Wearily I said, 'Mum, please don't start.'

'I'm not, dear!' Even more delicately, she paused again. 'But even if there *was* anything, you needn't worry that I'd be inviting him for the weekend after next. Though if I did I certainly wouldn't do another roast – I really don't know what he must have thought of that last one.'

'It wasn't that bad. He ate it, didn't he?'

'Well, yes, now you mention it. I always think you can tell a lot about a man from the way he eats. Look at Daddy – he'll eat anything. I never could do with men who pick at their food. Paul wouldn't touch onions, you know. Or broccoli. It just goes to show.'

I took the crack-of-dawn train back and went straight to work, which was frantic enough to take most of my mind off everything else. I got home feeling so weary I could have died.

I collapsed on the sofa with a large V&T and post-mortemed it all with Alix.

'At least you're on speaking terms again,' she said. 'And you've come out of it smelling of roses.'

'I won't tell you what I smell like.' Inelegantly I raised my arm and sniffed my armpit. 'This deodorant's been on since five-thirty this morning and I'm too knackered even to have a shower.'

'Don't, then. Go to bed and stink till morning.' Suddenly she frowned. 'You didn't forget to pay your hotel bill, did you?'

'Of course not! Why?'

'Something came from the hotel this morning. Hang on, where did I put it . . .?' After half a minute she unearthed a large white envelope from the kitchen. In a fancy green font at the top left-hand corner it said *Cranleigh Manor Hotel*.

'Probably inviting me for a weekend break,' I yawned. 'Or a sodding Medieval Night . . .' I opened it anyway and drew out a short letter and another envelope. The letter said,

Dear Ms Metcalfe,

We are forwarding the enclosed, which was found by the chambermaid after your departure. Possibly you overlooked it, as some hotel literature had also been pushed under the door. We trust you enjoyed your stay at the Cranleigh Manor and hope to have the pleasure of seeing you again soon.

I gaped at the envelope. It was smaller than the other, with *Cranleigh Manor* in the same green font. And smack in the middle was a bold black scrawl that said simply *Sophy*.

FIFTEEN

I ripped it open. In the same black scrawl it said:

> I'm three doors down, in 24. If you need to talk or
> the spooks are playing you up, give me a call – I
> don't care how late it is.
> Josh
> PS. I never thought you were desperate – just
> choosy.

My eyes were filling already, my throat constricting.
'He was there all the time. What must he have
thought?'

Alix grabbed the note and gave a despairing sigh. 'I
told you, didn't I? God, you're hopeless. Why didn't
you *see* it?'

Numbly I handed her the other letter. 'It was some
Medieval Night thing – I didn't even pick it up . . .'
With hideous clarity I suddenly saw that yellow flyer
exactly as it had looked on the blue carpet. I saw it in
the sharp focus, even down to a tiny white corner
protruding from underneath. Why the hell had I not
twigged?

When I told Alix she said, 'I suppose you were worn
out and not really with it, never mind your head being
full of K and B. Poor bloke – maybe he lay there half

the night waiting for you to call. For God's sake phone those Nixons and get his number.'

'*Dixons*. God, he must think I'm such a bitch . . .'

At this point Ace wandered in from the shower, clad in only a towel, and Alix filled him in.

'Told you, didn't I?' he said blithely. 'I knew he fancied you. I could tell.'

I didn't answer – already I was trying the Dixons but it was that loathsome answerphone again. In tears, I slammed the receiver back on the cradle. 'What's the *matter* with these bloody people? I can understand Tamara being out, but her parents? They're older than mine! They're supposed to be in, watching sodding *Emmerdale* and *Ground Force*!'

Ace said, 'Why haven't you got his number? I thought you phoned him last week.'

'She did, dickhead, but she wrote the number on a newspaper and they've all gone to the paper bank,' Alix said irritably.

'Maybe not all of them. Hang on a tick . . .'

Moments later he returned with a cheerful grin, a blackened banana skin, a Pot Noodle pot and two *Evening Standards*. 'Under the bed,' he grinned. 'Thought I'd seen a scrawl somewhere – is this it?' He handed me a *Standard* open at the horoscope page, with both Jerry's and Josh's numbers scrawled in the margin.

I could have kissed him. 'Ace, I'll never call you a slob again.'

Already I was jabbing numbers. After about six rings, a recorded Josh said sorry he couldn't take my call, and to please leave a message after the tone . . .

If the cretin who'd invented answerphones had walked in right then, I swear he would not have lived another minute. '*Sodding* answerphones!' I banged it down, in tears again. 'Why isn't he bloody well *in*? Why can't something be simple, just once in my sodding miserable life?'

'Maybe it's just as well,' Alix said tactfully. 'You're worn out and wound up. Try again later.'

'No. I'm going to leave a message now.' Already I was pressing 'last number redial'. After the tone I said, 'Josh, it's Sophy. I didn't get your note till just now. I didn't see it because something else had been pushed under the door, but the hotel forwarded it. I'm really sorry if you thought . . .' At this point my voice started cracking, my fragile control disintegrating like wet tissues.

'Sophy, *leave* it,' Alix said anxiously, but I was on autopilot to the bitter end.

'Why didn't you *call* me? Why didn't you come round? I was lying there, feeling like the biggest fool in creation and miserable as sin. Did you really think I'm the kind of bitch who'd ignore a note like that?' In full, tearful flood I went on, 'And I've got a clue for you, too – eight letters, beginning with D for Dickhead. Couldn't you see how I felt about you? I've wanted you practically since I first saw you – I've thought about you non-stop – and while I'm at it I saw you coming on the common that time and pretended to be asleep. I thought the babies were yours and all my fat was hanging out – why aren't you bloody well *answering*?'

My voice was cracking too much to go on, so

I didn't. I pressed 'end call' and looked up into Alix's horrified face.

'Blimey,' said Ace.

Alix said, 'Sophy, I *told* you to leave it! Haven't you ever heard about playing it cool?'

'I'm sick of playing it cool! I've been playing it cool ever since I met him and look where it's got me!'

'You'll put him off for life, going on like that!'

'Then at least I'll know where I stand! If telling him how I feel's going to put him off, I might as well forget it now!' I went for a bath, where my tears mingled with Ylang Ylang foam. Already I was wishing I could wipe the tape and start again, but it was too late. I collapsed into bed shortly afterwards, and he didn't phone back. I went to work next morning feeling leaden, as if my spark would never come back.

When I got home, late because of delays on the wretched Underground, Alix met me at the door, her eyes sparking more than I'd seen since she'd first Done It with Calum. 'He phoned,' she said. 'This afternoon. I'd nipped to the Pop-In but he left a message.'

'Something about his crossword,' Ace said. 'Gave the clue, too. He's a bit thick, if you ask me. I got it straight off.'

'Ace!' said Alix crossly. 'If you must listen to people's messages, it's not considered polite form to admit it.'

I wasn't listening. Already I was in the living room, turning the tape to 'play'.

'Sophy, it's dickhead,' he said. 'You're not the only one who has family dos to go to. I was in Kent last night for my old man's seventieth, which is why I

387

didn't get your message till this afternoon. Sorry to be a pain, but I'm still having crossword trouble. Hold on while I get the paper . . .' There was a short rustle. 'Here we are – fourteen down: *Object of intense and passionate desire, pursued and thought lost, but maybe found again.* Five letters, beginning with S. Have a little think, will you? I'll call back later.'

This was quite enough to make my eyes go all prickly until I realised Ace was still lurking by the door. 'Aah, init luvly?' he grinned.

Since there was nothing else handy, I threw a box of tissues at him. 'Push off!'

Laughing his face off, he disappeared.

I picked up the receiver and dialled. 'Hi, it's me.'

'Hi, me,' Josh said. 'Did you get my message?'

'If I hadn't, I wouldn't be phoning,' I said in somewhat wobbly tones.

More gently he said, 'So did you crack that clue?'

What with my gulpy throat and other symptoms of emotional disintegration, I don't quite know how I managed to talk at all. 'I'm not sure – I've never been much cop at crosswords. Maybe if you came over and helped me get my head round it . . .'

When I put the phone down twenty seconds later, Alix emerged from wherever she'd been listening and pretending not to. 'Well?' she grinned.

'He's coming in forty minutes!'

'Shit! Look, I'll go to Calum's – Ace!'

He put his head round the door. 'What?'

'You're going out too – take Tina to the cinema or something – I'll give you some money if you're skint –

388

only go and clear up your junk from the living room first and Hoover it – no, don't – you'll never do it properly – God, why didn't I do it before? Sophy, go and have a shower, quick – shave your legs – put on those La Perla knickers and don't forget to clean the loo – I'll tidy your room – go on, quick—'

Forty-three minutes later I was giving myself a final check in my cheval mirror: cream linen trousers and plain, hip-covering top in navy silk rib. Both smartly casual, and just what I'd normally wear for idling at home, of course.

Alix had gone mad with the Hoover, dusted my room and even changed the bed. It looked like something out of an advertisement, all smooth and pristine with the pillows plumped and the pillowcase corners tweaked out. Just the way I always did it, naturally. She'd blitzed the living room, too, disposed of tights drying on radiators and sprayed Spring Fresh polish to give an illusion of hygiene.

So by the time the doorbell actually rang I was sitting on the sofa with *Marie Claire*, pretending that we lived like proper people all the time.

I raced to the door. He was standing on the step with that crookedy little smile that made my heart turn over, and an armful of pink roses. 'Hi,' he said, giving them a wry glance. There must have been a dozen little bunches, not one big one. 'I'm afraid they're past their best. I bought them from a bloke at the lights and nearly told him to stuff them when I saw the state of them, but he looked like an illegal immigrant and it was starting to rain . . .'

389

'Oh, Josh . . .' For the second time that evening, my throat constricted. 'They're lovely – just a teeny bit droopy. Let me put them in water . . .'

Instead of an instant snog, then, he passed me the Cellophaned armful and followed me to the kitchen, where I unearthed a pair of scissors and started stripping off plastic and snipping ends off stems. 'There's a beer in the fridge, if you like,' I said, over my shoulder.

'I wouldn't say no.'

I heard him open the fridge and the hiss as he ripped off the ring pull, but no sounds of anything going down his throat.

'If you haven't eaten, I thought we might go out,' he said.

'That'd be lovely.' *Snip, snip*. I felt his eyes on me, non-stop. It felt like a re-run of Sunday morning, except that this time . . . 'There's a lovely little Italian up the road, if you like Italian.'

'Italian'll do fine.' After a moment he went on, 'Where are your friends?'

'Oh, out,' I said, as casually as I could, given my heart-thumping anticipation. 'They won't be back for hours.'

This was quite enough to send another squillion volts into an already charged atmosphere. And the faint 'tap' as he put his beer can down was like that firework bit, i.e., *Light blue touch paper and stand well clear*.

Just as he had in my folks' guest room, he came to stand just behind me. Just as he had before, he blew

390

very lightly on the back of my hastily upswept hair. 'Just how hungry are you?' he asked, as casually as you like.

Already I was going weak at the knees. 'Oh, not desperately,' I said, *Snip, snip*. 'Do you know, I think these'll be fine once they've had a drink. Are you?'

'Pretty peckish, actually.'

As I carried on snipping, he put his hands on my waist and brushed his lips against my hair.

God, it was lovely. It was so lovely, I wanted to keep the heart-stopping anticipation going as long as possible. 'I could probably find you a packet of crisps.'

He was so close behind me, I could feel the vibration of suppressed laughter as he brushed his lips against the back of my neck. 'I'm not sure I fancy crisps just now.'

I honestly don't know how I held out, but I carried on ripping off Cellophane. 'Twiglets, then?'

Again I felt that lovely, warm vibration. 'Is that all you're offering?'

Unsteadily I said, 'Well, if you can just wait until I've done these, I might be able to find you something more substantial . . .'

'I knew I should have told that guy to stuff his roses.' As his lips brushed the back of my neck again, his hands slid very lightly up the sides of my ribs, over the abundant sides of my 36Cs, traced circles over them with his fingertips, and down again.

'Dear me,' I said unsteadily, still snipping. 'Are you sure you're going to be able to last out?'

'I wouldn't bet on it. There's a serious danger that

I'm going to turn into one of those dreadful guests who help themselves.'

His hands slid behind me, stole under my top and up my back to my bra strap, which he unpinged with the deftness of a master. 'Are you going to leave those bloody roses alone?' he murmured.

The longer I stalled, the longer the delicious anticipation. 'I must just get them in water,' I said unsteadily. 'But do please help yourself. I'll be with you in a tick . . .'

Again I felt his warm, silent laughter. 'Let me see if I can speed you up a bit . . .' With a delicate, masterly touch, his hands stole forwards again under that silk top, up over the sides of my ribs, and traced more circles over my now unbra-ed breasts. And then, with a skill I can only describe as sublime, he applied a fingertip to the tip of each nipple. . . .

I don't think any element of foreplay has ever had such an instantly powerful effect on me. It sent instant, electric shocks straight to my *zizi*, as the Frogs call it. I can't think why there isn't a nice word in English; I've never cared for 'fanny', and anyway it's American for bottom, which could get very confusing in a cross-pond relationship. A girl at my junior school called it her 'front bottom', which is a prissy little mouthful, but I digress.

The roses lay forgotten as I turned around and responded with a hunger of a starving woman, as indeed I was. I seem to recall mentioning the kind of kiss that leads to frantic shedding of clothes and rampant coupling in under two minutes; well, that's how it was. Our mouths were held together by some sort of desperate suction as we struggled to tear each other's clothes off, nearly tripping over as we fumbled with buttons and tops and tried to discard shoes and kick ourselves out of trousers at the same time. I recall us both half laughing, him hanging on to me, as I hopped and struggled out of my trousers and he helped me get shot of my knickers.

We never made it to my pristine bed, so if you're the kind of kitchen-hygiene freak who constantly goes mad with the Dettox, you'd better skip the next bit. I never quite made it out of my top, either; it was sort of bunched up round my shoulders with my bra, and his shirt was unbuttoned but not off, not that we cared. Pinned up against the fridge, the important bits were gloriously naked and trying to get acquainted but there was a slight misbalance of height, which he addressed by the simple expedient of two hands under my bottom, hitching me up and transferring me to a perch on the breakfast bar. Well, I do like a man who has the muscle for this sort of caper.

The breakfast bar might have been made for the purpose. Like this, with my legs wrapped around him, we finally connected and I remember thinking my heart might actually stop with the ecstasy. I'm afraid to say it didn't last very long: he'd barely got going when I knew that any making-it-last stuff was beyond me. Still, there are times when only a quickie will do. He told me afterwards that he'd only thought, 'Thank God,' as he couldn't have held out either. Suffice it to say that the walls echoed with my orgasmic screams (I can get a bit noisy) and his gasps, of, 'Oh, Jesus', who I dare say has got used to this sort of thing by now.

Still wrapped, we stayed there a minute, letting our heart-rates get back to normal. I can still feel his arms around me, and the lovely, feel of damp, sex-heated skin on skin. I'd like to say that at this point we exchanged sweet murmurings and all that, but I can never rely on my body to co-operate with hearts-and-flowers stuff. My tummy let out a massive rumble, which made him shake again with lovely, melted-chocolate chuckles.

'Still peckish,' he said, brushing his lips against my forehead. 'That's the trouble with fast food. I meant it to be a five-course dinner.'

Half an hour later we walked half a mile up the road to that Italian. It was drizzling, but never have I cared less. Clamped together under an umbrella we talked all the way. I could have gone another three miles at least, except that I was starving.

It was a cosy, cheerful little place that managed to combine an easy, informal ambience with brilliant food. Several tables were in intimate, candlelit corners, and, as I'd hoped, we were shown to one of these.

Once the waiter had lit the candle and departed, Josh said, 'I think it's time I told you the real reason I was "amused", under that tree.'

'You were laughing at Mum, I suppose.'

He shook his head. 'She'd kill me if she knew I'd told you, but Julia didn't quite buy your story. She said . . .' Leaning closer, he put on a fair imitation of a conspiratorial female whisper. '"It all sounds a bit fishy to me. I think she might be gay and too scared to tell her parents."'

It might be very un-PC but I was monumentally put out. '*What?*'

'Well, she does get them now and then. Only they usually come right out with it.'

I had to lean forward and lower my voice, too. 'You didn't think I was gay, did you? When you first saw me?'

'I thought, well, if she is, it's a sinful waste.'

Phew.

Over fresh *tagliatelle* and little spinach pillowy things, all washed down with liquid Tuscan sunshine, we post-mortemed Kit and Belinda.

And me and Kit.

'I didn't think Tamara was bullshitting, not about him,' he said. 'Even at the wedding I thought you might want him back. You did ask me to look besotted.'

'I'd hardly ask you to look as if I made you puke!'

'And then you slunk off to talk to him.'

'I didn't! He was just there. I was about to sneak a very agitated fag.'

'Well, you can't blame me for thinking it. He's good-looking, in a good job, and he dumped you. In my experience these are three perfectly valid reasons for a woman to want an ex back.'

I had to admit, he had a point.

'But I guess I shouldn't have had a go at him,' he conceded. 'I feel a bit bad now, what with his old man and all that. But I meant it at the time – his poor-little-boy, please-forgive-me look was giving me the shits and I still wasn't sure whether you wanted him back or not.'

'I thought you knew,' I despaired. 'I thought it must have been so obvious.'

He topped up my glass. 'Maybe you're a better actress than you realise. Of course, I picked up something, but I'm not a mind reader. I wasn't sure I was more than a passing fancy you could take or leave.'

It came as something of a shock to realise that there do still exist men who do not imagine every woman alive is panting for them.

'But Kit's an idiot if he prefers Belinda to you,' he went on.

I could have listened to this sort of stuff all night. 'Come on – she's gorgeous!'

He held up his glass to the candlelight. It glowed like liquid rubies. 'See this? It's like comparing this to a strawberry milkshake. If he prefers the milkshake, good luck to him.'

No bloke had ever said things like this to me before. Well, maybe they had, but either I'd known it was the kind of bullshit they'd give to anyone stupid enough to fall for it, or else they were blokes I was already going off because they were wet, or whatever.

During an inter-course break I laced my fingers through his. 'I still owe you one for that brilliant lie on Sunday morning.'

'I owe you one, too, for Sunday morning.' In mock-ominous tones he went on, 'After flaunting yourself in that slithery job and leading me on shamelessly, you started twittering on about cups of tea. Have you any idea of the effect that kind of thing has on a gently reared lad who still takes his woolly bunny to bed with him?'

I bit back an unladylike snort. 'Very traumatic. You might well need therapy.'

'It was well above and beyond the call of duty,' he went on.

'Sorry,' I said meekly.

'You will be, when I dream up suitable vengeance.'

This was promising. 'Like what?'

'Wait and see.' He shot me a little wink from rivery, candlelit eyes I could cheerfully have drowned in. Any minute I felt sure he was going to turn into that gruesome old fart from the wedding, all wet-lipped and dribbly, and I'd wake up in a cold sweat.

After coffee and cognac we were still peckish so we went home for that five-course dinner. In my pristine bed, this time. We made love slowly. Languorously. Like a warm, erotic fantasy, only better.

And I should know.

While I lay basking afterwards, with his arm curled around me and his fingers playing with my hair, he mused. 'Where's that holiday camp they're packing you off to?'

'Wales. Near Brecon, I think. Why?'

'When?'

'September.'

'Then I shall have my vengeance.' His chest started vibrating in a highly suspicious manner. 'If it's the place I'm thinking of, an old friend of mine runs the courses. I'll tell him you need the grin wiped off your face. He'll fix up a few mud baths, dunkings in the river and so on. I might even nip down for a few days and watch.'

'Bastard.' I snuggled closer anyway. 'Neil was right, then. He said all the instructors were sadists.'

He chuckled. 'I dare say Neil's the type of cocky little sod who gets right up Rob's nose.'

'He gets right up *my* nose.' As I recalled Neil's remarks, an idle thought struck me. 'He said ex-*SAS* sadists.'

'Did he, now.'

Suddenly the thought wasn't quite so idle. Innocently I went on, 'But I dare say it was Neil's usual rubbish.'

'Talking out of his arse,' Josh agreed lazily.

'Obviously,' I said, still in innocent mode. 'Because if your friend Rob was ex-SAS, it might just follow that you were, too.'

'Ludicrous assumption,' he said, quite as lazily as before.

I don't mind telling you, this was quite enough to give me a piquant little *frisson*. I dare say I shouldn't say this, but I'm a secret sucker for all that macho stuff. Show me a man who signs up for evening classes in Getting In Touch With Your Emotions and I'll show you a puke bucket.

I knew it wasn't done to blab about it, but I thought I might tease it out of him. 'It's all right, I know you're not suppose to *say*,' I soothed. 'In case you get kidnapped and tortured to death for information, or whatever.'

He gave a little chuckle. 'You were doing a fair job of torturing me to death, not so long ago.'

Personally I'd have called it Prolonging the Ecstasy, though I will in all fairness admit that my highly skilled, Girl-On-Top stuff might just come under this category. I had suffered, too, though if you want to torture yourself to death, impaling yourself on a massive erection's a lovely way to go.

His chest was still vibrating under my cheek, and I have to say it felt lovely. 'If you keep that up till September, I might just ask Rob to be very nice to you, instead.'

September! If he was thinking that far ahead already, my cup was merrily runneth-ing right over. 'I'd rather you asked him to be very nice to poor old Jess. She's wetting herself at the very thought.'

Still vibrating, he dropped a soft kiss on my hair. 'Whatever you say, dear.'

I couldn't resist going on with the tease. In a confiding whisper I went on, 'The reason I asked about the thing you mustn't mention is that I always had this secret fantasy about being ravished by a you-know-what man. I think it's all that black that does it, and the balaclava thingy, and all that macho, crack-commando stuff.'

He was really laughing now. 'Sounds as if you indulge in some pretty dangerous fantasies. Get your granny to knit me a balaclava thingy and I'll come and ravish you in it. All right?'

I knew I'd got him, but I wasn't going to push it. 'I'll put it in my diary.'

After a moment I remembered something I'd been wanting to ask all night. 'What did you say when Julia asked you to step in?'

'What do you think? I said, "No way." But Julia can be very persuasive and she's done favours for me in the past.'

'I suppose she told you I was fat and screwed up, as well as gay.'

'You *are* screwed up, about your weight. Barely two hours after we met you were calling yourself a fat cow.'

I didn't fish here by retorting. 'Well, I am,' so he'd have to say, 'No you're not – you're just cuddly.' I had a feeling he'd say, 'Well, I've always had a thing about fat cows', and serve me right. 'I've just got a thing about my wobbly bits,' I said, with dignity.

Josh reached down and tweaked my bottom. 'So have I.'

It was better than Christmas.

Suddenly leaning out of bed, he grabbed his shirt from the floor.

'You're not going?' I asked, suddenly alarmed.

'Not unless you're throwing me out.' He drew something from the breast pocket. 'Here – I meant to give it to you over dinner. Julia had her cut, of course.'

It was a cheque, for not much less then I'd paid the agency for the first time. 'I can't take this! God knows, you earned it.'

'I don't want it. Give it to charity, if you like. How

about the Society for the Care and Resettlement of Inveterate T.O.P.s?'

'What?'

'Tellers of Porkies,' he explained.

Since I didn't know whether to laugh or cry I did a bit of both, which he stopped in the time-honoured way. Much pillow talk later, we finally drifted off.

Alix joined me in the kitchen at ten past seven, even though she wouldn't normally surface until half eight. 'I smelt the coffee. Has he gone?'

'Yes, you nosy cow – five minutes ago. He's got to see someone in Henley at nine.'

'You're looking very smug and pleased with yourself,' she grinned.

'So would you, I can tell you.'

She was still grinning. 'Well?'

'Twice,' I said, and we collapsed into adolescent giggles.

While she was pouring a coffee I went on. 'The cunning devil did think I'd be unable to resist a helpless bloke with two dear little babies. He was going to entice me off for a pub lunch and get me to admit I'd made Ace up.'

'Only it went a bit wrong.'

'Oh, well. It was almost worth all the agony for the ecstasy afterwards. He did think I was a bit of a headcase, whether I'd made Ace up or not. If I had, I was a headcase on that count. If I hadn't, I was a headcase to put up with him. So when he found me on the common and I was talking drivel in my "sleep", he went away thinking maybe it was just as well, there were plenty of nice, sane, female fish in the sea.'

'So why are you smirking like that?'

'Because he didn't want *them*, did he? He wanted *me*. He couldn't get me out of his mind.'

'Go on and smirk, then,' she grinned. 'I'll allow it this once.'

She joined me at the tacky Formica breakfast bar, which didn't look half so tacky any more, especially when he'd been sitting at it fifteen minutes back in only a towel, with his hair damp from the shower and a tiny nick on his chin from my blunt Ladyshave. I'd kissed it better, of course.

Alix said, 'Was he cursing you for a cow when you didn't phone him the other night?'

'I hope not. He was awake till around three thirty, but then he crashed out till ten to eight, when *he* phoned *me*, but of course I'd already left. He was hoping I might have phoned and he'd slept right through it. Then again, he thought I probably hadn't because I was still holding devastated candles for Kit.'

'So if the hotel hadn't forwarded his note . . .'

'It wouldn't have made any difference. He was going to ring me last night anyway, ostensibly to ask what had been going on with Kit and Belinda. Sort of test the water and take it from there. He said he doesn't give up that easily.'

'No,' Alix mused. 'He didn't strike me as the giving-up type. No problems in the balls department, if you ask me.'

I gave a replete little sigh. 'None whatsoever, believe me.'

After another mutual fit of giggles, Alix eyed the remains of Josh's thrown-down breakfast: a crumby plate, a tub of Olivio, and a pot of chunky marmalade. 'I bet you buttered and marmaladed his toast,' she grinned. 'And cut it up for him, too.'

'Of course. I'd have done him a couple of eggs as well, but he didn't have time. He said he'll have those next time, like tomorrow morning, and when I go to his place he'll bring me his best *oeufs au Josh*, in bed.'

'You never fancy eggs first thing!'

'I know, but I'll eat them even if they're horrible fried eggs with runny white on top.'

'God, you've got it bad,' she grinned.

I smiled serenely. 'I know.' For some reason I was recalling another kitchen conversation aeons ago, with Mum. *'When you met Daddy, how did you know he was the one?'*

'I don't know, dear. I just did.'

'The roses are gorgeous,' Alix said, nodding towards the two jugs that still sat on the worktop. 'There must be dozens of them.'

Funnily enough, they'd perked right up. If I'd needed a sign, that would have done fine.

'So where does he live?' she asked.

'Chiswick.'

'And what's this business?'

'He runs a security firm with a friend. They started off with personal security for the paranoid loaded, but it's mushroomed. I felt a bit bad when he told me, as

403

I'd imagined some Mickey Mouse outfit, halfway down the tubes. Still, at least I'll know where to go for some ugly great brute to keep me from raiding the fridge.'

'That'd never work. You'd only go to the Pop-In.' Idly Alix raised a leg from under her dressing gown and inspected it. 'My tan's all wearing off.'

'Good. It was making me sick.'

'Get some fake, then. A lovely all-over, fake tan. I'm sure Josh'll apply it if you ask him very nicely.'

'No way! I haven't let him see my worst wobbly bits yet. He's threatening a forced exposure.'

'Lovely.' She started another wicked fit of giggles. 'Nothing like a good old wrestling match before you give in.'

'I suppose it's tempting, as long as harsh daylight's excluded.'

'Candles, then. And wear things he can get off easily while you pretend to fight him off. *Stop it, I like it*, and all that.'

I wasn't sure I'd fight very hard.

On balance, things were really perking up.